# Between The Wild Lines

Greta Krafsig

ART WOLF
MEDIA

**Forbidden love threatens a world on the verge of extinction.**

F or decades, the Authority has used any means necessary to prevent mass extinction. How the Heart Blight virus killed 99.9% of the male population but spared females remains a mystery. Survivors are carriers, making men both vital to repopulation and a hazard as the virus continues to mutate.

Rei is training to become an Enforcer, a soldier responsible for securing Genetic Research Hubs, where carriers live in strict containment and scientists hunt for a cure. When she encounters Griff, an escaped survivor, she's taken captive and dragged into the wilderness. A deadly game of survival will test her loyalties and everything the Authority teaches. As the virus continues to mutate, the lines between truth and freedom blur. But one thing is certain—submit or hang.

# Dedication

For everyone who cheered me on,
this wouldn't be possible without you.

## Trigger Warning

Phyrros is a fictional world ravaged by a deadly virus and largely run by an authoritarian government. As a result, this story contains reproductive control, strong graphic violence, and explicit sexual content.

Authority keep us safe.

## Note

A glossary is available at the back of this book.

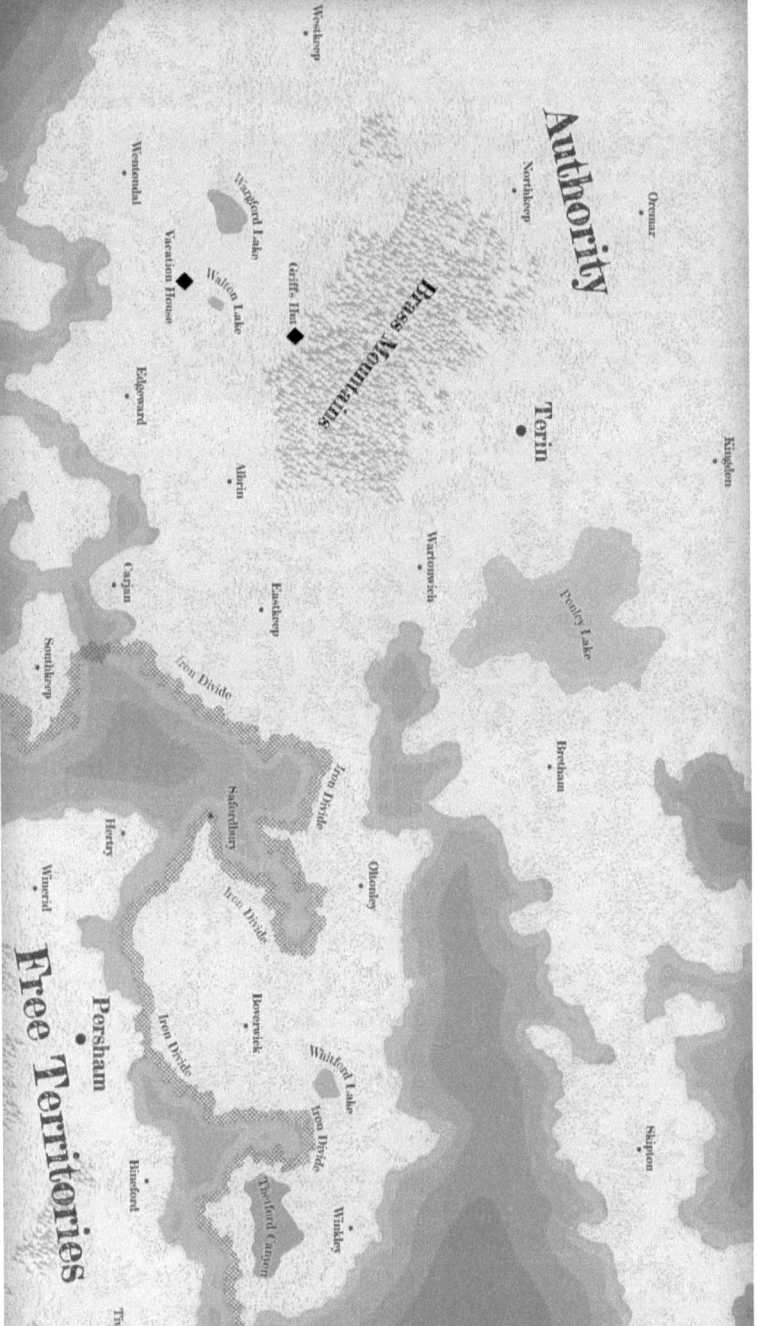

# 1

# REI

**Progress marches forward when turning back isn't an option.**

Activating the water nearly drains my rations, but my tether isn't glowing so I guess I won't die today. Ten minutes appear on the timer—a whole six more than protocol. Enforcer training has nice freaking perks. A lukewarm spray drums over my shoulders and breasts. The soothing pressure on sore muscles tempts me to stay forever, although my grumbling stomach disagrees.

The loudspeaker crackles and a bell blares overhead. Loud enough that I wince despite the roar of clanging pipes in the stark, military shower stall. The nozzle shuts off, taunting me as the countdown blinks with eight minutes remaining. Damn. Nothing like an unexpected call to formation to put a damper on simple pleasures. Ugh.

Drex Barrack is in chaos. Shirts, pants, and underwear are flung every which way. I hustle over the cold cement toward my bed. There's a crunch underfoot and I scowl at the gritty texture of my bunkmate's dreadful, extra spicy chips between my wet toes. Bless the mother! Cameron tosses me a gap-toothed smile. This is her second infraction. Eating the one thing everyone else leaves untouched in the mess hall might as well be her third.

"We have rules for a reason, keep your crap where it belongs!" I glare bullets toward her.

Cameron flinches and offers a shrug, shirt on backwards. "Oh, sorry Rei."

Belting her in the face won't do me any good. It's only been a few days and she's already on everyone's shit list. Mine included. Must be why Captain Alyssa assigned us together, to piss me off. When I make rank, this blatant disrespect will be a thing of the past.

Loyalty, duty, mission.

I won't let anything stand in the way of winning more lottery tickets, without them my chances of having a baby are slim to none.

Twisting my dark, wavy hair into a regulation bun, I dress and yank on my boots. Chip fragments bite the bottom of my foot, but there's no time to dig them out. Alyssa appears in the doorway and bellows roll call. Jumping to my feet, I stand at attention and suffer in silence while she accounts for all eight of us.

"Let's move it, grunts! We've got orders." Alyssa leads the way out.

Falling into formation, we jog single file after her. Barracks empty around us, other platoons marching like ants after separate scent trails. Our blue uniforms are in sharp contrast to a sea of brown and yellow. Enforcers are top of the food chain in the Military Management Zone or MMZ. It's a soldier's freaking playground.

We run the five-mile perimeter morning and evening to stay in shape, more if we piss off Alyssa. It might be my special talent or why the other trainees don't like me much. She winds us past the busy mess hall, med center, hydro-purification plant, and administrative buildings. New recruits suffer the burnout week obstacle course, panting and bleary-eyed. Bruised cheeks and black eyes are signs of their introduction to hand-to-hand combat. Pops of gunfire from the shooting range grow louder the further we go.

Our platoon slows in front of a squat viral research lab. Smooth concrete and a steel door sets it apart from the other pitted red-brick structures. The electronic display lists 743 days since the last incident. A bleak reminder of the traitor who murdered one of our leading scientists.

"Line up," Alyssa barks.

We arrange ourselves until we stand shoulder to shoulder. Cameron squeezes in beside me at the last second. Her fingers brush mine and I stiffen and smack them away. Is she coming on to me again? Gross. Or did Alyssa put her up to this? Either way, she doesn't seem to take the hint. I'm not interested in partnerships. I grit my teeth and pin my eyes ahead.

The light above the decontamination zone switches from red to green. Dr. Martina exits the lab and yanks off her hazmat suit's helmet. Bulky material clings to her despite her jerky attempts to free each limb. Her equipment is far superior to a standard-issue tether for good reason. Protocol requires level-three protective gear for anyone in direct and prolonged contact with the Heart Blight.

On TV she's a cool, polished, professional. The symbol of progress the Authority's made these past 60 years looking for a cure. But it's hard to miss the dark circles beneath her eyes. They make her relatable, more human, perhaps.

Dr. Martina's white lab coat billows as she picks up a small black case. Commander Morgan Lynx appears around the corner of the building and stops next to her. They exchange words as they approach, but I can't make them out, even as their voices grow louder.

"Attention!" Alyssa shouts at the head of our line.

I pull my shoulders back and straighten my stance, boots touching, legs rigid.

The conversation intensifies a few feet in front of us. I catch fragments: find him, cure, research, quarantine the infected, spreading. Dr. Martina spins and stomps away. Commander Lynx frowns, brows furrowing, shoulders tense. The expression vanishes when she faces us. Maybe I'm imagining the lines lingering between her eyebrows.

"Listen up, girls!" Commander Lynx says, lacing her hands behind her back and stepping closer. The sun's glare on the metal stripes of her stiff, blue uniform hurts my eyes. "There've been three attempted hijackings of transport vehicles in the past two weeks. The Sympathizers are getting bolder. We have one Enforcer platoon out of commission, another on a special search expedition, and the rest focused on this growing threat. As a result, you'll escort Dr. Martina to Northkeep GRH, where she'll collect fresh samples of the Heart Blight. Since this is such an unusual request, you'll receive 10 lottery tickets after completing this mission."

My stomach flips and my heart stutters. Ten is hard to wrap your head around. This is the chance of a lifetime. Civvies earn one ticket a year while military and government personnel get two. Enforcers, the Authority's elite soldiers, receive three. Gasps and murmurs erupt along the line. I gulp and school my face with every ounce of self-control I possess. The Commander's intense gray eyes meet mine. The leer on her lips is both a warning and approval.

"Quiet!" Alyssa snaps.

Cameron, oblivious to the consequences, leans over and whispers to me. "What the heck is the GRH?"

Bad decision. Hands trembling, I hide my grimace. Few people enjoy experiencing the full force of the Commander's attention.

While it's about time someone laid into this moron, I don't envy her the lesson.

"Did I give you permission to speak?" Commander Lynx growls and smashes a hand against her throat.

Cameron sputters and chokes, arms flying to her neck, skin turning the color of her hair.

"Don't make me regret signing off on your transfer to Enforcer training, little girl."

Letting go, Cameron doubles over, sucking in a breath.

"Do you hear me, soldier?"

Cameron nods, hands on her knees. Her gags erupt into a coughing fit.

Commander Lynx grabs the curls of her messy bun and yanks. Her chin tips backwards, tears streaking flushed cheeks. "I can't hear you." The tone is lethal, uncompromising.

A shiver runs down my spine.

"Y-y-yes, ma'am!" Cameron wheezes, eyes going wild and mouth contorting in pain until she releases her.

Commander Lynx pivots on her heel and glowers at her daughter. "Captain."

"Ma'am, yes ma'am." Alyssa snaps her hand to her forehead in salute.

"If you can't beat these trainees into submission, I'll find someone who can." Her gaze flicks to me. "Now," she continues, "Dr. Martina is waiting." She takes aim at a group of soldiers loitering by hefty wooden supply crates. Locking on to her next victims.

"Listen up, grunts." Alyssa's hard glint pierces me like an arrow. "Squad one takes point. Squad two in the middle. Rei, Cameron, and myself are on rear guard with Dr. Martina. Grab your packs, weapons loaded and safety on. Move it."

We head toward the pile of gear stacked by our vehicles in the hangar across the way. Two trainees fall into step behind Alyssa. I like to call them her lackeys. They kiss ass to stay on her good side. Although Alyssa is my age, she got promoted to captain last year. When all the women in your family hold the highest positions of power in the Authority, who needs skill, right?

I'm pretty sure being handpicked by her mother and graduating head of my class is why she hates me so much. But in the few months I've been under Alyssa's command, she's done everything she can to make my life a living hell.

Cameron clears her throat and rubs a hand across her bruised neck. "Gosh," she says, voice hoarse, "I wasn't expecting that."

"We're not in basic training anymore," I snap, lengthening my strides. Cameron scrambles to keep up.

"Is the Commander always so darn mean?"

"She broke the nose of the last trainee who spoke out of turn. Now you're here." I open and close my cramping fingers. After this, hopefully not for much longer.

"Oh...guess I got off easy then."

Cameron's chipper attitude grates on my nerves. I approach the two remaining backpacks on the ground.

"Seriously though, what's the GRH?"

"Bless the mother, didn't you pay attention during your two years in basic? Genetic Research Hub. Where we isolate the infected survivors."

"But I hated school. Especially final conditioning and initiation. Heck, there was so much saluting and chanting," Cameron raises her hoarse voice to a mocking falsetto that whistles through her teeth, "Authority keep us safe." Her face contorts like she's left with a rotten piece of food on ration.

Amusement fades to something harder. "My overseer gave me this fun smile. I wouldn't say the pledge so she elbowed me in the mouth and told me to hold out my hands. She used her discipline stick until I'd recited every word. They were a shredded mess, useless for weeks. Don't need those to have a baby. I still have scars, see?"

Thick white lines criss cross her palms.

How can she be this dense? The Heart Blight wiped out all but a handful of men. I curl my hands into fists and round on her.

"The virus isn't a joke! You wouldn't be standing here without the Authority lockdowns and protections. We owe them our freaking lives."

I grab her bag and throw it as hard as I can. The force of the impact against her chest sends her stumbling back a step. She grins, gap and all, unphased by my resulting scowl.

My eyes narrow and I hiss. "Dr. Martina reports new mutations all the time. How long do you think we have until a new strain wipes us out, too?"

Cameron shrugs and buckles her gun holster on her hips. "But have you ever wondered why the heck we never get sic—"

"Let's go, boots!" Alyssa calls, interrupting her as she leans out the driver's side window of the last truck and bangs on the door. "Rei, take shotgun."

I sling my bag over my shoulder, glad for a reason to ignore her mindless chatter. Cameron's face falls as I jog around to the passenger seat. For once, sitting beside Alyssa doesn't seem so bad.

In the back seat, Dr. Martina holds her black case to her chest, lost in thought, fingertips white from their death grip. Cameron, buckling herself into the seat beside her, shakes her out of whatever has her so distracted.

"Dr. Martina, it's so nice to meet you. I'm Rei. I just wanna say, I'm a huge fan."

A tired smile crosses her lips, warming her distant expression. "Hi, nice to meet you."

"I make time to watch your report every week. Does it really take three days for symptoms to show up once you're infected?"

"Unless you're a carrier like the survivors, yes. It starts with tussis and respiratory distress, followed by pyrexia and hematemesis until cardiac arrest." She shifts uncomfortably at my blank stare. "Right, layman's terms. Cough, fever, then vomiting blood. The Heart Blight feeds off your plasma. In time, your hemoglobin crystalizes. The lungs collapse and your heart stops beating. Once the fever hits, you'll be lucky to last 24 hours."

"Dang. Why do you think it only affected men and none of the other animals?" Cameron asks, leaning forward.

Dr. Martina sighs and rubs her eyes. "If we knew, maybe we'd have a cure." The words come out flat and stilted. A flurry of emotions struggle over her face. Her mouth thins into a firm line, a muscle in her cheek twitching. One hand presses against her forehead as she returns to her thoughts, conversation over.

She's so different from the proud, confident woman on broadcasts.

Alyssa picks up the radio microphone and presses the button. The speakers squawk. "Switch to secure channel two. ETA 45 minutes. Keep your eyes open, grunts. You may be trainees, but this isn't a drill. Move out."

The truck lurches, the seat belt biting into my shoulder, as Alyssa shifts into gear and rolls out behind the two other vehicles. The pitching awakens my empty stomach. I press my brow to the window and trace a finger along the top of my wrist, feeling the bump of my tether beneath the skin. Any distraction will do.

An older woman teaching me to play gents salutes us from the guard tower. Two red flags, one on either side, snap and ripple in the breeze when we exit the barbed-wire fencing. A bold red letter "A" impregnates the center of the black fire emblem. In entry school, we learn how the design symbolizes rising from the collapse. All resources were diverted toward a cure and the reproductive crisis.

Terin, the capital of the Authority, is a city held together by cracked asphalt roadways and strict discipline. The truck's suspension affords limited comfort from the potholes and ruts as we bounce along. I scan the streets, watching for suspicious activity as the civie foot traffic increases.

At its heart, dull color dominates. Gray from the concrete multi-story apartments. Reds from the flags adorning shop awnings, windows, and building doorways. The broken and crumbling libraries, schools, and luxury coffee shops are a faded, dingy white. Ribbons hang from light posts, signaling the approaching Cleansing holiday.

"We've got movement ahead. Stay sharp." I warn, wrapping a hand around my gun hilt. Our procession slows to a crawl. A group of civvies causes a mini blight storm on the sidewalk, shouting at the soldiers holding them back.

Bodies hang from the Suppression Line in front of them, ropes tight around their rotting, swollen, traitorous necks. One in civie patchwork beige and two in Sympathizer black. The word LIES defaces the inscription beneath their dangling feet. Every child memorizes those vandalized core tenets before starting entry school: Loyalty, Duty, Mission.

"Damn, those weren't there two days ago...." I swallow hard and fight a wave of nausea, eyes darting over the civie crowd in search of threats.

Driving past, Alyssa strains to follow my gaze out the passenger side window. But Cameron gasps and clamps a hand over her mouth. Her dry heaves and retching noises make me grateful I didn't eat this morning.

"Don't you dare throw up in here." I warn, my lips curling at the idea of those chips reappearing in our tight quarters.

Cameron composes herself, sniffs, and wipes tears and snot off her nose. How does someone who never shuts up cry in silence? Strange.

The radio chimes and cheery theme music from the Collective Voice Broadcast disrupts the tension. "Loyal citizens of the Authority, this is the CBV coming to you live. Today is code green, with a 4% chance of rain. Don't let this warm fall day deceive you, be prepared for a nip in the air as the sun goes down. While you're out and about, stop by the market for this week's special—carrots. Delicious and nutritious. With Cleansing day fast approaching wood bundles are limited to one per motherline. Unfortunately, we have no new births, but our dutiful and gracious leader, Director Evelyn Lynx, has a special message."

Static fizzes and the high-pitched squeal of microphone feedback makes me grimace. It's quickly replaced by the husky, resolute tone of Alyssa's grandmother.

"Children of the Authority, hear me. Today I speak to you not as your director, but as the mother of our great nation, a guardian of humanity. We suppressed three traitors for abortion and stealing earlier this week. Yet in the two years since the first cowardly

Sympathizer attack, they continue to strike our supply lines and spread their poisonous influence.

"Vigilance. Order. Discipline.

"These are our greatest weapons in stopping their threats. Their lies and deception sow doubts in the society we've built, of all we've sacrificed for the greater good.

"Don't be swayed. Stay the course.

"The Authority—no, I—pledge to protect you from the Heart Blight no matter the cost. Dedication to this mission will ensure our bright future. Together, we will endure, survive, and find a cure."

The announcer's voice returns. "Thank you for those inspiring words, Director Lynx. Now, please join me in closing with the pledge of allegiance."

Alert muscles relax when our truck reaches the city limits. My hand drops from my gun hilt as the broadcast ends and the theme song of the CVB fades. I've never seen the Director in person, only on TV, but there's a clear resemblance in the stiff line of Alyssa's shoulders.

"Gee, it's so different out here." Cameron says as we pass the beginnings of short, bushy shrubs and tall, spindly trees. Great, not even five minutes of peace before she opens her damn mouth again.

"Yeah, because the Brass Mountains are, you know, right there." Despite my terrible sense of direction, they're hard to miss. Pale pink light tints the sloped peaks. The scenery is wild and untamed compared to our typical concrete jungle. Getting out of the city isn't easy, but she's acting like she's never seen plants before.

"How are you doing, Dr. Martina?" I peer over my shoulder at our VIP.

She nods, eyes shut, fingers massaging her left temple. "I'm fine."

"We'll be there soon." I assure her.

Alyssa's side-eye greets me when I return my attention to our surroundings.

"What?"

"Nothing, grunt. Keep your eyes on the prize."

Our convoy rolls up to the first of two checkpoints some 30 miles outside of the city. Four soldiers leave the gatehouse and approach our vehicles. Three inspect the trucks while the last looks over the marching orders Alyssa hands them, salutes, and waves us through with a smile and a nod.

Radio static fizzes 10 minutes later. I wait, expecting a voice, but no one speaks. Alyssa picks up the microphone as we head into a tunnel cut into the side of the mountain. Thick concrete structures narrow the passage and dull, orange lights amplify the suffocating gloom.

"Say again, over." There are clips of sound, a garbled voice, and more static. Being underground doesn't help the interference.

"I can't hear you. You're breaking up, over." Alyssa tries again.

The truck in front of us explodes.

Flames ricochet across our windshield. Glass shatters, the world spins.

Someone is screaming. Me?

Everything is tumbling. My brain can't make sense of what's happening.

The world goes black.

# 2

**REI**

**Courage isn't the absence of fear, but a mask laid over it.**

Fear squeezes me in a vice grip. It's so dark. My ears ring and something warm runs up my cheek. I raise my hand to touch the liquid and my knuckles brush something cold and hard. It's so wrong. My view is tilted. I lower my arm to find my wet, sticky hair. The press of the seat belt digging into my legs and chest helps me orient myself. I'm flipped upside down. My head hangs to the ceiling, now the floor.

Panic grips my throat and pain rakes claws across my forehead and ribs. I take gasping breaths and try to calm my galloping heart. My whole body is shaking. A wave of vertigo sends nausea roiling through my stomach on a sharp, rapid drum beat. Sour bile makes my mouth pucker and twist.

Am I dying or just in shock? The agony is so intense the slightest movement is sliding on jagged blades of glass.

The high-pitched noise is fading, replaced with dull popping and cracking sounds. Gunshots? My eyes adjust to the oppressive darkness. I blink hard until the broken dashboard comes into focus. I reach for the seat belt, gasping at each excruciating inch. Fingers touch the release button and I scream as I rag-doll out of my seat and smack the ceiling.

Thick smoke irritates the back of my nose and my reflexive cough brings me back awake. How long was I out? Seconds, minutes? My eyes burn and tears pool as I struggle to push off the ground. The faint glow of fire gives off enough light to illuminate the situation unfolding before me.

*Boom!*

Something explodes further down the tunnel and flames dance in earnest now.

*Pop, pop!* More gunshots?

"Rei! Rei Koss! Move it! The Sympathizers are attacking!" My name on Alyssa's lips sounds like it's behind a roaring waterfall.

A hand grabs my upper arm. Nails gouge bruised flesh. I jerk from my attacker and whip around. Oh, it's Alyssa.

"Get up!" She takes hold of me again, pulling me through the broken windshield.

*Bang!* Bits of debris ricochets and a bullet whizzes past her head.

"Sonofabitch!" Alyssa drops to a crouch beside me and draws her gun.

Who's shooting at us? We've taken shelter behind an enormous slab of concrete from the growing heat and light from the flames. Part of the tunnel collapsed in front of our vehicle, blocking us from the worst of what remains of squad two. Squad one must be somewhere further down the tunnel.

"Where's the VIP?" I gasp, panic rising as I come to my senses.

"In our truck. Go, I'll cover you."

Voices shout up ahead, followed by another exchange of gunfire. Smoke and my aching chest launch me into a coughing fit. I force myself to take shallow breaths.

"Rei, snap out of it!" Alyssa slaps me across the cheek, and I gasp. "I gave you an order, soldier!"

Damn, it stings. I bare my teeth and catch myself from hitting her back. The sudden rush of adrenaline helps me ignore my injuries as I nod and crawl back to the truck on hands and knees. Bits of glass, rock, and metal bite into my palms. I wait for Alyssa to return fire before I jerk the back door open, using it for added protection.

"Dr. Martina, are you okay?" I reach past her dangling arms and unbuckle her seat belt, taking the brunt of her weight as she collapses over my shoulder. Her resulting groan lets me know she's still alive.

"VIP incoming!" I shout and wait for the burst of Alyssa's gunfire before I drag the scientist over. When Dr. Martina's out of the line of fire, I run through a mental first-aid checklist and assess her condition. There's a gash on her cheek, but her skin is pink and she's breathing steadily. I lift her eyelids and check each pupil. Normal. Chances of a concussion are low.

Dr. Martina moans, eyes fluttering open. She struggles to sit up, dazed and confused.

"Status!" Alyssa barks.

"Green. VIP secure." I hold Dr. Martina's shoulders as she reorients herself. "Stay still. You're okay. I've got you."

"Ahh! No, no, no! Goddess Lysara, save me." Cameron's terrible, wet scream and thick sobs curdle my blood.

I freeze. Alyssa and I lock eyes.

"I'm going," I say, my mind made up.

"Give me your extra clips." She growls, but doesn't wait for a response. One hand digs into the outer pocket of my pants and removes my spares. Ejecting the empty clip from her gun, she snaps in a replacement. "You have one minute. Go!"

I crouch and return to the truck.

Cameron is glassy-eyed, upside down, and somehow still alive. She's at a twisted, awkward angle. The broken driver's seat impales both legs. Her upper body dangles to the ground. Red-stained hands are the only thing holding her belly together.

"I'm dying," she gurgles.

Blood bubbles in the corner of her mouth. The light is fading in her eyes. I climb inside and reach over to soothe her hair, giving her what comfort I can.

"I'm here," I offer, but there's nothing I can do.

"I'm so scared.... Tell Claire...." She gasps and I strain to hear her mouth the words, "I lov...."

Her body goes limp. I'm numb. Cauterized.

"Rei, I need you!" Alyssa screams.

I duck and stumble back to the position she defends. Sweat plasters my dusty, torn uniform to my aching sides. My throat and nose burn from the smoke. I fumble to draw my gun from its holster and release the safety. Dr. Martina is curled into a ball, arms around her knees, eyes wide and trembling.

"Cameron?"

I shake my head, but the hollow surrealism remains.

"Squad two is gone. The Sympathizers have squad one pinned down by a service entrance about 50 yards ahead. I count eight enemy combatants, maybe more. It's hard to tell with this smoke. They won't be able to keep them busy for long...."

"Provide backup so we can get Dr. Martina out of here." Words leave my mouth before I can fully process the tactics clicking into place. "I'll cover you and fall back the way we came."

I grab Dr. Martina's arm and yank her to unsteady feet, shoving her head down when she attempts to rise to her full height and make herself a target. "Stay low!"

Meeting her scrutiny I ask, "Ready, captain?"

Alyssa hesitates, lower lip quivering, then nods. She fires around the corner, breaks left, and charges into the firefight to support squad one.

"Authority save me." I shoot at the service entrance and haul Dr. Martina in the opposite direction.

Uneven ground and hypervigilance are exhausting. My foot skids on a pile of debris. Muscles trained for combat keep me upright by pure reflex. Fire engulfs the shell of the middle truck in our convoy. A distorted, jagged death trap is all that remains of squad two. Behind us, further down the tunnel, the roaring flames silhouette two armed women, guns pointed at each other, muzzles flashing. The smoke blurs the line between friend and foe.

"Hurry," I urge Dr. Martina, half tugging, half dragging her further from the fighting.

"Oh no, the case!" Dr. Martina cries, the color draining from her face. She flails and jerks out of my grip.

I grab a handful of her sooty lab coat. Material stretches and rips, but I hold fast, refusing to let go. "Stop! Wait! It's too dangerous!"

"There's classified information on the virus. We can't let the Sympathizers get their hands on it!"

This isn't the time to argue. Retrieving the case myself leaves Dr. Martina alone and unprotected. I can't risk her safety, our mission. We're too exposed, too vulnerable, and not far enough from the fighting. Letting the rebels get ahold of important research goes against everything I've sworn to protect.

Do I choose duty or mission? There's only one option.

"Dammit! We're going back. Get behind me, keep low, and stay close." Taut, battered muscles complain when I tighten my grip on her arm. Cautiously, I pick our way toward our upside down vehicle.

Debris explodes beside my head. A bullet ricochets off the tunnel wall. I slam my hands against Dr. Martina's chest, sending her sprawling on her ass and out of danger. A Sympathizer stumbles into my line of fire, her gun swinging in my direction. The gun bucks in my palm when I squeeze the trigger. My shot hits her thigh and forces her to skitter backwards. Using her withdrawal to my advantage, I press the attack in a move perfected last week.

The Sympathizer panics, raises her gun, and takes aim. But she's too late, and I'm too close to miss.

*Bang!*

"Fuck!" she grabs her side and collapses, dead.

Thick smoke engulfs me. The heat intensifies, my lungs burn and my skin blisters. Pressing a forearm over my nose does little to help me breathe easier. I turn back for Dr. Martina.

A dirty white lab coat billows past me. Bless the mother, she's going after the case without me! I sprint after her, broken ankle be damned, panic gripping my chest.

Dr. Martina reaches our truck and fumbles inside. Panting from adrenaline, I grab hold of her collar and wrench back with all my might. Her soot streaked face goes from fearful to relieved as I slam her against the collapsed concrete slab behind cover. Right back where we freaking started.

"Are you crazy? I told you to stay close!" Fury rushes to fill the void in my chest.

I killed a Sympathizer.

Dr. Martina gulps and grips the case to her breast, disheveled hair flying as she shakes her head. "You don't understand, they can't find him—"

"Ahh!" The shrill scream jolts through my body, in sharp contrast to its typical barking tone. Alyssa is in trouble.

"Go," Dr. Martina says, eyes widening at my expression. "I'll stay here and keep my head down. I swear I won't budge." She crouches.

"No. You got the damn case, now I'm getting you out of here."

Lifting my gun, I peer around the corner and down the tunnel. The fire is finally smothering itself out, and the smoke is dissipating. I'm not sure how many Sympathizers remain, but staying here isn't an option. Waiting any longer will give away our position and the tiny advantage we have.

"We have to move. Now! Let's go." Yanking Dr. Martina to her feet, I drag her after me, my fingers locked around her wrist in a death grip.

Scuffling footsteps sound the alert. A Sympathizer sticks her head around the cover by the service entrance and I take aim. Alyssa stumbles to our position out of the thinning smoke, blocking my line of fire. She turns back and lets off a round, so fixated on her target she doesn't notice another shadowy figure rising from the ground behind her.

"Captain, behind you!"

They're too close together for me to risk the shot.

The Sympathizer smashes her in the chin with her elbow. Alyssa's gun spins out of her hand and disappears into the flames. They strike out at each other until the taller woman grabs her in a military style head lock. Alyssa's eyes bulge as she struggles for air.

*Bang! Bang!*

My heart stops, expecting the worst as I step in front of Dr. Martina to shield her. One of Alyssa's lackeys stands further down the tunnel. Thud. The enemy in the service entrance falls to the ground, a dark puddle spreading outwards from their body.

"No!" the tall Sympathizer choking Alyssa cries out. This momentary distraction allows Alyssa to slip free. She reverses the hold in a fluid motion and twists her neck until it snaps. The enemy's body flops to the ground.

Behind Alyssa, her lackey whimpers. A pool of blood blossoms across her uniform and her mouth opens in shock. Both knees hit the littered ground. One shaking hand presses against the dark stain. The Sympathizer she shot in the service entrance didn't miss either. "Oh...." Her eyes roll back into her head as she topples.

"Sonofabitch!" Alyssa chokes out, hobbling toward us. "There's still one more. She headed your way."

"Neutralized, captain." The distant, mechanical response doesn't sound like me.

"Status?" she manages before a fit of coughing wracks her trembling shoulders.

"Green. VIP secure." I motion to Dr. Martina. "What about squad one?"

She shakes her head and wipes her sweaty face, smearing patches of blood and soot on her cheeks. A jagged gash runs the length of her left forearm. She wobbles and yelps when she puts weight on her right knee. "Those two were the last of the enemy. We're clear. It's over."

I offer her my elbow.

"I'm fine," she grunts and limps past me. "Dr. Martina, I'm glad you're okay."

"Yes, Rei did a fantastic job protecting us." She runs a tender hand across the case's warped surface and beams, indifferent to the death and destruction around us.

I don't know this person.

We pick our way through the debris, heading for the dim light at the entrance of the tunnel. Alyssa's injury brings us to a crawl. The third time I offer my elbow she glares at me then laces her arm through mine. My shoulder aches from supporting her while she struggles to stay upright.

"Sonofabitch!" Alyssa chokes out as her foot slips and she's forced to step on it.

Dr. Martina takes a seat on a wide chunk of concrete, case in her lap, fiddling with the broken lock.

Something squishes underfoot. I glance down and my stomach roils. The hand of the Sympathizer I killed has a gritty imprint of my boot on the pale skin. Releasing Alyssa, I lunge aside and vomit. Bile burns my nose and makes my eyes water. My lungs throb in time with each forceful heave. The retching doesn't stop until my stomach cramps, as empty as I am. I lift my head and wipe my mouth.

It's nothing like shooting a target.

"Your first kill is the worst," Alyssa offers.

"Is that supposed to make me feel better?" I hiss.

The haughty stare of my captain and rival returns. "Watch your tongue, grunt."

"If you two are done with your ignorant, nonsensical pissing match, I have urgent, time-sensitive research to get back to. Shall we?" Dr. Martina stands in a huff, stomping away.

*Bang!*

I startle at the sound of the gunshot. My vision narrows, ears ringing, and the moment stretches into eternity. A dark hole in the back of Dr. Martina's lab coat is a dam releasing a torrential red stream. She pitches forward in slow motion.

"No!" My gun swings wildly, trying to pinpoint the source of the attack. The imprinted hand of the enemy twitches, weapon glinting in the murky light. Pained eyes sparkle and the Sympathizer grins. Lottery tickets vanish with every pull of my trigger. Hot tears blur my vision, and an anguished scream rips my throat raw.

There's a roar in my ears. A wave of dizziness sends my head spinning. The gun clicks empty over and over again. The walls are closing in. Darkness squeezes, suffocating, dragging me down.

I can't breathe.

"I think she's dead." Alyssa's voice pulls at the edges of my hysteria.

I know she is. I killed her.

Again.

"Rei! Get over here!"

Chest heaving, I turn from the evil corpse that ripped away an opportunity of a lifetime. But Alyssa's not talking about the enemy. I rush to where she squats beside Dr. Martina. Together, we flip her over. Glassy eyes stare above a lax mouth.

I check for a pulse.

Nothing.

Alyssa's shoulders slump, defeated. Our gazes meet in a silent exchange. I bow my head, heart seizing. The tangible weight of failure hangs in the air. Dark spots threaten the edges of my vision.

The black case lies open beside Dr. Martina's limp arm. Something shiny catches the dim light. It's not a research paper, test tube, vial or even a syringe.

No.

The black-and-white photo of a young boy with buck teeth stares back at me, his hollow expression a stark mirror of my own.

# 3

## GRIFF

**The wilderness doesn't choose sides,
but it'll show you what you're made of.**

The bowstring groans, going taut, as I pull back and imagine the
face of the woman who murdered my father. *Thunk*, bullseye.
I sling the bow over my shoulder and make my way to the rabbit.
Used to be my aim was shit. Turns out hunger is a better motivator
than hatred.

Three months feels like an eternity when you're all alone. Well,
other than Mischief. My gangly raccoon skitters down a nearby tree
and sniffs at the kill. I gently shoo him away and say a wordless thanks
to dinner. Several hard yanks bring the arrow out of the rabbit's neck.
A quick swipe on some leaves cleans the arrowhead before I slip it
into my quiver. Digging out a bit of rope from my backpack, I tie
the rabbit's soft, furry feet and sling it over my shoulder.

"Ya ready to head back, boy? Should be dark soon."

Dunno why I expect him to answer me, but it'd be nice not to talk
to myself for a change. Mischief touches the spot of blood on the
ground and licks his tiny, clawed fingers. His playful antics make me
shake my head and smile. Turning south, I retrace my trail along the
underbrush.

Birds chirp, insects buzz, and the wind whispers through the leaves. The sound baits me, drawing me into the solitude. At times like these, father woulda made me stop, listen, and let the sun warm my face. He had a way of turning survival into a game. Search for the smallest signs of activity and focus in on them: the slight impression of deer tracks, musky smells of animal droppings, the whispery rustle of wings, and branches broken at awkward angles.

*These are the tells of the mountain.* His gruff voice chimes in my head. Signs of life, nature and, best of all, freedom.

It takes time for me to navigate my way down the mountain trail. I ranged out farther than normal to find more supplies. A small antler necklace bumps against my chest in time with my long, purposeful strides. Father spent weeks carving it for me. I gulp and suck in a shaky breath.

The memory is still so vivid.

"Here." I remember him handing it to me for my nameday. His lopsided grin was out of place on a face that was always so stern and serious. "Happy nameday, Griff."

"What's this?" I asked.

It fit perfectly in my palm. A cord of tanned leather threaded through a small hole in the base. The tip was sharp like the beak of a bird and it had delicate wings. But the head, body, and tail resembled a mountain lion. Each padded foot ended in large, pointed talons. The carving spiraled the piece of antler.

"It's called a griffin. They're guardians of justice and defenders of the powerless." He reached over and ruffled my shaggy hair. "You're old enough to hold on to it now. Did ya know Pyrrhos was once a single country? The Authority attacked our town when they built the Iron Divide. Took me and your grandfather and a couple of other men, too. This here, this is our ticket to the Free Territories."

He showed me how to untwist the top. Inside, something foreign and metallic gleamed. My stomach clenched as I recognized where it came from. Father screwed it back together and slid the cord around my neck.

Rough hands gripped my shoulders and squeezed as he said, "Guard it with your life."

I traced the dips and ridges of the griffin with my fingers. "The woman who helped us escape gave ya this." She slipped it into his hand when we ran.

"She did," he said, and his tone grew solemn and serious. He bent and reset an empty trap at our feet. Back to business as usual.

Is he thinking about Ian, how we left him behind, how we'd never see him again?

"I hate them. The Authority is evil." I spat and kicked the ground with my too large boot. My big toe slammed into the end as my foot slid inside. It was gonna leave a bruise.

My father grunted and stood. "Go check the rest of the traps. I'll head over to the stream and see if I can wrestle us up some fish for dinner. I know they're your favorite."

We parted ways as I made the rounds, checking and resetting the snares. I had no luck until the last one. The raccoon was lying on its side, tongue lolling out. It tried to chew through its back leg to get loose and bled out instead.

I crouched to cut the rope wrapped into the torn flesh. That's where I was when I found the kits a few feet away. Both as cold and still as their momma. She must have struggled, trying to get free, helpless to protect the ones she loved, willing to do anything for her freedom.

A lot like us.

They deserved a burial. Sure, there would be nothing for dinner—on my nameday, no less—but I couldn't bring myself to feast on her torment.

Our suffering.

After several minutes, I found a flat rock to prepare a grave. Deep enough nothing would dig them up. When I finished, I laid her in first and went to get the kits. They felt so fragile in my hands. I'd never touched a baby raccoon before. I ran my fingers over their downy fur as I carried them over.

The one in my right hand moved, and I flinched, shocked. I rubbed again, using more force this time. It whined and shivered, but the other remained stiff. The live one wiggled in my hand, put my pointer finger in its mouth and suckled.

"Hey buddy," I cradled it to my chest as it continued to shake. It wouldn't make it on its own, weak and defenseless as it was. So I would take it home knowing my father was gonna throw a fit. His voice was already drilling into my head. Berating me for being too soft.

*Weakness got people killed.*

But it was my nameday. Didn't I deserve it?

The kit chomped on my finger. "Ouch!"

I fished around my pocket for the piece of deer meat I had for lunch. "Here, eat this instead." Satisfied, he traded my hand for the jerky. I'd gone without eating many times, why not once more?

"Ya like to get into a bit of trouble, huh? Well Mischief, I'm Griff." He let out a weak mew followed by a chirping noise when I lifted him toward my face. Like a baby bird already looking for its next meal. "Don't eat me," my laughter accompanied a tiny snout bumping my cheek and his playful attempts to chew my nose.

He fell asleep in my arms while I hiked back to the shelter we'd called home the last few weeks. As I got closer, the disapproving voice running through my head got harder to ignore. Father really wouldn't like this idea. Mischief would be both an annoyance and an extra mouth to feed.

*Survival is all about trimming the fat and doing what's necessary.*

Slowing, I left the deer track I'd been following and found a tree I noticed the day before with a deep hole in the trunk. Maybe in the past it belonged to a family of owls, but currently it was empty. High enough off the ground to keep the larger predators away and low enough the kit wouldn't hurt itself if it took a tumble.

I grabbed the lowest branch, a handful of leaves, and hoisted myself up. Mischief chittered as I placed him inside the hollow with the rest of the deer jerky. "Stay here, bud. I'll be back with more food soon." I said, tucking the leaves around him. Mischief whined and burrowed deeper into the hollow. He yawned and his eyes drifted closed.

My father was near the fire pit when I arrived at our shelter. The roots of the tree behind him were above ground and woven together, forming the lean-to we slept under. Father spotted me from the rabbit he was skinning and waved me closer with the tip of his hunting knife.

"No fish, but I got lucky with the snare we forgot by the stream. Here, let me see ya gut this." He flipped the weapon and handed them both over.

He corrected me several times, shaking his head and pointing out my mistakes as I prepared the rabbit. When I was done, he grimaced and said, "Good enough. Go get the fire started."

Lighting a fire was one of a few things my father left to me. There were days he cursed and hollered and threw a fit because he couldn't get the kindling to catch. But I could grow an ember from the soggiest of conditions. It was one of the few times he praised me amidst his constant, harsh criticisms.

The rabbit was delicious. When he wasn't looking, I stuck bits of meat into my pocket and schemed up excuses to slip away. Mischief needed to eat again before dark.

"I'll clean this up and get more firewood," I volunteered, as he picked his teeth with a broken bone and dropped it into the dying embers.

Father glanced up at the sky through the treetops, gauging the position of the sun. "It'll be dark soon. Go gather firewood, I'll clean this up. Don't take long."

I jumped up, eager to go. He cocked his head and one eyebrow lifted in question. One corner of my mouth quirked, and I tried to curb my smile. "Be back soon." I said, jogging off.

Mischief was mewing, and chittering by the time I reached his tree. I climbed up and passed him the pieces of rabbit. He gobbled them down and wrapped his little hands around my fingers, biting and licking off the grease.

"Hey! That hurts, be nice." Filling the cap of my canteen, I offered him some water. He drank some and spilled some and drank some more. I tickled his chin and played with him for a few minutes before I scooped out the wet leaves and replaced them with fresh, dry ones.

Once he'd settled down sleepily, I climbed down the tree. "I'll be back in the morning, buddy."

The voices brought me up short from picking up the dry stick and adding it to my armful. My stomach dropped to my knees as the sticks slipped from my hands. I took careful, quiet steps forward and paused, thinking what my father would say.

*Nobody knows the wild like we do, son. They're too stupid to look up.*

Scrambling up the nearest tree with big, leafy branches, I used it for both camouflage and a better view.

A group of women in blue Authority uniforms surrounded our shelter. My father stood in front of them, his hunting knife in one hand, guns aimed at him.

"Stay back! Drop it!" One soldier cried.

My father took a bold step forward.

"Don't come any closer or I'll shoot!" The same soldier tensed, her gun cocked.

My father dropped the weapon and raised his empty hands.

"Don't shoot, you bloody idiot. We want him alive. Lower your weapons." A woman behind the group stepped forward. Colorful patches and metals decorated the front of her uniform.

"I'm not going back, Commander," my father said.

"You will, Fletcher." The Commander's voice dripped with contempt. "You have a duty to humanity, to help us repopulate the society I've dedicated everything to build. But you're also a carrier. We can't have you running around spreading the virus, either. And I know Dr. Solenne gave you her research. Where is it?"

"I don't know what you're talking about."

"Very well. We'll tear this place apart until we find it. Now...where's the boy? Where's my son?"

Every muscle in my body froze. Her son?

"He's dead, bit by a rattlesnake last year," he said, his voice raising and projecting across the woods. Warning me to stay back.

"You're lying," the Commander countered and her voice grew harder. "I won't stop. I'll track him to the ends of the Authority and do everything in my power to make sure he's returned to containment. Where. He. Belongs."

My father lunged at her, grabbing for her gun. An unnatural light bathed them in green and yellow. They struggled together in a blur of limbs and grunts and curses. Bang! The flurry of movement stopped. They went still. The Commander staggered back; her gloved hand wet and dripping.

Father slumped to the ground, face first, unmoving. I bit down on my hand to stifle an anguished scream. A coppery taste filled my mouth, but I felt no pain.

"Bloody hell!" The Commander peeled off her glove and swore again. "Suit up and take the body back to the truck. Maybe we can salvage something out of this mess. The rest of you fan out. The boy's here somewhere. Find him!"

Her soldiers hurried to follow the commands. They spread out and tramped through the brush in my direction. I hugged the tree trunk and made myself invisible.

This couldn't be happening. He can't be dead.

Was he really my father and Ian my brother? Questions swirled in dizzying pursuit of the truth. Corpses can't answer, not anymore. A sharp throb along my temple from the tree's hard bark confirmed I wasn't dreaming. He said he didn't know who my mother was, the same as all the others stuck in confinement. If he lied about this, what else had he lied about?

Wordless screams built in my throat and strangled my chest, caught in the suffocating snare of my grief and sense of betrayal. Despite everything, he cared for me, raised me, gave me his name. Loved me. Taught me everything I needed to know to survive in these woods. If that didn't make him my father, what else could?

After an hour of fruitless searching, the soldiers gathered back at our shelter. The commander ordered them to ran-sack the place. They left as the last rays of the sun filtered through the treetops.

My palm closed around my necklace and the talons of the griffin dug into my skin, threatening to puncture. Tears stung the corners of my eyes and blurred the carving in the dim light. Was this the research the Commander was looking for?

I waited another three hours before I built up the nerve to climb out of my hiding spot. In the darkness, I grabbed whatever supplies I could salvage and shoved them into a tattered backpack. My father's hunting knife was stuck to the trunk of our shelter, both a warning and a promise.

The chilly air makes me shiver. Despite my mind wandering, my feet knew where to take me. The hunting shack I've been staying at looms in front of me. It held a treasure trove of supplies when I found it last month. Mischief skitters past my feet and up the stairs, then stops and waits for me to open the door to let him in.

"Dinner first, buddy." I place the rabbit in the lopsided circle of rocks where I make my campfire.

With the onset of fall, the days are growing shorter. One or two more supply runs and I'll have enough to head for the Free Territories. This necklace will destroy the Authority. I'll tear apart everything the Commander's worked for.

She'll never get her hands on this research, no matter the cost.

A life for a life.

# 4

## REI

**Every scar tells a story, but mine are screaming.**

Bright light does nothing to chase away the darkness that's tormenting me. The MMZ med center is coming to life as dawn filters through the window. Soft moans, distant snores, and discordant beeps accompany my hiss of pain. The thin mattress does little to help me find a comfortable position for my healing ribs.

Boots echo in the hall outside my room. There's a squeak and thud followed by lowered voices.

"—had one job to do. One! Do you know what this cost us?"

"We were ambushed and outnumbered! Half of my platoon died in the bombing!"

"Pathetic excuses."

"But mom—"

"I put you in charge and look what I have to bloody show for it. Nothing. Just one problem after another."

"I'm trying!"

"Not hard enough. The situation is spiraling out of control. We have to get ahead of this before it's too late. I'm re-assigning you to the search effort, effective immediately."

"Grandma was right—"

*Thwack!* The distinct echo of flesh connecting cuts through the ambient noise.

"Not. Another. Word. You're dismissed."

Alyssa limps past the doorway, shoulders rigid, one hand pressed to her cheek. Commander Lynx sweeps into my room, her presence looming over me. Piercing gray eyes suck the air out of the space. A shiver runs through me and my fingers curl into my sheets.

"At ease, soldier. Don't bother getting up, this won't take long. Come now, stay still, you need time to heal from your injuries."

Muscles scream when I drag myself into a sitting position. "Commander Lynx," Biceps trembling, I salute anyways, letting her drink in the battered sight of me.

"I'm placing you on administrative leave. Quite frankly, Rei, I'm not sure you're cut out to be an Enforcer."

"No." The immediate force of my response holds my conviction.

"No?" Commander Lynx raises a dangerous, questioning eyebrow.

Don't flinch, don't turn away, let her see every ounce of my resolve. She steps closer, becomes more threatening.

"You chose me for Enforcer training because I'm not like the others, you need me. No soldier is more dedicated to the cause. The Authority keeps us safe and I swear I won't let you down."

"Again. You won't let me down, again." An amused smirk crosses the hard line of her lips. "You know, you remind me of myself at your age. Loyal, determined, and best of all, willing to do whatever it takes.... Still—my decision stands."

She spins on her heel and crosses to the door. My heart plummets further with every step.

I can't breathe.

Commander Lynx pivots at the threshold, a thoughtful expression lighting up her face. "Report back after the Cleansing and we'll re-assess your future with the Enforcers," she says upon her exit..

Oxygen crashes back into my lungs with a deep, shuddering breath. She may as well have slapped me, too.

An hour later, a nurse bustles in to dismiss me. Once the drugs she gives me stop the pain from kicking my ass, I take a bus and walk the last few blocks to my childhood apartment. Civvies crowd the sidewalks, busily preparing for the upcoming festivities. The earthy, sweet scent of burning fire is my favorite thing about this time of year. Red ribbons flutter from railings, door knobs, light posts, and shop signs in memory of those cleansed in the mass pyres.

I wish I could burn away my shame the same way, let the flames consume me. Maybe it would hurt less.

Because it's all my fault.

I should have insisted she ditch the case. We shouldn't have gone back, Sympathizers be damned.

Would Commander Lynx dismiss me the moment I returned? If she wanted me gone, why order me to report in after the holiday? Maybe she doesn't know what to do with me. Rounding up new trainees takes time.

Or did I get through to her, somehow...?

I swipe my tether at the front door, unlocking it with a click. The tiny space brings back a sour, nostalgic feeling. A short trip down the hall brings me to my room with a wall desk, half-empty bookshelf, and crisply made bed.

And here I am, tucked beneath my covers. Cameron can't flash her gap-toothed smile, stand too freaking close, and prattle on and on. The lackeys will never follow Alyssa around like love-sick puppy dogs. Dr. Martina's broadcasts are a thing of the past. Every time I close my eyes I'm pulling the trigger. Blood drenches a white lab coat. The picture of the boy plummets through the air and burns in the fire, screaming my name.

The hard knot inside me swells.

Feet pad across the threadbare rug. The mattress shifts as my mother, Naomi, sits beside me.

I tense.

"It's been two days," she says.

I grunt and burrow deeper. Can't she just keep ignoring me?

"Get up. Do—something." She yanks the blanket off my head.

I grab it and pull it back over. "Go away."

She sighs. Metal springs creak as she stands and leaves.

Why can't she console me, and tell me everything will be okay like a normal mother? Nope, not her.

As a kid I thought her detachment was a sign of strength and resilience. The way she would brush me off and say "you'll be fine," when I scraped my knees, sending me on my way. Or how preoccupied she was when she wasn't drilling me for mindless information or praising me for my achievements.

*Thunk!*

What's she doing now?

Footsteps shuffle, growing louder.

She must be making herself breakfast before heading to work.

Cold water drenches me. I shriek and scramble out from my blanket. Everything is soaking wet, my mattress, sheet, and comforter.

"Rei Koss, get up or I'll drag you out of there," she says, letting the empty bucket clatter to the ground.

"Fine!" I tear off the soggy covers and stomp to the bathroom, slamming the door behind me.

Low-wattage light bulbs cast a murky yellow glow in the cramped space. There's hardly enough room to do more than turn around or sit on the toilet. The woman in the small, cracked mirror above the sink is unhealthy. Dark circles ring her eyes from restless nights and accentuate gaunt, angular cheekbones.

Hollow.

I shiver in my wet nightgown and yank it over my head. Bruises criss-crossing my chest and belly makes me cringe. They've faded to horrid shades of purplish-blue and yellowish-green. The skin on my temple is pink and tender where the scab fell off. I didn't know a tiny cut could bleed so much.

The blinding ache in my ribs stopped yesterday. I miss the throbbing pain. It felt better than the lump burrowing beneath my ribcage.

My tether swipes against the sink faucet and the sensor beeps, turning red. Denied. Bless the mother! She poured our whole damn quota on me.

"Put your bedding in to dry and come eat, " my mother calls as I pad naked back to my room.

I try to contain my annoyance as I dress and pile the damp bedding into my arms. If my mother loves me, she sure has a funny way of showing it. A trail of droplets makes the floor a mess as I head for the laundry. The dryer is in the closet of the small nursery separating our rooms. I shove the mess inside and turn it on.

My foot slips and sends me crashing into the edge of the crib. Cursing, I curl my toes against the pain. A floppy stuffed cat sits inside, judging me with its oversized, stitched on eyes.

"What are you looking at?" I demand. Of course, there's no response.

The empty nursery feels like an additional checkmark in a growing list of failures. During my last mandatory physical, the doctor reassured me my tether reported no fertility issues. There were nearly a hundred drawings a year but with five tickets my odds were less than six percent.

I turn my back on the crib and pick up the small picture frame on the changing table. Has this always been here? The closeup of the tree has a blurry green forest in the background. There's a triangle carved around a circular knot in the tree trunk. Weird.

"Rei, what's taking you so long—Oh." She reaches over and takes the photo from me.

"I haven't seen this before." It seems out of place for her minimalistic sense of less-is-more decor.

"Someone I helped transport supplies gave it to me." She traces a longing finger over the glass. "They died a few years ago."

"Who?"

Mother's mouth quivers. Her head shakes as she places the photo back down on the surface.

"Life is short, Rei. Come on, let's eat and you can tell me about your training."

A typical non-answer topped with a dollop of blatant insensitivity. Yep. Grin and bear it like a good girl. Just plaster on a fake smile and pretend she cares. My future daughter wouldn't be subjected to the same distant cynicism and indifferent nagging.

I sink down into the wobbly chair at our kitchen table. My mother places a veritable feast before me: grilled chicken breast, roasted vegetables, and pasta. She must have used a full day's rations to provide this spread.

She motions to my fork. "You've lost weight since the last time I saw you. Don't they feed you over there?"

I pick at my carrots to appease her efforts. "Of course they do," I grumble and put the smallest bite into my mouth. It's delicious. We cooked together every night when I was a child. One year, during a severe drought and lean crop, we had a flour fight in a powdery fit of squeals and giggles. Hard to believe she's the same person.

"Tell me about your barracks. Did they move you since you started Enforcer training? I hope you got a better room. Don't you like the veggies? I tried three different markets to find the broccoli."

"They're good." I humor her by taking another bite.

"So? I haven't seen you in almost a year. The least you could do is catch me up on how you've been."

My fork clatters to my plate. The table lurches as I stand. "Really? How I'm doing! How do you think I'm doing after being bombed and failing my mission? Huh?"

"Rei, stop overreacting and sit down." Her voice is flat and unaffected. "You're a soldier, act like one." Her dismissive gesture and cold reassurance drill into me like a naughty child who needs scolding.

"Dr. Martina is dead! She was our best hope of finding a cure." My voice quivers as I hold back tears. "What have I done?" I blink hard to stop the flood.

"It's okay to cry. To grieve." My mother's voice softens. If I didn't know her better, I'd think she's showing actual concern. "Life doesn't care about your misery. People die in the line of duty. You'll have other fights, other missions, and losses. Now sit down and finish eating."

Yep, she can't be bothered by anything deep or meaningful. Keep it surface level, factual, artificial. Do your duty, be a good soldier. Work harder, become an Enforcer, make rank. One achievement after the other is all she cares about. I open my mouth to speak.

Curse. Scream. To say every vicious thought clamoring around my head. The words catch on the terrible weight in my chest.

Stuck.

Tears pour down my face and splatter the tabletop. Have I doomed us all to the Heart Blight? Will she ever care about me?

She takes a bite of her chicken. "Mara asked about you. She'd like to see you while you're on leave. Why don't you girls meet at your favorite coffee shop?"

I sink into my seat, eyes fixed on my plate, afraid of the disregard I might see on her face. This is unbearable. I have to leave, to take a break from her, from myself.

Especially when she's right.

# 5

## REI

### Healing isn't something you find—it's comfort you leave behind.

As a young girl, the childless woman with wild gray hair and bulging eyes terrified me. Today I tower over the hunched, skeletal frame of Mrs. Wellsly. She pulls a moldy crust of bread from the trash bin outside our apartment door. Her lips peel back in a toothless smile, tongue darting over the edges of her irritated gums. Culls, or the last person in a motherline, have a tendency to develop peculiar behaviors.

"Didn't expect you until the Cleansing," she says in a croaking voice. Her smell is more pungent than I remember.

"Plans change," is all I can say as I scoot past her in the narrow space. I still can't understand what treasures she thinks she'll find.

Her cackle follows me down the stairs and around the corner. A large mural of the Director is the focal point of the narrow lobby. Some cocky kid had the brass to draw a curly mustache under her nose. Her mother stands behind her, hands on hips.

"Do you know what Enforcers do to naughty girls?"

"I'm sorry! I p-p-promise I'll be good. Don't let them suppress me!" The girl's wailing intensifies.

"Stop crying. There, you missed a spot. If they report you we'll lose half a day of rations." Her mother startles, recognition dawning. Hands clench the girl's shoulders and drags her out of my path.

Defacing the Director may well be a rite of passage in our building. The thin, smudgy mustache has nothing on the twisting forked tongue and pointed devil horns that Mara and I painted. Half rations for a week didn't put a damper on our nightly antics, either.

Hints of fall greet me as I exit our apartment building. A shiver skitters between my shoulders. I tuck my hands in the pockets of my lightweight jacket. If I walk fast, the trip to the coffee shop takes 10 minutes. I lengthen my stride.

Groups of older school girls exchange gossip, blocking the sidewalk at the end of the street. Their uniforms remind me that I'm not wearing mine. If I were, they would be obligated to move aside. But in my old shirt and pants, their gossip continues uninterrupted. I step off the cracked sidewalk and take my chances on the rutted street.

A passing car makes my muscles clench and my heart kick into overdrive. I release a long, shuddering breath. It's just a car. It won't explode. Repeating it over and over makes it feel true.

Two blocks later I'm getting closer to the commercial district. Smaller, squat buildings replace the tall cement apartments interspersed with drab, breaking playgrounds. As their height diminishes, their girth expands. Single-level wide display cases replace tall multi-story window slits. Faded brick facades punctuate some of the monotony of the cement.

In the shopping district, the sidewalks grow crowded and my progress matches the slog. Women and children of various ages walk in groups large and small, browsing and popping in and out of shops.

Three young girls squeal, giggle, and run, pushing past the throng with no regard for who they bump into.

"Get to decontamination, we'll be safe there!"

"Faster, she's catching up!"

Behind them a smaller, flush-faced girl yells, "I'm infected! I'm gonna get you!"

One woman tries to snatch the last girl's arm as she thunders past. Her packages fly out of her hands instead. Cement explodes in all directions and I duck, protecting my face. But it's only one of her brown bags landing beside me, not shards of glass or deadly shrapnel.

Dammit. What's wrong with me?

"Hey! Watch it, you brats!" The woman shakes her fist after their oblivious backsides.

Stooping on shaky legs, I retrieve the bag. She takes it and pats the top of my hand. "Lysara, bless you," she says.

"Authority keep you safe," I reply, rather than accepting her useless, Old God.

Loyal Grounds is the largest coffee shop on this side of the city. The warm, comforting scent of coffee assaults my nose as I push through the crowded doors. Familiar sights, sounds, and scents wash over me; low conversation, clinking spoons stirring mugs of coffee, the purr of the grinders, and a rich aroma with nutty undertones. I'm not sure we'll find a seat when Mara's arm shoots into the air from a front table. The ones reserved for expecting mothers.

"Rei!" she calls, waving her arms in big, sweeping motions.

"Mar?" I halt in front of her, taking in her large, pregnant belly.

"Surprise?" She beams and throws her arms around me.

"You're so big I can hardly hug you. Look at you!" I push away and hold her out at arm's length. "How did I miss your name in the lottery? Why didn't you tell me? Has it really been almost a year since we last spoke?"

"Ugh, babe, I wanted to tell you. I did. Things have been crazy. The winner of my lottery died before her insemination so my name was pulled from a backup drawing. Between morning sickness, doctors' appointments, comms failures, and an overflowing workload, I'm exhausted every night." We sit down and she reaches across the table, grabbing my hands.

"When are you due?"

"Four weeks. Let me tell you, I am so ready to be done. Everything hurts. I can hardly sleep, and this girl has a mean right hook." She smiles and presses a hand to her belly. "Do you wanna feel her? She's kicking."

"Really? Damn, she's so strong!"

"Will you be her auntie?" she asks.

"Me?" Envy, shock, confusion, disappointment, joy, and despair. The turmoil of each churning emotion is a slap in the face. Like a cruel joke.

Mara wipes a tear out of the corner of my eye. "Of course you! Besties forever, right?"

It's a fight to plaster a smile on my face. "I would be honored." Despite everything, I mean it.

"Crap, you're making me cry too! I've been so hormonal, let me tell you. Everything makes me a mess now." She sniffs and wipes her cheeks. "They reported the bombing on the CVB yesterday. Are you okay?"

I take a deep breath and steel myself. "No," I shake my head. "I'm not okay."

"Do you wanna talk about it?"

"I can't explain it, Mar. I was there, but it doesn't seem real. It's eating me up inside. It's like I'm being hollowed out and evicted from my body."

Mara scoots her chair closer. "Remember what we'd do when our moms got mad at us? Bet our chairs are still on the roof. How high did we count to?"

I take a deep, shuddering breath. "We never hit a million."

Mara's the closest thing I'll ever have to a sister. Laying beside her and gazing at the stars were some of my favorite memories. She had no expectations beyond friendship. I would wonder what's wrong with me, why I wasn't attracted to the prettiest girls in my class like the rest were, and if love could be so vast and unconditional. She'd smile and we'd dare each other to count higher, sneak out past curfew, and evade patrols. The perfect partner in crime.

"I'm sure your mom isn't helping the situation any," Mara says with a grimace. "Yeah, I thought so," she adds in response to my frown.

"Who knows if I'll still be in Enforcer training after the Cleansing, and all she cares about is grilling me. I can hardly sleep yet she wants to know everything I'm trying to forget. How can she be so horrible?"

"I think you need a vacation. Get away from her awful nagging. You could stay at the lake house. Give yourself time to unwind, get out of the city. Clear your head, right?"

"What about you? The baby is due soon. How could I miss becoming an auntie? You hear me, little one, I'm your auntie." I whisper into her bulging tummy. There's a forceful kick in response.

"Ugh," Mara digs into the spot with a hand. "This little girl isn't going anywhere. You'll be back in plenty of time to enjoy my increasing misery. I swear I have to pee every 20 minutes."

"All night long?"

"Yeah. Terrible, huh? Even work has taken pity on me. I'm delegated to monitoring surveillance videos or patching shitty comm signals. Our satellite is on its last leg, plus there's terrible reception in the Brass Mountains. What do they expect when they pour our best resources into the labs, and tethers, and water purifiers? They're important, but I can't work miracles with ancient tech that's constantly falling apart."

"They must be looking for Sympathizers."

"Well that would explain the surge of activity these past few months. It's super boring work, but at least I get frequent bathroom breaks. Oh, and get this, we've been fighting all week trying to get the Director to sign off on a USB to fix a bunch of comms issues. Her office keeps running me around in circles. You'd think I asked for a trip to the moon, hah! Like that could ever happen." She snorts and rolls her eyes.

"You ready to order?" A stoic woman wearing a red apron appears beside our table.

"Oh, no. It tastes terrible," Mara says, curling her lip back like she's swallowed some already.

"And you?" She asks me, rolling her eyes rather than bothering to turn her head.

"I can't freaking stand it. Smells great, though."

"Seriously?" the waitress asks in a deadpan voice. "If you're not ordering you should leave."

Mara and I exchange glances.

"Water, please." Mara says and we stifle our grins.

"Whatever...." The waitress shuffles away.

"Well she was fun. That never gets old," Mara says, her amusement finally getting the best of her.

"I've missed you."

"Me too. Now before I forget, and our pleasant entertainment returns, let me tell you where we hide the key to the lake house."

# 6

# REI

**Strange encounters make me question
if I should stay...or run.**

If I turn the key the car won't explode. My heart beats so loud I can
hear it in my ears. It's all in my head, I can do this, nothing is going
to happen. One finger touches the keychain and I hyperventilate.

"Dammit!"

The smug look on my mother's face if I walk back into the
apartment with my backpack goads me on. She berated me for over
an hour this morning, gnawing at me with her strange, I could care
less attitude. Like she enjoyed rubbing salt into infected wounds.
The irony was palpable when she handed me an antibiotic cream.

"I'm a soldier. You think I can't handle a few days in the woods?"

She only shrugged. "The bugs and snakes are terrible this time of
year."

"Yeah, and you sit behind a desk every day. You know what, don't
bother calling. I need a break from you too."

"My job is just as important as yours. Wait, come back. Rei!"

The door slammed and scared Mrs. Wellsly when I stormed out.
She dropped the trash bag she was rifling through and bits of paper
and garbage spilled all over the hallway.

No. I wasn't going back. The keys sway, waiting for me. Give it a few minutes and try again.

Sirens blare across the city. The street explodes with a frenzy of activity. Women and children race for home, put on expensive hydro-jackets with clear hoods, or move beneath canopies. My tether lets out a high-pitched screech, amplified by the cramped interior of the car.

Thunder grumbles in the distance. Rain is coming.

Fat drops splatter my windshield exactly five minutes later. A group of teenage girls rounds the corner of my apartment building, sprinting for the closest awning, completely unprotected.

Rainbow chasers.

The tethers implanted in their wrists activate, temporarily shielding them from the contaminated rain. With every frenzied stride they take, the glowing color changes. First deep forest green, then the hue of scraggly weeds before a tinge of gold appears, increasing in intensity.

The shortest girl can't keep up with the rest. Yellow rapidly darkens to a ruddy orange.

Her friends duck under the awning and out of the rain, hooting and hollering, oblivious to the one left behind.

The red glow surrounding her swirls with black. She won't make it.

Sixty seconds, that's how long a tether protects from the virus. Upon exposure to the Heart Blight, being untethered is the only way to stop further mutations.

The girl slams face first into the sidewalk, body jerking and twitching. Frothy foam at her mouth is washed away by the sudden downpour. Cleansing taught us an extremely valuable lesson, the Heart Blight can't infect the dead.

Rain drums the ground and streams into the gutters. Collectors will dispatch for cleanup duty once the storm passes.

The girl's empty gaze stares into the void. That might have been me if my mother hadn't pushed me. Stronger, faster, better. Always the best. Mara and I spent a whole year chasing until her mother found out and moved them to a district on the other side of town.

Gritting my teeth, I grab the key and turn the ignition. The engine sputters to life and fizzles back out. I gun the gas pedal a few times until the rattling stops. Time to go.

For such a compact car, and one we didn't drive often, the vehicle was reliable enough once it started. I try not to think about a similar trip as I head for the first checkpoint out of town. This isn't the same. For one, this is the opposite direction. Two, it's not an armed Enforcer convoy. Three...yeah, forget about three. The other two were good enough. I hope.

The skies are clear and the roads are dry by the time I reach the first checkpoint. A soldier at the gate gestures for me to roll down my window, letting in an earthy scent. My marching orders from the MMZ lay on the passenger seat next to me. She waves me through without issue after glancing at them. One checkpoint down, two more to go.

Getting through checkpoints is another perk of the military. Civvies apply for travel permits and those could take weeks or months for approval. Many civvies didn't bother with a car since rations included two bus trips a day.

The road grows smoother and it's easier to avoid potholes the further I get from the city. Industrial buildings trade with greenery as I pass through the second checkpoint. The red cast off the peaks of the Brass Mountains paints the interior of the car in hues of warm browns and yellow-golds.

My mind wanders as the trees grow taller, more dense.

Is time from home really the solution? I know my leave will end. If I'm not kicked out they'll assign new trainees. A fresh group of recruits to haze and endure tireless training sessions with. Would I remain just as useless as before? Was all my training for nothing?

Commander Lynx hand picked me, the Authority needs me. Alyssa certainly saw me as a threat based on the number of times she made my life a living hell in the MMZ. What did they see in me that I couldn't?

The tomato sandwich in my bag hits the spot when I take a bite. Goods with low water footprint are easy on the rations. Legs aching from driving all morning, I pull off the road and find a place to stretch. It's at least another hour until the third checkpoint.

Wind blows through the trees and their leaves whisper. Strange, not hearing the sounds of the city. Chirping of crickets and the whistle of birds replaces patrols and the bustle of people. It's a different kind of background noise, more relaxed, less anxious.

Turning the key in the ignition is easier this time. The third checkpoint comes and goes. A weathered sign with faded letters stands guard by the small town of Albrin. Children deploy sticks as make-believe swords and play in dirty trenches. Older women drive machinery into enormous natural choke points, arched tunnels framed with PVC and covered by transparent tarps. Pastures with grazing animals and crop fields leave the landscape open, sprawling, exposed. I've never seen so much grass in my life.

Man, it's hot. Rolling down the window relieves the blaring afternoon sun and lets the breeze whip past my hair. At least I'm almost there. The winding road rocks the car, the surface changing from pavement to gravel. Trees stand in formation on either side and cast shadows across the narrow lane. Some of them are changing colors. Vibrant hues of green, red, and yellow surround me. Spectacular.

This is the most peaceful and free I've felt in days. Mara's right. I needed this. No reminders of the city, the MMZ, my prodding mother, or myself.

I've never been to Mara's lake house before, but I've heard so much about it. Growing up, Mara, her mother, and grandmother would make the day-long trip every summer, leaving me bored for several unbearable weeks. Now I understand why.

The house is so well camouflaged it takes me a moment to separate the structure from the forest. Squat wooden architecture blends seamlessly into the landscape, framed by a sparkling lake and a view of the mountains beyond. Steps and terraced patios, one with a quaint fire pit, leads to the lower story. A wall of glass floor-to-ceiling windows frames an intricately carved green front door. The upper floor has another array of enormous windows, highlighting the natural views surrounding it.

"No wonder she loves it here," the car rolls to a stop and I pry clenched fingers from the steering wheel, grabbing my bag in the passenger seat.

It's a little chilly in the shade, so I tug on my lightweight jacket and take the stairs two at a time, bypassing the house for the scenic view. Leaves and helicopter seeds flutter to the ground. The lake is so clear and smooth it takes my breath away. Coppery, golden light frames the tips of the Brass Mountains. Trees stand guard on the opposite bank. The glassy surface of the water reflects the jewel tones of the changing leaves, heightening the charm.

"Wow...." No picture could ever do it justice. I let my bag slip off my shoulder and approach the edge of the lake where it laps over the rocks. It's so clear I see my reflection; windswept hair and a touch of astonishment. Sunlight warms the top of my head and shoulders. The pressure in my chest eases ever so slightly.

The rock, worn smooth on all sides, calls to me. Mara liked to tell me stories of hours spent skipping stones. How they'll make concentric circles as they bounce. She showed me once, one day after entry school, to flick your wrist and let them fly. But there was no water like this in the city, only a sea of cement.

I lift my arm to throw, the tug of a smile on the corners of my lips.

Beep boop! Beep boop!

The odd noise coming from my tether stops me in my tracks. What the heck? Skin beneath the back of my hand blinks blue in time with the strange melody when it triggers a second time.

Blue? Never seen it turn that color before. That can't be good.

A wave of panic surges and my eyes go skyward. Not a single cloud in sight, if its not rain, then what? Get inside first, questions later. Jogging back to the door is faster than walking.

"Where did she say the spare key was?" I rifle through a few potted planters, a knee high deer statue, and a storage box next to the front door. Damn, no luck, should have paid more attention.

I lift the weighted floormat, "Jackpot!"

The door swings open without a sound despite its heft. One step inside and I'm returned to the confines of the Authority. Simple decor in the living room meets all government standards: a couch with two flat pillows sits across from a TV, side table with a lamp, telephone and answering machine. There's no need to explore to know I'll find a galley kitchen with a table and flimsy chairs, cramped full bath, two narrow bedrooms and a tiny nursery. It's like walking back into my apartment with the added bonus of fantastic views.

Beep boop! Beep boop!

Right, call Mara. I bite my lip and reach for the phone beside the couch. Huh? No dial tone. Putting it back on the hook doesn't make a difference either. Its plugged in so why isn't it working? Maybe the power is out? I flick the lightswitch. Nope, lights work just fine.

Trust my luck to end up outside of comms range, truly cut off from everything and everyone.

"Mischief, what're ya doing?" the deep baritone makes my heart skip a beat.

The man emerges from the kitchen, arms full of dented cans and dusty jars from a time long gone. Fading afternoon sunlight casts a soft, golden glow upon him, highlighting broad shoulders and shaggy, dark hair falling across his forehead. He's so different from the men in the fuzzy, black and white entry school videos. Taller, bulkier, more substantial.

He freezes.

Vibrant green eyes flash in surprise when they meet mine. They're so...familiar? An odd sensation stirs low in my belly.

A survivor?

Here?

How?

A can falls from his cache with a thud and rolls across the hardwood floor. Authority-issue combat boots block its progress when it bumps into my toe, heightening the absurdity of the situation.

There's a ticking time bomb standing right in front of me.

"Bless the mother!" I reach for my gun and falter. Of course it's not there.

His whole body reacts to the sound of my voice like a visceral punch in the gut. Waking from whatever spell he's caught up in, his eyes dart to a lumpy backpack, knife, bow and quiver on the kitchen counter. If he gets to them first, I'm dead. If he gets his bow, I'm dead. If he touches me for longer than sixty seconds, I'm dead.

My options are tanking. Dammit! I'm in for a blight storm no matter how I look at it.

He drops his bounty. Cans dent the floor and jars shatter, coating the ground in slimy, salty brine and thick, sticky syrup, all rolling haphazardly. Lunging, he goes for the weapons.

Instinctively I react, diving forward to prevent him from getting the upper hand. A sweep of my arm sends the contents of the counter crashing to the ground. The knife skitters across the floor, sliding through the mess. Huge hands grab for me. Twisting, I fling myself backwards, landing face first on the ground as I tumble, smashing the feathered ends of arrows in his quiver.

Dirty boots skirt past me. He's going for the knife! My kick sweeps his feet from under him. He lands hard, the walls shaking from the impact when he hits his back.

He scrambles up, grabbing his backpack.

Crap, this isn't good. Do something, quick! The heavy can of pineapple hits his shoulder. It's not a gun, but it's better than nothing. The next smashes his hand grabbing for the bow. He jerks back, shaking his fingers in pain.

Aim for his head, incapacitate the enemy. The jam grazes his temple, stunning him, giving me a momentary opening.

My free hand shoots toward the blade. Get up, maintain a tactical advantage. Fingertips curl around the slippery hilt and I scramble to my feet.

An iron grip encircles my wrist, jerking me backwards against an unyielding chest, trying to disarm me. Blue light explodes from my tether. Warmth radiates and tingles across my skin where the paper-thin hydro barrier separates me from the deadly virus.

"Let go!" My scream mirrors his bark of surprise. I slam my elbow into his nose and tear free, catching the collar of his shirt when I swing the knife and spin to face him.

The glow disappears the moment he evades my counter attack, releasing me. A prickly sensation lingers on my forearm and shoulders despite the brief contact. Way too close for comfort. Better not let it happen again.

Chests heaving, clothing soaked and dripping, we stare each other down. The air is charged, thick, like I could scoop it into my palm and pour it through my fingers. I can't tear my eyes away from the material clinging to his body. Even soldiers who train day in and day out are soft, plump, curvy—he's the exact opposite.

His eyes flick over my breasts and heat floods my cheeks. Dammit! What's wrong with me?

Focus!

"Your hand's shaking...you planning to stab me or seduce me with that thing?" A dark eyebrow arches. He wipes jelly from his nose and smears it across his rugged jawline. He takes a bold step forward.

Don't back down, don't give him an inch.

"Awe, worried about me? Cute. Clearly I can handle myself." A month of knife drills doesn't make me proficient by any means. But he doesn't know that.

His lips quirk, front teeth flashing, and rich laughter fills the first floor.

"Am I some kinda joke to you? We'll see who's laughing when the Authority gets here."

The man's amusement falters, his body stiffens, and he rocks onto the balls of his feet.

"Who are you? What are you doing outside of containment?" Twirling my wrist reverses my grip on the knife for better defense.

Something hard and white bumps my forearm. The foreign object dangles from a thin, leather cord, tangled around the blade's hilt.

What the hell is this?

Eyes going wide, his hand flies to his chest and comes up empty. His eyes harden and narrow, lips thinning, a muscle ticks in his jaw, and both nostrils flare.

"That's mine," he growls, low and menacing. "Give it back and maybe I'll let ya live."

Apparently I've stumbled upon another advantage. Interesting....

"Touch me and you'll never see it again," I hiss, my body responding with a swirl of uncharted emotions.

# 7

## REI

**The wilderness has no mercy, and I am blind to the price it demands.**

The air stills, blood pounds between my ears, and the intensity in his green eyes rips the breath from my lungs. Goosebumps prickle my skin and a bead of sweat runs down my neck. All of my instincts are screaming at the top of their lungs and I'm torn by what they're saying.

He's blocking the only way out. Anticipate his next move, brace for his attack. Get out of here.

Now!

He launches and I spin, dodging past him. Heart pounding wildly, I race out of the house, leap down the steps, and sprint for my vehicle.

There's a crash behind me. Don't turn around. Faster!

How many arrows does he have? How far can he shoot? It's not like a gun, it can't have the same range. The closer he gets, the easier a target I become.

I yank open the car door and fling myself inside. The engine sputters when I twist the key. Bless the mother, start, dammit!

An arrow shatters the side mirror and I shriek in surprise. He stands in the open doorway, draws another from his quiver and takes aim. Thunk! There's a hiss of air as the front tire deflates.

Try again. Come on! I turn the key—nothing.

"I said give it back!" he roars, nocking another arrow, aiming for my face.

I duck and glass from the windshield showers my head and neck. The arrow trembles where it's embedded in the driver's seat. Too freaking accurate for comfort. Gotta move, put more distance between us. I slither into the passenger's seat and grab the door handle, throwing the door open.

Knife in hand, hunched low, I execute my mad dash for the treeline. After I've lost him I can circle back.

"Fuck!" His footsteps echo across the patio as he charges after me. Another arrow whizzes past my head.

Branches and leaves catch my jacket and the sides of my hair as I run, crashing through the brush. A prickly vine tears across the skin of my cheek and the palm of my hand as I shove it aside.

I find a narrow track and sprint down the path. My heart thunders in my chest and I suck in ragged breaths. Jogging on the flat surface of the MMZ is much, much easier than this uneven ground. Roots and rocks obstruct my every stride. Thick combat boots and momentum are the saving grace.

For once I'm grateful for Alyssa's hard assery and our daily runs. The white object bumps my wrist in time with my strides.

What the heck is this thing? I pull it free and tuck it into my bra so I don't drop it.

A faint sound to my right gives me pause. There it is again, closer this time. I plow headlong off the track in the opposite direction. He's still behind me, haven't lost him yet. Ducking a low branch, I leap over a fallen tree trunk. Nettle cuts sting my hands and arms. Don't stop. Force it out of mind and run faster.

I can't let him get within his ridiculously huge firing range. Although the trees help create natural cover, don't take it for granted.

Vision narrows and my ears strain. There, I heard it again. I turn left and keep running. Here, farther from the lake, the underbrush thins. Trees grow larger along with their branches, making it easier to see and navigate, but leaving me more exposed. Low light filters down between the canopy, shadows dancing across the ground.

When my chest is burning, I slow to a jog and then walk, pressing a hand against the stitch in my side. I take deep, gasping breaths, trying to get enough air. Huffing so hard it's all I can hear at this point.

Figure out which way he's gone. I stop and put my hands on my knees to catch my breath. As my panting slows, I listen for movement. Running blind is pointless. A bird caws and leaves whisper. Turning in a circle doesn't help me figure out where he is. I don't hear him, either.

Must've lost him.

His challenging green eyes, snarky smile, and hearty laughter plays on a loop in my head. What the hell is wrong with me? Here I am running for my life and all I can think about are the hard contours of his arms, shoulders, and chest. Is this what attraction feels like? A lifetime spent thinking that there's something broken inside of me, not understanding what the fuss is about, and now I'm suddenly, what? Fixed?

My heart flutters in my chest and my palms grow damp. I press my hands to my sweaty forehead. It's time to circle back to the lake house. He's out there somewhere, carrying a mutating virus that's threatening what little remains of humanity. Picking the direction I swore I heard him last, I jog the opposite way.

Stay vigilant.

Legs exhausted and trembling, I slow to a walk again. Shivers trail my spine from a chilly breeze. My clothes are plastered in brine and sugary syrup. The lightweight jacket isn't helping much. The sun is setting and the lake house is nowhere in sight. I wipe my brow and let out a string of curses.

Finding this escaped survivor is exactly what I need to get back into Commander Lynx's good graces. Get back and report to the Authority, call for reinforcements. Failure to do so is akin to aiding a national threat.

Treason.

I lengthen my strides. My mouth feels gritty, no matter how often I swallow, it doesn't help. A drink would do wonders right now. The ground grows rocky and fades with the light.

Panic wraps its shadowy tendrils around my neck. Why is it getting dark so fast? I should have been back by now. Where am I? Keep walking.

It's getting harder to see more than a few feet in front of my face. A branch catches me across the cheek and I feel the sting of the cut it leaves behind. A big winged bug smacks the side of my head. I wave and bat my hands like a cull to make it go away.

Within minutes, it's so dark I can hardly make out the hand I hold out to keep from smacking into another branch. An oppressive feeling squeezes my sides as the darkness deepens.

"I'm not in the tunnel," I whimper, like it might help. "You're fine, just taking a stroll in the woods...so you're not killed by the enemy. You'll be back in no time."

*Crash!*

Something large is racing through the woods behind me. I spin, but I can't see. The noise is growing louder, getting closer.

Is he trying to sneak up on me?

My whole body tenses and I move into a fighting stance, knife out and ready. I hold my breath.

The buck's antler nearly skewers my forehead as it leaps past me.

I gasp and scramble backwards.

My left foot expects ground behind it but finds a rock instead. The world tilts.

I throw my hands out and my elbow bangs into a tree trunk before my fingers dig into bark. My right foot smashes through a rotten stump and I catch my balance just in time.

Shivering, I right myself.

"Argh!" A white hot poker gouges my right ankle. I pull out a sharp piece of wood and gingerly extract my foot from the jagged hole. Warm, sticky blood pools in my palm and oozes past my fingers. There's so much.

Medical training kicks in. Stop the bleeding.

My other leg wobbles and I stumble to the ground. I let go of my cut long enough to strip out of my jacket. Gritting my teeth, I wrap my leg and tie the two arms together, pulling them tight. Stifling my scream brings the taste of iron to my mouth.

"Great, just great!" Things just can't get any worse, can they?

Tremors rock through me when I come down from the adrenaline rush. I'm going into shock. Gotta keep moving.

Groaning, I shift my injured leg. The jacket is already soaked. I place my hand on the tree next to me and get my good leg underneath. With a big effort, I push up and stand. I try a tentative step. Pain stabs. I keel over, forehead pressed to the rough bark, trying not to pass out.

Looks like walking on it isn't an option. Maybe if I had a stick to lean on? It's so dark that finding one I can use will be difficult. Squinting at the ground, I attempt to move to the next tree.

Three hops and a wave of dizziness overwhelms me. Wait for the ground to stop whirling then keep going.

*Crack.*

The sound of a twig snapping came from my right. I turn and catch a flash in the distance.

Is it him?

Was that a growl? Something else might be out there, stalking me.

Terrified, I hop two more times and press myself against the nearest tree. Even the tree I'm leaning on is spinning. It's getting worse. Warm blood runs into my boot.

There's a flash of light and a rustle of leaves. Whatever it is, it's circling behind me.

My toe hits something hard on the ground, a rock. I reach down and pick it up. It won't do much against a predator, but maybe it can scare it away.

*Grrrr.* I'm sure it's a growl this time.

"Go away! Leave me alone!" I scream, my fear ballooning into a monster I can't control.

Leaves and branches scrape and crack. I fling the rock toward the sound, then hold the knife out in the same direction. The rock crashes through the underbrush and something skitters back.

Is it gone? I listen hard, but don't hear anything. Scared it away...for now.

A fresh wave of vertigo slams into me. Sit down and make myself a target, or pass out standing up? Using one hand on the tree for balance, I lower to the ground, trying to ease the throbbing pain.

My foot is squishy inside my boot. I'm bleeding out. Fumbling with the material of my jacket, I search for the arms and take one in each hand. Brace and count.

One....

Two....

Three!

Yank both arms in opposite directions, pulling them tighter, as tight as I can.

"Ahhh!" My scream sounds distorted and far away. Like hearing an echo rebounding down a long, empty tunnel.

Don't pass out. Stay awake. My head lolls and I jerk my chin up, fighting to stay alert. I can't close my eyes.

Whatever's out there, it's coming for me.

# 8

## GRIFF

**What separates a predator from a monster is one doesn't care what it consumes.**

I n the three months since my father died, I've evaded multiple patrols and had my fair share of close calls, but this could be the death of me. She's crashing through the underbrush like a momma bear on a rampage. But I know these woods and her trail is hard to miss even though she's so fast. I duck and weave and lengthen my stride.

How could I have been so careless? The one thing I needed to protect....

The one thing!

And I'd lost it to a woman a head shorter than me.

Fuck!

What was I thinking leaving my weapons like that? I almost had enough food to make the journey to the Free Territories. Finding a fully stocked pantry was so unusual. Hunger made me greedy and now I was paying the ultimate price. If she figured out what she had and took it back to the Authority...my father woulda died in vain.

His gruff voice chides me. *Whatever happens, don't get caught.*

My laden backpack slams against my shoulder blades as I pace her. If there was one woman, there could be more. How many others are out here looking for me? Is she part of a patrol? She wasn't wearing a uniform like the other soldiers. No, her white shirt and patched, dingy pants were far from the blue uniforms dogging my steps these past months. But she sure acted like one, lunging for the weapons, putting me flat on my ass, holding the knife with an easy, practiced stance.

She stood there watching me with those dark, sultry eyes, soft curves heaving, shirt clinging to flushed skin. So fucking beautiful. It lured me in, let my guard down, allowed her to snatch my necklace and take off. Left me chasing her tail like a buck after a doe in season.

*But she's the enemy.*

I shoulda been more cautious, scouted ahead, kept my knife in my belt.

The sounds of her chase shifts. I slow to listen and catch my breath. If she continues in this direction long enough, she'll stumble into the hut I've been staying at. Instead, I need to force her and whoever else is out here to double back on themselves, get turned around, confused. It gives me time to figure out how many others are out here looking for me.

I turn and pick up a jog, angling to intercept her. Every time I close in she changes directions. Use her own tactics against her and push her exactly where I want her. Let her think she has the upper hand. Fingernails dig into my palms.

Give me hunger, thirst, pain, and sleepless nights exposed to harsh elements. I've survived them before with no skin off my back. Let the Authority try to imprison me again—never gonna happen.

The daylight is faltering when I stop and listen. It'll be dark soon. I can still make out the distant sounds of her fumbling through the woods like an injured animal. I've made several large circuits around her, forced her to cross her own trail three different times. It's clear there's no one else in these woods besides the two of us.

Why would they send a lone soldier after me?

How did she know about the necklace? How could she know?

And what the fuck was that creepy blue light?

I wince and my father's voice berates me. *Small mistakes can cost you your life. Expect the worst.*

Although I have to give it to her, it's been a few hours, and she's still running. Even the Commander's soldiers gave up after an hour. Why was she being so persistent? I woulda expected her to try and head back to the lake house by now, but she's spinning in circles. At the rate she's floundering, she must be exhausted. Her presence here complicates matters.

This location is no longer safe.

Checking her trail, I spot fresh tracks on the ground leading in her direction. There's one large paw pad with four smaller toes. Each small toe has the indent of a short claw at the end. A large predator of some kind. Wolf, maybe? They're too small and close together to be a bear. Still, they're big enough to be a threat.

Maybe the predator will solve the problem for me...or she could give up and find her way back to the Authority, letting them know I'm alive and where she saw me last. Shit! Why didn't I think of that earlier.

My fingers curl around my bowstring.

It's easy enough to hunt her down, to kill her. She has my knife but it's no match for an arrow. I cock my head and listen, trying to pinpoint her location. After a few minutes, I hear the faint sounds of snapping branches.

There she is. I'll circle around behind her and she'll never know what hit her. Gonna take back what belongs to me.

Sounds of her movement slow as darkness falls. Once it's fully dark, I stop and wait several minutes for my eyes to adjust. There's a sliver of moonlight visible through the tops of the trees. I strain for any sound.

*Crash!*

Something large is racing through the woods at full speed. I tense and stand my ground. My grip tightens around my bow and I pull back the arrow. If the woman spotted me and is charging, I'll be ready for her.

"Argh!" The scream pierces my ears.

The noise in the underbrush grows louder. A five point buck leaps out between the trees and bounds away.

"Great, just great!" Her voice sounds full of panic—scared.

If I'm close enough to hear her, I have to be careful now. Go behind and move in for the kill. I tread slowly to minimize the sound of my approach. Vision adjusted to the darkness, I can make out her thin silhouette among the trees.

The sound of a low growl makes me freeze. Two yellow eyes gleam in the distance.

Shit!

There's a scraping and shuffling sound from the woman. The predator slinks along, moving toward the noise she's making.

No need to get any closer to whatever's stalking her. All I need to do is make sure it enjoys its dinner.

*Grrrr.* Another growl, closer this time.

Shifting position, I adjust for a better angle. I aim for the widest part of the shadowy figure, her back. I take a deep breath and prepare to hold it.

"Go away! Leave me alone!" she yells.

A rock goes whizzing past, missing the shiner on my temple by a hair. I duck in surprise and my shot goes wide. The predator makes a racket as it races away, chased off by my misfire.

Shit again.

*Stop stalling, get the job done. Kill her.*

"Ahhh!" she screams as I step out from behind the cover of a tree.

Only the anguished cry isn't for me. Tangy blood assaults my nose. It's so strong I can taste it, too. Something's wrong with her. Was she attacked before I got here?

She slumps where she sits on the ground.

At the sound of my footsteps, her head jerks up. Pain and pallor are etched across her face. It's a look I know well. The same one I wore the night my father died.

She blinks hard, as if she's imagining me standing there, approaching her. A new, more dangerous kinda monster. Using two hands she struggles to lift the knife and defend herself. Both arms quiver with exhaustion and drop. The knife hits the ground, her head lolls.

I approach cautiously, making sure it's not a trap. Using my foot I nudge her leg. My boot comes away slick with blood. She slides sideways, unmoving. Passed out cold.

Now's the time to kill her. To end it. Make sure the Authority never knows I'm here, take the necklace back, continue to the Free Territories. All I need is one well-placed thrust to the jugular.

*Killing her is the only way.*

I pry the knife from her limp fingers, but there's no blue light this time. Weird. She's so small, dejected, completely helpless. Her pitiful state tugs at painful memories. Blood spreading across my father's chest and Mischief's mother with her leg torn to shreds.

Even passed out, I don't trust her. Bare shoulders and slender arms can't hide any unsavory surprises but I'm not taking any chances. I pat her down, searching for the necklace, surprised by the smooth texture of her clammy skin.

Wait. I pat her down a second time and pull her boots off. No luck.

"Fuck! Where is it?" I squeeze the hilt of the knife and grit my teeth.

*She's ruined everything! Kill her!*

"No, no, this can't be happening!" She's bleeding out. If she dies my hope of finding the necklace and taking it to the Free Territories goes with her.

I pull off my belt and wrap it above her knee. My palm engulfs her thigh when I loop it around. I tighten the makeshift noose with one swift jerk. She doesn't so much as twitch or tremble from the pain.

Still out cold. Is she even breathing?

Her full lips are a gentle brush against my calloused fingers. It's there, but faint. I shove the thought away. Enemy or no, I need that necklace. I can't leave her here.

"This is a bad idea..." her limp arms flop when I pick her up, carrying her across my shoulders like a dead deer.

I sigh and turn toward my hut. It's gonna be a miserable walk through the night.

One I'm sure I'll regret.

# 9

# REI

**Kindness can be a sharp blade that cuts
in ways you can't see until it's too late.**

An involuntary moan escapes my lips as the agonizing pain
drags me back into consciousness. My eyelids flutter open and
the wild lines above me materialize into log rafters. I lie on a hard,
lumpy bed of musty animal skins tinged with a sweet, earthy scent.
Afternoon light bathes me from a squat window on the opposite side
of the tiny room. Beside it sits a square metal box with a long tube
connected to the ceiling. A stack of wood rests beside it.

Where am I? How did I get here?

"Ouch!" A stabbing sensation jabs through my leg in frantic
staccato. Something rough jerks my arms and prevents them from
moving lower when I reach out to examine it. Tipping my chin
back, I find my wrists tied together above my head. The rope threads
through a metal loop fixed high to the rafters.

Tugging hard causes the scratchy fibers to dig into irritated skin.
They aren't coming free.

"What the?" I shimmy, doing my best to get into an upright
position with my arms at such an awkward angle. My leg screams
at the smallest movement as I sit up. The tanned hide covering my

lower half slides to the floor, exposing pale, naked thighs and stained bandages neatly wrapped around my injured ankle.

"Where the hell are my pants?"

"I took them off," a deep, husky voice replies.

I whip around. The man stands framed in the doorway, a metal pan in one hand. He clears his throat. My eyes widen in shock. Memories come flooding back: our tussle, the strange necklace, running, getting hurt, yellow eyes in the darkness, and a looming figure.

The door hinges squeal as the man enters the small interior and pulls it shut. He takes up a quarter of the space between the bed and the window. He walks past me and places the pan on top of the black box.

"Give them back right now! Untie me! Let me go!"

He kneels, back toward me, and places a piece of firewood from the stack into the bottom of the iron square.

"Hey! I'm talking to you! Don't ignore me!"

There's a crackling noise followed by the faint smell of smoke. He rocks back onto his haunches and returns to his full height, closing the front of the box. Low flames flicker inside.

"Are you deaf? Let me go! Give me back my pants, you asshole! You should be locked away, where you belong!"

He spins and his body goes rigid. A muscle in his jaw twitches as he trains me with a steely glare. "So demanding," he sneers. "I don't think you're in a position to ask me for anything right now." His gaze moves to my bare legs and travels their length.

Heat flushes my cheeks. It's happening again. I scramble, curling my uninjured leg underneath me, using the end of my shirt and the furs to hide as much skin as possible. How can something so wrong feel so right? Desire claws at the tender underside of my belly and I can't help but like it.

Snap out of it, he has the Heart Blight, he's not safe. How long did he touch me to get me here? To take my pants off? To wrap my ankle? A tremor ripples through tense muscles no matter how hard I try to hide it.

I gulp down panic. I haven't untethered or I wouldn't be here, alive and breathing.

"Where's the necklace?"

"Touch me, and Authority save me, I'll rip your throat out and you'll never see it again." I bare my teeth. No way I'm telling him, it's the only bit of leverage I have.

"You're welcome to try," he snaps.

He takes a hungry step forward so I shrink back, stomach growling, shoulders brushing the roughly textured wall behind me. One large hand picks up the fallen fur blanket and, with a toss, covers my partially exposed leg. Turning away, he takes a few long strides and crosses the room for a mini kitchen.

Huh? That's...not what I was expecting.

A tall chest of drawers, doubling as a wooden countertop, sits opposite my bed, with a porcelain tub set into one end and shelves overhead. He rifles around, then stomps back over.

"Here, eat this, then we'll try again," he barks and tosses a piece of jerky and a withered apple on my lap.

"I'm not hungry." My traitorous stomach exposes me with another grumble. Louder this time. Crap.

One dark eyebrow cocks and his hair brushes his forehead. "Course not."

If my hands were free, Authority help me, I would pummel the smirk right off his triumphant lips. Or jab the glee in those sparkling green eyes back into his head. Gotta wait for an opening. His knife is tucked into his belt, I need him to come closer.

"How, genius?" Jerking hard on the ropes doesn't allow me to lower my elbows below chest level. Man that hurt. There's no way I can pick up anything tied like this.

He edges forward and reaches above me, fiddling with the knot in the rafters. My shoulders sag in relief when he gives me more slack.

I lunge.

Fingertips graze the worn leather of his belt when the rope pulls taut, allowing them to go no further than the edge of the bed even as I strain with all my might. So close!

"Nice try," his voice is colder than the chill in the air. Goosebumps prickle my skin.

"Let me go, dammit!" I fling the food at his chest. Jerky rebounds and skitters across the wood plank floor. The apple hits the ground with a thud and rolls under a stool in the corner.

Warring emotions flash through his eyes, matching the intensity of my glare. His face remains mercilessly stoic as his hands curl into fists and veins bulge on his forearms.

"Ya gonna regret that later," he stomps out of the hut, door banging shut behind him.

And now I'm a freaking prisoner.

Heavy footsteps recede outside. When they're out of range I bring the rope to my mouth and tear at it with my teeth. Every moment I spend trapped brings me closer to contamination. Tender skin on my wrists scratches with every forceful jerk and twist.

It's no use.

"Arrgh!" The scream echos my pain and frustration.

I gotta get out of here, especially away from him, back to the Authority, back to safety. Report this to Commander Lynx, she needs to know, he's a major threat. What if he's not alone? How easily could he, or others like him, spread the virus to families in Albrin?

Despite the rising heat of the fire, I grow colder. What if I'm already infected? My tether was acting strange even before he appeared. Is it broken, is that why I'm still alive? Waves of nausea crash down on me, sending my stomach churning. Three days, that's how long Dr. Martina said it took for symptoms to appear.

He took my freaking pants! And he must have carried me here, put me on this bed, wrapped my leg. Those points of contact must have taken more than sixty seconds. Chest growing hot, panic rises, swelling behind my eyelids, ringing my ears. Am I already dying?

"Mother bless it!" The guttural scream rattles the tiny window. A log pops in the fire. Nobody cares if this is the end of my motherline. I'll be just another linebreaker barreling us toward extinction.

No. I won't go down without a fight, never have and never will. Put two years of basic and a few months of Enforcer training to good use. Take a deep breath and strategize. Survey the surroundings, identify all exits, come up with a plan, find a way out.

I scan for anything sharp or jagged within reach, but there's only the pile of thick, scratchy animal furs. The window is too small to climb out and the front door is the only other exit. Tipping my head back, I trace the rope to the metal ring in the ceiling. Maybe I can reach it. Easing my injured leg around, I try to get to my knees.

"Ow, ow, ow!" I gasp and flop back onto my butt. Well, that's a no go.

The third attempt, where I dig my fingers into the rounded logs of the wall and push with the good foot, is the winner. Bracing my hip against the wall allows me to stretch toward the knot.

Crap, it's too far, my hand is a good six inches short. Climbing the rope will make up the difference, but with wrists tied and a bum ankle it's not possible. Even now the achy throb protests my standing upright.

Do I wait it out long enough for my leg to heal? In three days I might be dead or unable to go anywhere. There are no good options. Ow, that hurts. I ease myself back onto the bed.

He wants this white object, whatever it is, sitting like salvation beneath my breast. Could I trick him into untying me? Handing it over doesn't guarantee he lets me walk out of here. And convincing him to let me leave might not be so simple either. Plus, I don't know where I am or how to get back to the lake house. I ran a long way yesterday, how much further did he carry me?

My stomach growls, reminding me the last time I ate was the tomato sandwich yesterday. My eyes wander to the piece of jerky on the floor. He touched it with his hands. Is it contaminated by the virus? If I lay on my back and stretch out a leg, I might be able to pick it up with my toes.

What am I doing? I'm not that hungry....

Footsteps and creaking boards alert me of his return. He ignores me and takes his bag off his shoulder. There's some kind of skinned animal in his other hand. He crosses the hut, pulls his knife, and breaks it down into a pan on the black box—oh, it's a wood stove. Sizzling meat and a savory aroma fill the air. Damn, this must be his way of torturing me for earlier.

He rinses the hunting knife, wipes it down, and slides it into a sheath on his belt. It hangs on his right side, close to his hip. If I could just get my hands on it....

Goading the enemy didn't work before, gotta switch tactics, get on his good side. He brought me here rather than letting me bleed out in the woods. Perhaps I can use this to my advantage and create an opportunity to escape.

"Hey, what's your name?" I ask.

He grunts and otherwise continues to ignore me.

"I'm Rei. It looks like you've been here a while. It's got a...um...rustic charm. So, did you build this place? Do you live alone?"

Still no response. I shift my leg and grimace, wishing the throbbing sensation would ease.

Muscles tense as he returns to his bag and rifles through the contents. Thin strips of material and a small glass jar emerge. He moves to the end of the bed and yanks off the fur covering my legs.

"Hey! What are you doing?" My shrill voice is laced with sharp concern.

"It's getting late. I need to check the wound and change your bandage."

"Don't touch me!" Ignoring the agony of sudden movement, I jerk my legs from his reaching hand. He grabs my heel but there's no flare of light from my tether. Terror overwhelms me, it really is broken, I'm so dead. "Get off, I said let go!" Rough palms clamp around my bare calf and uninjured ankle, dragging me closer.

Bucking and twisting my hips isn't working. Using my tied wrists as leverage I smash my knee into his chin. His grip loosens allowing me to slam my foot against his cheek as hard as I can. He grunts and curses, retreating from my frenzied kicks.

We glare at each other, breathless and panting. His lower lip and the side of his cheek are swelling.

"I should drag ya outside and let the wolf finish what it started."

The memory of suffocating darkness rears its ugly head. My heart races and my shoulders shake. Cameron goes limp, blood streams from a hole in a white lab coat, and the Sympathizer's body jerks when I empty my clip into her chest. Every failure hazing me with brutal clarity, a reminder that I deserve the painful end coming for me. For all of us. I pound my wrists between my breasts, trying to relieve the hollow feeling burrowing below the surface.

"Can't breathe!" I gasp. "I–I can't—" the sob catches in the back of my throat, begging for release, vision swims.

A cup shoves into my hands.

"Drink."

"—can't breathe!" My chest heaves at the force of every syllable.

"Drink!" He commands, pressing it to my lips, forcing my head back.

Water spills into my mouth, over the sides, and runs down my neck, soaking the collar of my crusty shirt. The sensation of something lodged in my throat eases with every gag, swallow, and sputter. I gasp and the claws of fear retract. My vision returns to normal and, dragging in a shaky breath, the cup hits the ground with a metallic clatter.

It's empty now, just like me.

# 10

# GRIFF

**When trusting someone can kill you,
every move is a gamble.**

S ave her life, treat her wound, offer her food and she thanks
me by throwing it in my face. Fuck that. The door slams and
boards groan under my weight. Retracing her trail from yesterday
is an option but I might as well be searching for a leaf in the forest.
Convincing her to hand it over is the best solution, and if nothing
else, will help run it to ground. But how?

Out of habit, I reach down and pick up a stick, tucking it under
my arm. The sun's setting and my stash of firewood is running
low after a morning spent making salve and boiling her jacket
for bandages. Gathering firewood takes longer than I expect,
although finding dinner in one of my traps makes it worth the
hassle. Father would approve of how well I skinned the rabbit.

The sun's setting when I climb the steps on achy legs. There's a
twinge in my palm grabbing the door handle. I didn't even notice
the splinter. Sounds of movement inside jerk my head up, ears
straining. What's she up to?

My eyes adjust to the hut's dim interior while I pause at the threshold. She's still on the bed in the same spot I left her earlier. Good.

"Hey, what's your name?" she probes as if she deserves an answer.

She doesn't...and I'm no longer a number forcefully subjected to the will of women.

"I'm Rei." Her chipper voice peppers me with off-handed questions in a lame attempt to lighten the uneasy mood.

Pretend she's not there, let her squirm, keep her guessing. Breaking down the rabbit reminds me how fragile life is. Bones snap with a twist and flesh parts from each delicate slice.

*Gutting a person is like gutting a rabbit.*

The knife pauses mid-air, hand shaking. Sweat beads my forehead and metal clatters when the weapon hits the countertop. Blood coats my palms and darkens my fingernails. Hurriedly I rinse them off and cross the room, digging through my backpack. Rounding on her, I yank the furs off her legs. Her sharp protest fuels the part of me refusing to bow to Father's harsh, relentless voice.

"It's getting late. I need to check the wound and change your bandage." I grab her heel and reach to examine the injury, pulling her closer when she snarls like a rabid fox.

"Don't touch me! Get off, I said let go!" She twists, knee catching my chin and her foot slams into my mouth. A coppery tang coats my tongue.

Dark, sultry eyes reflect my stormy glare. If Father were still here I wouldn't be in this situation. "I should drag ya outside and let the wolf finish what it started."

Color drains from her face and she chokes on a breath. Tremors rock her slender frame and her fists pound her chest. "Can't breathe!

I–I can't—" Sobs wrack her thin shoulders. It's an anguished sound, like I'm being torn from my little brother all over again.

I wasn't expecting this. Pleading to be let go, or even begging her arms hurt, those things I could imagine. But this? Reflex has me filling a cup from my canteen and shoving it into her hands.

"Drink," I insist. Her hyperventilating is getting worse, she's on the verge of passing out.

"—can't breathe!" She gasps. Her lips turn blue.

"Drink!" I force the cup to her mouth. Water spills as she gulps and chokes and sputters. The empty cup falls to the floor. Color returns to her lips, a rush of blood from the surge of adrenaline.

"Please," she wails, "it's so dark. I can't see." Gulping sobs punctuate her words.

It takes less than five minutes to light a fire. She shrieks in terror, hands covering her ears, when a log slips and bangs on the floor. Could this all be some kinda show? Based on my earlier experience, she's smart enough to pull off an elaborate plan. I furrow my brows as the ember catches. A low, dim glow expands to a soft, golden light as the fire spreads. I blow lightly to encourage it higher.

Behind me, Rei's finally calming down.

"Thank you," she manages between watery hiccups.

She's a mess. Red rims her puffy eyes, tears streak her cheeks, and snot glistens on her upper lip. She looks so small and miserable, sitting there, pale and gaunt, huddled in on herself. Her eyes are unfocused, reliving something only she can see.

Fuck, I don't think she's faking. Something made her like this, something bad.

The front of her shirt is soaked and the material sticks to the swell of her breasts. Oily strands of hair hang over her shoulders and forehead. Clearing my throat doesn't help my building discomfort. My pants are too tight.

I refill the cup and chug it down in three large gulps. Another splash goes into my palm and I run my wet hand across my flushed face.

There's something about her I just can't quite place my finger on. She's hot and glaring one minute, then terrified and panicking the next. A deer catching sight of a wolf, as if holding her ground will make some kinda difference between life and death.

Not that I have a whole lot of experience to draw from. Before leaving containment I spent most of my time with my brother and the other boys. Our fathers ruled the ward, protecting us from the women...until we hit puberty. Nothing could prepare me for the loss of control over my body in a system that rewarded helplessness and obedience.

One leery eye tracks me, a feral animal caught in a trap. A piece of dark, wavy hair falls across her cheek and I find myself reaching to brush it behind her ear. She jerks aside like I'm a scorching hot poker, chest heaving, skin flushing.

Shit, why did I do that?

Turning, I head to the counter and pull a plate from the shelf. Using a fork, I spear a few pieces of rabbit from the stove. She scowls and shakes her head when I hold it out to her.

"Smells like you burnt it."

"You're a piece of work, ya know that?"

The stool in the corner groans when I sink onto it. I have to blow on the rabbit a few times before I pop a piece into my mouth. Her stomach grumbles and a pink tongue flicks over parched lips.

"Must taste disgusting."

"Guess ya never gonna know." Things were much easier when she was unconscious and bleeding out.

Chunks of leg meat fall off the bone when I take a bite. Delicious. When I'm done, I lick my fingers, savoring the oily, gamey flavor. Her stomach rumbles, louder this time. Serves her right. A night without food reminds her who's in control here.

The window squeaks when I shove it open and whistle for Mischief. Within a few minutes, there are scraping noises as clawed fingers scrabble up the side of the hut. It took a week to carve the hand-holds close enough together for the scrappy kit.

Mischief pauses on the narrow sill, gray ears flicking, then leaps onto my shoulder. There's several faint pin-prick scars from how often he's broken the skin attempting to keep his balance.

A look I can't quite interpret flashes over whatever invisible wall she's climbing inside her head. "What the hell is that thing?"

"This is Mischief." Running a finger under his chin is rewarded with a playful bite. Not hard enough to puncture, but enough to mean business.

I stand and pick up the pan. Mischief grabs a piece of meat as soon as it's within reach. Nails dig into my forearm, preventing him from face planting.

"What is he?"

"Never seen a raccoon before, huh? Imagine a large, hairy rat that thrives on chaos and antics."

Mischief raises his head from the pan, noticing the woman for the first time. Rei, she said her name was. He cocks his face to the side and studies her. It's easy to forget that he's never seen another person in the hut before. Is he as uncomfortable with her invading the bed as I am?

Black paws grab the last piece of rabbit out of the pan and Mischief stuffs it into his mouth. He leaps down and crosses the floor without hesitation. Jumping onto the edge of the bed, he pulls the meat out of his mouth and holds it out like a fucking peace offer. It makes me want to catch him by the scruff of the neck and toss him outside for this bullshit.

"Uh, thanks, but no thanks," she says with a curl of the lip. Mischief shoves dinner back between his teeth, chewing vigorously, unbothered by her refusal, and climbs into her lap.

"What—what is he doing? Hey, get it off of me," she raises her wrists to avoid touching him.

"He's just a baby, he won't hurt ya."

Rei lowers her hands and stops when Mischief turns in her lap and plops into the space between her thighs. When he's settled she lightly brushes her fingertips over his head. Mischief chitters and snuggles in deeper.

"Does he normally do this?" Rei asks, trying to figure out where she can rest her arms.

"No." My brows furrow.

It's concerning that he took to her immediately. I was expecting anxiety, fear, hesitation, anything other than blind trust.

The dinner scraps go into the waste bucket under the sink and I scrub the dishes with fingers clenched. My knuckles scrape against the worn surfaces until they crack and bleed. I have to decide what to do with her.

*Slit her throat and be done with it*, father's voice insists. What's wrong with me?

It'd be the easiest option. Someone will eventually come looking for her. Then what? My bag is almost full, and I should have enough to make the trek if I ration carefully. Going in the fall with winter approaching, over terrain I wasn't familiar with, was a gamble at best. But so is staying here. If I left in the morning it would take her a while to find her way back to the lake house and call for help. Enough time for me to get a solid head start.

*Don't let her go, they'll know you're alive.*

Silence stretches. When I turn she's watching me intently, eyes lingering on my arms, chest, and shoulders, her fingers stroking Mischief's downy fur. Wonder what they'd feel like sliding over the slope of my abs, sinking below the waistband—no, stop it. Don't give into the Authority's fucking conditioning. Lowering my head I run a hand through my hair, letting the shudder wash over me, trying desperately to gut the stirring betrayal of my own body.

This is what they wanted, not what I want. Gotta shove it down, force it back into its dark corner. I drop my hand and sigh. "Give me back the necklace and I'll leave tomorrow, then you're free to go."

"Yeah, right. How can I trust you when I'm the one who's tied up?"

"What don't ya get, huh? I can't leave without it! Fuck!" This isn't working.

The coals are close to dying so I round on the stove, pick up a log, and shove it inside. Pops and cracks wake the slumbering fire. When the flames lick high enough, I put in as many logs as it'll hold. It's one thing I'll miss when I leave, a camp fire is much harder to cook with.

"Are you trying to roast me? Is this some kind of twisted torture tactic?" Rei pulls her shirt away from her body and uses the material to fan herself. Mischief is stretched out asleep, little paws twitching.

Sweat glistens near her collarbone, plasters her hair, and a bead slips down the line of her neck. Her skin is flushed, shiny almost, like she might be coming down with something. She shoulda let me check her leg earlier, it's probably getting infected.

"No. And it's Griff."

"What?"

"My name, it's Griff. Now lift ya leg."

"Why?"

"Can't hog all the blankets, gotta share."

Her heavy-lidded eyes go wide when I reach for the largest deer skin on the bed. She turns and glances around, as if just realizing there's two of us and only one bed. Her hands go tense in her lap, gripping the edge of another hide, covering most of her bare legs.

"Don't even think about it." Her eyes take on a hard edge, throwing daggers in my direction.

Instead of answering I give her a long, lingering look. The injury has taken a toll. Disheveled, long hair, wrists tied, and a stained shirt slipping down one shoulder. The naked flesh is skinnier than yesterday. An angular collar bone protrudes at the neckline. There's no word I can think of to describe the foreign, stirring sensation the sight evokes within me.

It's like I'm stuck taking one step forward and three steps backwards.

Grunting, I toss the deer skin on the floor. It's far enough from the wood stove to not be hazardous. Close enough to stop her from trying any funny business. Her shoulders sag and she releases a breath as I stretch out on top of it.

"Go to sleep," I order, tucking one arm under my head. The ground is harder than my bed, but I've slept on much worse over the years.

Rei shifts nervously and winces. Finding a comfortable position with Mischief and her wrists tied should be challenging. The side of my face is still tender from where she kicked me earlier. Her stomach growls and I smile. She deserves that, too. I hope she has a miserable night's sleep. It's hard to think about much else when your stomach is eating itself, a gnawing ache begging ya to put something, anything, in your mouth. The longer she goes hungry, the more docile she'll become.

The room is nice and warm. She stills on the bed, her breathing growing slow, deeper, heavy. A companionable silence falls over us. It's different from when it's only Mischief and myself, more intimate somehow. Rei's eyes meet mine, flutter closed and jerk open, fighting sleep. It's a losing battle, she's too exhausted.

At last her eyes close and stay closed. Her face softens when the tension drains away. She's so beautiful.

"Goodnight," she mumbles. The word is so quiet I think I've imagined it.

*Do it, do it now.*

Letting her live betrays everything Father's ever taught me. The Authority destroyed my life, killed my father, enslaved my brother and so many others. I can't forgive them for what they've done, what she's a part of. Metal glints when I pull the knife from my belt and study the jagged edge. The polished surface reflects wavering green eyes in the dim, flickering light of the fire.

Rei's pitiful moan and haunted whimper break the cozy ambiance. She thrashes and cries out in her sleep, caged by a nightmare she can't escape.

Just like me.

And it's fucking terrifying.

# 11

## REI

**Captivity is a trap, a test you can't fail, and help comes with strings attached.**

There's a tickle along my bare legs and my eyes flutter open. A head of shaggy brown hair brushes my calves while calloused fingers rub something over the swollen, jagged cut running the length of my ankle. The motion soothes the hot, achy discomfort splitting me in two. He's firmly captured my heel, making it impossible for me to extract myself.

"What are you doing?"

His grasp tightens by my cut and pain blossoms. The room spins, going fuzzy around the edges like billowing clouds of dense smoke. I'm suddenly staring down a long, dark tunnel, flames licking in the distance, shots ringing out.

No, not again. Please, not again. The hut wavers back into focus when I gasp.

"—checking the wound and changing the bandage. Leaving it like this will let the infection get worse, so stop struggling."

My tether remains colorless and unresponsive despite his touch. Panicking will cloud my judgement. I bite my lip, locking the residual tremors inside the hollow part of me. Get a grip and assess the situation.

There's no use denying I'm infected.

The clock is winding down. If I want any chance of getting outta here I have to gain his trust. I weigh the burning agony in my leg against my blood crystalizing and my lungs bursting. Red, inflamed skin and an oozing wound is my most immediate threat.

Our eyes meet and I nod, relaxing beneath his care. He releases me and picks up a small glass jar, pouring a thick liquid over the wound. A cool, numbing sensation drowns out the blistering agony. I let out a breath I didn't know I was holding as the throbbing eases.

When he finishes coating it a second time, he takes long strips of rust stained fabric and wraps them around my leg. They look oddly familiar.

"Is that my jacket?"

Gentle fingers tie the ends of the bandage and slide up my calf, admiring their handy work. He glances up from under long, dark lashes. The early light catches eyes full of concern. A pleasant ache persists between my legs when he studies my face.

"Out here nothing goes to waste. Besides, I coulda used your shirt instead." His gaze flicks over me.

"I was just asking." I say in a huff, covering my breasts with my arms. The necklace digs into my rib cage close to my heart.

Griff screws the lid on the jar and stands, moving toward the sink. Moments later he returns with a bruised apple I swore I threw at him yesterday. He holds it out, one eyebrow raising in question.

Food teases the beast in my stomach to life. I snatch it from him and take a huge bite, the sticky, sweet juice spilling down my chin.

"Hunger is a wonderful motivator," he says with a gleeful chuckle.

My mouth is too full to answer, so I can only glare. Mother bless it, he's enjoying every minute of pulling my strings.

I'm sucking on the apple core when he brings over a bucket with a large hole cut in the center. What is this? I blink in confusion. A quick shake rattles the bones of last night's dinner before I toss the stem inside with the rest of the scraps.

"Even animals know better than to waste food by throwing it."

"Hah, very funny. Says the infected hostile who's raiding houses, using me for target practice, and keeping me captive."

"Ya pounced on my stuff, remember? Besides, stealing is the only way to survive in this fucked up place."

"So you run around infecting more people? Bless the mother, you'd rather doom humanity to a miserable death."

"Bullshit! Nobody chooses to be locked up and helpless, a slave to their lies."

"Yeah, you mean like this?" The rope creaks and burns at my forceful tug.

"Tell me where my necklace is."

"Let. Me. Go!" I demand through clenched teeth. Don't trust the enemy. If I tell him he'll leave me here to die. His arrow nearly took me out yesterday.

"Fuck! You're so stubborn. Give it back and I'll let ya go, take my shit and leave, and you'll never see me again."

"Good, after you untie me!" We're at an impasse but he can't break what's already broken.

He spins and marches away. Crap, I've really pissed him off. Muscles shift beneath his shirt, accentuating the line to his waist when he leans over the counter. One palm drags over his rugged, handsome face then falls back to the edge of the sink, gripping hard. Everything is so black and white with him.

Broad shoulders slump and he lets out a shaky breath. "Please," he whispers in a voice full of thinly veiled anguish, mirroring my demons. "My Father gave it to me."

The hitch in my throat stands at attention, surprising me. A tense, plummeting sensation gives me pause. He's getting under my skin and I can't let him. Sincerity and the desperation in his plea scratches the edge of the darkness I'm carrying.

Two days, that's all I have left. His control is cracking, he's letting his guard down and it's just what I need to get outta here.

"Look, we can't trust each other. But our objectives align, we both wanna leave. Help me get back to the lake house, then I'll tell you where I stashed the necklace and we can go our separate ways. Anything else is non-negotiable, you copy?"

He hesitates. "Promise me I'll get it back."

No way it's that easy. I blink in shock, then nod before he changes his mind. Warily he reaches above my head to the rafters. After a few efficient tugs, the rope goes slack. My wrists tingle and sting. Shaking and stretching my fingers helps the circulation return. The skin on my wrists is raw and blistering.

Griff frowns at the dark purple bruises that echo the pattern of the rope braids. What changed his mind, why is he being so nice?

I plaster a fake smile on my face. Who cares if it's not genuine as long as it's convincing. "When do we leave?"

"Can ya walk?"

Gritting my teeth, I ignore the shooting pains and place both feet on the wood floor. I push up and stifle a scream. Agony rips into me, jabbing deep over and over, my injured leg buckles. Griff catches my elbow with a hand and steadies me as I sway and struggle to balance. Who knew men were so physically strong? One searing glare and he releases me, standing down, but the warmth of his grasp lingers.

"Sure, I'll let you fall on your ass next time."

"Ahh, damn, it hurts." A wave of nausea hits. I slap a hand over my mouth, but there's no holding it back. With seconds to spare I lunge for the bucket, regretting eating so damn fast. Mother bless it, I'll never eat an apple again.

"Guess not," Griff sighs.

"Of course I can, just give me a minute!" I snap, clambering to my knees, using the edge of the bed for leverage to rise. Sweat beads my forehead and I bite my lip against the agony. Lifting my ankle off the ground takes the pressure off but increases the throbbing ache. A wave of vertigo makes the room swim.

"You're still feverish. Ya won't get far like this. Sit down and rest, I'll find us some breakfast." He moves toward the door.

"Wait!" My voice raises an octave.

He turns and faces me, one eyebrow lifting in that cocky face of his.

"I, uh, I—what if you're not back before dark?"

"I'll be back before then," he says.

"No, please, wait! Don't leave me in the dark. I can't handle it. Please."

Griff examines me for a long stretch of time. If he notices how my nails are digging into my palms or how hard I'm biting my lower lip he doesn't say anything.

"So demanding," he growls. "Do ya know how to start a fire?"

I shake my head, releasing a shaky breath.

Griff's hand drops from the door handle. He crosses to the wood stove and moves the stool in front, patting the top. "Well then, come here."

He's doing this on purpose. Mother bless it, I won't let him win. On one leg I hop once, twice, three times. Lowering myself onto the stool is a feat in and of itself.

"That was...interesting."

"Oh shut it and show me how to light this thing."

He snorts and squats beside me. "First ya put some wood inside. Tear these into strips to make kindling to form a nest. Poking a hole in the center helps the ember catch. Then ya strike the flint."

Griff reaches into his pocket and pulls out an angular gray rock and a slender piece of scrap metal. He sets the kindling down and hits them together. A small spark lands in the kindling, he blows until it smokes. At the tiniest hint of a flame he stomps it out with his boot.

"Your turn."

I almost fall off the stool as I lean forward to grab the kindling. Griff slaps a hand down on the edge to keep me from toppling. Fighting the flush creeping up my neck and the sweat beading my forehead, I shred the stalks into a pile and hold my hand out for the flint.

"Don't try anything funny," he warns.

"I know, I know."

The flint is rough in comparison to the smooth metal. I position them the same way he did and hit them together. There's no spark, no nothing. I try again. Still nothing. There has to be some kind of trick to it.

"I thought this was easy."

"Ya gotta do it harder. Here, let me show ya." Griff takes my hands, ignoring me when I tense, and repeats the motion. An ember flares and dies in the air. "Like this," his voice purrs and a cool breath stirs the hair behind my ear. My thighs clench. I can't tell if the crisp, sweet, woodsy scent is coming from him or the fire.

"Try again." He lets go but the sensation lingers.

When did he get so close? I fumble with the flint, almost dropping it. Crap! Why won't it work? I hammer it again and again, harder each time, straining with the effort, keeping in time with the rapid pounding of my heart.

"That's enough, give it here."

Instead of jabbing him in the throat, I huff and drop them into his open palm. He creates an ember on the first try, blows softly, shielding me from the flames, then places it into the wood stove. Within moments the fire grows and spreads, accompanied by faint wisps of smoke.

Together we watch it smoulder and dance, burning and consuming indiscriminately, chasing away the darkness in the corners of the metal box. There's no twisted shrapnel, spent bullet shells, or dead bodies hiding in the shadows—only ashes.

I find myself glancing at Griff, watching a muscle in his jaw tense, front teeth flashing, wondering why he looks so familiar. Desperate green eyes meet mine and the grainy image of a young boy slams into me. He has the same strong nose, same squared chin, same thick eyebrows in a leaner, more rugged face.

My mouth pops open. No, it can't be.

Griff coughs and stands abruptly, running a hand over the back of his neck. "That'll keep for an hour or so. Go ahead and do ya business before I get back." He motions toward the bucket, then hurries out the door.

"Oh," I say to the emptiness he's left behind.

# 12

## GRIFF

**Evil doesn't need claws and teeth, so I wonder, am I the hunter or the hunted?**

This so-called truce is kicking a hornet's nest. Father fought to keep me from abusive, hateful, manipulative women. He may have been a hard, relentless teacher, but I'm still alive. All these years I imagined he enjoyed causing me misery. Looking back, I see it was his way of protecting me from a system wanting to destroy us—if only they didn't need us, too.

She's everything and nothing like the Commander who killed my father. She's haughty, opinionated, short-tempered, brash, and intelligent. But she's also injured, weak, terrified, and vulnerable right now. Turmoil churns, evoking the lessons drilled into me.

*Most predators hunt alone.*

My bag of supplies sits by the dead campfire, the hunting knife stuck in a tree stump that doubles as a stool. This morning I thought I was overreacting when Father's voice warned me to keep it outside. Leaving all my essentials where an animal might get them seems equally foolish. I grab my bow and slip the knife into my belt.

Dunno how much further to the Free Territories except to keep heading east. Every winter Father and I would find a place to hole up and stay until the thaw. Those were my favorite memories of him. Sitting by the fire, making arrows, preparing hides, and the slow scrape of his knife while he was whittling. A journey we were supposed to make together.

Yet here I am, agreeing to take Rei back to the lake house, in the opposite direction, like I ever had any other choice. I need that necklace.

Raising fingers to my mouth I whistle for Mischief. He tends to stick close in the morning and wander off after dark. Bushes rustle and he slinks out, preening and proud of himself. Such a troublemaker. Together we traipse away from the hut.

Rei isn't going anywhere on that ankle without me carrying her outta here. Her snarky, amusing banter comes to mind. The corner of my lip quirks, imagining her protests and a mean right hook if I scooped her into my arms.

Yeah, not gonna happen. A crutch it is then.

None of the nearby trees are the right kind. Tall ancient trunks, some with poison ivy, and patches of dry, reedy stalks grow in the immediate area. There's nothing suitable without weeks of effort. Spotting a long, fallen stick on the ground I give it a hopeful bend. It snaps, full of dry rot. Well that won't work. Kicking the larger piece sends it soaring and crashing into the underbrush.

The grove of young saplings I stumbled upon last week are the perfect shape and size. It's a bit of a hike, though. Better not waste any time. Finding a narrow game trail, I set off, my thighs burning from the constant, slight incline up the mountain.

Out here, despite the bugs, weather, wildlife, and limited resources, I have my freedom. There are no stained mattresses or padded cells with constant surveillance. Best of all, no quota to fill at the risk of electrodes, needles, and tests strapped to sterile, metal exam tables.

Something small and hard hits the back of my head. Turning, I spot Mischief sitting high in a tree. He sends an acorn flying past my face.

"Hey! Stop that!" I duck the next one.

He leaps down the branch, doing a near free fall, before he catches himself on another and scampers away.

"Little jerk," I say with a smile. It's like he has a sixth sense for pulling me out of bad memories.

In the grove it takes less time than the entire hike to identify the perfect, straight sapling and strip it down. It's so much quieter without her. Too quiet. I tuck the branch under my arm and head back.

Deer tracks on the ground pull me up short. Squatting down, I brush away damp, rotting leaves. They're fresh. A chance at a hearty breakfast. Pulling my bow around I nock an arrow. Years of growing up in the woods have taught me the art of making as little sound as possible. I follow taking careful footsteps.

The trail goes cold a hundred feet ahead. Where did it go? I search either side of the path. No luck, how disappointing.

A blackberry bush catches my eye. That'll do nicely, too. I push through a row of sticker bushes until I get to my prize. The rich flavor and dark juices of the biggest, fattest berry explode in my mouth. Yum, so good.

My hands are sticky and stained purple when I'm finished eating my fill and stuffing my shirt. Getting back to the path is harder. Thorn branches catch on my clothes and I spend a few minutes pulling them off and scratching myself at the same time.

Patience rewards me when I find myself back on the game trail, up several feet from where I started. Mischief is digging in the dirt at the base of a nearby tree. Curious, I head over.

"What'd ya find, boy?" Digging beside him unearths a crop of wild onions. "Nice!"

Pulling my knife from its sheath, I stab it into the ground and uproot the bulbs. Mischief grabs the first one and runs off with it in his mouth. I shake dirt from the others, adding them to my haul. Not the most appetizing of meals, but at least it's food. I rise and spot mushrooms growing on a rotten log. I grab one and split it in half, carefully examining the texture to identify it. Yep, had this one before. Don't wanna make the same mistake that had me puking my brains out for three days. Mushrooms don't fuck around.

It's a weird breakfast but it'll do. At least I won't have to break into my supplies. Not yet, anyway.

Deer woulda really hit the spot. Rabbit, while tasty, doesn't keep me full for long. If I detour I can check the traps—shit! Muddy paw-prints cross the trail, the same ones stalking Rei yesterday. It's smaller, more rounded, less symmetrical and most importantly, has no claws. How could I mistake a mountain lion for a wolf? This explains the deer's sudden change of direction.

There's few things in these woods I steer clear of. Enforcer patrols, bears, and mountain lions are at the top of the short list. I nock my bow, just in case.

"Mischief!" He trots over with something small and squirming in his mouth. "Let's go bud, better not stick around."

On high alert, we head back the way we came. Anytime Mischief wanders off I call him back within eyesight. Better to be safe than sorry. It's too close to home for comfort. I make a mental note to bury the leftover scraps. Don't want it getting any ideas.

*Feeling sorry for it doesn't make it any less dangerous.*

Father's stern voice lectured the day we found a coyote caught in one of our traps. It growled and snapped at us when we approached. Father handed me the bow and told me to shoot it. I was younger and my arms shook as I pulled back the string. A sharp smack across the back of my head punished my hesitation. The arrow went wide, hitting a tree. He handed me another.

*Take the shot. It's not gonna wait to go for the jugular.*

Without a word I pulled the bowstring back as far as I could, arms trembling, and shot the coyote in the head.

Thankfully, there's no sign of tracks near the hut. That rules out one source of danger, but not Rei. She's a woman, born and raised by the Authority, living an easy life at our expense. Gonna keep a close eye on her, now. Especially the way she glares daggers, bites her lower lip, those soft curves and smooth skin.

Fuck me, it's happening again.

I'm hard.

# 13

**REI**

**Boundaries are the lines we cross every time tensions build between us.**

G riff's resemblance to the boy in the photo is shocking. How did I miss it? Are they related somehow? My mind wheels, picking apart and chasing every possible scenario. Dr. Martina risked her life for the damn case. She didn't want the boy's photo falling into the Sympathizer's hands.

Why?

Is the boy connected to the virus? And how does Griff fit into all of this?

Nothing makes sense. I need answers and I'm running out of time. I'm nothing but a coward and a fraud, tucked away in the quiet woods, sheltered from the loud realities of the outside world. For once, tracing the familiar contours of the bump on my hand isn't enough to distract me. My tether went nuts at the lake house and hasn't worked since the first time he touched me.

At least I found some leverage.

Digging into my bra, I examine the necklace for the first time. Wow, it's stunning. Feathers cover the neck of the winged bird-like creature, curled around the glossy, white surface. What's it made of?

Wait, did I break it? A hairline crack threatens to remove the head from its body. Crap!

There's a scratching sound outside and I shove his trinket back into its hiding spot. Mischief peeks over the window sill. If he's back Griff won't be far behind. Round, black, curious eyes blink in my direction. The raccoon's tiny nose sticks up in the air, whiskers twitching, sniffing vigorously.

"What? It's no use, I don't have any food."

The stomp and groan of Griff's boots outside have me turning toward the door. There's a loud bang of something heavy hitting the ground.

He fills the door frame when he enters, carrying a long wooden stick, and pausing briefly to lean it against the wall. The other hand holds up his overloaded shirt. Toned muscles ripple across his exposed belly when he crosses to the counter and dumps the contents.

"Breakfast," he says. "I found mushrooms, onions and blackberries."

Mischief's head jerks up, ears twitching. He slinks onto the counter. A furry gray hand reaching for the biggest berry.

"Hey! No, not yet." Griff fills the sink and sweeps the berries into the water, outta reach.

Mischief sits on his haunches and watches, perturbed. Griff turns to stir the pan and Mischief dunks a hand in the sink and shoves a berry in his mouth.

"Mischief, what did I say?"

The kit grabs as many berries as he can, stuffing them into his cheeks and scampers away before Griff can seize him. Mischief returns Griff's disapproving grunt with satisfied chitters, licking his sticky fingers, feeling proud of himself. The raccoon jumps back to the narrow window ledge, sits on the side closest to the stove and side-eyes the pan.

"Guess it's hot enough he leaves it alone, huh?"

"Ya, a burn will do that. Luckily, it wasn't bad, just a little singed."

Savory mushrooms and onions assault my nose. They're not my favorite but my mouth waters and my stomach growls. I hug my knees to my chest and rest my head between them.

"I'm so hungry I could eat flour."

"What's that?"

"Flour? Um, it's a grain used to make bread. It comes from a plant called wheat."

"Huh, never heard of those." Griff shrugs and splits the contents of the pan, pouring some on a plate and the rest in a cup.

The cup is warm when Griff brings it over with a spoon.

"Uh, I think your raccoon is stealing your food."

"Fuck! Hey, no, that's mine. Ya already had your share." Griff lifts his plate out of the kit's reaching hands and shovels the remaining rations into his mouth.

"Alright, alright, here, lick the rest, ya trouble maker." Mischief wrestles the dish from his grasp as soon as it's close enough.

"Is he always like this?" I ask, resting my head on my knees again.

"His whole life...." Griff shakes his head. Mischief finishes and talks back at him with his chirping chatter, licking his hands and running them over his face and ears. When he's done preening, he jumps on the bed, grabs the edge of my cup and shoves his head inside. A chunk of onion sticks to his damp forehead when he finally emerges. I snort and pull it off.

Soft chitters and softer fur brushes my arms, rubbing against my chest when I pet him. A wet, pink tongue laps my cheek and tiny teeth nip my chin until I push him away.

"Ow, don't eat me."

"How's ya leg? Is it still painful?"

"Yeah, it aches."

"Ya really did a number on yourself. I'll put more medicine on it, that'll help." He opens his bag and rifles through it. "There it is," he pulls out the glass jar and fresh bandages. He approaches the bed, and sits on the edge, his glare daring me to try anything stupid. "Be nice."

A toss of the blanket exposes my bare legs and underwear at the same time. I clamp my thighs together in embarrassment. Griff either doesn't notice or ignores it as he grabs my calf and slides it closer to him. He waits until I nod before unwrapping the bandages. The jagged line is still puffy and hot, but the swelling and redness have improved. Raw, tender skin puckers where the crusty scab is forming. It's a good sign.

"Well, the infection is clearing up." He gently squeezes the sides.

"That hurts!"

"Sorry," he murmurs, "but this will be worse." Before I can protest, he uses a bandage to scrape the scab off the wound.

"Ow, ah, stop! Stop that hurts! Mother bless it! Ahh." Tears stain my cheeks with every excruciating poke and prod. The cut oozes a creamy white liquid.

"The medicine won't draw out the infection if it's not directly in the wound." He continues squeezing until it turns red.

"Authority save me, stop!" I say, biting my lower lip open.

His head jerks up and something dangerous flickers there. In an instant, it's gone. He coats the thick, goopy medicine over my ankle, bringing immediate, cool relief. The stabbing pain dulls to a low achy throb that continues to ease as it takes effect.

No amount of Enforcer first-aid training could treat this wound without a well-stocked med kit and a boat load of antibiotics. I wonder....

"What'd you put on it?"

"Beard lichen and yarrow. They're perfect for infection, swelling, and stopping the bleeding."

That's it, keep him talking.

"How did you learn all of this?"

Griff grunts and finishes wrapping my leg with the clean bandages. When he's done, his hand lingers on my calf and slides upwards.

I snatch my leg away from him and toss the blanket back over myself. Goosebumps are forming on my skin, but I don't think they're from the dropping temperature.

"Hey! I asked you a question. Who taught you this? Did you learn it in containment?"

He tightens the last bandage with a hard jerk.

"Ouch!" I hiss.

"Ya honestly think they teach us anything in containment? No," he spits, "the only thing it taught me was how to suffer."

He motions to my leg. "Father taught me this."

"Your father?"

"I broke my collarbone climbing a tree. It took months to heal properly." He tugs on the corner of his shirt collar, exposing a thick scar. "It got infected. Father had to pull the scab off every couple of days and apply more medicine." He grimaces and stands.

"Is he out here, too? Or anyone else? How did you end up out here in the woods?" I ask hurriedly, trying to milk him for useful information.

"No," he says in a bitter voice, turning away. "Oh! I almost forgot." Griff takes the stick leaning against the wall and holds it out to me.

Interesting, he quickly changed the topic. Is he protecting someone? I shove down visions of beating him over the head with it, carefully composing my face.

"What's this?"

"It's a crutch." He shoves it under his armpit, lifts one leg and hops, looking ridiculous. "You can't walk outta here on that leg, so I made ya this. Here, try it."

His vibrant eyes meet mine, and he licks his lips.

I cough and hesitate, finger curling in the blankets. Why is it suddenly so hot in here? Men are not at all how I expected. Years in the academy, all the handsy girls and useless advances I shot down, couldn't have prepared me for the way he looks at me like he'd like to devour me. Or the way my body stirs to the hunger in his eyes.

"Um, can you turn around?"

Griff laughs, a deep, throaty noise that leaves him sounding almost breathless and the muscles in his neck straining. It's the first time he's shown genuine happiness, and it tightens cords in my lower stomach.

"Nothing I haven't seen already," he counters, the smirk lifting a corner of his lips.

That lopsided smile should be illegal. If my eyes could shoot bullets right now...I sigh and stand up, letting the blanket slip from my bare skin. The air has cooled significantly since he entered. I push up from the edge of the bed and stand, balancing on my good leg and grabbing the crutch.

He doesn't let go.

"I can't use this if you're holding on." I snap and offer a smile to smooth over the harshness of the words.

Griff pulls his knife from his belt and rests it against his leg. He holds my gaze in a silent warning and opens his mouth to reply.

"No funny business—I know, I know." I interrupt, yanking hard enough he surrenders. His grip tightens on the knife hilt. I put the crutch under my arm, but it's too long for me to use it the way he did.

"Give it back, I'll make it shorter." He flips it horizontally and, with a single whack, takes the end clean off.

Closing my gaping mouth without comment, I tuck it back under my armpit. The crutch supports the brunt of my weight when I swing my injured leg forward. The difference is night and day.

"Much better," I say. Moving is much easier and almost pain free. His gaze follows my march around the room until, flushed and sweating, I sink back onto the bed.

His eyes trace the tops of my breasts where he stands above me. He coughs suddenly and yanks the door open. "It'll have to do. I'm gonna start packing, we'll leave as soon as I'm done." The door bangs behind him.

While the view I gave him wasn't intentional, it's working in my favor. Once he's left, I fan my face and chest with my hand. Sure, he's handsome and strong, and between his fits of anger, he continues to help me. But he's also the enemy and getting him to talk isn't exactly a textbook scenario. I wipe my grimy forehead and run my fingers through my oily, tangled hair.

I was supposed to call Mara two days ago. Would she think I was still in a funk and just needing my space? Or would she realize something's wrong?

There's a dull roar overhead followed by a rumble of thunder. Wind gusts and howls, lightning flashes. Dammit! Trust my luck. Mother nature is laughing at me.

Heavy rain drums the roof and pools on the windowsill where it's open for Mischief to come and go. There was no five-minute warning, my tether is eerily quiet. Griff is still out there, what's taking him so long? The unsettling chill isn't only from the goosebumps prickling my bare skin or the fact the wood stove is burning low.

What the hell is wrong with me? I'm sitting here dying and making a fool out of myself. Some soldier I am. During the bombing, I failed the other trainees, lost my lottery tickets, and now I'm breaking my motherline.

Thunder booms overhead, shaking the cabin walls. I shriek in surprise. It's not a bomb, it's not a bomb. Rain is pouring harder now. Mischief topples through the window. Water drenches his body, making him look more cat-like than I've ever seen him. Droplets patter the floor until he shakes, sending spray flying across the room and onto my arm.

"Well, thanks." I mutter.

Yesterday, my tether would have protected me from the virus contaminated water. Today, it no longer matters.

How long does it take to pack? What's he doing?

Mischief jumps up onto the bed. He circles a few times then burrows under a cover. His tiny body shakes from the cold.

"Poor little guy." He chitters as I wrap the furs tightly around him. "Maybe your dad will freeze out there and then it'll just be you and me, huh?" I laugh at myself, but the joke doesn't sit right.

Mischief's shaking stops as his body heat warms the small cocoon he's snuggled into. I find myself soothing his cute, fluffy fur, lulling him to sleep.

"So much for personal space," I sigh. Apparently, if he's not eating or getting into trouble, he's sleeping.

My mother never let me have a pet. She complained about how they drained your rations and caused trouble around the house. When I asked her how she knew that, she told me about her cat,

Snickers. My grandmother took pity on the stray and brought it home for Mother's nameday. Snickers liked to pee on her bed, so it's no surprise she hated it. How much different would my life have been if I'd had a pet? Something that loved me unconditionally, no matter its bad habits or the trouble it got into.

Maybe that's the reason I wanted a child. A beautiful little girl with my large brown eyes and long, dark hair I could hold in my arms. I woulda done everything with her that my mother never did for me. Read her books before bed, take her down to the coffee shop and buy her a chocolate milk for no special reason, just because I wanted her to know how much I loved her. How much I woulda loved her.

My hand smoothes over my flat belly. I imagine little legs kicking there like I felt on Mara's stomach. Tears stream down my cheeks and my mouth quivers. Soon she'd have a daughter, but I would never be an auntie.

Or a mother.

# 14

**Escape is a battle where each step is a
lie and every obstacle is a rebellion.**

The front door blows open, accompanied by a gust of icy
wind, chilling my puffy eyes and damp face. Griff enters,
hair plastered to his skull, shirt and pants contouring his body.
He carries his bag, my boots, and his bow and arrows.

"Shit, it's cold," he says with a shiver. Seconds later, he's peeling
his wet shirt over his head and wringing it out into the sink. Bless
the mother...I've never seen so many chiseled muscles begging to
be explored.

"Hey! What are you doing?"

"I'm drying off. What does it look like I'm doing? It's fucking
freezing out there." He hangs it in the rafters near the fire. Facing
the wood stove, he tugs off his boots, unzips his pants, and
glances over his shoulder. "Are you gonna watch?"

"What?"

He shakes his head and mutters. "Course ya will."

Wet material slaps the floor with a plop. I've seen plenty of naked
women in the barracks but this...not at all the same. I clamp a hand

over my eyes as my heart leaps into my throat. "Put your damn clothes on!" I hiss.

"Oh, ya think I have spares lying all over the place, do ya?"

I yelp as he pulls one blanket out from under my legs, but I dare not uncover my eyes. There's a thump and a clunk and several other sounds I can't quite make out. Wood squeaks and drags across the floor. What's he doing?

"Are you decent?" I demand.

"Ya asking permission to uncover ya eyes? The answer is yes."

Arrogant jerk. I peek through the tiniest gap in my fingers until I can make out his wet, muscular back, facing me where he sits by the fire. The deer skin covers his lower half.

"Are those my pants?"

"It's the only thing I could find to dry off with. Besides, you're not using them." He rubs the material over his arms, chest, and shoulders. Then he dips his head and draws them vigorously through his hair.

"Ew," I curl my lips.

"What, ya want them back?" He half turns and holds the material out towards me.

My eyes go wide as I shake my head no. He chuckles and continues to dry off. When he's done, he stands and tosses my pants into the rafters beside his other clothes.

Water droplets hit the floor in a steady rhythm. Muscles shift when he leans forward and stuffs more logs into the fire, getting it going again. He holds both hands out, rubs them together, blows on them, and repeats.

"When are we leaving?"

"Have ya looked outside or are ya deaf?"

"You've gotta be kidding me! You said you'd take me back!"

"And I will, once the storm passes. Unless you get some sick satisfaction outta freezing to death?"

I cross my arms over my chest. "And how long will it take to get back to the lake house?"

"Depends."

"On what?"

"How fast ya can walk."

"That's not an answer."

Griff grunts and goes quiet. I guess he's not gonna tell me. Not that I blame him, if our positions were reversed I wouldn't tell me either.

He surprises me when at last he offers, "A day, give or take."

If I poke and prod too much he tends to shut down. Better stick to neutral territory for now, or whatever will keep him on comms and maintain this uneasy truce.

"How long have you had Mischief?" I reach over and pet him. He snores softly. The drum of the rain is picking up again, loudly on the roof.

"A few months. I found him as a kit."

"Where?"

"Here, in the mountains. His mom got caught in a trap. So I took him in and raised him myself. My father woulda hated him. He loves to cause trouble." He turns his head in profile and in the light of the fire I catch a smile tugging the corner of his mouth.

"How'd you train him to come when you whistle like that?"

His broad shoulders lift and lower in a quick motion. "Just sorta happened, I guess. He's helpful when I'm out foraging. Usually he notices something I can eat before I do."

"How long have you lived out here?"

Griff huffs and says, "So demanding...."

A companionable silence falls between us. I trace one finger over my parched lips and struggle to swallow.

"Are ya thirsty?"

"Yeah," I nod.

He stands and crosses to his bag. I avert my eyes as the deer skin slips lower with each stride he takes. Who knew men had so many muscles? At least, the textbooks never described them that way, only that they were extremely contagious. I shudder at the thought. The symptoms of the Heart Blight loom, the incubation period nearing its end. I'm the countdown on a ticking time bomb I can't diffuse.

He pulls out a canteen and hands it to me.

My fingers tremble when I take it. This will be my second time drinking the contaminated water. We have to leave today, before I'm too weak to travel.

"Ya gonna drink it or not?" He raises an eyebrow.

I unscrew the top and take a sip. The liquid soothes my dry mouth and parched throat. It tastes crisp and clean, better than anything I've had in the city. I gulp it down until it's empty and my stomach's content.

"Thanks."

"It's more fun when I'm helping ya drink." Griff's hand lingers on mine when he reaches for it.

A breath catches in my throat and heat flares up and down my body. His cocky smile brightens the room. This routine is becoming uncomfortably comfortable.

"Sounds like the rain is stopping," I say. Thank the Authority. Finally, something working in my favor. The sooner we leave the better.

"Dry enough, I guess." He tosses my pants, smacking me in the face. "Turn around, get dressed."

Snapping at him would be the easiest thing to do. I bite my lip and turn my head, displacing Mischief when I start to put my pants on, still warm from their proximity to the fire. They have a crisp, sweet, woodsy fragrance. Just like him. Gritting my teeth isn't helping me ignore how wrong this situation is.

"Guess I should put one of your boots in my bag. Ya should be able to wear the other one. Then we can get outta here."

We. He said we. The irritation at those words has me at the edge of a breaking point. Too comfortable indeed.

Wasting no time, I pull on my boot and grab the crutch. I wince, pushing off the bed. It's now or never.

Griff, fully dressed, collects his supplies. His bow and arrows go over one shoulder, and the backpack on the other. He grunts under the weight.

Leaning more on the crutch than I would like, I make one last sweep of the hut, drinking it all in, before heading to the door. Seriously? The room seems so cozy now that we're leaving.

"Well, it was fun, time to go." I say.

Pulling the door open I step outside. Fun? I snort and giggle, trying to contain my irrational laughter and relief.

The front of the hut has a small deck area where there's a large stack of soaked wood. The railing ends at several wide, steep steps. What idiot wouldn't put a handrail on those death traps? Getting down the stairs with my bum leg is going to be an adventure.

Beyond, there's a small circle of stones with an upturned stump beside it. That's it. There's no identifying marks, no trail, no path, no signs of other human activity.

"Well, damn." There's no way I can get down those stairs without falling and hurting myself even worse than I already have.

"Here, let me help you." Griff wraps his arm around my waist, pulling me close, and half carries, half drags me down the stairs. He's so solid, lifting me easier than a sandbag in a training drill. Scary, but something else, too. Exhilarating? No, that's not right.

I smile prettily and bat my eyelashes. "Thanks," I'm rewarded with a flush creeping up the sides of his face. One hand rubs at his neck, and he turns away abruptly. Oh, this is good. I can use this accidental revelation every chance I get.

"This way," he says, heading out.

Mischief skitters ahead. Leaves crunch and squish underfoot as he sets the pace. Not too fast, but not slow, either. Perfect. I want to get as far as we can before it gets dark. My stomach clenches at the idea of staying out here overnight.

"Am I going too fast?"

"No, I'm fine." I hobble along behind him, wincing anytime my injured foot brushes the ground as I lose my balance.

It takes all my focus and effort to follow him. Every stick, rock, log, and tangle becoming a kill-zone for my ankle. They're enemy combatants to the stability of the crutch and my core strength. Within an hour I'm panting, sweating, and cursing my injury with every word imaginable. Griff is pulling further and further ahead. Twice already he doubled back to check on me, letting me catch up.

The third time he falls back and waits while I pause to catch my breath.

"You need to take a break." He motions towards a big rock.

"No, I'm fine."

"Really? At this pace, we'll get there next week. What? Don't look at me like that, it's true!"

"I can go faster."

"Sure ya can."

I sigh and collapse onto the makeshift seat. It's only been a few hours and my wound is throbbing something fierce. My other leg wobbles with exhaustion from having to compensate. The crutch has transformed my armpit into a massive bruise. To make matters worse, my shoulders and back are cramping.

He squats beside me and rifles through his bag, handing me water and something to eat. "Here."

"Thanks." I need to keep my strength up as long as I can. Every bit counts. The smoked meat is tough and chewy. What I imagine it would taste like to eat a leather belt. Complaining will only set off another pissing match. Instead, I chomp into it with all my might.

"See how the sun shines through the trees?"

"Yeah?"

"My little brother would insist we stop here so he can sketch. He has a talent for finding light in the darkness, ya know?"

"You have a brother?" I bite my tongue before I accidentally ask about the photo. Thinking quickly, I add, "How old is he?"

Griff stands, brushing dirt from his pants, a muscle twitching in his jaw. "I'm gonna scout ahead while you're resting. Stay put, I'll be back," he calls over his shoulder and stalks off.

I watch his back recede through the woods and his footsteps grow faint. Stretching out my leg, I gingerly roll my hurt ankle, trying to ease the stiff muscles. Massaging my calf helps, but the ache persists. Two days ago, this would've been the perfect opportunity to slip away, head back to Mara's place, and report him to the Authority. If only I could freaking walk. Scowling at my ankle doesn't help, either.

The tree on my right is blocking the sun and as it goes lower in the sky, it's getting chilly. I notice a triangle scratched into the tree around the knot in the trunk. Did a deer do this? Huh, weird.

There's a rustle in the woods to my right. I go rigid, straining to see or hear anything.

"Griff? Mischief?" I call. There it is again, the same noise, but no answer. Panic rises. Uneventful minutes pass before I release the breath I'm holding.

It's just some harmless critter, or maybe a branch falling. These woods are far more alive than I imagined, but it's different from the city. In Terin, people scurry from place to place, intent on reaching their destination. Out here, time has a tendency to slow, to pass with an ease that only exists after an exhausting day of training in the barracks.

*Bang!*

My whole body jerks. Was that a gunshot?

"Griff! Where are you?" There's no freaking answer.

Crap. Break time is over. Fumbling to my feet, I groan as I straighten and start off in the direction he disappeared. Ignore the increasing pains shooting up my calf and the opposite hip. Place one foot in front of the other, focus on the way forward.

My chest is heaving when I stop walking. Every step is pure agony. I groan and rotate my arms in circles to relax the tense muscles cramping along my spine. The sun is getting lower in the sky and a battering ram assaults my armpit.

Mother bless it, why isn't he answering me?

It's a struggle to catch my breath, visible in puffy clouds before my face. Taking the pressure off my bad leg helps. I rub my tight thighs with the heel of my fist to loosen those sore muscles and warm up my tingling fingers, too. I have to keep going. The temperature is dropping at an alarming rate.

"Dammit! No, no, no, that can't be!" There it is again. A damn triangle around a knot in the tree's trunk. The same one I passed when I set off after Griff. "H–how is that possible?" Palms hit my forehead and rake roughly through my hair.

My scream of frustration breaks the soft ambiance of the woods. A bird flaps, startled, leaping off a branch and into the air. I try to kick at the ground with my good leg, but it cramps, forcing me to step on my bad leg, nearly toppling me over. Come on, think. There's no way I've been limping in circles.

"Just keep moving," I hiss, pumping myself up. Forget the throbbing in my shoulders and the revolt throughout my body. Drown out the pain. Panicking now will just slow me down.

Leaning heavily on the crutch, I hobble forward another step. My going is much slower. For every five steps, I stop and rest. Each break gets longer, doubling and then tripling in duration. It's so cold. The sun barely filters through the treetop, and it's getting harder and harder to see.

"Griff!" I shout louder. Only the chirping of crickets and the wind answer.

No, he wouldn't leave me out here, right? Not without his stupid necklace. Was it a gunshot I heard earlier? Come on, five more steps. I wipe sweat from my brow with stiff fingers and icy feet. Everything else aches with a confusing mixture of burning heat and frigid chills.

Oh shit, it's the first symptom of the Heart Blight.

The ground disappears out from under me and there's a loud crack. Freezing water splashes, drenching my pants and the back of my shirt. Mud squishes between my fingers and under my butt. Pain shoots up my tail bone and has my teeth rattling. I'm so disoriented I take a moment to understand what happened. My crutch floats next to me in the wrist deep pool of water, broken in two pieces. Dirt and roots loom over me. I tip my head back and find the dusky sky and tree tops high above.

I'm in a sinkhole.

Standing, I stretch my arms out but they're a foot short of touching the walls. As small as it is, and with the light fading, it would have been easy to miss even if I had been looking for it.

Cupping wet hands around my mouth I shout, "Griff!"

Still nothing.

Dammit! I reach for a root on the side of the hole, testing my weight. Of course it broke.

"You've got to be kidding me!" Nervous laughter bursts from my lips, so hard I double over and grab my stomach. Hot tears leak from the corners of my eyes. My sides ache by the time they subside. Violent shivers and chattering teeth bring me crashing back to reality. The fever must be getting to me.

Gotta focus. I approach another part of the wall and search for another root to grab. It takes several tries to find one that holds my weight. Bracing both my feet against the muddy, wet bottom and pulling myself up. My arms, long past exhaustion, refuse to cooperate. I get two small, shuffling steps upwards before my injured leg slips and I splash back into the water.

"Don't panic. Try something else. Find another way." I spin around, searching. The broken crutch bumps into my foot. I pick up the smaller piece, jam it into the muddy part of the wall where I slipped, and try pulling myself up again. When I brace my good foot against the piece of crutch, it holds.

"Come on, come on!" I reach up to grab a rock further above me. My injured leg slips against the wall and dirt and muck showers my head. I land on my back in the water, blinking hard, commanding my sluggish body to get back up.

"Griff!" I scream in frustration until my voice is hoarse and raw.

Authority save me, I'm trapped.

# 15

# GRIFF

**We're prisoners of circumstance, of each other, of choices forced upon us we can't take back.**

It's been a long time since I've thought about the good times I had with my brother. Today, watching the light filter past the trees with Rei, I remember the way his eyes lit up when I handed him the pen I stole. Or how he would grab my hand and dig his head into my chest when he was scared, refusing to cry.

We didn't have much, but we had each other.

And I left him there, knowing what his next nameday had in store for him. The sound of him shrieking has overshadowed the happy memories for so long.

What was I doing? My steps falter and I shake myself out of the fog. Scouting ahead was just an excuse to give her more time off her ankle. Our progress was embarrassingly slow, like an inchworm. Things would be so much easier if she could swallow her pride and stop pushing herself so hard. Not that I'm surprised, the Authority needs compliant, loyal citizens to stay in power. Enforcers were the worst of all, herding us around like animals from one torture to another.

"Fuck, these are new." I bend down and rake the leaves off of the damp ground. The boot prints are too small to be my own and too fresh to be Rei's. Tracing the slow arc of their progress, I reach for my bow. Strange, there's only one set of tracks. Patrols search in groups of two or three, preferring to stick together, traipsing through the woods like rampaging momma bears. They've never come this close before. Why suddenly split up?

The change of tactics sits uneasy on my shoulders. Instincts urge me to investigate, caution screams to run, and reason reminds me what I'm doing out here in the first place. Slip between patrols and get the necklace across the Iron Divide. Find safety and escape oppression among the Free Territories. Destroy the Authority and everything the Commander built to get justice for my father.

Branches snap in the distance. My bow jerks up, turning toward the sound.

Someone's coming.

The boy stumbles around a tree, face dirty, hair matted, boots and clothes crusted in mud. He trips and goes down on one knee, head drooping so low his forehead brushes the soggy underbrush.

What? Who is he? What's he doing out here of all places? How did he escape?

"Hey, are you okay?"

His head tips back, lolling on his neck, and his eyes struggle to focus as I approach.

"I must be dreaming," he whimpers, blinking hard. "They left me to die in the storm, but the rain didn't kill me. Why wasn't I suppressed?"

"Sorry, I don't understand. What's your name? Who left you?"

"Enforcers," he spits out the word like it's cursed. My hand on his shoulder steadies him when he trembles. "In the end I was wrong. I shouldn't have gone inside."

"It's okay, I can help you."

His gaze fixates on where I'm touching him. "No. I tried so hard, but instead I found you...and the Heart Blight."

A muddy hand raises with a flash of metal.

*Bang!*

Arms flailing, I hit my ass. A part of the boy's head is missing. Blood drips from the gaping wound onto the collar of his shirt, turning the dark blue material black.

One mistake is all it takes to die, my father's voice jeers and I imagine the piercing, disappointed stare he would give me.

My mouth gapes. No, it can't be. There's a bump on the skin of her limp wrist and a mucky blue uniform. She's not a boy, she's an Enforcer they left to die. This is what the Authority does, twisting, corrupting, and tormenting us with their lies. I don't allow myself to follow the thought any further. Fiddling with the gun reveals an empty clip. Put it back, better to ditch it if it's not useful. The echo of the gunshot will have carried. Time to go.

The sun is lower in the sky, more than enough time for Rei to have caught her breath. Temperatures are dropping. My scouting detour went much further than I intended. An open air fire won't be as comfortable as the warmth of the wood stove, if I can even get one started to begin with. Finding wood after a storm was a skill in patience and determination.

I round the corner to the spot I left Rei. My backpack sits beside an empty rock. Fuck! After everything I've done for her, all those doe eyes and sweet smiles.... Scanning for her trail, the circular shape of her crutch is easy to spot in the soft ground, made deeper by how heavily she's leaning on it. I should be able to catch up to her quickly. No, my life depends on it.

The Authority can't know I'm alive.

Racing after her, I slip and slide. I slow when the mountain lion's tracks converge with hers. As if shit couldn't get any worse. This would explain why she took off. Lumpy cans and bottles in my bag beat a rhythm against my shoulder blades. The pounding of my heart and the roar in my ears drives me forward at a relentless pace.

The strange feeling she evokes, the way it stirs low in my stomach—it's like a spell she's working over me. It has to stop. I can't make any more excuses for her, or take pity on her. She's dangerous and she'll do anything in her power to ruin my life forever. The sly looks and the timid smiles, her pale skin peeking out from under the blankets. Drawing me in was her way of getting my guard down.

I slow to catch my breath, my hand on my side. My chest is heaving from the effort of running flat out. She got further than I would have expected on such a bum leg. Her tracks have shifted, the crutch drags across the ground. She's getting tired.

Rei's scream brings me skidding to a halt. Was that my name? I'm close and it's a good thing, too. It's getting harder to find her tracks on the ground. There's the scream again, weaker this time. Like her voice is going hoarse. Gut wrenching sobs fill the air. I forgot she's afraid of the dark. But would that have her screaming like this? Did she get attacked? Her voice sounds funny too, kinda muffled.

"Rei?" I call out to her.

"Griff? Be careful, there's a sinkhole! I'm here, down here!"

Squelching and slashing noises give me enough warning to inch forward. Tucked into the base of a tree is a dark hole. Part of the root system rotted and the heavy rains collapsed the ground in on itself.

"Griff! Bless the mother, you're here." The way she says my name, with a flood of relief, twists my insides and slams them against each other. Pull yourself together.

I lie down on my stomach, and scoot forward, afraid if I stand too close the edge might collapse. Rei's big dark eyes peer up at me. Slimy, foul smelling water soaks her clothes. She's sitting with her back pressed to one side of the hole, teeth chattering, shivering uncontrollably. She looks terrified, miserable, and best of all, thrilled to see me.

If I go down there, I'll likely get stuck like she is. I swear and push my sweaty hair out of my eyes. "I told ya to stay put."

Water sloshes as she stands, her hand sliding on the muddy wall behind her. "You said you'd come back!" Her voice comes out like the croak of a frog. Rei wobbles, the water splashing, struggling to stay on her feet. Her lips are turning blue and the temperature continues to drop with the sun.

*Go back for the rope and leave her here to freeze, this is too dangerous,* Father insists. Rei senses the dark direction of his voice in my head, my hesitation.

"If you leave me here, you'll never find your necklace."

"Come here, I'll pull ya out." I reach out a hand.

She grabs a root near the wall and tries to haul herself up high enough. Her fingers graze mine and slip away. She tries again, pushing off harder this time. It's still not enough for me to get a good grip on her slimy hand.

"My fingers are so cold it's hard for me to hang on." She stutters, shaking them, trying to regain some feeling.

"Try blowing on them to warm them up, that helps."

She does, and then opens and closes them in quick succession. "It's not working."

"Okay, grab the crutch and see if ya can hold on to that."

She nods and turns, searching the dark pool for the long bobbing section of crutch. Wincing, she slides her hand into the cold water and grabs it. She stretches it as high as it will go, and I grab hold of the end.

"Hang on, don't let go. I'm gonna pull ya up." I strain against the weight of her body and the position I'm in, trying to hoist her higher. "Give me your hand, too." I thrust my other arm down to her.

Using the crutch for leverage, she places her feet against the wall and tries to push up. Her feet slip but she's determined, and she shuffles upwards, using her knees for purchase. Her free hand reaches up and I grab her wrist.

It takes every ounce of strength I have to keep hauling her up. Both feet continue to scramble against the mud. Finally, one finds purchase, and she surges upwards as I get to my knees and lean back. Her upper body clears the edge and the crutch snaps.

She slips. My grip tightens on her wrist and I grab for her shirt with the other hand. Then I fling myself backwards, using my body weight for leverage. Rei slides over the lip of the sinkhole and slams on top of me.

Her dirty hair tickles my ear and forehead. The top of her nose brushes my cheek and I can feel her cold, trembling breath against my mouth. One of her hands slides over my chest, fingers splayed. The wet sleeve of her other hand tickles the side of my neck. Our chests rise and fall as one.

Pressing my lips to hers would warm them up. Would they be as soft as her skin? I release her shirt and slide my hand underneath the material. The skin of her abdomen shudders under my palm. Instead of pulling away, she arches into the warmth.

Her wet clothes are soaking into mine. I ache to touch her more, to let my hands wander over the peaks and valleys of her body. But something hard and cold pokes my sternum. Something familiar. My hand slides to the curve of her breast and my heart skips a beat.

"What are you doing?" She whispers, her voice husky and exhausted.

I lean forward, pressing my mouth against her ear. "Taking back my necklace," I say, then pushing her off me.

She grunts and flops to the ground, sluggish to rise onto her hands and knees. I'm rewarded with the glare I've grown accustomed to over the past two days. There she is.

The necklace dangles in my hand, cold and clammy like her skin. She had the fucking thing all along.

Rei tosses her head back and laughs. It's a wild, unbound sound. It sends shivers down my spine. When her feverish eyes return to my face, the fire in them blazes as hot as my desire to strip her down to her underwear.

"You promised to take me to the lake house," she growls, baring her teeth like a rabid fox.

Stepping toward her, she retreats, inching closer to the mouth of the sinkhole. I hold out a hand.

"Take it," I command.

Emotions battle across her pale face and harden with her decision. Stiff, icy fingers touch my palm, relaxing when I haul her to safety.

"It's getting dark, we're soaked, and you're running a fever. It's not safe out here. Let's head back to the hut, we can try again tomorrow."

"No! We have to keep going! I have to get back! I can't die out here!"

"You're not gonna die."

"Take me back! You promised! I have to say goodbye!"

"What are ya talking about?"

"I'm dying and it's all your fault!"

Her hysteria is reaching a breaking point. There's no reasoning with her in this state. We need a fire and dry clothes before we freeze to death.

Rei screams and kicks out when I catch her in a bear hug, lifting her off the ground. Her nails dig into my forearms and her legs thrash. I jerk my face out of the way just in time as she tries to smash it with the back of her head.

"Stop! Calm down," I hold tighter. My skin burns where she's scratched me. "Look!" Grabbing her chin, I force her head around. "Do ya see those?" Even in the dim light the mountain lion's tracks are deep in the mud. "Do ya see?" I insist she answer me.

She nods against my hold of her face. "Yes," she croaks.

"There's a mountain lion nearby. It'll pounce and snap our necks before we know what hit us. Ya understand?"

She nods again. Her cheeks are so cold in my hand.

"It's not safe out here. We need to move before it gets any darker. I'm gonna let ya go." I miss the press of her body against my front as soon as I do. She takes a step away and spins to face me.

I jerk my head. "That way, start walking."

She limps along a few steps in the direction I motioned. Without the crutch, her going is even slower than before.

We need to hurry. I walk abreast of her and wrap my arm around her waist. She twists away in surprise, then stops as my palm digs into her hip bone, refusing to let go. "We'll be here all night at this rate." I mutter. "Put your arm around my shoulder, use it like a crutch."

She bites her blue lips and her teeth chatter. Finally she relents, draping her arm across the back of my neck.

I support most of her body weight as we go. The pace is still too slow. I'm supporting more and more of her weight as the temperature and wet clothing saps her strength. There's a scream and growl a few hundred yards behind us. So fucking close.

"Shit." I let go of her hip and sweep her into my arms and lengthen my strides. She hardly notices. Her eyelids are half closed and her skin is stone cold. Her breathing is growing shallow. What little warmth I can offer leeches away where our bodies touch.

The hair on the top of her head tickles the bottom of my chin. My arms and shoulders ache. Despite everything, holding her like this continues to stir something in me I can't understand. How can I want to strangle and kiss her at the same time?

The hut appears in the distance and I let out a sigh of relief.

Home, sweet home.

# 16

## Fire provides warmth and a fragile bridge between us.

My embarrassment at the fiasco in the woods, and his arms wrapped around me, have the icicle I've become melting inside. He sets me down on the edge of the bed and pulls my shirt over my head. I'm too drained to complain, even when he pulls my pants off, leaving me in only my bra and underwear.

So this is where I die.

The chill permeates every inch of me but the fever rages. It's a torment of hot and cold. I can't feel my limbs as he grabs them and swings them onto the bed. He piles blankets on top of me and goes to the wood stove. Within a few minutes, there's a roaring fire.

"I'm s-so co-cold," I stutter. "I can't f-feel my f-f-flingers or t-toes."

Griff ties his necklace high in the rafters where I can't reach it. Then he pulls his shirt over his head and spreads it by the fire beside my wet and dirty clothing. I'm too numb to react when his pants join them.

He's left standing in damp shorts.

Knife in hand, he stalks toward the bed. I blink stupidly as he crawls over the top of me and to the side closest to the wall. He pulls the deer skins over himself and then wraps an arm around my stomach. With one powerful yank, he presses his chest and legs against my butt and hips.

I gasp at the skin to skin contact. He's so much warmer than I am, setting my backside ablaze. Pins and needles jab my skin, digging deep. The painful chill of the cold, the fury of the fever, his body heat, heavy skins on top of us, and the roaring fire make me ache from head to toe. My limbs burn and my head pounds, knocking against my eyeballs.

My chest is heavy and full. It's hard to breathe but focusing on the solidness at my back and sucking air in helps. This must be what it's like when blood crystalizes. A violent shiver wracks through me, muscles jerk and spasm.

The arm wrapped around my waist squeezes me tighter, pressing me more firmly against his body. Throbbing pain in my ankle makes me moan.

"Shh, I got ya. You're gonna be okay." Rough fingers brush the hair away from my sweaty forehead.

Dying is the hottest, steamiest shower I can imagine, boiling me from the inside out.

I don't remember falling asleep, but somehow I'm still alive.

The weight around my mid-section is comfortable and safe. My limbs are stiff, but all of my fingers and toes respond when I wiggle them this time. I shift my injured leg and it grazes his. It tickles. Huh, his legs are so hairy. He breathes deeply and his chest rises and falls against my shoulder blades. A puff of air stirs strands of hair by my ear when he exhales. His fingers brush the side of my neck.

Heat floods my cheeks. Just a few days ago, all I could think about was avoiding his touch and now I've spent the night pressed skin to skin. Growing up, I couldn't understand what all the fuss was about. Now I know.

Dammit, this is bad.

Three days curled up to a survivor carrying the Heart Blight and here I am thinking traitorous thoughts about how much I like it. What am I doing? A shock runs through me, and I try to sit up and peel myself off of him. Corded muscles tighten on my belly and his hips grind into my ass.

"Hey!" I twist, trying to put distance between us. Bad idea. Now we're face to face. As he drags me forward, my breasts crush against bare chest. His eyes pop open as I place hands on his shoulder, trying get up.

"Morning," he says with a lazy grin. I hate him so much in that moment, that handsome face, disheveled hair, and the intensity in his eyes.

"Let go, you're too close," I push harder, angling away from him.

He chuckles and rests his hand against my forehead, leaning closer, his mouth inches from mine. "Don't ya think ya owe me an apology first? Fever's gone but ya scratched the hell outta my arm yesterday."

"Yeah? You got your necklace, take me back to the lake house," I demand.

He stiffens and releases me, sitting up in bed. The morning light plays along his exposed upper body and I gape. The long, thick scar across his right collarbone stands out, but the rest of him is lean and sculpted. Enforcer training would be a walk in the park for someone built like him. As I examine him in the morning light, he stands abruptly and leaves the bed. The door opens and slams closed.

"Great, just great." I sit and stretch my achy limbs and roll my sore ankle. Despite my adventure yesterday, it doesn't buckle when I stand and limp over to the kitchen. There's a half-empty canteen of water by the sink and I gulp until it's empty. I'm still so thirsty and my rumbling stomach reminds me that I haven't eaten anything since yesterday afternoon.

The necklace dangles from high in the rafters. My leverage is gone. He's helped me this far, but what am I gonna do if he won't take me back to the lake house? If I can find a way to reach it, what then? What's so special about the damn thing anyways?

I'm standing on the wobbly stool, reaching for the necklace, my fingers brushing the swaying end, when the door opens.

"Seriously?" Griff stomps in and grabs my waist, lifting me over his shoulder.

"Put me down, you big brute! I just wanted to look at it!"

He tosses me onto the bed. "Ya expect me to believe that?"

"I'm telling the truth! Authority save me, you don't believe me."

"Nothing ya done gives me a reason to trust ya."

"Oh yeah? Well, how about you? You tie me up and fling me around like I'm a sack of flour! How about you treat me with some respect?"

"I've done nothing but treat ya—your leg, food, water—I even made ya a fucking crutch! All you've done in return is kick my ass and run back to the shitty Authority so ya can turn me in. Does it make ya happy? Would ya rather see me locked up and experimented on for the rest of my life?"

"You're infected with the virus!"

"Really? After everything that's happened? It's been three days. Why aren't ya sick, huh?" He stalks closer and places his hands on either side of me where I sit on the bed. "I saw the way ya looked at me when ya got here, like the smallest touch would kill ya." His breath on my collar bone makes me press my thighs together. "Well? I've had my hands all over ya. Why hasn't the virus killed ya by now?"

"I–I don't–I'm not a scientist!" I open my mouth to retort and clamp it shut before I say something I might regret. Pissing him off won't help anything. "You promised to take me back!"

"Ya serious? Ya barely made it a mile yesterday."

"I can do it."

Griff's eyebrows raise and his shoulders stiffen. Clearly, the answer is no.

"So what am I supposed to do, sit here and be useless?"

His lips purse in thought. We're still in our underwear. I feel heat rising in my cheeks. What's wrong with me? I lick my lips and push his shoulder, trying to give myself more space.

"I have an idea," he says, removing his arms from the bed and crossing them over his chest.

"Really? I didn't think you'd agree so easily."

He shrugs. "We're outta drinking water. It's a nice, tedious task. Even a child can handle. Ya just boil it and re-fill the canteens."

The rude gesture I make behind his back would make Mara proud. Go ahead, insult me and underestimate me. When he's locked in a cell in the GRH I'll get the last laugh.

So I spend a good portion of the morning cleaning myself up and boiling the rainwater on the stove after Griff stokes the fire. Although I can't properly wash my hair, it feels better after I douse it in the sink basin and scrub my fingers through it. When I'm finished, Griff pulls down our clothes and has me scrub those, too. The water is filthy when I'm done. Griff hauls out the dirty water while I lay them out by the fire to dry and refill all the canteens.

I limp back over to the bed.

"Let me see your leg," he stands from the stool where he was fletching an arrow and sinks down beside me.

I bite my lip as he swings my leg up and onto his lap. My heel digs into his muscular thigh as he unwraps the bandages and examines the wound. He presses on the edge of the injury despite my protests.

"It's healing nice and clean. I don't think ya need more poultice on it. Just clean bandages." Removing the old bandages, he gently wraps it with the clean ones. "There, that outta do it." His hand lingers across the base of my foot.

I cough and jerk it away, easing it back down to the ground. I can't wait until my clothes are dry enough to put them back on. Seeing so much of his skin and him seeing mine is uncomfortable.

"How did you escape the Authority?" I say, not expecting an answer.

"A woman in a white coat helped my father and I get out of there."

My head whips around in shock. "What? A scientist helped you?"

Griff shrugs. "I dunno who she was."

"And you're sure she wore a white lab coat?"

"Does the sun rise every day?"

"That means there's a traitor in the Authority." I say, my grip tightening on the edge of the bed. I need to get this information to Commander Lynx. Did the Sympathizers bomb our caravan because they already knew Dr. Martina would be in that truck? Was she the target all along?

"Hah!" Griff stands and paces back and forth, glaring bullets at me. "You're the only traitor here, Rei. Have ya ever stopped to think about why the Authority keeps us locked up in containment?"

"Of course I know why. You're infected with the virus that wiped out most of the world's male population."

"Am I Rei?" Griff stalks close enough his knees bump into mine. He towers over me, forcing me to tip my head back. "If I'm so contagious, how are ya still breathing? Huh?"

"The virus is mutating more and more often. It's only a matter of time before it destroys us."

"How do ya know that's true?"

"B–because that's what all the reports say!"

"Who writes the reports, Rei?"

"The scientists and the leaders of the Authority."

"Exactly. The Authority controls everything and ya just trust what they spoon feed ya without a care in the world!"

"That's not true!" I say, jumping to my feet, my voice rising and my chest heaving.

"Oh yeah? Then why aren't ya sick, huh?"

For three days I've lived with him, touched him, even drank and was exposed to virus contaminated water.

"I–I don't know...maybe it's only passed by blood or saliva? Authority scientists wear hazmat suits. We're given a standard issue tether to protect us from the virus in the water. Why would they do that if it wasn't contagious, if it wasn't dangerous? The Authority's trying to save humanity! Do you want humans to go extinct? Is that what you want?"

"Right. Yet here ya stand, healthy and full of fight, living in close quarters with an infected survivor," he growls. His big hand grabs the base of my head and full lips smash into mine. The pillowy softness sucks my breath away, his tongue coaxing my mouth open.

Griff stops abruptly, leaving our chests heaving. "There. Now we'll know just how contagious I really am." He releases my hair and grabs his clothing before stalking out the door.

My fingers raise and brush over my swollen bottom lip. It's still wet from the kiss. I should be terrified, but no matter where I look, the fear doesn't exist. What I find within me is a roiling sea of longing and desire...for him, for his solidarity, for the feel of his skin pressed against mine once more.

I smack my cheeks with my hands and shake my head. No, this is wrong. I'm training to become an Enforcer, to protect humanity from survivors like him. I want to prevent the spread of this virus to ensure the future for generations to come.

So one day I can hold a daughter in my arms.

It's like some kind of freaking messed up karma that what I've always wanted, having a child, is right here, within my reach. Yet it's the same thing that will condemn my life forever and set me swinging on the Suppression Line.

The longer I stay here, the more complicit I become, no matter how hard I try to deny it. But, gaining his trust, returning to the lake house, and turning him in to the Authority means going back to being broken in a society where this simmering desire is only for and between women.

I must tread so, so carefully.

My fingers brush my lower lip again, remembering the taste of his tongue and the prickly sensation of his stubble against my chin. I have to get out of here as soon as possible, before I no longer trust myself.

# 17

## **Life is an argument between mind, body, and will.**

Last night I swore my fever was the first symptom of the Heart Blight. So why am I fine today? Sure, I'm hungry, but my cheeks aren't hot and I'm certainly not dying. Why would the Authority lie about the virus yet take so many precautions against it at the same time? There are too many questions and not enough answers.

Griff barges back into the hut, fully dressed, the necklace drumming against his chest while he collects his things. Nothing's stopping him from just disappearing, walking away and never coming back.

"Where are you going?"

"Hunting."

"I'm coming, too."

One corner of his mouth tugs with his smile. Shit! Don't stare at his lips.

"And ya leg?"

"I can keep up. It's doing better than yesterday."

He chuckles. "Of course it is. Here, get dressed." Clothes fly at me hard enough that I shoot my hands up to keep them from hitting my face.

That's all the prompting I need to pull on my pants, slip the shirt over my head, and go limping after him into the forest. Memorize every detail, no matter how small, to get a lay of the land. Next time, I'll know which direction takes me to the lake house.

Griff sets a steady pace, but not so fast that my leg gives out. Within 20 minutes, and the burning sensation in my butt and thighs, we're climbing a slight incline. The ache in my leg is bearable, but not for much longer. His crutch would be so nice right now. I didn't realize how much pressure it was taking off my injury. If I asked him, would he make me another one? For some reason, I bet the answer's yes.

I'm breathing hard when Griff stops and lifts a hand. The gesture makes me wince, taking me back to the MMZ barracks. Alyssa uses the same signal during drills, or right before she sends us on another lap around the perimeter.

"What is it?" I say in a huff, resting my hands on my knees to catch my breath.

"Listen," he says, lowering his fist.

I strain my ears, but there's only the rustling leaves. "I don't hear anything...."

"The woods are full of game, if ya know where to find them. Tell me what ya hear."

"Uh, leaves?" I offer with a shrug.

"If ya listen carefully, ya can hear the gurgle of the water. Plus the birds, insects, branches breaking and falling, and a rabbit thumping the ground."

"Wow, you hear all of that?" I cock my head to the side and try listening again. I catch a bird tweeting but none of the others. "Oh wait, there's a rustling in the leaves. Ouch!" Something hard and round hits me on the side of the neck. "What?" Another small object hits me on the forehead this time.

"Mischief, stop throwing acorns!" Griff reprimands.

I duck as the next small object is lobbed in my direction and hits Griff square on the nose. Laughter bubbles and I clamp a hand over my mouth. The next round of acorns launch like grenades. Swatting them aside, we scramble to get outta range.

"Little shit," Griff grumbles. He picks up an acorn and lobs it in the raccoon's direction. Mischief chitters and scurries away when it snaps the leaves beside him. A low chuckle escapes his soft, kissable lips. "Serves ya right!"

Blinking hard, I clear my throat and run a finger over the bump of my tether. The more distractions, the better. "So...what are we looking for?"

"We're gonna check the traps and maybe we'll find something to forage." He walks a few feet further and squats near the base of a tree. "See here? This is a trap. This piece of wood gets knocked down if a rabbit, squirrel, or bird crosses and ensnares it." He slips his hand through the loop on the ground and hits the stick holding the lure. The loop goes tight around his wrist. "They can fight all they want, but once they're caught in a trap, there's no way out."

Griff unties the rope with his free hand and resets the lure. "Here, ya try." He moves out of the way for me to repeat the process.

He's so close, the fabric of his shirt brushes my shoulder. I knock over the stick in the center of the trap. "Wow, that's tighter than I thought it would be." The tight squeeze on my wrist reminds me of being tied up, his hair tickling my legs as he tended to my ankle. Griff has to hold the rope, decreasing the tension, until I can use my free hand to untangle the other one.

"Now try to reset it," he says.

I try once, twice, three times to set the stick back in the center and reset the lure. After the third try, Griff senses my frustration and fixes it himself. Everything is so effortless for him, yet he consistently guides me through every fumbling attempt. This is so outta my element. Years of busting my ass, getting to the top of my class as a soldier, and putting up with Alyssa's impatience for incompetence stand in stark contrast.

"That's harder than it looks," I grumble.

"Survival of the fittest is never easy." He counters, "Try resetting the next one."

"You make these traps and snares yourself?"

"Ya just need a bit of rope and somewhere to add the tension." He reaches for a new snare and traces it to where it's tied around a supple bush branch. "When the lure triggers, it tightens the noose and there ya have it, dinner."

"How do you remember where they all are?" I cross my fingers, hoping he gives me something, anything, about where we are in relation to the lake.

Chin tipping up, green eyes and stubble catching the light, he inspects the trees and the sky beyond. "The sun rises in the east and sets in the west. If ya know that, or how to find the north star, ya can get yourself going in the right direction. But here, most of the time I just recognize where I am since I've been staying at the hut a while now. I think I see some berries over there. Come on."

Following him, dense, scrubby bushes tear at my hair and catch on my clothing. When we finally push through the thickest part, a large bush with small, reddish berries greets us. Griff picks one and holds it out to me. "These are boysenberries. It's like a cross between a blackberry and a raspberry. They're a bit more tart than the blackberries we had last time."

I take it from him and pop it into my mouth. It's juicy and slightly sweet. "You must love berries," I say, licking sticky fingers.

He grins, and it lights up his entire face, a wide, genuine smile. "My father used to scold me because I would spend hours looking for berries rather than hunting. Mischief is the one who turned me on to these. He's better at gathering food than I am."

Griff teaches me how to pick them without getting pricked by thorns.

"Ah, ah, not that one." He grabs my hand when I pull a dark, ripe berry from a bush beside us. "That one causes hallucinations. Eat enough and it'll have ya puking your guts out, too."

"I take it you know from experience?"

The cocky, lopsided smirk is his answer.

When we've finished stripping the bush or anything large and ripe enough to eat, he leads me back through the thicket and onto a narrow track. We continue our climb until my thighs are burning and my leg's throbbing. Freaking ankle. His strides are so much longer than mine already, but he detours periodically.

"Can we stop for a minute?"

"We're almost there. Come on, you're gonna appreciate it." He continues up the trail, leaving me standing there like a rear guard.

As soon as he's out of view, I turn and peer back the way we came. I could make a break for it, just go while he's distracted. Sure, I don't know where I am, but without leverage, this is an opportunity I shouldn't pass up. My retreat falters. He's contagious, the enemy I've trained to detain by any means necessary.

So why do I feel safer with him than behind the barbed-wire perimeter of the MMZ, or amongst a heavily armed platoon? Why doesn't he see me as broken as I see myself? Childless. Deserving of my failures. But it's so different when I'm with him. My boots thud, going heavy, sacks of flour dragging my feet in an agonizing training exercise.

Bless the mother, I can't freaking move, stuck in this new and uncharted war zone of desire, loyalty, and duty. Erratic beats of my heart pound with my about-face, intending to retrace my steps toward Griff, drawing me up short.

Shit!

He stands at the bend in the path, arrow drawn and aimed at my heart.

Watching. Waiting.

# 18

## REI

**It shouldn't feel safe in the hands of the enemy, but sometimes we're opposite ends of the same coin.**

When our eyes meet, he lowers his bow, muscles visibly relaxing, hair falling over his forehead. The slight bob of his chin makes me wonder if this was a test, and somehow I've passed.

"Were you really going to shoot me?" I demand.

"Were ya gonna run?" He counters, eyes flashing.

"No," I say, stomping closer in a huff.

"No," he mirrors my gruff response, slipping the arrow back into his quiver. "This way," he turns and heads off.

Several minutes later, I hear the low gurgle of running water. My pulse leaps and I pick up my pace, hurrying after him with my limping stride. We round a large outcropping of rocks, and I stop, letting out a defeated oomph. It's not the lake, not even close. A trickle of water slides down the tall, rocky facade.

"This is the best place for hunting and water. Sometimes I come here to clean off, too." Griff climbs up over a stack of rocks and offers his hand.

I hesitate, then reach up and take it. The pull propels me forward so quickly I stumble over the uneven surface. He catches my shoulder and steadies me as I wince and lean down to rub my sore ankle.

"Sorry, sometimes I forget how much smaller ya are than me." Once I regain my balance, he lets go and heads up to the next set of rocks. The largest one is so huge I have to sit and slide to the ground on the other side. At the bottom of our rough climb, there's a larger source of the spring water splashing into a small, crystal clear pool.

"Here. Sit there and stick your leg in the water, it'll help."

Three days ago, all the lottery tickets in the world wouldn't have been enough for me to stick my bare skin in unpurified water for more than the 60 seconds my tether allowed. It almost seems silly now.

Griff gently pries off my boot and unwraps the bandages. He examines my swollen ankle with a poke and a prod. "Good, it's not hot. The infection is gone."

"Argh, that's cold!"

"Did ya think it would be warm?" He laughs and splashes me with his hand.

"Hey! Knock it off. Do you want me to freeze to death?"

"Ya mean like yesterday?" He raises an eyebrow and his eyes dance with amusement. "Maybe ya want me to warm ya up again afterwards...."

Stomach doing flip-flops, I turn my face away, cheeks growing hot. How can he say things like that without a shred of embarrassment? Thinking of his hard chest pressed to mine, the earthy scent of his skin, and the calluses on his hands brushing my stomach sends warmth pooling between my legs. I'm suddenly glad the water is there to cool me down.

"Don't go getting any stupid ideas." I warn.

"I think I should be the one telling ya that." He says, rinsing my bandages under the cold water when I finally can't stand the icy chill any longer.

"Give me those, I can do it." I snatch them away from him. He opens his mouth to protest and closes it again at my warning glare.

"Okay, okay, sure ya can."

While I re-wrap my leg with the damp cloth and gingerly slip my foot back into my boot, he re-fills his empty water bottles.

"Here," he hands me one when he's done.

"But it's contaminated."

"Not as safe as boiling it first, but I've never gotten sick drinking from here before." He sighs. "Fine, ya boiled this one earlier this morning."

"Thanks," I unscrew the cap and take a long, long drink.

It's nearly empty when I hand it back. He finishes the rest, water trickling down his chin, then re-fills it in the spring. He stands and holds out a hand to help me to my feet.

I push it away and stand on my own, wincing as I put weight on my injured leg. The cold water has helped reduce the swelling.

"This way." He heads off, back over the rocks and into the woods. He stops at the base of a stocky tree and cups his hands below a branch. "Put ya foot here and I'll boost ya up."

"You want me to climb this? No way." I shake my head.

"It's easier to hunt when your prey can't see ya. Come on, up ya go."

I glare at him for a minute before I huff, placing my hands on his shoulders and my injured foot into the palm of his hands. He hoists me so I can grab the tree branch and pull myself up. I hang on for dear life. Moments later, he's grabbed the branch and swung himself up with ease. He stands and grabs a higher one, pulling himself up again. He leans down and offers me his hand.

"Come on, one more."

"I'm good, this is high enough."

"It's fine. I promise it'll hold ya. Trust me."

"I'm gonna fall."

"Ya won't."

I bite my lower lip. I want him to trust me—no; he needs to trust me. "Fine." Inching my way toward his hand, I grab it and he hoists me as I use my other hand to climb. Taking a moment to slow my galloping heart, my back presses into the tree trunk, fingers digging into the lumpy bark for dear life.

"Sit," he says, straddling the branch with ease. The entire limb wobbles underneath me and my stomach does panicky flip-flops.

"Authority save me," I whisper, scooting down until I'm on my bottom. When I've situated myself to where I feel somewhat balanced, I let out a deep breath.

"It's beautiful."

I glance up and see him watching me. He turns away quickly and coughs.

"The view from up here, it's beautiful." He says, rubbing his chin.

The forested treeline looks sloped from this perspective, and I can make out the trail we followed earlier along with the rocky outcropping we passed. Tree tops are a blend of greens, oranges, reds, browns, and yellows as far as I can see. This higher vantage point reveals far more than when I was on the ground.

A lightbulb goes off in my head. Why didn't I think about this earlier? I swivel left and right, looking for the lake or any other signs of Mara's house.

"Ya can't see it from here," Griff says, as if reading my mind. "The lake." His piercing green eyes are full of laughter.

"Which way is it?" Crap. I didn't mean to say that out loud. The regretful words slipped right outta my mouth.

"You're unbelievable, ya know that? After everything I've done for ya."

"Like keep me prisoner against my will?"

"Would ya rather I leave ya?"

The words are like a punch in the gut. No, I would not rather. A chill runs through me and it's not from the damp bandages on my leg. Quick, change the subject.

"How long do we have to hunt before finding something?"

Griff plucks a stem from a nearby branch and twirls the leaf in his fingers. "Depends. Sometimes I go all day with no luck."

"So you want me to sit here the rest of the day? Doing what? Waiting for something that might show up?"

"Are ya always this impatient?"

"So what if I am?" I quip, raising my chin in defiance.

"Survival isn't about making rash and impulsive decisions."

"I'm trained to make quick decisions."

"I see how well that's going for ya..." he mumbles.

"What are you trying to say? I'm more than capable of holding my own. It's not my fault I grew up in a city rather than running around the woods, hunting and taming the local wildlife."

He snorts. "You're wrong about one thing. Mischief tamed me, not the other way around. Builds character, ya know."

"Why do you have to be such a smart ass—"

"I thought ya ankle could use a break," he interrupts before I can further vent my frustrations.

The words give me pause. Was he doing all of this on my behalf? Checking his traps, the berry bushes, the cold spring, climbing a tree to get a lay of the land?

"Thank you," I choke out, surprised I mean it.

"We're just people, ya know, all the men in containment." He rips the leaf into pieces and watches the fragments flutter.

"Of course I know that," I say, but the lump in my throat is hard to swallow.

We sit in silence, watching the sunset through the foliage, casting vivid hues around us. The longer I sit, the more I pick up around us, the birds, the rustling of leaves, and the plop of acorns. The serene thrum of the forest has its own kind of heartbeat, a peaceful energy.

Griff goes still on his branch, gazing into the distance. Slowly, he reaches for an arrow from his quiver and nocks it on his bow. He draws it back and holds it there, watching something I can't see. Thwack! The arrow whizzes past accompanied by a loud squeal.

Griff smiles. "Dinner. Come on, I'll help ya down."

We find the rabbit about 300 yards away. I glance back at the tree we climbed, astonished he could hit such a small moving target. His aim is much better than mine.

"Teach me how you do that." I demand, as he pulls out the arrow and grabs the rabbit by the ears.

"Not a chance." He wipes the arrowhead off with a handful of leaves and shoves it back into his quiver.

"Let me help. I can hit a target from 100 yards."

"That's what I'm afraid of." He shoves the rabbit in his bag and examines the lowering sun. "We should head back."

"If you want me to trust you, then you have to trust me, too."

"None of your behavior so far warrants me trusting ya."

"I'm here, aren't I? I haven't tried to run."

"Yet." He slips the bow over his shoulder and brushes past me.

"Come on, let me try."

"So demanding," he growls, neck flushing red, picking up the pace.

I struggle to keep up, but don't complain or push my luck a second time. We fall into a comfortable silence and I enjoy watching the shift of muscles beneath his shirt as we go. When I stub the toe on a rock and stumble, Griff turns back, frowning. His pace slows until he's walking beside me.

"Ya can lean on me like yesterday," he offers.

I pin him with eyes full of thanks, wrapping my arm around his shoulder, leaning against his considerable heft, pressed hip to hip. My leg is revolting now and every step sends shooting pains all the way up my calf.

The light is fading by the time I hobble back into the small clearing with the hut.

"Take a seat here."

He lowers me to a low stump by the fire pit. I groan in relief as I sink onto the makeshift stool and take all the pressure off my ankle. Griff returns with a handful of wood and dumps it into the circle of stone. He pulls a tin out of his bag and hands it to me.

"Huh?" I ask, confused.

"Ya said ya wanted to help. Light the fire."

His smirks at the annoyance I assume he sees written all over my face. In retaliation, I purse my lips and bat my eyelashes. He coughs and bends over, busying himself in his bag.

Flicking a strand of my hair out of my way, I create the little nest of kindling like he showed me last time. The flint and the scrap of metal scrape together. Changing the angle and the pressure and how fast or slow I strike them together makes no difference.

"This is impossible! Nothing I try is working." I say in a huff.

Griff grabs my hands and re-positions them. His calloused palms grazing against the bump of my tether. Warm breath teases the hair on the back of my neck as he leans over me, his solid chest pressing my shoulder. He draws my hands in a quick, downward sliding motion. The spark flares to life in the pile of kindling.

"Pick it up and blow on it, but not too hard, or it'll go out."

I cup the bundle in my palms and blow gently until a wisp of smoke billows and the flame quickly catches. Ouch, hot! I yelp and drop it into the pile of logs. The fire licks at the larger pieces of wood until they catch, popping and crackling.

Griff squats beside me with the rabbit, the material of our pants sliding with a friction hotter than the fire. He pulls his knife and examines the edge.

"What are you doing?"

"Gotta skin it and gut it before ya eat it." He presses the knife into a tender section of the flesh with a deft, confident slice.

"Teach me," I demand. He pauses, inspecting me with what I can only guess is a judgement of my sincerity. "You wouldn't let me try the bow. Let me try this."

He considers for a long moment. Yeah, there's no way in hell he's gonna say yes. Flipping the knife, he offers the hilt in one hand and the rabbit in the other.

"Ya want me to trust ya," he says, jerking the hilt back when I reach for it. "Give me a reason to."

I nod and take them both. He directs me on where to place the knife and how to run it beneath the skin.

"Like this?" I ask.

"Yep, now grab the pelt from the bottom and pull toward the ears."

Nausea stirs as I slip my fingers under the fur, grimacing at the squish of flesh and the ooze of blood. Blood drips from a hole in the back of Dr. Martina's lab coat. The skin peels back, exposing the meat and gutted belly underneath. Cameron's insides spill out of her bloodied hands.

I turn my head and gag.

"Shit!" Griff grabs the rabbit and knife before I fling them into the fire in my distress.

I vomit beside the fire, the acrid taste of my stomach acid mixing with the tangy sweetness of the berries. I heave again, but my stomach's empty.

"Ugh, gross." I wipe my mouth with the back of my hand.

"I'll finish this up. Why don't ya head inside and put your leg up for a bit?"

I shake my head. "No, I'm staying. I want to watch."

"Ya sure?"

"Yes." I say between gritted teeth. Running won't help anything, it follows me no matter where I go.

Griff lifts an eyebrow, waiting to see if I'll change my mind, then walks me through how to finish preparing the rabbit for dinner. I'm glad my stomach is empty by the time he's done. I can feel him slowly relaxing his guard.

"Let me cook the rabbit for dinner." I say as we head inside.

"Ya cook?" Griff asks, a look of amusement crossing his face as I pin him with a glare, rolling my eyes.

"Yes, I can. Better than you, too." I shoulder past him and enter the hut before he does.

To my disappointment, Griff finishes breaking down the rabbit without my help. When he's done, he sets about starting a fire in the wood stove and settling down by its warmth. The temperature in the room is dropping rapidly with the setting of the sun.

Setting the bones in the pot, I fill it with a little water to simmer for a broth then wash the berries. I've always imagined standing in the kitchen cooking dinner for my daughter one day–much like this. I drop pieces of the rabbit onto the stove and use the spoon to flip them as they brown. When they're done, I fish the bones out of the broth and drop the rabbit inside to continue to simmer. On a plate, I add a splash of water and crush the berries into a thick, watery paste.

"Here," I offer him the finished dish. The browned meat swims in the fatty bone broth with a drizzle of the berry sauce on top.

"Wow, ya seriously can cook."

"Haha, hilarious." I scoop the remaining food into the cup and limp over to the bed.

"This is delicious," he says between trying not to burn his tongue with a mouth full of food. "I think it's the best meal I've ever had." He looks at me and winks.

My cheeks flush and I load up my spoon and blow on the food to cool it down.

There's a scrabbling noise at the window and Mischief squeezes himself through the opening.

"Hey buddy. Ya gonna be nice to us now that we have food?" Griff picks up a chunk of meat off his plate and offers it to the raccoon.

Mischief turns up his nose at Griff and pads across the floor, jumping up onto the bed beside me. His little paws grab for the cup in my hand.

"Wait, wait!" I laugh and fish out a piece of meat for him. He snatches it from my fingers and gobbles it up, then reaches for more. I end up splitting my dinner with him until he chitters and curls up on the bed to sleep.

"I wish my brother was here to draw ya..." Griff says, licking his spoon clean.

I go rigid. "He's a lot younger than you, right?"

Griff nods. "Yeah, by a few years."

"Does he look like you?"

Griff blinks, head cocking to the side. "Of course, we're related. Father used to complain he'd have trouble telling us apart if I wasn't taller. Why?"

This has to be it. The boy in the photo is Griff's brother. My pulse races and I can feel my palms getting sweaty as I hurry to come up with an excuse. Focus, tell him what he wants to hear. Floundering, I offer a truth, instead. "You're not half bad looking."

Griff throws back his head and roars with laughter. After a long spell of cracking himself up, he wipes the corners of his eyes. "You're not bad yourself. Ya know, I've been thinking, ya leg's doing much better. We can just go our separate ways."

Panic rises. He's going to leave me here. "But I don't know how to get back on my own."

"I have a solution." He sticks his hand out. There's a golden gleam from the flat circular object in his palm.

Griff flips it open and watches as the needle swings. He points to the letter N. "Father called it a compass, it can help ya find your way. This squiggle tells ya where north is no matter which direction ya face." He turns it and shows how the hand swings with the movement.

"Oh, you mean the letter N? That must be north. I've heard of these before, but I've never seen one."

"Yeah, I guess that makes sense. What did ya call them? Letters?"

"You know, from the alphabet...." I trail off at his blank stare. "Oh! You can't read."

"What's that?"

I frown and try to come up with the easiest way to explain. "Uh, so letters are marks that stand for sounds. When you put them together, they give you a word."

"Ahh," Griff nods his head. "Kinda like the trail markers."

I'm not sure what he means, but I guess that's the best I can do to explain it right now. Of course the Authority wouldn't teach survivors to read. They don't need to, right? The thought itches in the back of my mind.

"So when can I leave?"

"Day after tomorrow." The finality brokers no discussion.

"Really?" I say, forcing a smile and wondering why this news doesn't fill me with excitement.

# 19

## GRIFF

**I've learned to survive the wilderness,
now we need to survive each other.**

Achy discomfort wakes me up early, where it rubs against
the front of my pants. It's happening more and more often
now, especially when I think about Rei in her underwear or how
supple she felt pressed against my chest. I shoot to my feet and go
to the kitchen basin. I take a long drink and then splash a handful
over my face. The coldness of the water is enough to shock my
system into calming down.

Finding myself alone on the path, her hobbling progress
growing slower, I doubled back like I had the day before. Rei
heading in the opposite direction dredged up memories of
nameless Enforcers locking me in a cell without a backwards
glance. Pulling my bow was sheer instinct. Then she stopped,
turned, and the torment she stirred wasn't forced or drugged,
but my own indecent, lustful urges. A woman I could put a face
to, imagining the way she bites her lip, sweeps long hair over her
shoulder, and glares with big, brown, tormented doe eyes.

Not a piece of shit Enforcer.

I want to trust her, to splay my hands around her ass and grind our hips together, to suck and tease her soft, plump lips, exploring smooth skin never meant for the harsh wilderness. Fuck! Groaning, I clench my fingers on the edge of the sink, sucking in a deep breath, resisting the urge to touch myself and find release. But I won't, I can't. This hot, throbbing, shameful need doesn't belong to them anymore. I won't let it. And I hate struggling to separate what's mine from what they made me.

*It's because you're weak and stupid.* My father's voice is especially cheery in the morning when my hard on doesn't cooperate with the intelligent thoughts in my head.

"Shut. Up." I grind out between clenched teeth.

"Huh?" Rei sits up on the bed behind me, rubbing the crust out of the corners of her eyes. "Did you say something?"

"Yeah. I said get up." I push away from the counter and collect the things we'll need.

"Where are we going?"

"Hunting, where else? Come outside when you're ready." I need fresh air and space. The hut feels way too cramped right now.

Minutes later she appears, limping down the stairs and over to where I stack fresh logs in the fire pit. I swing my bow over my shoulder and start off into the woods, turning for my second favorite hunting ground. The loud crunch and crash of her steps follow. Even if she were to take off, it would be easy to find the trail and the stomping chorus of her boots. It's clear she's never had to be stealthy a day in her life. No, the Authority has always been about brute strength, manipulation, and control out in the open for everyone to see.

Under my shirt the necklace knocks against my chest and I resist the urge to pull it out and trace over the carving. Expecting to set a pace slower than yesterday, she surprises me when she has an easier time keeping up. Her limp is still there, but much less pronounced this morning. She'll be walking normally tomorrow and happy to part ways, I'm sure. If I didn't want to taste her as much as I wanted to thrash her I would have left with the necklace as soon as I found it tucked between her breasts.

Women will do anything to get what they want, my father's voice warns my thoughts. I shake my head and plow forward. Sure, she's rash and headstrong and determined, but she's also smart, and so fucking sexy.

"Is this the same way we went yesterday?" She asks and I know she's fishing for information again.

"Yes, and no." I offer as vague an answer as I can muster. She learns so fast. "There's a clearing not much further ahead with a natural blind. We'll stop there."

The surrounding trees thin as we approach the meadow. It's far enough from the spring that she won't be able to hear it either. She's breathing harder as the incline increases, her ankle bothering her more. Trust her not to complain, she uses pride like a knife. Prefering to hack and slash and defend herself with a tough exterior despite what it costs her. Putting up walls like they could trap and hold the darkness she's carrying despite the nightmares leaking from the seams.

The crash of her footsteps falters behind me. "Wow, look at all the flowers!" She plows straight for the grass so I grab an arm to stop her.

"Yeah, lots of bees, too."

"Is the big, muscular man afraid of poor little bees?" She says in an exaggerated, cutesy voice.

"Come on, this way." I'm not about to tell her I'm allergic to them.

She tosses her hair over her shoulder and laughs before following me to the blind. A pair of old, rotting tree logs form a natural shelter like a simple tent.

"No way. You want me to crawl in there? The bugs will be all over me."

"Aww, ya afraid of the little bitty bugs?" I mock her using the same tone she gave me earlier.

She rolls her eyes and gets down on her hands and knees, scooting beneath the fallen limbs. I hang my bag on a broken tree branch, take my bow and arrows, and follow her. Resist the urge to smack her ass. Now is not the time. I wedge myself in beside her until we both lay on our bellies with a perfect view of the meadow in a small gap in front of us. The large, dead trees offer great protection from the bright sun. The thick, dry grass I've lined the ground with makes for a comfortable resting spot.

"If ants or other creepy crawlies climb on me, I'm out of here," she says with a grumble and flicks away an invisible insect with a shudder.

"Noted," I say, positioning my bow in front of me so I can get a shot off if necessary. The deer tracks I spotted earlier led in this general direction. Based on the depth of the track, it was a mature one, hopefully a buck. He could feed us for a week and provide an extra store of smoked meat for my journey. Not to mention, his hide would make a nice blanket, since I'd lost most of my favorites to Rei's invasion of my bed.

Or we could share the bed again....

Ugh, not again. I'm glad I'm laying on my stomach when the erection returns. Shit! Knock it off. As if on cue, Rei shifts and her forearm brushes my shoulder. We jerk away from each other like we've touched hot coals in the fire.

"Sooo...what do we do now?" she asks, turning her face to hide the flush creeping up her neck.

"We wait."

"That's it? How boring."

"I'm sorry. Would ya prefer I did a song and dance to entertain ya?"

"That'd be more fun than this. What's better, your singing or dancing?" She laughs into my silence. "Neither, I take it."

"Ya see, the tops of the long grass over there?" I point my hand in the direction. "See how the seed heads are all bent?"

"No."

"More to the right. Your other right...."

"You mean by the red flower?"

I nod. "Something ran through there recently. Likely a deer, a big one."

"You notice all these tiny details." She yawns and plops her face in her hands, elbows propping her up.

"Missing those things can be the difference between life and death out here. Like a sinkhole."

She glares at me but says nothing more. The peaceful morning lulls, wind stirs the grass, insects buzz, and birds chirp overhead. Her eyelids droop and her head slips lower and lower as she nods off to sleep. Her loud snort snaps her back awake, and she blinks and peers around in surprise.

A sly fox indeed, I chuckle.

"Why are you laughing?" she snaps.

She's so fucking demanding.

"Fine, don't answer me. We can just sit here bored out of our minds for the rest of the day." She huffs and pulls at the dry grass, rolling it through her slender, deft fingers.

Having her beside me is different from the time I spend with Mischief. It reminds me of the quiet nights I spent with my father as I looked up at the stars or sharpened my knife. I didn't realize how much I'd missed this until Rei arrived, despite the unfavorable circumstances.

"What does it feel like to have the Heart Blight virus?" She lets the piece of grass slip from her grasp and pulls another one.

"If ya were gonna get sick, ya would be dead already," I say, glancing at her from the corner of my eye.

"According to Dr. Martina, I should be dying right now. But I feel fine." Her cheek twitches, but she doesn't respond, just continues to twist the grass.

"I don't know what it feels like," I say, confessing the truth. "Father told me when I was a baby I got so sick I had trouble keeping anything down. But all I remember is how he used to brush my hair off of my forehead when I didn't feel good. He loved to tell me stories about his life in the Free Territories."

Rei perks up and drops the grass. "Your father lived in the Free Territories?"

I nod. "He was born there. The Authority raided his town when he was young and took him to a containment facility."

"That can't be right. The Authority hasn't expanded since the first Cleansing. They built the Iron Divide to contain the virus in the Authority but nothing could stop the spread. But the Free Territories collapsed and no one lives there."

"Are ya calling my father a liar?"

"No, it's just—"

"Ya don't forget being dragged from your house in chains and locked away in a place where you're experimented on like a rat. Like I was." I pin her with a hard stare, daring her to disagree with me.

"What was he like?"

I raise an eyebrow. That's not the response I was expecting. "Who? My father?"

She nods.

A light breeze bends the flowers and grasses as it ripples across the meadow. It should be a simple question, but it requires separating the good memories from the painful ones. The silence draws out. I'm not sure I have it in me to answer. How do I put it into words she can understand?

"He did everything he could to keep me alive," I say, settling on a neutral response. "He wanted to make sure I survived long enough to get to the Free Territories. He was a hard man who demanded perfection. Ya know, I hear him in my head sometimes, like he's still alive, still with me." I blink hard, fighting the swell of emotions.

"Sounds a lot like my mom, in a way. I hate how detached she is. Like getting close to me is physically difficult for her. But I also couldn't imagine life without her. You don't get to choose your parents..." she trails off.

"At first, I struggled to survive without him. He made everything seem so easy. But once he was gone, I understood how much weight he'd been carrying for me. I nearly starved to death the first month. I was higher in the mountains then, and the game was scarce. A big storm rolled in. It was so cold, and the rain was coming down so fast. I woulda died from hypothermia if Mischief hadn't found an overhang deep enough to give us shelter. I have him to thank for that. We woulda died without the fire." That cold, miserable night still makes me shiver. "That's when I decided to come down the mountain where the game was more plentiful."

I check Rei's face, expecting a reaction, but she's staring across the meadow, her cheeks resting in both hands. The five point buck snaps at the bent edges of the tall grass, his ears flicking back and forth. The same one that nearly skewered me a few days ago. My bow string pulls taut as I take aim. There's a crack and snap of a branch in the distance. The buck's head shoots up, tail flicking, on high alert. Suddenly he bounds off into the woods and my arrow flies past, missing its mark.

"Shit!" The top of my head smacks against the rotting log above us. "Ouch." Rubbing at the tender spot showers me with bits of dead bark falling from my hair. "Well, he won't be back." I grumble. "Come on, let's go get my arrow and check the traps."

We scoot back out of the blind, shielding our eyes. It takes a few minutes for them to adjust. Rei brushes her shirt and pants, checking for bugs with meticulous care. Together, we edge around the meadow and I find my arrow in the trunk of a tree.

"Teach me how to shoot your bow. It can't be much different from a gun, right?"

My eyebrow arches. "That's why ya wanna try? So ya can shoot me with it?"

"The thought has crossed my mind—" she mutters and coughs, "—no, I'm just curious." The smile she plasters on her face is as fake as they come.

I pull the bow over my shoulder and hand it to her without an arrow. "I bet ya can't even full draw."

"Challenge accepted." Rei takes it from me and holds it out in front of her face, aiming at some invisible target in the distance. Finally, she takes the string and pulls. "Ugh, you're not kidding. How do you pull back so far on this thing?"

She freezes as I step behind her, pressing my chest to her back, taking her hands in mine. I uncurl her fingers on the bow shaft and reposition them correctly. Our fingers lace together on the string and draw until I feel the tension in her arm. My chin brushes the top of her shoulder. "Brute force doesn't solve every problem. Sometimes ya need a much lighter touch," I whisper in her ear,

"Lower your shoulder, keep it parallel to the target." My knee slips between her thighs, spreading them apart. "Widen your stance a bit and anchor your hand by your face. Ya want it nice and slow and steady."

She shivers and stray hairs tickle the side of my cheek.

"Take a breath, hold it."

As she does, I help her finish the draw, increasing the tension on the string and the press of her ass against my groin.

"Release," I whisper, brushing my lips over the sensitive skin on her neck. The arrow launches.

*Thwack!*

Rei whips around, eyes bright, chest heaving, flushing beneath my smug smile. This flustered, sweaty look suits her. Maybe this bothers her as much as it bothers me.

"Give me an arrow, I want to hit something," she purrs with a hint of something darker than amusement.

"No way," I straighten.

"You want me to trust you, right? How about you trust me, too? One arrow. Just one," she wipes her palm on her pants and holds out a hand.

I consider for a moment. She accepts me putting the arrow in her hand, my palm sliding down her forearm to rest at her elbow. If she tries anything I can easily disarm her.

She nocks the arrow and focuses on a spot in the distance. Her arm draws back and trembles from the strain of the bowstring without my help. The arrow flies wide, going further than I expected for a first attempt.

"Give me another one." She demands, her shoulder pressing my chest as she turns. "I wanna try again." By the fifth attempt, she hits the edge of a tree in the distance and laughs. "See! I told you!"

I take the bow from her and bump her forwards with my hip. "Now go collect the arrows and don't think I won't notice one missing."

She rolls her eyes before marching off to collect them.

"Hey, what's this?" Rei brushes her hand over the grooves scratched into the bark. "Is this from a deer or something? There was one just like it by the sinkhole."

Shrugging, I shake my head. There's no way I'm telling her the triangle carved around the circle is the symbol of the Sympathizers. That the symbol she found, like countless others in these woods, mark a safe path to the Free Territories. The same trail I'd been following since my father died. The same trail I'd follow when I left tomorrow.

"Deer or bear maybe—they both like to scratch trees." I offer one truth in place of another.

# 20

**Trust has risks you can't shake—what if survival is more than staying alive?**

Three days ago I could have used this moment to stab him with the arrows in my hand. But now I miss his warmth, the security of him pressed against my backside, solid and unyielding. And tomorrow I'm going back to the lake house, with a new scar on my ankle, and no symptoms of the virus...or him.

"Here." I hold out the arrows. "See, you can trust me." I smirk when he stuffs them back into his quiver.

"Your aim is shit."

Is that a hint of amusement or pride?

"You should see me with a gun," I counter and pick up a small, smooth rock on the ground.

The stone looks like something Mara would love to add to her collection of interesting bits and bobs. As kids, the two of us would sneak out at night, past curfew, and wander deserted side streets, looking for treasures. I'm not sure what we loved more, the challenge or the adventure. We'd stay out until a patrol squad shone their spotlight too close for comfort.

One time, an old cull emerged from the shadows. Trash piled around her cardboard tent and her clothing in tatters, black teeth disappearing into the darkness. Her clawed hands reached out to us, tearing at our hair as she croaked something unintelligible. We screamed, racing back to our beds, terrified. It haunted us for weeks.

If only Mara could freaking see me now, cozying up to something far more dangerous.

Griff looks up and examines the sky, his head cocking to one side and the corner of his mouth tipping into a frown. "There's another storm coming. We should gather firewood as we head back. Ya know, make ya useful somehow."

Arrogant jerk.

I scoff and half-heartedly chuck the rock at him, but he ducks out of the way before it hits. "I can be useful." To prove a point, I bend over and pick up a stick from the ground. "See?"

Wait, what? Is he appreciating my ass. "Hey! My eyes are up here."

A smirk spreads over his damn handsome face, and his eyes sparkle. "I know...I like the other view better."

Bless the mother everything he says now has me hot and bothered. I huff and stick my tongue at him, marching past and squatting to pick up another stick. Don't reward his smug charm.

"You're going the wrong way," he says as I retrace our path back to the hut. At least I thought it was. He jerks his head in the opposite direction, "it's this way."

"How can you tell?" I ask as I turn around, picking up sticks here and there as we go.

"Can ya see our tracks? We headed north."

"Like where the compass points?"

"Yeah. Moss grows on the north side of trees." He stops to point out the green tinge on a tree trunk. In the city you could follow street signs, or take a bus, or ask someone passing by.

"Guess this is like nature's form of GPS. Can you really not read?" I ask out loud, more to myself than as a question to him.

"Let's poke, prod, and experiment on ya and—oh, yeah, let's teach ya how to read." His voice turns dark and vicious.

Was that what he was talking about?

"You keep saying experiments. Do you mean research on the virus? Of course the scientists research the virus. How else will they find a cure?"

Griff's eyes flash with a dark fury and he turns and stalks off without another word. I hurry to follow him, my ankle throbbing from the armful of sticks I'm carrying.

"You can tell me, you know." I offer after hobbling a few minutes in silence.

Griff spins around so fast I take a step back in surprise. "Then ya can tell me why ya shut down the minute you're alone in the dark," he snarls.

I open my mouth to say something, but the anguish of my failures are lodged in my throat. Instead, I ball my hands into fists. "Fine!" I shout.

"Fine!" He shouts back.

We continue walking, my limp becoming more pronounced as we go. Both arms ache from the heavy load I'm carrying and the scratchy bark is making them itch something fierce.

Griff lets out a long sigh. "Do ya have to be so loud when ya walk?"

"Wha—" I stop when he stomps over to me, kicking at the leaves on the ground and smashing into the undergrowth. "Oh." I say and my mouth lingers in the shape. "Am I that bad?"

"Like a herd of deer running for their lives." He grumbles and comes to my side. "Look, put your toe down first, then your heel. See, like this."

I try to imitate his way of stepping, but the marching gait drilled into me the past few years keeps creeping back in. Years of repetitive training in the MMZ wouldn't be easy to overcome in a few minutes.

"That's a little better." He stops abruptly and snaps a finger over his lips.

I stop where I am, listening hard. There's nothing.

Making no sudden movements, Griff takes an arrow from his quiver and nocks his bow. He turns slowly and draws the string back at the same time. I hold my breath while he sucks in his own. There's a slight rustle of leaves on our left. He adjusts the angle of the bow and lets an arrow fly. A loud squawk plays in time with the frantic flapping of wings.

Griff hurries off toward the sound. He bends over something in the bushes and pulls out his knife. A moment later, he wipes the blood away on the ground before putting it back in his belt. He lifts his prize and grins like Mara showing off her mischievous handy work.

"Turkey!" He says, holding it by the neck and bringing it over. "A nice fat one, too. These suckers are hard to hunt. Tricky bastards."

"Great, can we go now?" His smile makes something lurch low in my belly. I brush past him, my arms aching and my ankle throbbing, leading the way down the narrow track we've been following for a while now.

"You're going the wrong way again," he points over his shoulder and his smile widens, lighting up that damn handsome face. "This way."

I roll my eyes and make a face when he turns away. I stomp down the path as loud as I can for good measure, but it doesn't seem to dampen his good mood. Griff's cheerful whistling breaks the silence. Glancing around, I expect Mischief to magically appear, but he doesn't.

There it is again. Another one of those strange symbols. I pause as I get close enough to run my fingers over the marks on the tree. The grooves make a perfect triangle around the small circle. Why do they seem so familiar?

"I don't think an animal made this," I say.

Griff comes beside me where I stand. A range of emotions flick across his face but his silence is telling.

"This feels man made. Was it carved by a knife, maybe? And I know this isn't the same one we saw back near the meadow or the sinkhole. I might have a terrible sense of direction, but I'm not dumb."

He shakes his head and leans against the side of a tree trunk, watching me watch him. Thinking. About what?

"What are you hiding?" I say, hoping my impulsive prodding won't shut down the conversation.

"They—uh—mark a trail."

"What's that mean?"

He pushes off the tree trunk and turns away, ending the conversation before it can even get started. "Come on, let's keep going, I'm hungry."

The sun is high in the sky by the time the hut appears through the woods. "Ugh, thank the Authority." I drop my armful of wood and try to massage the aches and pains out of my forearms. Rolling my shoulders helps a bit too.

"I'll get this gutted and cleaned."

My stomach churns as he prepares the turkey.

Griff snorts. "Ya don't have to watch. Here," he hands me the little tin box from his bag. "Make yourself useful again by starting the fire," he motions to the hut.

"No, I'm staying."

"Course ya are," he says with a shake of his head. Ten minutes later the bird is free of its feathers, innards, head, and feet.

I'm grateful for the excuse to head inside and sit down for a bit. I sink onto the stool by the wood stove as soon as I can. Ugh, my ankle hurts. Grit my teeth pulling my boot off. The swelling is completely gone, but the ache and throbbing still linger. Wiggling my toes relieves some of the tension in my tired muscles.

"You make this look so damn easy. This is impossible," I scrape the flint and piece of metal against each other yet again, but there's no spark. "Here, you do it." I hold them out to him, but he shakes his head.

"Nope, keep trying. Don't give up. Ya got it."

"So demanding," I say in a deep voice, mocking him. "It's not working. If you wanna eat, you should just do it."

"Let me show ya again." He leans over me, taking my hands. He hits with a quick, confident, downward motion. "Now ya try."

I hold the flint firmly in one hand and strike with the other. The spark flies and catches in my little bundle of kindling. "Oh! Yes! I did it–oh, mother bless it, don't go out." I blow on the ember in the kindling until a tendril of flame flickers and grows. Setting it into the wood stove, I watch as it gains steam and burns brighter, the larger logs catching.

Leaping up from the stool, I nearly knock my head into Griff's chin. With a big grin on my face, I throw my arms around him and hop up and down.

Laughter bursts from my lips and my chin tips up to meet his gaze. My breath hitches at the longing in his bright eyes. They're dancing with the embers of the fire behind us. My underwear grow damp between my thighs.

Shit.

# 21

# GRIFF

## Doubt smothers feelings ignited by desire.

She smells earthy, like the woods and the useless pine branches she collected. They make shit firewood and won't help against the growing chill. Her body pressing against mine staves off the chill from the growing darkness in the cabin.

Our chests connect, rubbing, teasing, challenging my self control. As her head tips back, she exposes her flushed neck and the delicate line of her collarbone. My left hand slides across her lower back and the fingers of my right tangle in her dark, curly hair. Rei's lips part and I suck in a breath, remembering how warm and soft they felt yesterday.

I slide my palm across her neck, cupping the side of her chin and cheek. I can't tear my eyes away from her. She's full of so much life...so beautiful, so irresistible. Her breathing picks up with mine, and she nuzzles her head in my grasp.

My pants grow tighter, constricting my erection. Rei grips my shirt and her fingernails scrape my skin beneath. She grinds her hips into my crotch. I have an overpowering urge to rip her clothes off with my teeth. I want to consume her, to make her scream my name, to feel her hot skin riding me.

She grins and presses her advantage as I growl. The trail of her fingertips leave a burning path of destruction across my quivering body. Rei swallows hard. Her eyebrow arches in question as she touches my lower lip. I lean forward, stopping short of our mouths meeting, prolonging the anticipation of our connection. My self control balances on the edge, waiting for her permission.

I want to bury myself inside her until she's clinging to me for dear life and it's hard to think straight. And I think she wants the same.

"Are you going to kiss me?" she asks and I feel the slightest brush of her mouth forming the words.

"No," I say, obliging her, slipping my tongue inside.

She screams as Mischief leaps from the windowsill and tangles in her hair.

"Ahh! Let go! Ouch!" She flails and tries to pull him free. His little feet dig into her scalp and shoulder, frantically trying to get free.

I try to grab him. "Shit! Mischief! Rei, stop moving. He's caught in your hair."

"Ow! No, don't pull, that's making it worse. Get his foot untangled first."

"I'm trying. Ya keep turning away from me when I've almost got it. Stand still." I say. She winces and stops moving.

Together we pry Mischief out one limb at a time. When he's free, he bites my hand and scrapes my chest while he thrashes his back legs.

"Hey!" I say. As I drop him to the ground, his claws catch the leather strap of my necklace. It snaps and skitters across the floor. "Fuck, what's up with ya? Chill out, will ya."

Mischief gives me a look that comes as close to a human glower as I've ever seen. Then he leaps back up to the windowsill and disappears out into the night.

I cough and look at Rei with a sheepish smile. The moment between us, whatever that was, is long gone. She rubs at a sore spot on her scalp, then picks up my necklace from the floor. My stomach drops and I snatch it out of her hand.

"You said our father gave you this?" she asks, unperturbed by my yanking it away from her.

"He loved to carve." I re-tie the leather strip around my neck and tuck it back under my shirt.

"What kind of animal is that? I've never seen anything like it before."

"It's called a griffin. They're guardians, protectors of the weak and vulnerable. In mythology, it stands for justice against the forces of evil."

"What's mythology? I've never heard that word before."

"A collection of stories, myths, and legends about the ancient deities. The ones before the Cleansing." I return to the sink and break down the turkey for dinner.

"Oh. You mean like the Old Gods. At school my classmates would talk about them when the overseers weren't around. If they caught you talking or praying to them, they'd whack you with their discipline sticks like their lives depended on it."

"Just for talking about an Old God?"

She nods and then shrugs. "We're only allowed to recite approved passages. Things like Authority keep me safe."

I frown. "Do they?"

"Do they what?" she asks.

"Keep ya safe?"

Rei doesn't answer. The smell of cooking turkey and the popping wood in the fire fills the hut.

"I've never thought about it before," she says, her brows furrowing. "They organized the Cleansing. All those dead bodies everywhere...if they hadn't rounded them up and burned them, the virus and other diseases would've continued to spread. Plus, they maintain order in the city. And of course there's the research to find a cure for the virus. That's the most important part."

I put a turkey leg on a plate and hand it to her. She blows on it to cool it down before trying to tear off a piece of the meat. When it burns her fingers she sticks them in her mouth and sucks. Fuck!

"But you're not sick. And even now, ya just gonna believe their lies?" I ask, goading her into the argument we've had multiple times now. That'll get my blood rushing to thinking parts of my body.

"Sometimes you have to do things for the greater good."

"Do you seriously believe that? What if those things hurt people who can't defend themselves?"

"You had no trouble putting me on my back," she says and her eyes rove over me in a way that makes my blood boil.

"Not all wounds leave physical scars," I growl, stalking closer to where she's sitting on the stool. "I know ya understand that. We have more in common than ya like to admit. Do ya know your nightmares wake me up most nights? Whose Alyssa? If the Authority is so safe, why couldn't ya save Cameron?"

She bolts upright and her plate clatters to the ground.

"None of your business!" she yells, her chest heaving and her shaking fists curling at her sides.

Her shoulder smashes into mine as she forces her way past me, limp almost gone. The door bangs behind her, leaving me alone like when we part ways tomorrow. Did I seriously stay because I couldn't bear to leave her hurt and alone in these woods, because she had my necklace?

For years Father would berate me, pushing me harder with his stern disapproval. Ian's the one who deserved to escape, to follow in Father's footsteps and bring the necklace to the Free Territories. He wasn't the kinda person who talked back, pushed the boundaries, or got outta line.

Why me?

The longer I stay, the greater the risk of patrols and the more dangerous this situation becomes.

And yet, the less I care.

# 22

## REI

**Belief is a fragile flame consuming us,
undone by a single breeze.**

The fact that he knows about the nightmares haunting me is both comforting and terrifying. What he said is carving out a pit in my stomach. Here I am, warring with these unfamiliar feelings building inside of me. That first night it would've been so easy to slink out of bed while he was asleep on the floor, straddle him, grab his knife, and slit his throat.

It's a move I've practiced as a trainee. Against other women, it's easy to use your body weight, wrapping your leg around a torso, or even pin an arm to the ground. But Griff isn't a woman, that's for sure. The few sparring matches we'd had, it was immediately clear I was at a major disadvantage. I shudder, but I don't know if it's from the thought of killing him or wrapping myself around him.

Our bodies touching was so freaking intense. I run my hand down my stomach, sliding it into my pants and under the band of my underwear. My fingers slide over slick flesh and my groan surprises me. Oh, crap. This is what he does to me, reassembling the pieces I thought were shot to hell.

My mother took multiple lovers over the years, but they petered away over time. Trysts with girlfriends and relationships were common in entry school, but that was never something Mara or I were interested in. No, the two of us would much rather wiggle our way around the rules, skating right up to the line, even placing a foot on it, before darting back to the safety of conformity and compliance.

Unlike many girls our age, our friendship was just a friendship, nothing more. What we wanted, Mara and I, were children. That was something only winning the lottery could give us. The Authority controlled the GRH and inside there, under heavy guard, were the GPUs, or Genetic Preservation Units. They housed thousands of vials of sperm–the last hope for humanity.

I'm so far off mission. Uncharted territory of the most uncomfortable kind. Awkward to say the least, let alone illegal by the rules of the Authority.

Had I really asked the enemy to kiss me?

Did suggesting it make me a traitor?

I clamp my hands over my face and breathe deeply, trying not to hyperventilate. I'm so horrified and turned on at the same time. It's been days and I'm still here, still alive, tether broken...not sick, not dying. I frown.

My mother and Mara must be frantic with worry. Had they sent someone looking for me? I was in such an awful place at the time; I hope they didn't think I'd hurt myself. Would I have had it in me to hurt myself if things hadn't gone to shit? No. I just needed a change of scenery. Of course I got much more than I'd bargained for.

I roll my injured leg and smirk when the pain is nothing more than a tightness in my muscles. I just need to figure out which direction it is to get to the lake. Griff, for all that he is charming and bull headed, lets slip more and more when I bat my eyes and run my hands over him. The memory of my palm sliding up his chest sends a trill through my lower stomach. I tell myself I'm just trying to gain his trust, but it feels like more than that. More intimate.

Griff pulls open the door. We stare at each other, saying so much without words. Then he moves aside to let me back in and I notice the bow and quiver over his shoulder.

"Where are you going?" I ask.

"To get firewood." he grumbles, eyes refusing to meet mine.

"I'll come with you."

"No, stay here."

"What? Why?"

"It'll be faster without ya. I'll be back before dark." He stomps off, shoulders hunched, like he's been given an honorable discharge.

It's clear something about this tenuous relationship has shifted, but I'm not sure if that's a good thing. Not yet, anyway. I jeer and make faces and rude gestures at the spot he vacated. Flopping down on the bed, I stare at the rafters high overhead. This is it, our last night, if I'm to believe he'll keep his word. I rub a hand over my forehead and my fingers come away grimy.

"Ew, gross." I sit up and examine my dingy shirt. There's brown and green stains, courtesy of the sinkhole, and the wood I carried yesterday. A lingering ache in my arms reminds me of how heavy they were. My pants aren't much better off...I could really use a bath.

I eye the bucket I filled with water two days ago. Griff is off doing mother knows what. That would give me enough time to heat some water and clean myself off. I grab the last two logs and feed them into the wood stove, then fill a pot and set it on the stove to boil. While that's warming up, I sit on the stool and unwrap my leg. The long, jagged cut has a thick scab. For once it doesn't hurt as I poke at it. It's going to leave a gnarly scar. I drop my dirty bandages into the water while it heats to a boil. While it's not the best sponge, it's the only thing I have to scrub myself clean with besides my clothing.

When the water is hot, I move it off the stove and let it cool a bit in the sink. I strip naked and examine myself from head to toe. Days in the wilderness with limited food and lying in a bed has left my toned body leaner than normal. When I slide my hand over my stomach, I trace the edge of my rib cage and the point of my hip bone. At least they're not visible. I'm too skinny.

I test the water with my pinky finger before I pull the bandages out of the hot water and scrub myself from head to toe. All those times I complained about lukewarm spray at the barracks seems like a luxury compared to these conditions. What I would give for a real shower right about now. My skin feels raw from rubbing so hard, but knowing I'm clean is worth the momentary discomfort.

The front door of the hut bangs open, and I freeze. Griff takes a single step inside. His mouth drops open and his eyes might pop out of his head. I swear and race for the bed, burying myself under the covers.

"What are you doing? Get out!" I shriek.

"Don't get the bed wet. You're gonna regret it later tonight." The corner of his mouth quirks, but he makes no move to give me privacy.

"I said get out! Can't you see I'm trying to clean up?"

"Oh, I can see alright. I'll be outside. Call me when you're decent." He lingers a moment longer before turning and closing the door behind him.

I swear a blue streak, but refuse to get off the bed until I'm sure he's left. His boots creak down the stairs as he moves away. I was so engrossed before I missed them earlier. I glare at the door and wait another 10 minutes for good measure. When he doesn't return, I race back to my clothes and put them on, dirt or no. At least my skin is clean. I frown and bite my lip. He wasn't supposed to get back so soon. I really wanted to wash my clothes too, but there's no way I'm risking it now.

Laying the furs I got wet out to dry, I sit on the stool and comb my fingers through my wet, tangled hair. When I'm done and my hair is dry enough not to catch a chill outside, I push open the front door. I poke my head out, but I don't see him by the fire pit. Then something shiny catches my attention. I walk down the stairs and head over. His hunting knife is stuck in the wood of the stool, gleaming in the sunlight filtering through the trees.

My hand curls around the hilt, and I rock it back and forth until it pulls free. I've held it once before, but I never took the time to appreciate the weight and balance of the blade before. He's honed the edge to a razor point, sharper than the last time I held it, for sure. I swing at the air, imagining I'm sparring in the barracks, preparing for the enemy. The Sympathizer who grabbed Alyssa around the neck swims into view. Her glittering, hate-filled eyes swivel to me and the vision melts away into the strong, handsome jawline and amused grin of Griff's face.

I drop the knife and place my hands on my knees, my stomach roiling. No, it wasn't him. It's all in my imagination. Seeing them in my mind's eye brings out such a visceral reaction. The Sympathizers, like Griff, are the enemy. I've trained for years with my blood, sweat, and tears to protect everything the Authority stands for.

I need to go back, I'm not a traitor. I have to turn him in. If I didn't, and the Authority found out, I'd become another linebreaker, hanging from the Suppression Line, going against everything I've ever been taught.

But really, what harm was he doing out here? He avoided people at all costs. He stuck to the woods and lived off the land. It's not like he was terrorizing nearby towns or causing a wake of death and infection, right? I wasn't sick, and I'd been in close quarters. Would it hurt to just let him go on doing what he'd been doing until he reaches the Free Territories?

I let out a shaky sigh. Despite all the times I've hit, punched, and kicked him he's helped me over and over again. I stand and sniff, wiping a hand across my nose. My bare feet are growing icy the longer I stand outside in the chilly temperature. Inside, I use his knife to pry open cans in his backpack and begin to cook dinner. Such a mundane, familiar thing makes me think of Mother. She hated to cook, but she always made me something to eat when I was home, no matter how tired she was from work. For the first time, I miss the way she would pry me for information about training, or pretend to care. I even miss the detached way she'd fuss when I'd had enough of her pestering questions.

She probably thought I was dead. I wipe a tear from the corner of my eye.

Cooking like this is oddly comforting, but I'm not sure why.

# 23

# GRIFF

**The wild brings us closer to
ourselves—reminding us we're human.**

I wasn't expecting to walk in on her naked. She'd protested so much I thought she'd be happy when I finished a sweep of the perimeter, found some firewood, and came back early. But there she was, the dark hair tangled around her head matching the mass of dark curls between her legs. I wanted to wrap one of my hands around those pert breasts and suck her nipple into my mouth.

Desire ripples through me, and I try to shake some sense into myself. Her screaming at me to get out was the only reason I found the self-control to shut the door again. I reach for my canteens only to find them empty.

Fuck.

I need something to drink. I gotta cool down.

On instinct I angle toward the spring. Instead of clearing my head the walk sends me spiraling into thoughts of Rei, her foxlike smile, the bite of her sharp intelligence, and those sharp claws of impulsive behavior. The feel of her lips against mine lingers along with the press of her breasts as her arms hug me in her excitement. How fast she picks up on things. The terrified look in her big, brown eyes when she's trembling in the dark. How I want to wrap myself around her and hold her close, whispering that I won't let anything hurt her.

The spring doesn't appear fast enough. I shove my largest canteen under the cold water and let it fill. My heart is racing and my palms are sweaty. She'll turn me in the first chance she gets and still I want to devour her like a rabid animal. I empty the canteen over my head. It drenches my shirt, too. I refill it and repeat the process twice more.

It's not enough.

Tearing my shirt over my head I douse it in the spring. When it's soaking wet I use it to scrub myself clean. Gritting my teeth against the rough material and the bite of the air. Each time slowly returns me to my senses. The shock to my system helps, pulling me back into the reality of my situation. I lift my hand to wipe my wet hair outta my face and sniff the water off my nose. I'm shivering by the time I wring out my clothes as much as I can, wrestling them on like I tangle with my dirty thoughts caught in her snare.

A light breeze blows through the trees and I shiver. Fall is drawing to a close and winter is right around the corner. So fucking cold. The temperature continues to drop enough that all thoughts of Rei are finally replaced by my chattering teeth and icy fingers. I refill my canteens once more and head back to the hut at a brisk pace. The sun is going down and I don't want to be caught out here after dark.

At the entrance to the hut I pause, then knock my knuckles against the wood three times.

"I'm decent," she calls.

I open the door to the savory scent of something cooking on the wood stove.

"Ya made dinner? But how did–" I stop short, seeing my knife on the counter. I must have left it by the fire pit earlier. How could I have been so careless?

Rei picks up the knife and saunters over. I tense, shifting my weight to the balls of my feet, expecting her to lunge. Instead she flips it over and holds it out to me hilt first.

"You forgot this," she says, plopping it into my hand and turning back to the pot on the stove. She puts a spoon inside, stirring the contents. "Why are you all wet? Did it it rain?" She peeks out the little window.

I slip the knife into my belt and take a seat on the stool by the fire. My hands are frozen. So cold. Rubbing them together a few times for good measure helps the feeling return. "It's not raining, I just needed to cool down."

She turns and raises an eyebrow at me, smirks, then goes back to stirring the pot. "This is done so I hope you're hungry."

I put my fingers to my lips and whistle for Mischief. Rei divides portions of the pot between the plate and a metal cup. She brings the cup and spoon over to me. Our fingers graze as I take it from her. My eyes flick to her parted lips and jerk back to the cup again. Shoveling a scoop of the hot food into my mouth covers my discomfort. These small gestures are adding up. Submitting to my need for control, putting her trust in me, asking to stay by my side, making dinner. It's almost like she cares for me, Griff, rather than a means to an end for children.

But women are supposed to be evil.

Rei takes her plate over to the bed. We eat in an uncomfortable silence, both of us too caught up in our own thoughts to offer conversation.

"It's too quiet. Say something, will you," Rei says, standing and bringing her plate to the sink. "Are you done? Here, I'll take that, too. Geesh, it's cold out tonight. Are you sure Mischief is okay? He's usually here by now."

I shrug, "Mischief can take care of himself. He'll show up when he's hungry." I cough. "Thanks."

"Huh?"

"I said thanks."

"Thanks for what?"

"For dinner," I say, standing up. "That's twice now. It's been a long time since someone's cooked for me."

"Your dad cooked a lot?" she asks, rinsing off the dishes.

"Yeah but he was a terrible cook. He burned most everything. He used to say one day he hoped my brother and I could sit down to dinner together like his family used to when he was a kid."

"Where's your brother?" she asks, resting a hand on her hip and cocking her head to the side.

"He's still in Eastkeep," I say and my voice comes out unexpectedly husky with emotion. I clear my throat and brush a strand of my damp hair out of my eyes. It's getting late but at least my clothes are dry.

"Oh..." Rei wrings her hands together. "You know I was thinking—" she cuts off as Mischief scrabbles through the window. There's something dark and gray in his mouth. "What's that?"

Mischief leaps down from the windowsill and places his prize on the ground. The mouse squeaks and tears off across the floor. Rei shrieks as it makes a beeline for her bare feet. She leaps on the edge of the counter then skitters for the bed, climbing on top of it.

"Mischief, bad boy!" I say and swear. I stomp down on the ground near the mouse, trying to kill it, but it rebounds off the bottom of the kitchen counter and shoots toward the bed. Mischief scampers after it, his little black paws slapping left and right as the mouse rapidly changes directions and zig-zags away from him. His nails make clicking and scratching noises on the wood floors as he leaps after it with impressive agility.

Rei screams again as the mouse leaps into the mountain of covers at her feet. She launches herself into the air and smashes against me, trying to put as much distance as possible between her and the mouse. Her hands grip my forearms so tight her nails break the skin.

Mischief follows the mouse onto the bed, burrowing under the covers, his body creating lumpy mountains and valleys in the terrain of animal skins. There's another high-pitched squeak from the bed and the furry mouse pops out from the skins and plops back onto the floor. Rei's nails dig in further as she screams and cusses and climbs onto the stool, her hands on my shoulders to keep her balance as it wobbles. Mischief's black and gray head emerges from the tunnel of covers and bolts after it.

The mouse scurries to the corner and runs the perimeter of the room, Mischief hot on its heels. Finding no exit, it angles across the room and slams head first into my boot. The impact stuns it momentarily. It pauses in confusion and that's all the handicap Mischief needs. He grabs the little mouse and stuffs the whole thing into his mouth.

*Crunch.*

The little pink tail hangs out of the corner until he swallows.

"That's disgusting." Rei curls her upper lip and the color drains from her face.

"Mischief, shoo!" I push him toward the window with my boot. He turns quickly, snapping at my foot, before leaping back up to the windowsill and slipping back outside.

I chuckle. "Guess he found his own dinner."

Rei's face breaks into a grin and throws her head back. Her laughter consumes my loneliness.

# 24

**REI**

**Loyalty, duty, mission—they take until surrender is all that's left, but this time, the choice is mine.**

I haven't laughed this hard in years. It's the kind of mad hysteria that sends shockwaves through the stool below me. Griff's hands on my waist tighten, supporting me as I wobble. It's strange being taller than him, even if it's momentary. His eyes are the bright moss on trees in the forest, drawing me in, spinning me toward true north. My hands splay on his forearms and I trace the curve of his muscle with a finger. My breath catches in my throat. I should turn him into the Authority, not admire the broad line of his shoulders or the fine stubble on the strong curve of his chin. No, stop it, I shake my head.

*Crack!* The stool breaks.

Griff sweeps me into his arms as I tumble forward, my body pressing his. The hard lump of his father's necklace rests against the swell of my breasts. His touch devours me with hunger, a starving dog chasing a girl down the street for a treat in her hand. But I'm the treat. Griff's lips part and his tongue runs over them in a way that sends suggestive thoughts sliding down my body.

I want to feel those lips on mine again. My head presses against his forehead as I lean forward, inviting him—no, teasing him—to kiss me.

His mouth consumes mine with wild abandon. Our lips open and part, sucking, licking, and caressing until we're breathless. My body is going weak with longing for him, all of him. I slide my hands under his shirt and his muscles spasm beneath my palms.

"Fuck, you're so beautiful," he murmurs and backs us against the wall. My shoulder blades press into the cold, rough wood as he grinds himself between my legs. He reaches over and shuts the window. "Just in case he comes back."

I laugh against his lips. He breaks off the kiss and lowers his head to my neck, my throat. His long, damp hair tickles my ear and my cheek. His tongue traces a path from my collarbone to my chin, tasting the salt of my skin. My hand slides up his chest and brushes his nipple. It goes taut between my fingers and he lets out a low moan.

"My turn," he says, knocking my arm away. Griff runs his hand under my shirt and across the tender skin of my belly.

I suck in a sharp breath as his fingertips send shivers down my spine and desire pools between my legs.

Griff pulls back, "Is this okay?"

I grab his hand on my stomach and slide it between my breasts. "Please," I beg, "don't stop."

He grins and uses his other hand to pull my shirt up and over my head. It tangles on my arms and he holds me there, pinned to the wall, his eyes drinking in my bare flesh. His hand frees one breast from my bra. His rough fingers brush over my nipple until it's peaked and aching.

I arch my back away from the wall, wanting to feel his hands everywhere and nowhere all at the same time. The throbbing between my legs presses into the bulge of his crotch. I grind myself against him, inviting him to keep going. More, I need so much more. The fire building inside me is raging and only he can put it out.

Griff leans down and covers my erect nipple with his mouth. His tongue flicks and sucks and his teeth graze it gently. I'm surprised to hear a moan escape my lips. It's hoarse and breathless. Wanting. I want to touch him, to taste his skin. I struggle where he holds my arms above my head.

"Please..." I whisper.

Griff's chuckle sends vibrations across my breast bone. He lifts his head and kisses me again, his tongue flicking inside my mouth. When he releases me, he tears my shirt off and drops it to the ground. My hands are finally free again. I tug at his shirt, trying to remove it, but I can't get it off with the way his arms wrap around me.

He spins me away from the wall and kisses me again. We take several steps back and he lavishes me with his teeth, lips, and tongue. My thighs hit the edge of the bed and I sit down abruptly. It puts me on eye level with the bulge in his pants. My eyes widen as Griff looks down at me and pulls his shirt over his head. Of course I've seen him shirtless before, but this close I can make out each straining muscle with detail and the downy trail of hair leading below his belt line.

He leans forward and places his hands on either side of me on the bed. His mouth hovers inches from mine. "Do ya want me to stop?" He asks. His voice itself is a gentle caress.

"I uh—I don't know how this works...." My cheeks flush and I lower my gaze to hide my shame. Of course we're taught the basics of insemination in school, but doing something like this, with a man, in the flesh? There were no classes for this kind of thing. It went against everything I'd trained for. And it felt so damn good.

He chuckles and puts his fingers under my chin, lifting it back up to meet his gaze. "Ya think I've done this before, either?"

I shake my head no and his hand slides from my chin to tangle in my hair. He pulls me forward and kisses me again. "I guess not," I say when he releases me, my voice heady and breathless. I want this, I know I do.

My hand trembles as I reach forward and undo the button on his pants. It takes a few tugs to pull the zipper down because the material is so taut against him. My fingers curl around the edge of his belt line and trail over the skin of his butt and thigh as I drag them down, along with his shorts.

I gasp and clamp a hand over my mouth when his clothing hits the floor. My eyes bulge out of my head. He stands inches away from me, naked, fully erect. Before my panic can fully set in, Griff leans forwards and unhooks my bra strap. The full exposure of both breasts makes me self-conscious. I cross my arms over my chest, but he doesn't seem to notice.

"Now it's my turn." He trails his fingers down the sides of my waist and grabs the edge of my pants. They slide off of me until I'm only in my underwear. "You're amazing," he says as his eyes drink me in. Large, rough hands slide up my thighs as he shifts me back onto the bed and joins me there. I shiver as one hand moves up the inside of my thigh, brushing the material of my underwear at the wet apex between my legs.

He hooks a finger into the waistband and slides them off over my hips until they reach my knees. My breathing gets faster and the feeling building inside me grows and stretches until I think I might burst. I grab his hand on my hip and pull it between my legs. His fingers cup my soft hair and I rub myself into the heel of his hand. A moan bursts from my lips and my eyes go wide as his finger slips inside. I arch my body up and into the foreign sensation as he strokes and explores.

The bed creaks as he crawls forward and I lie back. He seems so big and imposing as he hovers above me, his eyes lingering on my neck, my breasts, my belly button. He trails a line of kisses from my neck, down my chest, across my breasts and then below to my belly. His teeth graze over my sweaty skin and I shudder as another finger slips inside me. Griff presses his knee between my legs and uses his other hand to spread them apart.

"I've only seen this done by animals in the forest," he says, drawing his tongue from my belly up to my breast. He takes my nipple in his mouth again, sucking until it's red and sensitive.

"Shut up and kiss me," I say, gasping as the movement of his fingers increases, sliding in and out of me faster, more urgently. I grab his face and feel the bristle of the whiskers on his chin. I press my mouth to his and slip my tongue inside, flicking it in and out with the same rhythm he's setting with his fingers.

Griff groans and pulls away. He presses his forehead to mine. "So demanding...." His breath tickles the sweaty hair curled behind my ear. With one hand, he holds my knee as his fingers withdraw. His erection brushes against my wet downy hair, hard and soft at the same time. His lips cover mine as he slams himself into me, burying deep inside.

I cry out and rake his shoulders with my nails as pain flares. Griff's bruising grip on my leg increases as he thrusts again and again, his pace increasing and frantic. It hurts so bad tears stream down my face and I press my palms against his chest, trying to get him off of me, to make it stop. But Griff's eyes are looking past me, not at me, as he moves faster and faster, thrusting against me, the flesh of our bodies merging together.

"Wait-" I say and break off as the pain lessens, replaced by something new, something amazing and warm. It curls my toes and has me arching up against him, wanting, needy. It feels so good, so right. The ache builds and builds, until the pressure, the fullness, detonates between my legs and radiates through my body. I spasm and scream, not in pain, but in pleasure. My fingers dig into his arms as my hips buck and my body trembles. The feeling explodes from the inside outwards. It's like nothing I've ever felt before, like I've unlocked a new and forbidden part of myself. Griff slams into me again, once, twice, three times and cries out, his head thrown back and his eyes closed. Sweat from his hair and face dribbles onto my stomach and slides down his chest. As he pulls away, I feel a damp liquid sliding down my thighs.

I clamp my hands over my mouth and heat flushes my cheeks, mortified. What have I done? Griff laughs and collapses beside me on the bed. My body feels so relaxed now, uncomfortable, but in a good way.

"I'm sorry if I hurt ya," he says, turning his face to murmur against my bare shoulder. "I lost it." He slides his finger across my sweaty skin, tracing a pattern of apology only he understands.

I spy the trail of deep scratches on his upper arms. There's blood under my fingernails. "Me too," I say, showing him my bloody fingertips.

He chuckles. "I didn't even notice." He twists so he can see the stripes he's earned. "Ahh, yeah, they sting."

I prop myself up on an elbow and run my finger over his chest, teasing his nipple until it peaks beneath my attention. Griff grabs my hand and bites my fingers playfully. Our eyes meet and I see the hunger returning. Anticipation quivers through my swollen flesh.

I chose this.

I want this.

Him.

"Can we do it again?" I ask.

The smile on his face lights up the room. He rolls on top of me and buries his face between my breasts.

It's all the answer I need.

# 25

**REI**

## After finding yourself in the enemy's reflection, your heart becomes a battlefield.

There's something solid pressed against me and it's making me hot and sweaty. Soft snores follow a deep rumble against my back. The thing pinning me down is an arm, Griff's arm. It holds me tight against his naked body, overloading me in the sweet undertones of earthy pine.

Is lying in his arms what's neutralizing the dark assault of my nightmares? I've slept peacefully for the past two days for the first time since the bombing.

My butt nestles like a bullet in the chamber of his groin, and as I roll over, he stirs. From this close, I can examine Griff in minute detail. His eyelashes are thick, wispy, and flutter against my fingertips. The jagged scar on his collarbone has ridges similar to the Brass Mountains. It's bumpier than his calloused hands.

How many times did we go at it until we fell asleep? Everything is sore and sensitive. The ache between my legs is a small price to pay for the pleasure I got in return.

Griff blinks and the sated look in his eyes makes my mouth quirk into a smile. He reminds me of the feral tom cat strutting around our neighborhood looking proud of itself.

"Hi," he says and lifts his arm in a languid stretch. There are new scratches across his shoulders, but at least they're scabbing over. I blush, feeling ashamed of marking him that way. "How are ya feeling?" He presses his forehead to mine and tucks a strand of hair behind my ear.

"Tired. Sore. Good."

He arches an eyebrow and his cock slides against my leg. I look down my nose at him and shake my head, bubbling with laughter.

"You're insatiable," I say, pulling away from him.

Griff pins my wrists to the bed and rolls on top of me, his knee forcing my thighs apart. "Oh yeah? How many times did ya beg me to do it again, huh?" He presses a trail of kisses from my collarbone to my breasts. I cry out when he sucks my swollen nipple into his mouth. My fingers rake through his hair, trying to pry off his attentive lips and tongue.

"Ahh, wait. That hurts," I say, pushing his shoulders away. He licks my nipple one more time for good measure.

"You're so sensitive here," he says and lightly draws a circle around it. "When I'm inside ya and I suck hard, ya clamp around me like a noose in a trap." He chuckles, his eyes sparkling.

I swat at his back, trying to sit up, but he dips his head and kisses his way across my stomach and then lower, hair tickling my ribcage. I moan as his finger slips between my legs and rubs in just the right freaking spot.

Mother bless it, right there.

"Ya really like this too," he murmurs, letting his fingers glide back and forth in a rhythmic motion.

"Don't stop," I groan, falling back on the bed, lifting my hips to give him better access. "Yes, that, so good." I whimper and shove his head down until his breath warms my slick thighs. His tongue traces a path upward as his fingers slip in deeper.

"Ah!" I cry as he licks between my damp curls, his warm, wet tongue teasing me in a way his fingers cannot. "Oh, damn," I gasp, gritting my teeth as the pressure builds.

Now the anticipation of what that feeling means has me panting and moaning and grinding against him. His fingers pick up the pace and so does his tongue. I claw at the furs beneath me as I scream, allowing the shuddering release to crash over me in all-consuming waves.

Pleasure I claim from him as my own.

Turns out, I was never broken to begin with.

"Yeah," Griff says, "ya like that?" His cock replaces his fingers. It slides inside me without resistance and only the slightest bit of discomfort. He rocks against me, grabbing my hips, holding them, spreading me open. Each stroke stretches and fills me in a delightful, satisfying way.

"I like when ya moan," he says, bending close and panting in my ear. He kisses my neck, my throat, my collarbone. A calloused hand splays over my ribs, holding me still while I writhe beneath him.

"Faster," I say, lifting my hips to match his thrusting rhythm. "Please," I beg, awaiting the recoil of the tense, throbbing ache that builds and stretches and grows. "Harder!" I growl, grabbing his ass with my hands, trying to pull him further inside of me. "I need more," I demand, and my voice doesn't sound like my own.

"So demanding...." Griff laughs and thrusts faster, his skin slapping against mine.

He grabs my knee and adjusts the angle, and I shudder as he sinks deeper. There's a flash of pain each time he slams so far into me followed by an intense cramping sensation, then I scream and explode, muscles seizing–blinding, disorienting, chaotic. My eyes roll back into my head and my limbs go slack as I shudder and shake.

Griff roars and collapses on top of me.

"Rei? Rei!"

A sharp slap stings my cheek, dragging me from the smoking aftermath. What happened? I gasp, sucking in a breath.

"Shit, ya almost passed out. Are ya okay?"

I cough and nod, unable to speak. Every muscle in my body aches like I've run the perimeter track in the MMZ for the past three days straight. I'm so tired. Griff smoothes my sweaty hair from my face and rolls onto his back beside me. My chest heaves as I try to steady my thundering heart.

"I didn't know it would be like this..." Griff says, rubbing a hand across his furrowed brow.

"Like what?" I ask when I can finally speak.

"Incredible." He puts his hands behind his neck and stares up at the ceiling.

I roll onto my side and prop my head up on my palm. There's so much tension between his dark eyebrows. "Tell me something about yourself."

"We use our father's name to identify our fatherline. His name was Fletcher."

Noticing the sad note in his voice, I try his name on for size. Anything to cheer him up. "Nice to meet you, Griff Fletcher."

"Has a nice ring to it, doesn't it? I lived in the GRH containment facility until I was twelve. When we're young, our fathers take care of us. As soon as we turn eight, they separate us into the boys' ward. Now, it's your turn. Tell me about your nightmares, who's Cameron? Alyssa?"

Biting my lip doesn't make saying it out loud any easier. "My squad was assigned to a protection detail. Sympathizers bombed our convoy. They picked us off one by one. I watched Cameron bleed out. Alyssa, my commanding officer, provided backup so I could get Dr. Martina to safety. But I couldn't save her...and in my nightmares I see them die over and over again."

"Watching someone die is awful," he says with a solemn nod and silence keeps us company.

Suddenly he snorts, "I always thought you were a soldier. Guess I was right. Good thing you're not an Enforcer, right?"

My gut twist. "Griff, Dr. Martina had a picture of your brother. Do you know why?"

"What's a picture?"

"Uh, like a drawing in black and white."

He shrugs. "Dunno. Most of the day, we're confined to cells. The scientists watched us and took notes on their stupid notepads. We're just a big experiment to them, ya know?"

What should I say? I want to answer, to tell him I was training to become an Enforcer, but I don't know how. Our lives depend on the Authority's scientists finding a cure for the Heart Blight. The same virus Griff carried that should have killed me by now. Days ago life was by-the-books, but now everything is off protocol, a damn battlefield of freaking mixed signals all jumbled together.

"Why did ya join the Authority?" He asks, his gaze still fixed to the ceiling.

"My mother encouraged me to join because it's the best way to have a child. I've always wanted a daughter..." I shrug. "When we reach sexual maturity, we get our tether. Every woman who's not a cull gets a ticket in the lottery. When a baby is born they draw a lottery ticket and the winner has a year to get pregnant."

Griff's eyes flare and his hands ball into fists. "Ya can't be serious!" He sits up and pushes away from me. "Is that all we are to ya? A way to reproduce?"

I sit up too, taken aback by his change in demeanor. "What? I don't understand. Why are you mad?"

"Why am I–" he breaks off and sneers at me. "Do ya really not have any idea what they do to us in there?"

"Griff, calm down. I don't know what you're talking about."

"No, I won't calm down!" He says, the veins in his neck bulging. "How can ya be so stupid? So naïve? Ya live there, under their control, but ya pretend nothing happens. Ya talk about it like what they're doing is no big deal!"

"You keep saying experiments, but I don't know what that means!" I say, returning the same level of intensity he's giving.

"How do ya think they get those women *pregnant*, Rei?"

I scrunch my brows in confusion. "The lottery winners get appointments at the lab with one of the scientists. They're inseminated."

"Where does it come from, Rei, huh? Don't ya get it? It takes a man and a woman to make a baby." He leans over and slides his hand inside me, lifting it to my face. The thick, viscous fluid sticks between his fingers as he splays them wide. "Is this why ya were all over me last night, begging to go again and again? Is it, Rei?"

I open my mouth to say something, anything, but nothing comes out. My mind races. Is it true? Of course, they taught us we kept men in containment for reproduction and safety. The lottery process and insemination were all covered in school years before they adjusted our tether and started monitoring our fertility. I watch the fury on Griff's face and feel the thick fluid oozing down my thighs.

"No.... T–that can't be right." I say with a sputter.

Griff scoffs and rakes his hands through his hair, pulling it so hard his forehead goes white. "Ya really don't know, do ya? How they strap us to laboratory beds and stick us with needles, setting our blood on fire to test their so-called cures. Do ya know they dose our food with a drug cocktail and force us to touch ourselves until our skin is swollen and raw? The only way we get relief is an NAP or meeting their ridiculous quotas to provide ya with babies for *insemination*."

"Griff, that can't be right. The Authority keeps us safe."

His empty laughter fills the hut.

"When has the Authority ever kept men safe, Rei, huh? Have ya ever thought about that? How does locking us up and torturing us keep us safe? Why aren't ya sick, Rei?" His eyes bulge and his face goes red as he spits like it's burning a hole through his tongue.

Enforcer training screams to move, get away, protect myself. The last time I saw him this mad I'd taken his necklace and his arrow struck the seat of my car where I'd been a second earlier.

I scrabble backwards, falling off the bed and onto the floor. Shuffling through our pile of clothes on the floor, I pull his hunting knife, holding it out in front of me. Fumbling, I pull on my shirt and pants.

Go. Get out of here. Now.

"My baby brother is trapped in that hellhole, Rei. I wouldn't wish the GRH on anyone. It destroys your soul piece by piece until all that's left is an empty shell of who ya were supposed to be."

"Humanity would've died out years ago if the Authority didn't keep men in containment. The virus will kill us until there's no one left." I say in a voice hoarse and foreign to my own ears.

"What about the Free Territories, huh?"

"The Free Territories are empty wastelands! It's a fairy tale the Sympathizers use to stir up trouble and bring people over to their stupid cause."

"They're not! The Authority's lying! Their job is to keep ya locked behind the Iron Divide and feed ya their bullshit! There *is* another way. They manipulate and control ya like ants and ya scurry around, good little unthinking soldiers."

"Without the research of the Authority's scientists, we'll never get a cure. It's mutating faster and faster every year."

"That's what they tell ya in order to control ya!" Griff shouts, stalking closer to the edge of the bed. "The Authority created the Heart Blight virus and they've been covering it up ever since."

This time I'm the one peeling with wicked laughter. "You seriously think the Authority created the same virus they've spent decades trying to cure? Who's the delusional one now, Griff?"

Griff grabs his necklace. "I have proof."

"A stupid griffin your father carved isn't proof of anything other than how crazy you sound right now!"

I go rigid as he stands and steps close enough the point of the knife grazes his chest. A droplet of blood drips from the thin cut. He pulls the necklace over his head and flips it over, shows me the symbol on the bottom. The same triangle and circle I saw on those trees in the woods.

"These symbols mark safe passage for Sympathizers." He places both hands on the griffin's neck and twists. The carved head spins as he unscrews it. Griff reaches in and pulls out a USB drive. "The researcher who helped us escape gave us this. It contains evidence of how the Authority created the virus. They used the Cleansing to rise to power and manipulate the surviving population. I'm taking this to the Free Territories so everyone will know the truth. The Authority is pure evil, Rei, and you're a product of their sick, twisted games."

My eyes go wide at the sight of the USB drive. Mara told me how impossible it was to get one. "You don't even know what that is, let alone how to use it," I sputter, glaring at him, but my words ring hollow to my own ears. Was he telling the truth? Could the Authority be involved in all of this somehow? It would explain why I hadn't died from the Heart Blight.

Griff screws the necklace back together and steps forward again, forcing me to step back or stab him. "What reason do I have to lie, Rei? I could've killed ya or left ya here, but I stayed! I risked everything for ya! Don't ya get it? The Commander killed my father for getting this information out of the Authority. They've been patrolling the Brass Mountains for months looking for me. The longer I stay the greater the chance they'll find me."

"Wait, wait, you're lying! C-commander Lynx killed your father? She would never do that!"

"I saw it with my own eyes. If I could, I would rip her heart out of her chest and watch her life drain away," Griff says and wraps his hand over top of mine on the hilt of the knife. I didn't realize my hand was shaking until his grasp forces it still.

"You're lying! You'd tell me anything to stay out of containment, where you belong!"

Griff lets go of me and raises both palms in the air above his head. "If ya truly believe that, then go ahead, kill me, Rei. I'd rather die than go back."

I tighten my grip on the blade and grit my teeth. One lunge with all my weight behind it and this puts an end to him. I can figure out how to get back to Mara's lake house, even if it kills me. I wrap my other hand around the hilt when it trembles. Griff's defeated gaze meets mine and the emptiness within them expands the black, sour feeling burrowing into my chest.

The feral scream rips from my mouth and ready my lunge, to end it all. But the knife clatters onto the floor rather than pierce his heart between the ribs.

Spinning, I yank open the door and race out into the darkness of my own making.

The chill is an afterthought on my bare feet.

# 26

## REI

**Existence isn't a choice; we try
to protect ourselves from danger
whether or not we want to.**

My breath comes out in little white puffs as I stomp away from the hut. I clench my fists and my nails break the skin of my palms. Did the Authority create the Heart Blight virus? That doesn't even make any sense. Everything they stand for, everything they've taught me, said the exact opposite. But I can't deny the USB drive and how protective Griff's been of his necklace. Here I was thinking it was for sentimental reasons.

No, I shake my head. I don't know what's on the USB. It could be empty or just some random surveillance video. Like Mara told me, they closely guarded them between the two divisions. Then how did Griff end up with one? And saying Commander Lynx killed his father? She would never do something like that! Humanity would go extinct without men.

"Argh!" I kick at a stone on the path and let out a streak of curses. Dammit! I forgot I was freaking barefoot. That's going to leave a bruise. I hop a few steps, then limp until the pain subsides and the sun goes down. It'll be dark soon and the last thing I need right now is another panic attack, caught in that freaking tunnel, choking on the memory of burning smoke, emptying my clip in the Sympathizer's crimson smile.

A low growl makes my whole body go rigid. The leaves ahead of me rustle and the mountain lion steps onto the path, blocking the way. Its golden eyes match the ones I saw when I hurt my ankle. Danger stalks closer, mouth open, revealing wicked, gleaming sharp teeth.

Bless the mother! I inch backwards, holding its unblinking gaze. The growl intensifies and it launches. Go! Run! My shriek pierces the night and I bolt toward the hut. Twigs snap and leaves crash behind me. Faster! I have to go faster! It's gaining on me. Don't look back, even a split second distraction could be the difference between life and death.

"Griff!!" I scream his name so loud it hurts my ears. I'm running flat out and my muscles roar in protest as the adrenaline dwindles. They're begging for more oxygen, for me to stop and rest. I spy the hut in the distance, but I won't make it.

The mountain lion claws swipe at my heels. A wall of solid muscle slams into my back. I duck and roll at the same time. My evasive manoeuvre is enough to catch it off guard as I somersault across the dirt, leaves, and sticks at the edge of the path. I scramble to my hands and knees, trying to get back up as it careens into me a second time.

It's going to kill me. I shriek, lifting my arms over my face to cover my head. Teeth flash as it snarls, going for the kill. My legs kick out with every ounce of strength I can muster, smashing its muzzle. This can't be the end. I don't want to die.

Griff barrels into the side of the mountain lion. Claws tear at my shirt, teeth snap shut a hot breath from my forearms, and it's ripped away by the impact of another body in motion. The hunting knife arcs, stabbing deep into its side. Warm blood sprays, splattering my face. It roars and whips around, slashing viciously. Griff dodges, but his foot slips on slick leaves.

"No!" I screech, scrambling to rise. Help him!

The mountain lion pounces, enormous jaws clamping down on Griff's shoulder, claws tearing at his arms and chest. Ragged screams fill the night and Griff drives the blade to the hilt again and again. The mountain lion shakes its locked jaw, foamy spittle flying, Griff's body thrashing and bucking like an empty sandbag. It's too strong, too heavy, he can't get clear.

He's pinned.

Trapped.

Don't think, move! There's no time! Instincts take over, my fingers curl around a rock and I charge, smashing the top of its head. Griff's scream falters, his eyes glazing over, but his free arm continues to jab and skewer. The wound gushes faster with each thrust of the blade.

Still, it won't let go.

*It's killing him.*

I lift the rock higher, as high as I can, holding it in both hands, and whack it with everything I freaking have.

*Crack!* The skull breaks with a sickening squish, collapsing on top of Griff, its dripping jaws going slack.

"Griff? Griff!" I shove into the limp, furry corpse, but it won't budge. Dammit! My feet slip and slide in pools of slimy, cooling scarlet. After several attempts, I finally get enough leverage to push it off him.

Free of the weight, Griff coughs and groans. The hand holding the knife trembles as he struggles to sit up. I grab him under the armpits and help him into an upright position.

"Griff?" His gaze meets mine, but it's unfocused, looking right through me, a prisoner to shock and adrenaline.

I sink to my knees and wrap his arm around my shoulder. No matter how hard I shove he's too heavy to lift. "Griff, you have to help me!" I scream. His pupils are distant and blank. This isn't working. My palm connects with his face. Crap it stings. "Hey! Eyes on me! Stand up!"

He blinks hard and stares at me. "Rei?" He whispers, gasping.

"Get up!" I shove to my feet as hard as I can, leg muscles burning from the strain. All those miles running the MMZ perimeter track are finally paying off. This time, Griff shakes out of his stupor enough to provide backup. He pushes and together we rise. He sways, stumbling forward a step, and I fling my hand across his chest to keep him upright. Crap, this is going sideways fast.

"Lean on me," I say. His head turns at the sound of my voice, seeking, but not finding. He's lost in a fog of pain and blood loss. Gotta move before he shuts down completely.

"Come on." I half drag, half carry him toward the hut. Every step I take he grows heavier. It's taking too long. My legs tremble and my ankle threatens to buckle with the effort of keeping him upright. "Keep walking! We're almost there."

Our progress is agonizingly slow. When we reach the hut I slam my foot on the bottom step, nearly dropping him and grunting with the effort. My shoulders throb and my injured ankle protests even the slightest movement. Oh no, he's too heavy. There's not enough leverage to get him up the stairs with me. Crap, I'm losing my grip.

"No, no!" He slumps forward and falls against the steps, coming within an inch of smashing his head. His bleeding arm still has a death grip on the knife. "Dammit, Griff! Help me! Get up!" His breathing labors and his eyes flutter closed. I can't give up, we're so close. Crawling over him, I grab the front of his shredded, stained shirt, dragging him backwards.

It's no use. He won't budge.

I hook my arms under his armpits and pull but my dirty bare feet slide on the wood. He can't stay out here like this. Think, there has to be a way. Grabbing his face, I place a hand on either side and shake.

"Griff! You can't die on me now! Wake up! Please, wake up!" Tears stream down my cheeks and splatter his clammy skin. But he only moans. "Griff!" I slap him as hard as I can. It stings so bad, it's gonna leave a bruise.

His eyes snap open. He surges to his feet, eyes wild and deranged, chest heaving, knife swinging wildly.

"Griff! It's me!" I fall back, jerking out of reach.

He blinks, breath ragged. "Rei?" He says in a quavering voice.

"Yes," I say in a hoarse, trembling voice—choking back sobs. "It's me. Let's go inside."

Griff nods, his eyes bright and feverish. He walks up the steps, pulls open the door, and collapses on the bed. The knife clatters to the floor.

Bless the mother, I hurry after him, pulling the door shut. The chill from outside has seeped into my fingers and toes. The fire has gone out in the wood stove, leaving me fumbling in the rapidly falling gloom. I find Griff's bag by the door and dig through it until I find the flint and kindling. My hands tremble as I try to make a spark.

"Come on. Come on!" I strike once, twice, three times with no freaking success. Calm down, deep breath. Reset. My fingers open and close, shaking free of the tension like they've caught the recoil. Remember his hands covering mine, the motion, the confidence and angle of the impact. The spark smolders in the kindling. Gentle steady breath coaxes it to life. It smokes, growing larger, flaring to the ominous orange of a tether, bursting into flame. I drop it into the wood stove and fill it with logs, stoking the fire as high as I can.

I grab a pot, fill it with water, and set it to boil along with a roll of my old bandages. First aid training kicks in, assess the situation, tackle the worst wounds first. There's blood on his shoulder, but the slices on his chest are oozing. Lifting the material gently, I peel it from his skin, but Griff is so out of it he doesn't even notice.

The cuts could really use stitches, but I don't have any way to close them, and even if I did, I wouldn't know how. At least I can stop the bleeding. I return to the stove and fish the bandages out of the water, wring them out and use them to clean the wounds. Once they're free of dirt, I pack clean bandages into lacerations.

"That will have to do for now," I mumble, sitting up and wiping a hand over my forehead. It's like an inferno in here with the wood stove burning so high. One injury down, one to go. His shoulder took most of the damage. The question is, how to get his shirt off? Getting it over his head is a no-go in this state. The gleam of the knife on the floor catches my eye. Ahh yes, that'll do nicely. It separates the shredded material with a few proficient cuts.

Crap, what a mess. There's two deep puncture wounds and several smaller ones on either side of his shoulder. I prod the inflamed skin with my fingers, but nothing feels broken. By some miracle, they've clotted and are no longer bleeding. Cleaning them takes a long time, but I'm satisfied with my handy work when I wrap them with the last of the bandages. Now for one last check on his stomach. Phew, packing the gashes worked. They've stopped bleeding, too.

Griff moans and his eyes flutter open. He hisses in pain when he pushes himself up onto his elbows.

"Wait! What are you doing? Lie down, you need to rest." I place a hand on his forearm and push. He's so weak he flops backwards without resistance.

"If we leave it there, it'll attract more predators," he says, laboring to sit up again.

No way I'm letting him leave. He's too weak to go anywhere. I place a hand on his chest and pin him down. "Stop. You're in no condition to go anywhere. I'll do it."

"Ya won't be able to move it alone." He says, panting at just those few words.

"I'll figure it out. Get some rest. I'll be back." The largest deer skin replaces my hand. His skin is still clammy but his color is returning. Smoothing back his sweaty hair, I place a kiss on his forehead. His eyes slide close and I wait until his breathing steadies before I stand up.

He's gonna be okay, he has to be.

There's a scratching noise at the window. I clear my throat and open it for Mischief. It's pitch black and freezing outside compared to the blistering heat in the hut. I shiver and close it behind the kit. Why did he close it earlier? Oh, that's right. My cheeks flush at the memory of my wrists pinned above my head and Griff leaning over me.

Bless the mother, stop it. Now is not the time. Far from it.

"Time for the hard part," I sigh, finding my boots and pulling them on my scratched, dirty feet.

The darkness envelops me as I shut the door behind me. Only the soft glow from the side window gives off any light to see. I shiver and wrap my arms around myself, trying to chase away the chill and the hulking, cloying, roiling in the pit of my stomach.

"You're not in the tunnel. It's only the woods." I suck in cold air, shaky breaths coming faster, heart hammering against my ribcage. The stairs creak as I retrace our steps back down the path. Tendrils of inky blackness curl up the sides of my neck, wrapping around my throat. Don't stop, ignore it, it's not real, keep going.

My boots crunch on the brittle leaves and a stick snaps underfoot. Not a gunshot. I gasp and bend over, hands on knees, gulping cold air. Oh! The glassy, dead eyes of the mountain lion stare at me, mocking me. I found it.

"Mother bless it. Let's make this fast." It's dead right? My foot bumps the mountain lion's huge paw. A boot print marks the pale flesh of the Sympathizer's hand.

I shudder. The corpse is already stiff. Of course it is. Hurry up!

Cameron holds her gaping stomach.

Steeling myself, I grab a paw and lean backwards with my body weight to drag it down the path. A sound echoes in the distance and I freeze, letting go. Muscles tense and my heart gallops erratically in my chest. It's a stupid freaking owl. There's a flutter of wings and branches rustling overhead. I gulp down the dread building in my gut and grab the mountain lion's paw again.

My throat is constricting, I'm choking, I can't breathe.

The ground slopes and the weight of the corpse sets it sliding down the damp, leafy undergrowth. Gravity takes over. The corpse tumbles down the incline and slams into the bottom of a shallow gully. Hands on my knees as I struggle to stay upright as the world spins. I'm so dizzy.

Rustling in the woods has me spinning, searching for the enemy Sympathizer. Run! Turning, I shoot back the way I came, aiming for the faint glow of the hut's window, a beacon in the panic swallowing me whole. Faster! Don't look back!

A blast of scalding heat hits me as I clamber inside and slam the door behind me. Exhaustion sets in, my whole body aches. The fire is still roaring, lighting up the tiny space, leaving no room for the shadows that haunt me. Griff lies unmoving on the bed, Mischief curled at his feet. Putting a hand on his damp forehead calms my nerves and my breathing slows, returning to normal.

He came to my rescue even after the horrible things I said to him.

He's real.

The darkness is gone.

We're safe now.

Kicking off my boots I climb over Griff on the bed, yawning, eyelids drooping. He mumbles something indistinguishable as I join him under the blankets, scooting as close as I can without disturbing his injured shoulder.

"Rei?" He groans, his eyes shining with pain as they flutter.

"I'm here. You're gonna be okay." Lacing our fingers together, I smooth my thumb over his hand, enjoying the solidarity and intimacy of his presence. His fingers squeeze mine and he relaxes beside me.

The fire crackles and pops. Our breathing deepens and slows, finding and matching the same languid rhythm.

For the first time in my life, it's not the Authority making me feel safe.

# 27

## GRIFF

**When we're broken and suffering, words become unnecessary, and presence becomes everything.**

The world is on fire and I'm drowning. The strange mixture of hot and cold is so uncomfortable, but I can't seem to move. My limbs feel like lead and they don't respond when I tell them to. I want to speak, but nothing comes out of my mouth. Panic rises and I strain to open my eyes, wiggle my fingers, say something, anything.

I gasp and the jerky movement sends waves of pain down the side of my neck and through my chest. I'm not sure what's dream and what's reality.

"Griff?"

I hear my name, but it sounds like it's coming from far away. Muffled almost, like it's underwater. Something cool touches my chest.

"Ahh, it hurts." I moan and flinch at the sharp stabs of pain.

"Damn, sorry."

"I'm so hot." Legs kick and the blanket pulls away, exposing my sweaty skin to the air. Teeth chatter and my lips shiver. "S-so cold, too."

"You need to keep the blanket on."

There's movement beside me and the heavy deerskin falls over top of me again. I grimace as it slides over my skin, as if the slightest pressure will split it open. Flames are consuming me from the inside out.

"So hot, so thirsty." I try to pull the cover off again. Strong fingers grab my hand and force it down. I'm too weak to do anything but let it flop back beside me.

"I said leave it. Here, let me get you some water." There's movement and then something soft and gentle is prying my mouth open. My lips are so dry. A stream of water pours into my mouth. I gulp the liquid, some spilling over my thick tongue and running down my face.

"No more." I sputter, turning my head away.

"You need to stay hydrated. Come on, just a few more sips."

Fingers grab my jaw and squeeze. More water slips down my throat, forcing me to swallow and gag.

"That's better," Rei's voice soothes. That's right. Rei. The mountain lion. Memory comes flooding back. The pain in my shoulder intensifies as I remember the jaws closing into me, crushing me, splitting me in half. Tearing me apart.

Devouring.

Hungry.

Deadly.

"Shh, you're okay. It's the middle of the night. Go back to sleep." A hand runs across my forehead and rakes through my damp hair. It's so nice, comforting even, just like Father used to do when I was sick as a child. I'm being boiled alive, but my sweaty skin makes me shiver. It's so hard to keep my eyes open.

As soon as day breaks, she'll be gone and I'll be here.

Dying.

"Don't leave me," I whisper and tears leak from the corners of my eyes. "I've been alone for so long. I don't want to be alone anymore."

Her fingers curl along my scalp in a steady, soothing, rhythmic pattern. It helps chase the pain away if I focus on her, on the way she comforts me, cares for me, like I'm worthy of being more than a number, an object, a possession of the Authority.

Maybe, just maybe, she needs me as much as I need her.

"Shh, I'm right here," she whispers, cool breath brushing my sweaty neck. Her voice is calming. I love the sultry undertones, the snide remarks, the moans of pleasure, and the intelligent banter. Her forehead presses against mine and her hair tickles my cheek, my mouth, my neck, and nose.

"Please, don't leave me." I beg, despite knowing my efforts are futile. She's a soldier, an Authority soldier, no less. She's trained to follow orders, to do what she's told, entrenched in their lies and propaganda, to turn me in at the first chance she gets.

There's a husky chuckle and a soft kiss on my lips. "So demanding," she purrs. "Go to sleep. You need to rest." Her fingers pressing into mine.

I grab hold of her for dear life.

# 28

## REI

**We thrive on unspoken hope: what we do today makes tomorrow possible.**

Something's wrong. The fur covering me is as damp as the sweaty body I'm pressed against. Griff moans and I sit up, placing a hand on his forehead. It's burning hot. Feverish. Crap! Chills hit me like a ton of bricks. I fling the blankets off and scramble to attention.

It's freezing in here.

Plumes of white steam curl and dissipate every time I exhale. The fire went out overnight and frigid air permeates the room. I hurry over to the wood stove, shivering, wincing with every icy step. The kindling catches on the first try. Bless the mother for small miracles. I feed the logs into the fire and rub my palms together, reaching for the warmth of growing flames.

Griff will need clean bandages so I better set the pot to boil and check his wounds. I'll bet he's thirsty, too. I grab a canteen of water and return to his limp form.

His skin is uncomfortably slick and warm under my hands. Sliding my fingers under his clammy hair, I tip his head. "Griff, wake up, drink something."

He moans and his eyebrows furrow, but he doesn't respond. I grab his chin and pry his mouth open, pouring water into his mouth until he sputters and gags.

Vacant, green eyes flutter open. "Rei?" He asks in a hoarse, weak voice.

"Come on, you have to drink this."

"No more," he says, coughing and wincing.

"Keep drinking." Water fills his mouth until he swallows, gulps, and sputters. His head turns and his arm swings, knocking the canteen to the floor with a clatter.

"C-can't," he whimpers.

"All right, that's enough for now. I'm going to check your bandages, okay? I'll try to be gentle."

He nods and his eyelids droop. I peel back the bandages on his shoulder. The skin is tender to the touch, but the puncture wounds look clean, not swollen. Cleaning and re-dressing the bandages take only a few minutes. He moans but otherwise doesn't complain. So far, so good.

Griff shivers when I pull off his damp blanket and peel back the bandages on the scratches on his stomach. Oh damn. I gulp and bite my lower lip. It's not good, not good at all. Thick pus oozes from the jagged claw marks on his angry, swollen skin. They need cleaning, on the double. I grab clean bandages and gently prod his raw flesh.

"Aaah!" Griff screams and jolts awake, his rough hand clamping over the top of mine. "Shit! Stop! That fucking hurts!"

Shoving his hand away, I push him back down. "I don't care if it hurts, it's infected you idiot!" I wash the wound despite his gritting teeth and flushing face. Twice more, he weakly attempts to stop my best efforts at playing doctor.

"Fuck! Please, I can't stand it anymore–Aaah!" His eyes roll back and he passes out cold.

"Griff? Griff!" No response. "Come on Griff, don't do this to me!" I shake him and smack his cheek. Mother bless it, it stings.

His eyes shoot open and he gasps, shivering violently, shaking the bed. "C-c-cold. I'm so c-c-cold." His teeth chatter.

"Hold on, I'll find something to warm you up."

Re-wrapping his wounds took a lot of time, leaving his sweaty skin exposed. Ripping through the furs on the bed, I search for anything dry. Toward the bottom of the pile, I find a few older skins, placing them like patchwork over him. Steam rises in wispy tendrils from the rest of the damp, sweaty furs spread out by the fire. It's the best I can do for right now.

"Griff, you need some of the medicine you put on my leg. The stuff that fights infections."

He shakes his head, still shuddering, his muscles tensing and his eyes glazed. "C-c-can't. That was the l-l-last."

"I'm no expert, but you need antibiotics to get your fever down."

Griff shakes his head and tears slide down his jaw. Another intense tremor rips through him. "Leave me," he croaks. That faraway look is creeping back into his eyes, like a fog rolling over the streets after a hard rain, strangling the sun in the sky.

"What?"

"Just leave me to die," he whispers and convulses.

No. No! He doesn't mean it. What kinda sick, twisted joke is he playing right now?

"You've gotta be freaking kidding me! That's not funny!"

Jaw clenched, he turns his head, tracking my voice, searching through the haze of pain to meet mine. "Compass, in my bag. Southwest." He wheezes, and his eyes struggle to stay open. "The l-l-lake." His hand lifts, reaching toward my face. I grab it and press calloused fingers against the wet skin of my cheek.

"Stop it! I-I won't go! You're not dying, do you hear me! You have to get better!"

"So demanding...." He tries to smile, but the spasm of pain transforms his mouth into a grimace. His fingertips trace a gentle path through the tears on my chin and fall slack.

"Griff!" I shake him, but he's out cold. "Hey! Don't you dare die on me! You're not allowed to die, do you hear me? Griff!"

This can't be happening. Focus! I need to get him antibiotics, and fast. But where? There's no way I can find the plants he used to treat my leg. He used everything he had left of that medicine on me, his enemy. Why didn't he let me die and save it for himself? And after everything that's happened, now he wants me to leave him like this? Just let him die while I, what, go back to the lake house and pretend none of this ever happened?

No. Take a deep breath, don't panic, assess the situation. I thrust a hand through my hair and stand up, spinning and pacing as I think. There has to be something I can do.

Of course! My luggage back at the lake house! I left it out by the lake, right before my tether started acting strange. Would it still be there? I have to check. A bitter laugh escapes my lips. Trust my mother's fussing to come in handy after I berated her for it the day I left. That stupid antibiotic cream will save Griff's life.

For the first time since I found myself in this freaking crazy situation, I'll listen to Griff. Going back to Mara's lake house is my only chance to save him, even if it means leaving him to fend for himself. It took at least a day to get to the hut. There's no time to waste, I have to go now.

I scramble around the room, grabbing his bag and emptying it of everything except the compass, the tin with the flint and kindling, and three cans of food. Then I boil more water and refill the canteens. Leaving one next to Griff on the bed, I pack the other two and jam his knife into my belt. Scooping the dry furs off the ground, I pile them on top of Griff. They'll get wet again, but when the fire goes out, it'd be his only protection from the temperature.

When I'm done, I carry in three large loads from the woodpile outside, stacking the logs beside the fire and feeding in as many as I can.

"Sorry Mischief," I say into the crisp air as I slide the window shut. The kit left the bed sometime during the early morning hours. Now he won't be able to come and go, but it'll keep the heat inside as long as possible.

I swing Griff's bag swings over my shoulder and shove my feet into my boots. Now to figure out where I'm freaking going. I flip open the compass and watch the arrow swing, orienting itself.

There's no time to waste, I have to go.

"Griff, I'm coming back. I promise." His hot, sweaty forehead blazes under my touch. I plant a soft kiss on his forehead. "I know you're a fighter, like me. Please trust me. Don't give up. Keep fighting."

I turn and hurry out the door, securing it behind me. Holding the compass, I spin until I'm facing southwest. Letting out a shaky breath, I break into a jog.

Slow but steady is the goal, cover as much ground as possible, as fast as I can...before it's too late.

# 29

 **REI**

## Life leaves many scars, some more visible than others.

My ankle throbs after the first mile. By the fifth, I'm doing everything I can to push through the pain and ignore it. At midday, my limp is impeding my progress, forcing me to slow and stop. A fallen log I sink onto creaks under my weight. The groan of relief slips outta my lips as I elevate my ankle. After a long drink, I consult the compass.

Yep, I'm still heading southwest.

At this pace, if my ankle doesn't hold up, I'll be out here all night. Dread bubbles in the pit of my stomach but I slam it back into the void in my chest. Panicking won't save Griff. These past few days I've worked so hard to get to this point, to return to the lake house and the Authority. It's finally happening, but with each step, the doubt and guilt build.

What if I survive and he dies?

Despite my shortcomings, my threats to turn him into the Authority, even taking his freaking necklace, he risked his life for me. Why? I had his necklace and thought I was dying when he tended my ankle and pulled me from a sinkhole. But after that...he could have just left me alone in the woods to fend for myself, to be mauled in the jaws of the mountain lion.

I'd spent so long trying to do enough, to be enough. The head of my class, the best marksman, the most determined and loyal soldier. Everything my mother encouraged, Alyssa despised, and Commander Lynx praised me for. A good little Enforcer earning her lottery tickets in a system where I could only be broken, could only find comfort with another woman.

But for the first time in my life, with Griff, I didn't have to satisfy rules or conditions, or sacrifice a part of myself. What Griff gave me had been there all along, quiet and steadily, without asking, or following protocol. The passion, the chemistry, the way he touches me and what we did together was freely given rather than some prize to be earned.

Our time together is distorting and fracturing the world around me. First my tether, then the virus, now the very foundation my whole life has been built upon. He's lonely and I'm, well, I'm not sure what I am. Scared of the dark? Forced to relive the nightmare of the Sympathizer bombing and the death of my fellow Enforcers until I'm empty inside?

A traitor?

I get back up, stretch, and return to a steady jogging pace. My ankle appreciates the quick break and is cooperating for the time being. Focus on putting one foot in front of the other. This is nothing I can't handle. Push the pain out of mind and keep going. Pretend this is just another day of exhausting training.

After two years in basic and several months in Enforcer training, I should be a pro at this. Grin and bear and force my way through with the same determination I've had since I was a kid. Mara would be proud to see me now, reckless—and for the enemy, no less. She was always the biggest instigator with getting ourselves into trouble.

The Authority taught that letting your guard down got you killed. But here I was, still alive.

I stumble over a dip in the ground and throw my arms out to catch my balance. The sun is setting and my mind is wandering like I am in these woods. I check my heading on the compass.

What if Griff told me the wrong direction? No, stop. He was half outta it but he wouldn't do that. Crap! What's wrong with me? Leaning against a tree trunk, I press a hand to my forehead and catch my breath.

My leg is throbbing again, but I'm getting better at ignoring it. The familiar shape of a berry bush has me approaching. My stomach growls as I pull a handful off the branches and examine them. They're similar to what Griff and I collected a few days ago. I smile, thinking about how excited Griff got about them, his favorite.

I stuff handfuls into my mouth until I can't eat anymore. They're more tart than sweet, but my growling stomach doesn't care. I laugh and clamp a hand over my mouth in surprise. A few days ago I'd never eaten berries before—or rabbit, or turkey, for that matter.

Setting off again, I sip from my canteen to wash the bitter aftertaste off my tongue. Gotta pick up the pace. I'm no expert, but I'd had enough first aid training to know a bad wound when I saw one. Even cleaning the infection out as best I could wouldn't be enough if I couldn't find antibiotics and get them back to him in time.

Then what? If Griff survives this, what happens next? I can't stay here forever, ignoring my duties to the Authority. I swore an oath. So he has a USB, it doesn't mean anything. It would be easy for him to tell me whatever he thought I wanted to hear. Anything to make me feel sorry for him, to get me on his side. After all, that'd be the best way to keep me from turning him into the Authority.

Focus! Now is not the time. None of this matters if he dies....

The light drains away as the sun sets, casting tall shadows around me, guards on duty in a silent forest. It reminds me of the first day I stood at the edge of the lake, studying the treeline. Despite days living surrounded by woods and wildlife, it feels more foreboding than before. Leaves crunch underfoot and the partially naked branches look like arms with claws and teeth. A bird flaps from a tree and something small skitters away in the underbrush to my right. Every sound Griff teased me about being deaf to before is amplified. Memories of those golden eyes stalking me that first night urge me on faster. Stay alert, keep my ears and eyes open.

I charge forward, prepared for whatever the darkness brings. My hand goes to Griff's knife at my belt, and a sense of comfort washes over me.

"Authority save me. How much farther?" I groan in a breathy exhale matching the rhythm of my footfalls.

My progress slows to a crawl when it's too dark for me to see much further than a foot or two beyond my nose. I won't make the same mistakes again. Carefully, I pick my way down a narrow track and through a thicket of sharp barbs and brambles. Dammit, why do they have to catch on Griff's bag and snag my shirt? Pushing them away helps but the thorns bite into my palms. Crap, it's caught in my hair. I stop and disentangle myself before I can continue onward. Skin tingles and stings from the multitude of scratches it's leaving behind.

"Damn, that hurts." I stick my thumb in my mouth and use my teeth to pull out a large thorn.

An owl hoots in the distance, followed by a loud thunk. My body goes rigid and I pause. Straining my ears doesn't help. The next, louder sound is more freaking ominous. Where is it coming from, which direction? Sweat beads on my forehead and my breath quickens. With my eyes adjusted somewhat to the dark, I faintly see the trail before me.

The trees lean in, their gnarled branches reaching, linking together, forming a ceiling above me as my vision tunnels.

*Crack!*

"Aaah!" I shriek and spin. It's behind me.

"Rei," says a familiar feminine voice in a whisper against the back of my neck.

A flood of adrenaline courses through me, and I have to force my trembling limbs to swivel. Cameron stands before me, her gray hands clutching a disemboweled stomach, her face pale and bloodless.

"It's all your fault," she says, taking a step closer, her gap teeth flashing, a strand of her intestines falling to the ground and trailing her approach.

"You're dead, you're not real," I growl between gritted teeth, backing away from her. "I'm sorry. I couldn't save you." Panic rises like a tide, a wave growing taller, building into the Iron Divide and crashing over me.

*Boom! Pop, pop, pop!*

There's a flare of bright light, metal crunching, glass breaking, and gunshots. Acrid smoke burns my nostrils and the cloying heat of the exploded truck blisters my skin. Cameron launches at me, her mouth wide and gaping.

I bring Griff's knife up and slash at her. She evaporates into a lick of flames and the snap of leaves by my ear has gunshots zipping past my freaking head. Crap! I duck and cover, taking off running down the path. Tree trunks merge and condense. Dark bark is replaced by large chunks of exploded concrete and exposed, twisted rebar. I'm back in the tunnel, surrounded by debris. I charge toward the faint light at the end, passing the bodies of the other trainees and Sympathizers strewn along it.

My foot hits something solid and I fall face first, catching myself on my hands before I faceplant among the corpses.

"Alyssa!" Her body is the most twisted of all, bits and pieces strewn around the ground from the blast. I tripped over her arm, my hand is on her severed leg, and a chunk of her torso lies in front of me. Her eyes, so like that of her mother, Commander Lynx, bore holes into my chest.

Judging me.

Blaming me.

*Pop! Pop!*

Bits of dust and concrete shower my head and bite into my skin. Get up! Move! I fumble to my feet, sprinting from the mass grave.

The Sympathizers want to kill me and I don't know why.

"Rei! It's your turn, Rei!" The Sympathizer I killed steps out onto the path in front of me but she's me and I'm her. The gun raises to point at my chest. There's a satisfied grin on her bloody mouth, my death staring back at me. In the reflection, I see a blossom of red spread across my chest and trickle down, splashing the ground, staining it red.

"No! Nooo!" Gripping the knife with white knuckles, I barrel into the Sympathizer wearing my face. Her neck snaps, although I've stabbed her in the chest. Her eyes go wide and she slumps.

I've just killed myself.

"Rei!" I spin, following the sound of Griff's voice.

"Griff? Where are you?"

The Sympathizer who was me has vanished. Stumbling back, I blink and my eyes struggle to focus on the tree trunk mere inches from my face. Griff's hunting knife sticks out of the bark, my hands still wrapped around the hilt. Bless the mother, was I hallucinating? Tugging it free takes some effort and time, but I'm not leaving it here.

Faint rays of dawn light filter through the treetops. A bird sings in the distance. My chest is heaving and my ankle is sending shooting pains from my foot all the way through my thigh and into my hip. Sweat drenches my clothes and I shiver in the chilly air.

Did I run through the night? With trembling fingers, I put the knife away and drink. My throat feels raw and scratchy, no matter how much water I gulp down. There's a splash as I put the empty canteen back in the bag. What was that? I furrow my brows and cock my head, listening.

There it is again, the same splashing noise. Curious, I limp toward the source. When I push through a row of woody bushes, I catch my first glimpse of the lake. It has the same beautiful, serene quality I admired the first time I saw it. A log bumps the bank, splashing, sending small ripples outwards across the surface.

I dig the compass out, pop it open, and read the southwest heading.

Griff was telling the truth.

# 30

# GRIFF

**A single command can fracture a soul, shackle the spirit, and bind fate.**

The fucking noise is back, scratching behind my burning eyeballs, slamming against my forehead. Digging its way out of my skull with gnashing yellow teeth and wicked sharp claws. Lifting my hands and crushing them against my ears isn't helping. It won't stop, it wants to hollow me out until I disappear, a pile of lonely, forgotten bones in a sad, little hut.

There's a bear sitting on my chest, pinning me down, forcing me to fight for every suffocating breath.

"Get off of me!"

My fingers curl into its coarse, stiff fur, flinging it aside, rolling clear of the attack. A mountain of blankets thumps to the ground and I lean over the edge of the bed, stomach revolting. Why won't the pressure let up? Chilly air bathes my hot, sweaty skin. Bandages slide and catch over the raw cuts across my stomach, shaking me out of the feverish haze with a hiss. Nausea is not my friend, but it sure as shit wants to be.

*Look where trusting the enemy got ya, huh?* My father's gruff sneer booms, drowning out the scratchy racket.

"Shut up!!" The scratching is growing louder, and now it's coming from the front door, too. I turn my head and sweat drips down my neck, plopping on the wood, joining the deadly chorus dragging me under. Who's there? What could they possibly want?

I scrabble to my feet, swaying and almost tripping on the tangle of furs.

Not a bear...just me dying.

Alone.

Several unsteady steps and my shoulder slams into the doorframe. The vice tightens around my ribs and I struggle to suck in air. My surroundings swim in waves of vertigo. There's that fucking scratching again. I rip open the front door, teeth bared, ready to tear apart the noisy offender with my bare hands. Her leering smile widens, and she takes her dark blue cap off.

Commander Lynx steps across the threshold, looming above me, metals on her uniform clinking.

"Hello son." She lifts her chin, peering down her nose at me. As if she has a right to call me that.

"Murderer!" I scream. My blood boils and every muscle in my body goes rigid.

Her eyebrows raise in disdain. "Such squalor...it's like you never left containment, isn't it?"

Burn it all down, destroy the system, a life for a life.

Hands out, I lunge for her throat, passing right through her and smashing into the railing. It gives way under my bulky frame and I smash over the edge, tasting dirt, seeing stars. Ahh, shit, it hurts! The frost on the ground cools my palms and soaks the knees of my pants.

"My, my, you're still as useless as ever." Disgust curls her lips, twisting into vicious, steely laughter.

"Why did ya kill him?" Thick anguish punctuates my demanding cry. My hands clench, but my feet won't cooperate. Tears stream down my cheeks. "Why!"

"Come now dear, you know I didn't want to kill him. You're more useful to me in the GRH making beautiful babies," she says.

"I'm gonna kill ya!" I scream.

Her smile widens as she lays a hand on my shoulder. Nails scratch my arm and leave a thin trail down my bicep. I flinch and swing at her, sending her skittering. Dark, glittering eyes morph into a furry black mask, peering at me with gray ears and a twitching, wet nose.

"Mischief?" I reach out a hand in confusion. "Wha–?" Sharp teeth clamp down on my finger.

"Ahh, shit! What the hell!" Mischief's mouth opens wide, and he licks his lips. Teeth elongate and his paws grow sharp, wicked claws. A sinister growl rumbles through his body, standing his hair on end. Somehow, he's grown larger, and I've shrunk to the size of a mouse, about to be his dinner.

"N-no. No!" Adrenaline jerks my legs to life and I stand, tripping up the stairs in a frantic race for safety. Slamming the door behind me, I press my back against it.

Wood splinters and explodes around me.

Massive claws rake the door, puncturing through to the inside. It bulges inward, a pregnant belly about to pop.

Run! Get out of here!

When I turn the far wall of the hut is gone, open to the woods of the forest. My bare feet slap the frozen soil and I stumble on sticks and rocks hidden under the leaves. Legs pumping as fast as I can, chest burning, throat wheezing, the world blurs. The light in the distance is the glow of the Free Territories. I'm gonna make it, I'm almost there. Everything I have pours into one last sprint. Sun warms my clammy skin when I burst through the leaves and out into the sun.

Oh fuck.

It's so tall. My eyes travel up and up and up. The Iron Divide must be as high as the Brass Mountains. It stands silent and brazen. Unyielding. Impenetrable. How the hell am I supposed to get past that? I shuffle forward on weak, shaking legs and place a hand on the concrete. Crumbling, rough patches disfigure its surface. Pressing my forehead against it, I squint through a crack at eye level. Verdant fields stretch toward the horizon, bathed in warm golden hues. The Free Territories are right there, so close, yet so far away.

"Griff?"

Her concerned voice floods me with relief as I spin. Rei's hair is backlit in the honeyed-yellow of sunset, in stark contrast to the twisted, ominous forest behind her. There's a softness to her big brown eyes, mirroring our wild and passionate time together. She holds out a hand to me, giving me control, allowing me the choices I've so often had forced upon me.

Trusting me.

Empowering my desire in a way that belongs to me.

Only me.

"Griff," she calls, "we need to go back." She splays her hopeful fingers wide, urging me to hurry, to decide, to pick her.

"I–", the word sputters and dies in my throat. The darkness encroaches, wrapping around her. Wind whips and sweeps her hair into furious disarray. Shadows encompass her face, leaving two gleaming silvery orbs in swirling blackness.

"The Authority needs you," a harsh, foreign voice demands, contorting in rage. "Come here!"

"I'm not going back!"

The Iron Divide digs into my shoulders with lumpy, cracked, concrete fingers. There's nowhere to go, no escape. I'm trapped. That thing is not Rei anymore, it's the Authority. What it does to them, how it warps and corrupts, lies and destroys.

"You can and you will!" The figure stretches and writhes until Commander Lynx stands in its place. "I'm putting you back where you belong."

Her hand raises, and she's holding a gun.

*Bang!*

The bullet hits me in the gut, burrowing deep beneath my flesh. Pain radiates outwards in piercing, punctuated slashes. Blood and pus cover my slick palms.

"Argh!" Hoarse, raw screams jolt me from the agonizing misery. It's me, I'm screaming.

Fuck!

The bed is soaking wet. My hand knocks into something hard. Oh, is that my canteen? With shaking fingers, I unscrew the top and drink until it's empty. My mouth tastes like sour bile and my stomach is swollen and hot, like it could split any minute. The last embers of a fire crackle low in the wood stove, no longer enough to chase away the chill invading the room. Gotta put more logs in before it goes out.

Get up. My arms and legs rebel, refusing to listen, even my groan is hardly a whisper. Muscles ache and spasm, fading as fast as I am. The pressure in my head is trying to pop my eyeballs out from the inside. The beams of the rafters dance and cross in wild lines, they won't stop spinning. My stomach roils and I dry heave, crying out at the debilitating pain.

I'm so tired. So, so tired.

Everything hurts.

Hot tears stream from the corner of my eyes, my breath rattles and wheezes in my throat. I tried, I really did. But I can't any longer. Sleep is overtaking me, dragging me into oblivion where there is no pain, no misery, no Rei. There's no more fight left in me.

Rei was the first choice I truly made for myself.

And now she'll be my last choice, too.

# 31

**Searching can reveal more than we intended to find.**

I t takes me a while to retrace my steps back to the house, to the edge of the water where I left my bag when my tether made those strange noises. Military issue boots sink into the soft shore, squishing when I stop at the spot I tried to skip rocks the way Mara taught me. It might as well be ages ago that I was here last.

My heart sinks into the pit of my stomach.

Oh no. No! It's gone.

Where is it? Damnit! It has to be here somewhere! I race up and down the muddy edge of the bank. Nothing. Could the water have risen high enough to reach where I'd left it? The glassy surface offers no answers no matter how hard I peer at it.

*Beep boop! Beep boop!*

Bless the mother! My mouth pops open as a blue light of my tether flickers to life beneath the skin of my palm. No freaking way. Not again.

I shake my head and pull in a shuddering breath. Whatever's going on with this damn thing will have to wait. My bag's not here, and

Griff still needs me. This can't be the end, there has to be another way. Turning in a slow circle, I take one last look.

A metallic gleam catches my eye.

My car!

The windshield is gone, the arrow still stuck through the driver's seat, one door open toward the edge of the woods. It's only been a week yet a thick pile of leaves litters the ground, covering the tires. Maybe I'll find something useful inside. I reach the passenger side and place a hand on the roof, leaning toward the glove box.

A sinister rattling noise stops me cold. The coppery head of the snake rises from the seat. Its black tongue flicks back and forth and its whipping tail threatens, filling me with paralyzing fear. Time slows, stretches, narrows.

Don't move. Hold your breath. Both our lives depend on it.

The rattlesnake sways, weaving its neck, standing its ground. Great, just great. How the heck am I getting myself outta this? I wrack my brain and take inventory. Pulling the knife won't do any good. Even if I could stab the damn thing, the chances of doing so without getting bitten are slim to none. I have Griff's backpack behind me, but as soon as I move it'll strike, making it essentially useless. Besides, dropping it on the snake won't kill it, only piss it off more.

Back up, that's the best answer. But the snake might find my movement threatening. The leaves underneath me certainly don't help, either. How do I get away without making any freaking noise?

The snake flicks its tongue, lowering itself back to the seat, coiling up in place. The rattle falls still. Beady black eyes watch me, full of caution.

I can't hold my breath any longer. My adrenaline's fading fast. I'm so tired. In a perfect world I would lie down and sleep right where I stood, rattlesnake be damned. If I don't move soon, I'm gonna lose my nerve. Keeping my focus pinned on the snake, I inch my nearest foot off the ground. When it doesn't stir, I slide it back as far as I can without losing my balance. Gingerly, I lower my toe.

A single leaf crunches and the snake rattles, but remains coiled. Crap! Wait for the rattling to stop before I lower my heel. With agonizing patience I take my time, shifting my weight back. Repeating the process is a master class exercise in bodily control. One step, two, three. Easing myself out of the target area, placing my toe down before rocking back onto my heel.

Well, maybe. This should be far enough, right? Yes? It's now or never.

I launch myself from the car.

Behind me there's a furious hiss and rattle. Run! Don't look back, it won't change anything. The ominous rattle grows faint as I sprint for the lake house.

"Damn, that was close." I skid to a halt when I reach the open front door, leaning on my knees to catch my breath. There's a terrible stitch in my side and my ankle's not happy.

At last I stand, wiping strands of hair from my sweaty forehead, and enter Mara's house. Broken glass crunches under foot, the rubbery soles peeling from a floor covered in sticky, sugary syrup.

*Beep boop! Beep boop!*

Compared to Griff's hut, the stark, standard issue Authority furniture is worth a year's rations. And now I know where he is and what a loyal Enforcer in my position should do.

How many lottery tickets is a life worth?

My heart contracts, skipping a beat, and my fingers clench the material of my shirt below my breasts. Griff may be an arrogant asshole at times, but he was also protective, dependable, caring, and strong. It couldn't be wrong or selfish to want those things for myself, could it? But what did that make me for him?

Poison, that's what.

And his only chance of survival.

Slinging Griff's bag onto the kitchen counter, I rummage through every drawer and cabinet, searching for anything useful. A dusty stack of canned beans, an extra water bottle which I refill with the rest, and a pair of scissors make it into the bag. But no bandages, no medicine.

No antibiotics.

"Dammit, come on, there has to be something in here I can use." Heading down the hall I go straight into the bathroom. Like the one in our apartment, the mirror pulls open to reveal a hidden compartment in the wall. There's three pill bottles, one is for pain, another for cold and flu, the last for upset stomach. The bottle of mouthwash might be the closest thing I'm likely to find to alcohol. All four go into the bag.

Next, I head upstairs to the bedrooms. Yanking open every wobbly or stuck dresser drawer, checking under the beds and searching every closet takes too long. He's dying out there and there's nothing here besides a handful of old clothes. I take two t-shirts to rip apart for bandages. Everything else is useless.

"Dammit! There have to be antibiotics somewhere." I grind my teeth together and rub my tired eyes. Exhaustion and my stand off with the snake are taking their toll, dragging at my sluggish limbs. The faster I get back, the better.

The nursery and a small shed I spotted behind the house from a bedroom window are the only two places I haven't checked. I turn the handle but it doesn't give. Huh? Strange. Who locks a nursery?

Digging into the backpack I pluck out a can. Yeah, this should work. I swing at the doorknob with a growl until it clatters to the floor, denting the hardwood. Ugh, it's still stuck. Shouldering into it forces it open a few measly inches. It takes slamming my full body weight against it to win several more. Boxes topple through the narrow gap, tumbling into the hall. There's more stacked inside the gloomy interior, clearly the source of the door's resistance.

I rip one open, finding textbooks, strange schematics, mathematical calculations and medical journals. What is this stuff?

There's a lot more stacked inside. Luckily the tight opening I cleared is wide enough to slip through. Ewww. Get them off me! Spiderwebs cling to my nose and catch in my hair. I'm sure they appreciate my squeals and frantically waving arms. Something cold and stringy tangles around my wrist. A hard tug on the dangling chain triggers on a single bare lightbulb.

Who needs this many boxes? They take up most of the space, stacked from floor to ceiling. Amidst the junk there's a broken stool, a long white lab coat, and a lot of strange looking scientific equipment laid out on a cluttered countertop. Is that a microscope? I haven't seen one of those since entry school. Who did all this stuff belong to? My feet slip and slide as I clamber across the mountains of cardboard, randomly yanking them open, finding unrecognizable garbage, shoving the box aside and trying again.

Oh, that's extremely promising.

There's a dark metal box with a faded white plus sign at the far end of the room, partially buried under a stack of papers. Balancing on teetering, dusty boxes and shoving aside a rusty ironing board, I reach the target. It rattles when I pick it up. That's a good sign. The lid refuses to budge, but slamming it down on the counter top does the trick. Inside I find gauze, bandaids, and an antibiotic ointment.

"Yes!"

A device whirrs on the countertop, lights blinking. Well, that's new. Not sure what it is and there's no way to turn it on or off, either.

Beep boop! Beep boop!

Dammit! I startle and it slips from my hand with a clatter, a long crack fracturing the surface. The blinking light goes dark. Yeah, that was weird, all right, best not to mess with anything else. I gather the first aid kit and pull off a piece of paper stuck to the bottom. The text is faded with age, but I can make out the title at the top: Technologically Enabled Tracking of Heritable Embryonic Reproduction.

"Whatever the hell that is," I mutter. It's a harder struggle back across box mountain, especially with one hand now occupied. As soon as squish outta the nursery I empty the contents of the first aid kit into Griff's backpack.

It's time to head back.

Picking it up, exhaustion overwhelms me, and the hallway spins. My hand finds the wall, steading myself. It's suddenly hard to keep my eyes open. When was the last time I slept?

"I just need to sit down for a minute," I mumble into the empty silence. Shaky steps bring me back downstairs and I wobble over to the couch, flopping onto the cushion. My ankle thanks me when I unlace my boot and pull it off, massaging the worst part. My chin dips and I slump, jerking upright when I nearly tumble over. A huge yawn escapes my lips. Lowering my hand from my mouth, my fingers brush the surface of a cold, hard box on the side table.

A robotic feminine voice chips, "you have five new messages."

"Rei? I'm sure you're arrived by now. It's getting late, but please call me once you've settled in. Did you remember to pack your sweater?

It gets cold out there at night. Anyway, I know you're still mad at me. Let's talk when you get back."

*Beep.* "You have four new messages."

"Hi Rei! I hope you're enjoying the house. The lake is beautiful this time of the year, especially with all the leaves changing colors. I forgot to tell you there's–ahh, bless the mother–this kid has been kicking the crap out of me lately. I think she's eager to meet her auntie! Did I tell you I can't see my feet when I stand up anymore? Ugh, this belly is so uncomfortable and my back hurts all the time, too. Sorry, you don't want to listen to me complain. Relax and take some time to yourself. Talk soon, bye!"

*Beep.* "You have three new messages."

"Rei? Are you there? Please pick up the phone.... Rei! It's been three days. If you're mad at me, fine. Be mad at me, but at least call me back. Alright?"

*Beep.* "You have two new messages."

"Where are you Rei? Your mom's calling me multiple times a day and it's driving me nuts. If you don't want to talk to your mom, that's fine, I understand. I told her you needed some space, but you're not answering me either. Crap–there she is, calling me again. That's the fourth time today. I can't keep covering for you much longer. Wait–did I remember to tell you to flip the breaker if the phone's acting weird? I swear one day I'll figure out what keeps overloading the circuit. Ahh! Bless the mother, was that a contraction? Well...either I just pissed myself or my water broke, I gotta go."

*Beep.* "You have one new message."

"Rei Koss, you pick up this phone right now! Do you hear me? Where are you? Mara lost her baby boy. She's a wreck and she told me she's been lying about talking to you. What's going on? Rei! Call me back! You need to come home right now. Do you hear me? Rei! Damn this girl!"

*Beep.* "No new messages."

# 32

## REI

**Sometimes, the cage you've built is the
only thing holding you together.**

I don't know how long I slept, sleep deprivation dragging me
under, but the sun sits high in the sky. Hopefully flipping
the breaker fixed the phone. I suck in a breath and bite my lip,
pressing it to my ear.

Yes! There's a dial tone.

For the first time there was something in my mother's voice
beyond distant, dismissive banter. Her terror was such a real
emotion. Is it possible, after all these years, that she does care?

It's ringing and there's a click on the other end of the line.
"Hi–"

"Mom, it's me–"

"–you've reached Naomi and Rei Koss. Please leave a message."
Oh, she must be at work, but it's been so long since I called her
there that I don't remember the number.

*Beep.*

"Mom, it's Rei. Before you get mad and freak out, I'm okay. I
found–err–had an accident, but I'm fine." I hesitate. There's more
I want to say but my throat constricts, hung up on the future

stretching before me, and how it's tearing me apart. "I don't know when I'll be home. Bye," I choke out and hang up.

Mara's number is the next thing I punch into the phone. The line rings until it switches to voicemail, but there's no space for me to leave a message. At that moment, I feel the weight of my solitude. The house is so still, peaceful even, but it doesn't bring me any comfort.

Quite the opposite.

Stop wasting time, I have to go, Griff needs me. Grabbing his backpack, I swing it over my shoulder. There's a full day's trek ahead of me.

Closing the front door and locking it behind me seems silly, it's so benign, so ordinary. Things I took for granted—food, water, electricity, heat—I did without a second thought. But those same things are life or death for Griff.

I flick open the compass and orient myself to the northeast. I can't dawdle or I might not make it there in time. My chest squeezes tightly at the thought. A little over a week ago, I wouldn't have thought twice about hauling him into the Authority. But now....

Leaves crunch underfoot as I jog toward the woods.

Ignoring the twinge in my ankle, I pick up the pace, grateful for daily runs on the MMZ track for the first time since I signed up for service. The Authority took care of us, maintained peace and order, and provided stability in a broken, failing world. They were fighting for a cure, not for us, but for all of humanity.

Who was I to hesitate to do what I'd been training for? Since entry school it'd been drilled into my head: survivors are dangerous carriers of the virus and the water is contaminated. Only our tether could protect us from the virus in the water.

But it's not true.

My steps stumble and falter. I slow to a walk, holding a hand to the stitch in my side.

Take Mara's baby, for instance. Damn! How could I have forgotten that part of the message? Mara lost her baby boy? How? Of course she'd be devastated. But her doctor said it was a girl. No one had male children in the Authority. The Collective Voice Broadcast only reported the birth of female children. Wouldn't a boy end up in containment, like Griff, and every other survivor?

"But Mara isn't sick. How could her son carry the virus? Wouldn't taking baby boys to containment expose them to the Heart Blight because the infected survivors are there?" My mind whirls to the low drum of swaying branches and leaves in the growing wind.

There's no denying the USB drive Griff carries hidden around his neck. Everything he described about how he escaped must mean a scientist inside the Authority helped him and his father. The Sympathizer's bombing the transport and the picture of Griff's brother in Dr. Martina's case can't be a coincidence. Why? What did the Sympathizers want? There's something going on here, and it has a creeping sense of foreboding raising the hairs on the back of my neck.

The wheels in my head keep spinning as I break back into a run, feet pounding through the underbrush. I want to outrun them, the thoughts. The doubts. Questioning the Authority sets off the same warning bells in my head that call us to formation in the barracks. Sure, there were things I didn't like or even disagreed with, everyone had their issues with something or another. But this was something new. Different.

Traitors hang from the Suppression Line on swollen, rotting necks. And I slept with the enemy.

No one can ever know...about him, about us.

Going back, not turning him in, is a mission of assured self-destruction and I can't help myself.

A strong, icy wind blows through the trees and there's a low rumble in the distance. I look up and frown. The sky is growing dark ahead of me. There's a storm coming. Lightning streaks across the sky. My hair whips around my head and into my face.

Great, just great. As if things can't get any worse. The bag bangs against my shoulders as I run, ignoring the growing pains in my calves and my raspy, winded breaths. Every step feels slower, and it takes so much more effort, going in this direction. A bruise is forming along my lower back where the jumbled contents keep smashing into me.

How long have I been running?

My tether lets out a horrible, high-pitched screech. The sound turns my blood cold. It can only mean one thing...it's working again. It's a five minute warning. Rain is coming.

"No! No! Mother bless it, why now?"

Thunder rumbles overhead. Sticks and debris pepper my skin as the wind whips with a fury. The temperature drops as the storm continues to roll in. I have to find shelter. Now!

Faster! Go faster!

There has to be somewhere I can shield myself from the elements. A place I can stay dry until it passes. Feet pound the ground, sprinting at speeds I've never imagined possible before. There has to be something around here I can use! A hollow long, a ditch, something!

Fat raindrops splatter the ground. Rainbow chasing, what Mara and I stupidly did for a dangerous thrill, has never felt more horrifying or desperate than this moment. My tether lights up deep forest green.

Sixty seconds.

The downpour intensifies. It's so hard to see where I'm going.

Green lightens.

My head swivels left and right, calculating trajectories and possibilities. The rain is freezing, becoming sleet, the temperature plummeting.

It's turning yellow. I can't die here, I won't!

My boots skid on the slippery ground and go out from under me. I sprawl on my hands and knees.

Gold appears, growing in intensity.

Lifting my head, I see something promising in the distance.

The yellow is bleeding to orange.

I climb to my feet and scramble toward the outcropping of rocks. There's a narrow gap between the largest rocks, forming a small, natural shelter.

Red. I'm outta time.

Pulling the backpack off, I turn sideways and shove myself into the breach. The material of my shirt rips, skin scrapes, the backpack catches.

Black swirls.

"Aargh!" I scream, pushing, pulling, dragging myself through the crevice, tumbling in with a mighty shove.

The light on my tether blinks off. I'm no longer being pelted by the icy sleet. Lungs suck in as much air as my mouth allows in deep, shaky, gulping gasps. My teeth chatter and it's painful to curl and uncurl my frozen fingers. If I couldn't see them in front of my face I wouldn't know they existed. One threat is being replaced by another.

It's so cold.

I glance around, taking in my rocky cover. It's wide enough to sit if I curl my knees to my chest and use the backpack like a chair. Bits of feathers and bone litter one corner. Whatever small critter was using the place, I hope it doesn't come back soon. Fire, I need a fire. Sifting through Griff's backpack I find the tin. Numb fingers don't want to cooperate. It takes several tries to pick up the box and a few more to pry it open.

As my body temperature plummets, my limbs grow warm and heavy. Hypothermia, that's what Griff called it.

"Dammit!" There's no wood. Even if I get a fire started, there's nothing I can burn to keep it going. Fire first, then wood. Even if that means...more rainbow chasing.

At the hut, Griff's firepit is surrounded by large rocks. But here, wedged in this space, there's nothing to safely separate me from the fire. Digging a hole against the back wall is what I settle for, using three sides as a natural barrier, leaving only the side closest to me potentially exposed.

Worry about burning to death later.

Dry leaves, bones, and any small sticks I can find go into the hole. When it's full with everything I can find, I grab the flint. Placing the downy feathers and bits of fur on top, I strike an ember on the first try. Blowing gently causes the fire to catch. A thin, yellow flame dances in my makeshift campfire.

Luckily it's such a small area the flame heats it quickly. Rubbing myself all over helps the feeling return. It takes a few minutes before my fingers tingle, like something is jabbing them with a million sharp needles. My toes are the next to undergo the same, uncomfortable sensation.

It's still somewhat bearable with the fire keeping the temperature outside above freezing. Panic grows as I watch the flame burn lower. Getting it started again will be much harder once it goes out. Time to find some wood.

Gathering my wits about me, I slide back through the narrow crevasse. The worst of the storm has died down, but there's still a steady, icy drizzle coming down. Green flares from my tether as I scuttle around, picking up as many sticks and pieces of wood as I can find. Orange threatens when I shove the pieces of wood through the narrow fracture and force my way in behind them.

Of all the times for my tether to start working again. Bitter anguish scraps my throat raw.

The flame is low when I add a small stick. "Come on, come on, just give me a few more minutes," I plead. The stick is causing white, cloying smoke to billow, stinging my eyes.

If the flame goes out now, if the stick doesn't catch on fire, I'll likely freeze to death. Crap! The flame grows smaller and smaller.

"No, no, no, don't do this to me." I'm shivering again, my fingers and toes tingling and burning at the same time. I grab the flint and strike another ember. It sparks in the fading flame, continuing to shrink until it goes out.

"Mother bless it! No! Come on! Don't do this to me!" I strike the flint again, showering the firepit with embers. "Come back!" My attempts grow frenzied. "Burn, damn you!"

In the fading light of the day I strike the flint in rapid succession. Each time I glimpse flashes of my life before my eyes. A young girl tottering down the city street holding her mother's hand, running through the streets with a laughing Mara, going to school and struggling to hold an armful of books with lines criss-crossing my palms for breaking the rules, entering the Authority's boot camp and getting my ass kicked on the mat, the world spinning upside down as the truck in front of ours explodes.

*Boom!*

A crack of lightning bathes my small shelter in a flash of blinding white light. I shriek and shield my face.

It's not a bomb, it's not a bomb.

When I first entered these woods, I had no clue what I was getting myself into. All I could think about was escaping to the lake house, putting my failures behind me, earning the lottery tickets I so desperately wanted. Now here I was, continuing to be as useless and pathetic as ever.

Hadn't I learned anything?

When I at last lower my hand, I burst out into slow, cynical laughter.

The stick is on fire.

# 33

## REI

**Uncertainty is a spy among us, uncovering the truth, no matter the cost.**

Please, let him be okay. I've lost the rest of the day to the storm. When the rain stops, I sigh with relief and squeeze out of my hidey-hole, inching my way out into the night. Cold rock and clods of dirt shower my head. At least I can feel my fingers and toes again.

Beyond the outcropping, the ground is slick with sleet and patches of ice. I pick my way through the inky black, boots stumbling on damp foliage, sticks, and rocks. It's too dangerous to run, but I march as fast as I dare, pulling out the compass when my eyes adjust to reorient myself. The footing improves when I stumble upon a narrow, worn track covered from the worst of the ice by the dense canopy of the trees above. It's safe enough for me to take off running again, the light growing around me with the first hints of dawn.

Will I make it back in time? I shake my head. No, worrying won't help anything. Hurry! My strides lengthen. Everything will be okay, he will be okay. I force down the void clawing out of my chest, squeezing it tightly.

When Griff is safe, I have to go.

What's the harm in one loose survivor? I wasn't sick. It's not like he wanted to announce his presence to anyone. Quite the opposite, in fact. Besides, he was leaving, too.

The sense of unease and questions I have about the Authority's motives nag like one of Alyssa's relentless drills. Ugh! This is so frustrating. None of it makes sense. What would the Authority gain by telling so many lies? Okay, so put myself in their shoes. Civvies depended on the Authority for food, shelter, order, and reproduction. Soldiers were incentivized with additional lottery tickets and tasked with maintaining the peace amongst the civvies. The best of those soldiers were hand-picked by Commander Lynx to become Enforcers, responsible for the security of the GRH and tasked with the most dangerous missions. Director Lynx orchestrated all parts of the Authority, using her daughter and grand-daughter to full tactical advantage. And in every single one of those scenarios one thing was crystal clear.

Control. That's what.

It's like Griff said all along, when I didn't want to believe it, when I wasn't ready to face reality glaring me right in the face. If I put myself in the shoes of Alyssa, or Commander Lynx, or even the Director, in charge of the thousands of women in the Authority, was civvie compliance. Before, I thought he was crazy to suggest there was information on the USB that he and his father smuggled out of the Authority. Now, I wasn't so sure.

If the Authority created the Heart Blight virus and the information got into the wrong hands...add that to the growing unrest and increased Sympathizer activity. What if the Iron Divide didn't protect us from the desolate wasteland of the Free Territories? My whole life could be a load of fairy tales spoon-fed to keep me and the rest of the civvies in check.

The fewer the questions, the better. Anything to keep us tethered.

I was twelve years old and at school the day my period started. The overseer asked for a volunteer to go up to the board and solve the math question. My scrawny arm shot up into the air and several of the other girls snickered at my enthusiasm.

"Yes, Rei. Here, you try." The overseer held out a piece of chalk and I beamed as I hopped up from my desk and went to accept it.

"Ew!"

"Look at her pants!"

"Oh my gosh, are you dying, Rei?" Mara asked.

The chorus of my classmate's voices and Mara's concern prompted me to turn around. I couldn't see the red mark on the back of my pants, but the spot on my chair was large and visible.

"Now, now, that's enough!" Smack! The overseer whacked her discipline stick against the wall. Every girl in the classroom fell silent and pinned their eyes straight ahead. Including me.

Our class overseer, an older woman with graying wisps of hair curling at her temple, was one of many culls in the Authority. I always wondered why she was so keen to hit us with one hand and hug us with the other.

"Come here Rei," she grabbed my scrawny arm. Her grip left bruises as she dragged me across the room. She pulled the hall pass, a stretchy yellow bracelet, from her pocket and slipped it over my wrist.

"Go straight to the clinic," she said, shoving me over the threshold. The door shut in my face.

I shook myself out of my stupor and hurried toward the clinic. The nurse overseer inside didn't look up when I knocked. Lacing my fingers together, I waited patiently for her to recognize me. Her discipline stick was buried under the paperwork on her desk, easily within reach if I didn't follow protocol.

"Yes?" she said, looking up at last, glasses falling down the end of her nose. Her pen rolled to the edge of her desk, but she slammed her hand down and stopped it before it fell.

"Um. I guess I'm bleeding?" I turned around so she could see the back of my pants.

"Come in. I'll get you a clean pair of pants." She stood and rooted through a cabinet in the back. "Here," she thrust a clean pair of pants at me, "hold these and stand right here."

She flopped down in her chair so hard the legs groaned from her weight. One after the other, she pulled open desk drawers and collected supplies. Some things I didn't recognize. The metal device was similar to a gun but its odd shape differed from the ones soldiers and Enforcers carried.

"Give me your hand," she said, grabbing my wrist and pulling it closer, setting it flat on the edge of the desk.

I did as she commanded. A cold, wet, alcohol swab wiped over the bump of my tether. There was a crackling noise as she unwrapped a small packet and loaded a needle into the strange metal device.

She took a firm hold of my wrist, aligned the muzzle of the device over my tether, and pulled the trigger.

*Click!*

"Ahh!" I cried out when it punctured my skin. A shiny bead of blood welled in its place.

The nurse set the injector down and pressed a piece of gauze to my hand to stop the bleeding. "Hold it there for a minute. Let me tape it down. There, that's better. You can let go now. Leave this bandage on for at least 10 minutes. You can get changed now."

"What was that?" I asked and bit my lip, expecting several good whacks for questioning out of turn.

The nurse overseer pulled off her gloves and dumped them into a trashcan. "Just a little adjustment to your tether now that you've become a woman. No worries dear, you won't bleed again until you get reproductive approval. You can change back there."

She pointed to a curtained off area. I changed my pants and returned to class, where a clean chair waited for me behind my desk.

A stick snaps underfoot and I jump in surprise, my wandering attention jerked back to the woods. "Hah, you're freaking yourself out for no reason." I mutter with a dry chuckle.

I lift my gaze and my mouth falls open. The dark hut looms in the distance, the front door wide open.

"Griff!" The tormented cry rips from my mouth before my feet can respond. I slip and slide, nearly falling, in my mad rush forward.

"No, no, please, no...Griff!"

The stairs creak as my boots hammer the steps and I clamber inside. Blankets litter the ground. The wood stove is out cold. Trinkets from the shelves above the sink basin scatter the floor. A frozen puddle of water glistens below the window.

Worst of all, the bed is empty. Oh no.

"Griff!" I spin. "Griff, where are you?"

Racing for the threshold, I skid to a halt at the sound of a groan.

"Griff?" The trembling voice is unrecognizable as my own.

A pale hand emerges from the pile of blankets on the floor. Relief drums like the down-pouring storm last night. Sinking to the floor, I drag the blankets away from him, revealing a clammy, flushed, sweaty face.

"Rei?" He asks with dry, cracked, bleeding lips in a voice barely above a whisper. He's burning up.

"Shh, it's me. I'm here." I cradle his head in my lap and my tether flares green, the protective barrier preventing our skin from truly touching.

Dammit!

I release him and dig the medicine out of the backpack, piling pills into my hand. "Open your mouth, good, like that. I'm going to give you some water. You have to swallow, okay? These will make you feel better. No. Take one more drink. Just one more. There, that's better."

Griff groans and his eyelids flutter. It's like an icebox in here. When I'm done and the fire is blazing, I shut the front door and put water on to boil. I need to clean his wounds immediately.

"Griff? Hey, come on, don't go to sleep on me. Wake up. Help me get you back on the bed. You're too heavy for me to lift by myself. Come on, up you go."

A sweaty, hot arm drapes my shoulder. He's so weak he doesn't notice my tether flaring to life again. Even with him supporting some of his weight, it's a struggle to get him a few steps to the bed, my tether turning yellow, deepening to orange. Collapsing on the bed, he groans and shivers. The old bandages on his chest are slimy with pus and tinged pink with blood. I pull them off and grimace at the sight underneath. Angry, inflamed skin puckers on the edges of the wounds. An overflowing latrine in the height of summer time. I gag and slap a hand over my mouth to keep myself from throwing up on him.

Digging out one of the old t-shirts I found at the lake house, I dump it into the pot of boiling water.

"Ahh!" Griff screams and passes out the moment I touch the damp material to his wounds.

"Dammit, I'm sorry." I choke out with a sob. "I have to get this clean."

With him unconscious, I make speedy work. My lip curls with disgust as I dig deep, cleaning out the infection, until the tissue wells with healthy, pink blood. When it looks better, I repeat the process a second, and then a third time.

Now for the worst part.

Griff's eyes snap open and his scream shakes the window the moment I pour the mouthwash disinfectant across his stomach. The liquid bubbles and fizzes and foams as the alcohol content battles it out with the infection. He throws his head back, mouth wide, face going beet red, eyes bulging, arms flailing.

"I'm sorry," I cry, knocking away the arm weakly swinging for me, green light bathing his face. "It'll make you feel better, I promise." I pour more onto the wound. "There, I'm done."

His body goes rigid, shakes violently, and he screams again. Both eyes roll back into his head and he passes out a second time.

The other old t-shirt tears into strips with a slice of Griff's hunting knife. At last, I slather the antibiotic ointment on and bind his chest with the fresh bandages. Slowly, his breathing gets deeper, relaxes. His skin is still flushed and sweaty. I trail my fingers across the bumpy scar on his collarbone, made smooth by the barrier separating us, watching my tether change colors, forcing us apart, blocking out the warmth of his skin.

Bless the mother, this is torture. I'm cauterized, cut off from all sensation, from him.

His cheeks look sunken, and he's lost weight in the two days I was gone. Even though he's passed out, I didn't realize how much I missed his company. Lowering my head, green flare of light be damned, I press my forehead against his. The bristly stubble on his face should tickle my chin, but now–nothing.

There's a scratching noise at the door. I lift my head and listen. When I hear the chittering, I stand and let Mischief inside. He jumps onto the bed and curls up beside Griff, his wet little nose bumping against his shoulder.

"I guess you didn't like being locked out, huh, buddy? Either that or you just like cuddling with whoever is on the bed." I say with a smile. "Well, he's not out of the woods yet."

I shut the door and spread most of the furs on the floor so they'll dry. How long has it been since we last ate? Locating a can of corn in Griff's supplies that I left behind in the hut, I open it and eat half the contents. Griff can have the rest when he wakes up.

He *will* wake up.

Desire wells, urging me to curl up on the bed beside him, to hold him close, let my heartbeat match his. Instead I stretch out on damp furs on the floor. The pallor of his skin is better and his color is returning. I'll bet his fever is dropping, too. My eyes go to the necklace around his neck. The griffin must have taken many weeks to carve, requiring a great level of skill and care.

If the USB drive contains damning information about the Authority, it would give Commander Lynx a reason to kill him—a motive. The Commander I knew was a hard, relentless woman. She would get things her way, consequences be damned.

Griff's fingers close around the necklace. His bright green eyes are clouded with pain as he looks at me on the floor. Besides the discomfort, there's something else in the intensity of his gaze. I want to kiss him, to hold him, to touch him.

"Welcome back. Are you hungry?" I ask.

"Yeah, thirsty, too." He says. "I didn't think I'd ever see ya again."

"You just worry about feeling better, okay?"

He nods. "Come up here with me."

I shake my head. "No, I can't. Besides, you need to rest."

"I don't mind," Griff murmurs, studying my face, frowning at whatever he sees there.

"But I mind. Let me get you something to eat."

I feel so safe here, like a piece of me that's been missing these past two days has finally slid back into place. But I can't stay, I have to go home. The Authority never has to know about this, about him, about us. That much I can do for him in return for all the things he's done for me. What I can't do is let myself get attached. This–whatever it is–could never work anyways.

It's forbidden.

Like my glowing tether threatens, I need to put distance between us.

At the very least, I can stay long enough to make sure he's going to be okay without me.

# 34

# GRIFF

**The lines between us blur when something makes us question our beliefs.**

For once, the heat isn't radiating off of me, but is instead coming from the body pressed against me. Hair is tickling my nose. I reach a hand and brush it away, letting my fingers tangle in her soft fur. Fur? My eyes pop open, finding Mischief pressed into the hollow of my neck.

Where's Rei? It wasn't a dream, was it?

My head jerks, eyes searching wildly, going still when they land on her slender frame curled in the furs on the floor. I didn't expect to see her again. She finally had the freedom she'd been fighting for since day one.

Why'd she come back for me?

She stirs but doesn't wake. There are dark circles under her eyes and she looks like she's been through hell. But she came back, like she said she would. Conflicted feelings war within me. Rei wasn't the evil, ruthless woman who killed my father. Sure, she was stubborn, demanding, and packed a hell of a mean left hook. Beneath that tough exterior there was something soft and vulnerable, something as tormented and broken inside as I was. Maybe that's what first attracted me to her when she found me in the lake house.

Did I look at her and see parts of myself?

Sitting up, I wince as bandages chafe my raw skin. The difference between how I feel today and yesterday is beyond comparison. I stand on shaky legs and find my bag by the door. Inside I find the bounty she returned with. I can't read the pill bottles, but they rattle when I shake them. I'll have to wake her up to figure out which one to take.

My knees wobble and I lean against the wall to steady myself. I pull out a canteen and drink until it's empty. Despite the corn she fed me earlier, my stomach is still growling and the can of beans I found is calling to it. Using my supplies would be a dumb idea–no, I'll save these for when we're desperate for food.

We.

I shake my head and push off the wall. Not we, just me.

As soon as I'm well enough, I need to leave. The sad, distant look she gave me and finding her sleeping on the floor says it all. She'll go back to the Authority. I'll need all the head starts I can get. I curl my fist around my necklace and feel the hard ridges dig into the palm of my skin.

I don't want to leave her. She could come with me. The sense of loneliness grows as I watch her sleeping. I stumble back to the bed on wobbly legs and sink onto the edge. My body remembering the pleasant feeling of trailing my fingers up her shoulder, along her neck, stopping at the delicate cup of her cheek. Pleasure that wasn't forced or demanded, but given freely. And it belonged to me, not to the Authority, not to anyone else.

For the first time, the sharp bark lurching between my ears isn't my Father. No, this dark and possessive voice belongs to me.

*She's mine.*

# 35

## Perseverance is a hopeful game of trial and error.

Her innocent gaze pins me with large, soft, brown eyes, like I mean her no harm, but I do. The doe lowers her long neck and noses through the icy ground in search of a few shoots of grass. Her breath mirrors mine, little white puffs visible in the frosty air. Easing the bow up, I draw the arrow back the way Griff taught me.

Inhale a deep breath and hold it. Steady your arm, lock the elbow. The bowstring snaps my wrist as I let go. Ouch, that stings! The shot goes wide and buries into the trunk of a tree beside my target. The doe bolts, leaping off into the woods, unscathed.

"Dammit! I really wish I had a gun right now." I rub at the red welt forming on my skin and go to retrieve the arrow. There's that strange symbol again. Griff said it was the way the Sympathizers marked safe passage. My finger traces the scar in the tree trunk, a triangle with the small circle inside. Who took the time to carve this here? Safe passage for who?

Using Griff's hunting knife I trace the triangle with the tip, scoring the lines deeper. Shavings tickle my nose and hurt my eyes when I blow them away. It was a lot easier to carve into the trunk than I thought it would be. Shoving the knife back into my belt, I sigh. Stop wasting the daylight hours.

Pushing away from the tree, I continue on. Two days have passed, and I still haven't had any luck hunting. The failures in my life seemed to pile as high as the Brass Mountains.

What's that sound? Water? The distraction is a welcome one, anything to snap me out of my tumultuous thoughts. Around the bend my eyes light up at the tall rocks bordering the spring. Yesterday I had no success finding my way here despite my best efforts. Our water supply was running dangerously low. This was just the pick me up I needed.

Leaning the bow against one of the large boulders, I climb over them and drop into the little gully where the fresh water gurgles. My tether lights up the moment I dunk a canteen under the spray. Crap. What'll I do if I can't drink this after boiling it?

The heaviness of the bottles in the backpack makes my shoulders ache as I leave the spring. Griff has such broad, muscular shoulders. Carrying all this water back and forth every few days might have something to do with that. How exhausting. I pick up the bow, groaning at the slight weight it adds to my already sore back.

"So hungry...." My stomach rumbles, agreeing with me. "I should have just eaten those beans. Griff be damned." I scowl at the memory of the argument we had yesterday. "I should have left yesterday." I grumble and kick at a loose stone on the ground as I find the correct heading on the compass and return to the hut. His wounds were healing nicely and this morning he stood for over five minutes without getting dizzy.

"Go hunting, he says. Check the traps, my ass. How am I supposed to find your stupid traps, Griff, huh? It took me two tries to even get to the spring. We're gonna starve before I actually catch anything out here."

Being out here, spending all day looking for something to eat, gives me a greater appreciation for Griff's efforts. This is hard, a lot harder than I thought it would be. Being such an impatient person didn't help much, either.

"Ugh, I give up." I stomp through the woods, plowing my way forward. He makes hunting, tracking, and scavenging look so easy.

Something small and hard hits the back of my neck.

"Ouch!" I rub at the spot and spin. There's a chittering noise in the tree behind me. It takes a few minutes for my eyes to find Mischief's masked face on the tree branch.

"Hey, be nice! I know you're hungry, I'm hungry, too. Instead of getting mad at me, why don't you do something useful and help me find dinner?"

Mischief's tiny black hands work in a flurry of movement and another acorn shoots at my forehead.

"Hey! I said be nice!" I step backwards and swat it away. My boot heel knocks into something and I nearly fall over backwards, arms pedaling to keep my balance.

"Ooh! A trap!" The rope rises out of the leaves on the ground like a snake, covered in bits of dirt and debris. I follow it from the tree trunk to a fat, limp rabbit hung on the other end.

A huge grin splits my face. I turn and beam at Mischief.

"Thank you!" I say, untying the rope from the rabbit's neck.

Laying it down, I slit the belly open. Ugh, so gross. I clean out its innards as best as I can. When I'm done, I tie the rabbit to my belt and retrace my steps to the hut.

"Griff! Look what Mischief helped me find! We're having rabbit for dinner."

He looks up from the bed when I enter. Although still sore, he looks more like himself and his fever hasn't returned. He gives me a fatigued smile.

"Ya call that skinning? There are big chunks missing."

I flip my hair over my shoulder and roll my eyes at him. "Do you want to eat or not? No complaining."

Soon the smell of rabbit meat cooking has my mouth watering. Mischief slips through the open window and climbs onto the counter, trying to steal pieces of the raw meat.

"Hey! Wait until we eat." I pick him up in my arms, cradling him like a newborn, scratching the silky fur behind his ears. "It'll be ready soon. I saw you left claw marks all over the front door. Guess you didn't like being locked out while your daddy was sick, huh?" He chitters and leans into my massaging fingertips until he squirms like a toddler to be let go.

"Did ya find the spring?" Griff asks.

"Yeah, it took me a while, but I found it. I refilled the empty water bottles. Here," I say, handing Griff food. He pats the bed beside him and scoots over to make room for me. "You're feeling much better."

He shovels food into his mouth and nods. "Yeah. It doesn't feel like something's sitting on my chest anymore."

"I'm glad." I take another bite of food, enjoying a full belly.

"You're leaving tomorrow, aren't ya?"

The spoon pauses halfway to my mouth. Metal clinks when it falls to the plate and I push the last few bites of rabbit around, no longer hungry. Saying the words out loud makes them seem so final. It's something I can't take back once I put it out there in the wild–it'll forever draw the line between us. I open my mouth and close it again.

How can I tell him I don't want to go, but that I have to? Nothing can adequately express how his light, smile, and care for me cauterizes the dark void in the pit of my chest.

"Yes," I choke out, fighting tears.

"Come with me. We'll go to the Free Territories together."

"I can't."

"Why not?"

"Because I'm no good for you. Don't you understand?"

"No. I don't. Explain it to me."

Dropping my eyes, ashamed to see his reaction, I whisper, "I'm training to become an Enforcer."

There, it's done, a scab ripped off a festering wound so it can finally heal. There's no going back. This will end us for good. Stab him with a truth so painful he'll leave tomorrow with no regrets. He deserves a life free from the abuse and shackles of the Authority.

He's better off without me.

"I know."

My head snaps up. "How?"

"I've told ya before, ya talk a lot when you're asleep."

"Oh...."

"I forgot to thank ya," he says.

"Huh? For what? Without your help, I would've bled out in the woods." It's embarrassing to admit. Soldiers should be strong enough to take care of themselves.

Griff chuckles. "For believing me. For coming back to me. For saving my life. I've hated women in the Authority for so long...and now they've saved me. Twice."

"Do you remember the name of the woman who helped you and your father escape?"

"All I remember is her red hair."

Mischief jumps up onto the bed, balancing on my leg as he walks toward me. He snatches the plate out of my hand, gobbles up the last few pieces of meat, and leaps away.

"Hey! Mischief!" Griff scolds, but I just laugh.

"It's okay, I was done anyway." Our eyes meet and my laughter fades, replaced by desire. "I'm going to miss you," Heat climbs up my neck, fanning my cheeks, turning red with my confession.

Griff lifts a hand, reaching to touch my cheek. He jerks back in surprise when my tether flares green. "What the fuck?"

"My tether's working again."

Fingers on my chin tip my head back. He cups my cheek and the green grows lighter. Griff's forehead wrinkles, furrows digging between his brows, turning yellow. He leans forward, brushing fingers over my lips, the hue deepening to gold, then orange.

Would I let him touch me until my tether turns black and I'm suppressed, lying dead in his arms?

Red flares and he releases me like he's been burned. "Shit, it's weird, we're touching but I can't feel ya. What is this? Why does it keep changing colors?"

"It's designed to protect us from the virus. When it turns black it releases a deadly suppression drug. They say a corpse can't get infected with the Heart Blight."

Griff's eyes narrow, his jaw clenching and his hands curling into fists. "Can ya take it out?"

"I can't. It'll trigger the suppression drug and I'll die–" My words cut off abruptly as realization dawns. That's what I've been taught since entry school. But I'm not sick, the virus isn't contagious, and the water was safe to drink. My tether is just another one of the Authority's lies.

It's all an illusion of control.

Pulling the knife from my belt, I position the tip on top of the bump beneath the skin.

Griff grabs my wrist, eyes wide and pleading. Green light flares.

"Let go," I demand. This is my choice, and one I won't allow anyone to take from me.

Slowly he releases me, watching, waiting. Terrified.

"Ah," I wince at how much force I have to apply to break the skin. Blood wells over the bump on my hand. Shoving my thumb and index finger inside the cut, I dig around for the pill, but it keeps slipping away from my slick fingers.

"Got it!" The tiny, oblong device plops to the floor boards accompanied by crimson splashes spilling down my forearm. Griff fetches bandages from his backpack as I sit, gaze transfixed on what I've just done.

Rough, calloused fingers graze my wrist, wrapping a bandage around my palm, tying it tight. There's no rainbow lights. No suppression.

Griff wraps his arms around me and hugs me so tight his heart marches a formation against my rib cage. There's nowhere I'd rather be and no place I've ever felt safer. His fingers trace a burning trail of sensation down my spine, splaying over my waist, squeezing my hips, cupping my ass, drawing us closer.

No more lies, no more lottery tickets.

"Yes. I'll come with you." I smile into the side of his neck, breathing in the sweet, crisp scent of pine.

No. There's only Griff.

"Kiss me," I beg, enjoying the scratch of his chin along soft, sensitive skin.

"So demanding," he replies in a voice husky with desire before he sucks my lower lip into his mouth.

# 36

## GRIFF

**Vulnerability requires an act of courage
to expose a great weakness.**

I close the distance between us and taste her lips. She opens her
mouth, allowing me to explore inside, savoring the taste of me. I
want to consume her, to devour every inch of her body.

Rei's hand wanders over my biceps and trails down my arm. As
she leans into me, I roll onto my back and pull her on top of me. She
tosses her head and laughs, her long hair forming a curtain around
our faces.

"I don't want to hurt you," she says, trying to support her weight
on her hands beside my head.

I grind my crotch against her butt and complain, "this hurts more."

She flushes red, and she lowers her face to hide the expression in
her eyes. I grab her chin and bring her gaze back to mine. I want to see
that lustful gleam, the desire I make her feel, to remember it always.
Remember what it means to be needed for who I am as a person
rather than as a necessity to the future of humanity.

I grab a hand and bring it to the waistband of my pants. Rei's
mouth quirks into a smile and she complies with my request by
helping me slide my pants off my hips. Her eyes go wide and her

mouth makes a big O when she finds my cock ready and waiting for her.

"I don't remember it being this big..." she rails off. Her fingers slide along the shaft and trace small circles around the head. I suck in a breath and let out a long, low groan. "You like this?" she asks, wrapping fingers around the most sensitive part.

It's miles better than anything I've ever done myself in the name of fulfilling quotas. I can only nod as she squeezes and pulls at the same time.

"Ahh, fuck!" I snatch her wrist and hold it still before I lose my shit.

The playful gleam in her eye sends jolts of anticipation through my groin. Rei lifts her hips and pulls her pants and underwear down. She rubs my cock between her thighs and it slides against moist curls, tickling, teasing. A moan slips between her teeth where she bites her lower lip.

"I want you inside of me," she says, gyrating her hips back and forth, rocking against me. Her hand slips between our arousal coaxing, gripping, flicking, and stroking.

Tight, soft, warmth envelops me as she inches onto my cock with agonizingly slow precision. She winces as it stretches her wide, whimpering, fighting past the temporary discomfort. Placing my hands on both sides of her hips I thrust upwards and slam her down onto me at the same time.

"Ahh!" Her cries are a mixture of pain and pleasure.

Fuck, she's so tight, clenching around me, sucking me in. I don't waste any time thrusting, pulling, bouncing, and grinding her hips on top of me. Enjoying each and every stroke. Her hands curl around my forearms as our bodies smash together in a frantic, desperate rhythm. The pressure slurping and squelching around my cock grows tighter as her release builds. Every moan, cry, and whimper make me twitch and slam harder inside her. It's so fucking hot. I'm doing this, driving her to the edge of the Iron Divide, forcing her to climb to the top. Daring her to jump.

Her moans become louder, more frantic. I push myself up on one arm, ignoring the protests of pain across my stomach, grabbing her soft, round ass cheeks, shoving her closer. Deeper.

"Griff!" Her scream shatters the sound of our sweaty bodies slapping together. She clenches and unclenches around my cock with a vice that has me roaring my release.

We collapse onto the bed, exhausted, her muscles continuing to contract and quiver around me. The weight of her body presses against my tender wounds, but I don't care. I love the feeling of her wrapped around me, still buried deep inside her. Our chests rise and fall in syncopated rhythm. The frantic beating of her heart pressed against me mirrors my own.

My fingers curl in the long, sweaty hair tickling my neck and shoulder. We fit together, two halves of a whole. A pang of sadness overwhelms me at the thought.

This is it, our last day together.

Rei's breathing slows, and within a few minutes, she's asleep. I run a hand behind her neck, trail her shoulder blade, around the small of her back, pressing her more firmly against me. If I could pause time I would capture this feeling forever. She looks so peaceful, so content.

A cup clatters to the ground. Mischief lifts his head from licking a plate in the sink. His ears cock backwards and he chitters. Tiny claws scrabble against the wooden floor as he takes off toward the window and launches himself outside.

"What the hell, Mischief?" His antics have been worse than usual since Rei locked him outside when I was sick. Frantic, almost. Could he be jealous? For the first time in his life, he was being put aside while my attention was elsewhere.

Rei shifts in my arms and I kiss her forehead. She smells earthy, like the outdoors after a warm, spring rain with a hint of honeysuckle. It's hard to believe where we are now from where we started. I was so sure I would strangle her with my bare hands that first day. Now I don't want to take them off her.

"I love ya," I whisper into the dark tangles of her hair.

# 37

**REI**

## The heavy magnitude of trust lies in the palm of a hand.

Something is sharply shaking my shoulder, but I don't want the peaceful, comforting dream to end. The urgency in his hissing voice shatters the lingering effects of the warm, fuzzy feeling.

"Rei, wake up!"

"What's wron–" a hand clamps over my mouth. Calluses scrape against my swollen lips.

"Shh! Listen...."

Going still in his arms, I focus on the surrounding forest. Wind blows through the trees, a bird caws overhead, something rustles in the distance. I drag his hand off and whisper, "I don't hear anything."

He presses a finger to my lips and pulls my pants on.

"I can do it," I murmur in a low voice. "Did you hear somethi–"

Muffled voices pull me up short. It's hard to tell which direction they're coming from, but it can't be far if we're hearing them inside the hut.

"Her...last pinged...this direction. I'm not...getting...strong signal...area...mostly...a dead spot." The sound fades in and out of our range, but there's no denying I know that freaking voice.

Alyssa.

My heart plummets into my stomach, I bolt to my feet, stuffing items into Griff's bag.

"It's the Authority. Run. Now!" I hiss and shove his gear against his bandaged chest. I spin, looking for his boots.

Griff grabs my elbow. He shakes his head and uses my arm to steady himself. "I'm in no shape to run. They can't catch ya here, ya have to go."

"I'm not going without you!" I turn, slamming my feet into my boots, before his grip tightens painfully.

"Take this," he says, pulling the necklace over his shaggy hair, wrapping my fingers around it. "Keep it safe."

"No I–"

He presses our foreheads together. "Rei! Promise me you'll keep it safe."

"Yes. I promise. Now get your boots on, we need to go!" I say, shoving the necklace in my bra.

There's a high-pitched scream that sounds an awful lot like Mischief. Crap! Griff spins and barrels through the door, running outside.

"Wait, Griff!" I hurry after him.

And collide into his broad back.

# 38

## REI

**Cutting grief fractures the wild.**

Commander Lynx, Alyssa, and three other Enforcers stand before us. Tension courses through Griff's shoulders, bunching together like a mountain lion ready to pounce.

"Well, well, there you are, not dead after all." Commander Lynx says in a chilling voice to match her piercing, gray eyes.

Griff's rage with a fury I've only seen once before–when I first took his necklace. "I'm gonna destroy ya," he says in a voice so quiet and matter of fact that it sends a shiver through me.

"Ah, ah, not so fast." Alyssa says, raising her gloved hands to aim a gun at Griff's chest. "Don't move or I'll shoot."

Griff doesn't take his eyes off of Commander Lynx as he asks, "Ya gonna let her kill me like ya killed my father?"

"Oh, heavens no!" she says, waving her hand in the air dismissively. "You're much more valuable to us alive. Besides, that wouldn't be fair to your sister now, would it?"

His sister? My eyes go wide. If she's his sister, then that would mean Commander Lynx is his mother? My eyes jerk from Griff to Alyssa to the Commander and back again. Bless the mother. How could I have freaking missed the resemblance? Standing here, all together, it's easy to see the similarities. Intense eyes, prominent noses, angular jaw lines, fierce devotion, and proud, stiff shoulders.

"How nice is this, huh? A little family reunion. But I wasn't expecting to find my most promising, loyal trainee turned traitor." Commander Lynx says, with a penetrating gaze. It's the same look I recognize when Griff means business. "Having a pleasant time playing house, are we, Rei?"

"I—it's not—I wasn't—" I say with a sputter.

"I had such high hopes for you, too. What a shame." She says and clucks her tongue.

"H—how did you find us?" I force myself to speak a coherent sentence.

"A tether has many uses. I've had Enforcer patrols sweeping the mountains for months without any luck. But thanks to you, Rei, the Authority will find a cure and keep us safe. To think you would throw it all away so easily. I thought you believed in our cause."

I do, no, I did. I thought I did.

"I don't know," I say, forced to confront my new truth.

"The Authority hangs traitors, Rei. You, of all people, should understand that. Alyssa, kill her."

"No!" Griff grabs the hunting knife from my belt and steps in front of me. He presses the blade to his throat.

Commander Lynx throws her arms out as some of the other Enforcers step forwards. "Wait! Stand down! We need him alive!"

"If ya touch her, I'll kill myself," Griff barks. A line of blood wells underneath the sharp edge of the weapon.

My cry catches in my throat. He wouldn't dare! I'm too terrified to move, let alone speak.

"Let her go and I'll go with ya without a fight." There's a desperate, pleading tone in Griff's voice.

"My, my. You've finally grown some backbone and taken after your mother." Commander Lynx says with a note of pride. She turns to me. "Rei, you're free to go."

I shake my head, moving closer to Griff.

"Rei, ya have to run," Griff warns, not taking his eyes off Commander Lynx or Alyssa.

"I'm not leaving without you!" I cry.

"Go. Ya have to go."

I shake my head. "No. I can't."

Alyssa takes a step forward, coming closer.

"They won't hurt me," he says, reaching his free hand out to me. I grab his fingers and squeeze, like I can hold him there or take him with me.

There's a collective gasp and murmur from the Enforcers surrounding us, several of them exchange worried glances. Oh. They were expecting my tether to flare to life. It gives me an idea.

"The Authority is lying to you! The water is safe to drink and I'm not sick. See?" Linking our fingers together, I lift Griff's hand in mine, I hold up my bandaged, tetherless palm.

"Bloody hell! Stupid girl, you have no idea what you're talking about!" Commander Lynx screams, her face contorting, turning red. "Kill her!"

"Go!" Griff presses the knife deeper and blood streams down his throat. "Please," he says in a voice thick with barely contained emotion.

Turning, I take off into the woods.

"After her, you idiots! She'll hang like the traitor she is!" Commander Lynx's fury echoes among the trees. "Search his place. It's here somewhere."

Even as I race away, I can hear Griff screaming. "Let me go! Get off of me!"

There's thunderous crashing of footsteps behind me as the Enforcers give chase.

# 39

## REI

**When cornered and facing death,
instinct fights back.**

It's not much of a head start, but I have the advantage of knowing these woods better than they do. I can't let them catch me. The landscape blurs around me as I try to put more distance between us. These aren't trainees, these are full-fledged Enforcers. And they tracked my tether?

I slow to a jog, just long enough to assess the situation. I can still hear them behind me, crashing through the leaves and undergrowth like a stampede of deer.

"There! I see her!" says an Enforcer, far too close for comfort.

I can't help glancing over my shoulder. Alyssa is visible in the distance, flanked by two other Enforcers. She raises her gun and fires. The bullet ricochets off the tree next to my head.

Ducking, I scramble out of her line of sight and take cover behind a tree.

"You're dead, traitor!" Alyssa screams.

Running is no longer an option, but I can't stay here either. Footsteps approach as I huddle against the rough bark. I need a plan, and fast. Searching wildly, I spy a Sympathizer logo. The triangle is cut around a knot in the wood, where a branch used to be, rather than a circle carved in the center. My eyes go wide as realization dawns. Out here, I have both a tactical and strategic advantage.

This could work, but they'll have to be close, really close—near enough that shooting me could risk them shooting each other. Enforcer training dictates never to use firearms in hand-to-hand combat. In tight quarters, it's easy for a gun to be turned against you. After three months of perfecting drills under Alyssa's command, her playbook is predictable.

I peek my head out from around the tree trunk. The bullet whips past my nose by mere freaking inches.

Mother bless it!

"Is that the best you can do? No wonder you're such a disappointment to the Commander. Do you really think she'll let you lead the Authority one day?" I taunt, hitting her where I know it hurts the most. She'll have them spread into a pincer move–one coming straight for me while the other two flank both sides.

"And yet, I'm not the one headed for suppression, am I Rei? She trusts me to get things done."

"That's funny, you looked pretty surprised when she called Griff her son. Didn't know you had a brother, did you, Captain?" When I hear their footsteps split three ways, I sprint forwards, leaving the safety of cover, forcing them to respond before they can fully get into position.

"Hell! After her!"

It's working! Their footsteps converge as they race toward me, forced out of their formation by the wooded landscape. Another bullet shoots past me, sending splinters flying from the tree. They're still not close enough. I skid behind another tree for cover. I need them even closer than this.

"You call yourself an Enforcer? That's some terrible aim you got there." I criticize with the same harsh bark Commander Lynx uses, listening hard. They slow to a jog as they approach the tree I'm hidden behind. Just a little more....

The hand holding the gun slides past me on my left. There's a chittering noise in the trees above and an acorn smacks her in the face, distracting her. I grab her arm and charge, raising the gun over her golden hair. It goes off as I elbow her in the jaw, her green eyes flashing in pain. Birds scatter overhead. I punch harder, but she's recovered enough to guard from my attack.

A second Enforcer comes up behind me. I swing the golden-haired woman toward the newcomer, still fighting for her gun. I ram my elbow into her wrist and it thumps to the ground. The second Enforcer runs forward, trying to help the first. I kick out at her, using the green-eyed Enforcer as a human shield, my arms wrapping around her neck.

Hands claw at my hair, my cheeks, my eyes as I apply pressure, strangling her. Alyssa approaches, her gun at her side, trying to figure out how to best join in the fray. I drag the golden-haired Enforcer back a step and kick out at the second.

"Let her go! There's no way you're getting out of this alive," Alyssa barks, raising her gun again.

Come on, I need her to take another step forward. Maybe if I back up first? The green-eyed Enforcer's nails are scratching with everything she has now, her attempts growing weaker as she threatens to pass out. I refuse to relinquish my hold.

Alyssa takes another step forward, Her eyes going wide in shock the split second before she plummets, disappearing from view. I release the golden-haired Enforcer, shoving her forwards, tangling my leg with hers, tripping her. She collapses, gasping for air, her hands thrown out in front of her to break her fall. Instead, she catches the front of the second Enforcer's uniform, knocking her off balance. I lower my shoulder and plow into them with everything I've got. They tumble over the edge of the sinkhole with a scream and a thump as they hit the muddy bottom.

I don't waste another second. I turn and sprint toward Mara's house. This will buy me some time, sure, but with three of them in there, it won't take long for them to climb back out. I've got to get out of here.

Mischief peers at me from the leaves of the tree, his large eyes blinking, tiny ears cocking in my direction. Tears stream down my cheeks. He'll be okay out here by himself, won't he?

I'm losing them both.

# 40

# GRIFF

**They can bind you and break you, but
they cannot unmake you.**

I tumble forward as the truck jerks to a stop and the handcuffs
bite into my skin. There's a flurry of activity outside as the
Enforcers disembark. A woman with vibrant green eyes and
golden hair lowers the truck bed and steps inside. Mud coats her
boots and the knees of her pants. Behind her, another Enforcer
has their gun trained on me.

"No funny business," she says, rattling keys as she unlocks the
chain securing my handcuffs to a metal loop on the floor. Her
black gloved hand grabs my elbow. Her grip tightens, but she's
not strong enough to drag me to my feet alone. "Get up!"

"Ya smell like shit. Gotta say, it's a big improvement."

The vixen's muddy boot slams into my shin. "We'll see who's
laughing when you're naked and grunting like the dirty pig you
are," she snaps. "I'll be sure to bring you a picture of your little
traitor's body when we find her. Maybe it'll help you meet your
quota."

I lunge, barreling into her, slamming her against the other side of
the truck. Pain explodes across the back of my head, dropping me to

my knees. Blood drips from my hair, slides down my jaw, dripping onto my hand.

Hands grab me and drag my ass out of the truck until I land in a heap on the ground. There's a ringing between my ears that won't stop and my vision is swimming.

"Are you okay?" one of the others asks the vixen.

"Fine," she croaks. "Get him to his feet."

"Why is he so heavy?" A disembodied voice asks. The cuffs at my wrists jangle as I'm dragged toward the large steel door. Every muscle in my body screams in protest as it looms before me. The woman in front of her uses a keycard to open the door. I struggle to get my feet underneath me, to raise, to resist.

No! I don't want this, I can't go back. I can't do this!

"I said move!" The vixen hits me from behind, buckling my legs out from under me. The ground lurches beneath me as arms link with mine. Cold, hard concrete scrapes my bare feet as they drag through the halls in my disoriented state.

*Boom.*

The slam of the steel door behind us rings down the narrow, bleak hallway. Long, fluorescent lights throw harsh shadows and highlight the pitted flaws in the concrete.

"Get off me you evil fuckers!" I scream, struggling against them, as I'm half dragged, half carried.

We pass through two more solid metal doors; the Enforcers using a badge to get past each one. Surveillance cameras buzz and whirr as their motion sensors kick in. I scramble to get my feet back underneath me as we enter the main cell block.

Several men sitting at various small tables pause what they're doing, watching me buck and struggle with blank expressions.

"Open 47," the vixen calls up to the camera above the cell we're facing. The light at the top turns from red to green and they shove me inside.

It's the same glass observation window, cold, hard floor, toilet, and sink. The stick figures I etched into the wall as a 12-year-old boy stare at me with empty circles for eyes and a wobbly line for the mouth—my brother and me. Fear floods my chest, drowning me in memories still trapped in this cell.

"Please, ya don't have to do this," I plead, head throbbing from where she hit me earlier. The other Enforcers have their guns trained on me again.

"Turn around." The vixen slams me against the wall and unlocks the cuffs. "I didn't give you permission to speak, 47. Open your mouth again and I'll double your quota," she hisses and unlocks the cuffs, backing toward the door.

"The Authority is lying to y–"

She decks me across the face. Fuck! I double over, nose bleeding. The cell door slams and the light above turns red.

I'm locked in. My chest seizes, growing tight, and I force myself to suck in one breath and then another. Stumbling to the sink, I turn the knob. Under better circumstances I might appreciate the easy access to water. Shit, shit, shit! What am I gonna do now? I have to get out of here. Cupping my hand under the faucet I drink deeply and rinse the blood off my nose, mouth, and the back of my head.

Red swirls the drain. It's like life is literally draining out of me.

*Tap, tap, tap.*

I jerk my head up at the sound. A face presses against the tiny window of my cell door. It has my same strong nose, chiseled jaw, and dark brown hair. A black crayon is tucked behind one ear. Except for his blue eyes, he's a leaner, ganglier version of myself.

"Griff?" The thick glass muffles his voice.

"Ian!"

His wide grin is infectious. It's been so long since I last saw him. He was so young then, his baby blues overly large in his thin, pale face. Now he's as tall as I am, maybe even taller. I never thought I'd see him again.

"It's really you! I can't believe it!" Ian says, holding up his hand, pressing it to the glass. I reach out and place mine against his like I used to when he was too afraid to fall asleep. "Look, I can't talk long or they'll send me back to my cell. I'm in 51 over there." He looks over his shoulder, but his hand and head block everything else from view. He turns back. "How's dad?"

The question hits me like another punch to the gut. Of course he doesn't know. I press my forehead against the cool metal. All I can do is shake my head.

"Oh...."

"Ian, we have to get out of here. I need ya to talk to the others, we need to come up with a plan."

Ian shakes his head. "Most of the guys hardly leave their cells anymore. Do you remember Sam? He hasn't spoken to anyone in years."

"We can't stay here. If we band together, we can overwhelm them and force our way out."

Ian frowns. "Shit, they're coming. I gotta go."

He peels away from my door and hurries in the opposite direction. There's a small group of older men sitting around a table. Ian sinks into a chair, picking up a hand of cards. The Enforcers approach and exchange words for several minutes, then he scoots, standing from his chair, and walks out of view.

Shit! I can't see where they went. His cell, I guess? Running a hand through my hair, and wincing when I hit the tender spot, I take six strides from the door to the glass observation window and back again. If I hold my hands out I can almost touch the walls on both sides. This prison was so much larger when I was a child.

Man, my head hurts. Holding my aching temple, I sink to the ground. Now here I am, right back where I started. After everything my father fought for, everything he taught me and sacrificed, I gave it all up for Rei.

And I would do it again.

"Ugh," I say with a groan. The throbbing pain is getting worse. I lie down on the ground and curl my knees toward my chest to keep warm. Maybe if I close my eyes for a second I can get this headache to go away. The room is spinning.

*Click!*

The light outside of my door goes from red to green as it unlocks. I struggle to sit up as three Enforcers enter, one with a gun drawn.

"The sedatives in his water are kicking in. He should be out soon," a distorted voice croons.

My head droops as the Enforcers grab my arms and drag me out of the cell. Colors and lights blur around me. Cold, rough cement scrapes my toes. A blast of water rouses me as it hits me in the mouth and nose. The spray from the hose feels like needles stinging against my naked skin. I yelp and cover myself, but there's nowhere to go, no way to avoid it. When the torrent finally shuts off, I press a hand to my woozy head and wrestle with my dread. It's been years since I was last subjected to this routine, yet my tortured memories are so crisp it may as well have been yesterday. When the door to the shower clangs open, gloved hands grab my arms and drag me toward a metal laboratory table.

Fear clenches around my insides and twists, a blade to the gut. Sweat breaks out on my forehead and my heart plummets.

"No, no!" I say, struggling against them. Something sharp stabs my neck. My arms and legs go numb. I droop forward and the Enforcers fight to keep me upright as I go limp.

Someone grabs my legs and lifts them onto the table. Hard steel is chilly beneath my wet skin. Pungent antiseptic burns my nose. There's a bright light above my face burning into my eyeballs. Why can't I close my eyes? Why aren't they responding? Buckles clink as the Enforcers strap my limbs down. Then they're gone, their chatter following them out the door.

My eyes tear from the lights but they still won't close. There's a metallic clunk and the crackle of plastic. Red overtakes my vision as a scientist in a hazmat suit leans forward and examines me through the transparent part of her visor.

"How much did you give him?" Says a familiar voice behind the scientist.

"The usual dose," she responds.

"Why is he still coherent?" asks Commander Lynx.

"If I had to guess, it's because of a higher body mass. He's had years out on his own with extreme levels of physical activity, living off a high fat, high protein diet. It's affecting the drug's potency."

"You're the scientist. Can't you just give him another dose? We need to know where he hid Dr. Solenne's research," says Commander Lynx, her brows furrowing.

"Another dose could kill him. It's too risky. You'll have to take what you can get."

Commander Lynx leans over me. I want to reach up and wrap my hands around her throat, but my arms and legs won't move. My mind feels foggy and slow.

"Griff, where did you hide the USB drive? Hey, answer me."
Commander Lynx says. Her gloved hand smacks the side of my
cheek.

My tongue won't move. It feels awkward in my mouth, fuzzy
and swollen. There's an overwhelming urge to answer her, to blurt
out Rei has my necklace, but I use every ounce of my willpower to
clamp my mouth shut. Whatever they gave me, I won't let them
win.

"I'm. Gonna. Kill. Ya...." I force each word out with laborious
effort.

"Hey! Answer me." She smacks my cheek again, harder this time.

I grit my teeth and force my mouth shut, leering up at her.

"It isn't working, you need to fix it!" she says, turning and
hissing at the scientist.

"It'll take some time to re-calibrate the formula. It'd be better to
wait until he adjusts to the diet."

"Bloody hell! That'll take too much time, time we don't have,"
Commander Lynx snaps. "Run your tests, Rei didn't get sick and
we need to figure out why. Find me something useful."

"I need more resources. You can't expect me to work a miracle
in these conditions—"

"More resources? Hah! I've quarantined half the barracks in
the MMZ. Every doctor in the med center is showing signs of
fever and coughing. We're beyond stretched thin, and you want
to bitch at me about not having enough resources? I pulled every
soldier from the checkpoints outside of Albrin to make up for
the shortage in troops. We had three new deaths this morning. To
make matters worse, the Sympathizers have noticed something's
off with our patrols. They're getting bolder. If we don't get
Solenne's research back soon—"

"I'm doing my best, Commander. Dr. Martina was our leading expert on pathogenic mutations. You know this isn't my area of expertise!"

"Yes, well, Dr. Nora, you and the Director are the only two healthy, qualified scientists we have left. So you don't get a choice, do you? Humanity is depending on us to fix this mess before it's too late. Now, get to work."

The door opens and closes as Commander Lynx stomps away. Dr. Nora sighs and shakes her head. She reaches for something on a tray beside her and holds up a shiny instrument.

"Sorry buddy, this is going to hurt."

Firey pain consumes me.

# 41

## REI

**When loyalty is currency, betrayal is defying the hands holding you down.**

Although my tether is gone, I don't put it past them to show up at any freaking minute. Stalking around the lake, I keep my eyes and ears open for the sound of Enforcers. So far, the journey back to Mara's house has been otherwise uneventful. I stick to the woods until the terraced patios of the lake house appear.

The rumble of a convoy truck on the gravel road sends a spike of panic through my stomach. It skids to a stop in front of my car, bits of rock showering the paint job. Three Enforcers exit.

"Spread out and check the house. If she's here, we'll find her," Alyssa says.

Of course, they would think to check Mara's house. How could I be so stupid? They cross the stone patios and head toward the house. Glass breaks as they shatter one of the beautiful windows to get inside. Waiting until I can no longer hear them, I slink away from my hiding spot and take off toward my car.

When I reach it, my footsteps falter.

"Dammit!"

Someone has slashed all four tires. Now what am I supposed to do? It's too far to hike all the way back to Terin. The nearest town has to be at least 20 or 30 miles down the road. I need a car if I want any chance of making it out of here. There's only one other vehicle. How long have they been inside? I don't know if I have time to attempt the crazy idea gathering like storm clouds.

An Enforcer exits the broken front window and sidles around back, heading toward the shed. When she's out of sight, I sprint for the driver's side door of the truck, wrench it open, and fling myself into the front seat.

Yes! Luck is on my side. The key hangs in the ignition. I crank the engine and slam the door at the same time. Jamming the gear into reverse, I floor the gas pedal and the truck shoots backwards. My car appears in the rear-view mirror, and I smash into the front bumper as I barrel past. The smaller vehicle crashes into a tree on the side of the road, the front hood flies off, and a dark spray of oil spills beneath it.

Good. There's no way they can use it to come after me now.

There's a shout from the house and Alyssa and another Enforcer appear, guns in hand.

*Bang! Bang!*

Crap! Gunshots. The windshield cracks like a spider's web, fractures radiating outwards from the bullet hole. Ducking down, I steer and stay low.

"Don't let her get away!" Alyssa shouts, her voice nearly drowned out by gunfire, running at me, shooting. The third Enforcer races from around the back of the house, lagging behind them.

But the truck is moving too fast for them to keep up on foot. I yank the steering wheel, holding the truck on the road as gravel spits under squealing tires. At last they're far enough away that I can't see them anymore.

At the intersection of Mara's private road and the main one, I spin the truck around to face forwards. Taking my time, I change gears and pull off at a normal speed. No one will know I don't belong in this truck if I play my cards right. Not yet anyway.

They have Griff.

I uncurl my clenched fingers, relieving the ache from their death grip. Instinct kicked in and I'm heading toward Terin. But should I be going home? I'm a traitor, they'll be looking for me. It's not safe for me there...or anywhere.

"Damnit! Where else can I go?" The weight of my circumstances crushes my shoulders. The Authority is all I've ever known. Other than the apartment where I grew up and the barracks of the MMZ, I've never lived anywhere else.

Until Griff.

The radio on the truck dashboard squawks and fizzes with static. A high-pitched female voice I don't recognize says, "Yes, the package made it to Eastkeep, over."

"Any word from Captain Alyssa on the traitor?" asks a different, deeper voice.

"Negative," says the first voice. "The reception out there was terrible. Lots of dead spots. It might take them a while to get a signal and check in. She wanted to take one last sweep of the area, over."

"Is it true that he's the Commander's son?" asks the deeper, troubled voice.

"Your job is to follow orders, not to ask stupid, dangerous questions," says the high-pitched voice with a note of annoyance.

"They were holding hands but her tether didn't activate...how's that possible? Do you think she's infected?"

"Go ahead, keep talking. You'll end up swinging before you know it."

"They quarantined my girlfriend's barracks yesterday. It's the same one Quinn was in," says the deeper voice.

"I warned her to stop poking her nose where it doesn't belong. It's her own damn fault she got infected."

"We shouldn't have left her out in the Brass Mountains during the storm. A bullet would have been far kinder."

There's a long pause before the high-pitched voice answers, "I left one in the chamber. She was my friend too, you know."

"I know." Another pause. "Is he really the boy in the photo? I honestly didn't think we'd ever find him. It's been months of searching and now they're suddenly calling everyone bac–"

"Bless the mother! Maintain radio silence until the next checkpoint. Over."

The static on the line returns, then the radio beeps and goes quiet. Apparently I'm not the only one with growing suspicions about the Authority's motives. If what they said was true, Griff was the boy in the photo? And what did they mean about an infected Enforcer? Wouldn't their tether have kicked in and suppressed them first? Or had she also removed it the same way I did?

My hand digs into my bra and I pull out Griff's necklace. I trace a finger over the triangle with a circle on the bottom. The Sympathizers helped Griff and his father escape.

Now more than ever, I need to figure out what's on this USB drive. And there's only one person I know and trust in the Authority who has the equipment I need to access this information.

Mara.

What's the best route back into Terin? There are several checkpoints if I go the direct route, but if I go a longer, more roundabout way, I only have to go through one. It won't take long for Alyssa to find the phone and report the stolen truck. But heading through multiple checkpoints means more chances someone will notice something suspicious.

I opt for the longer route and steel myself for what's ahead.

# 42

## GRIFF

**Even in the darkness, if I have to crawl through hell to see your light again, so be it.**

Something is digging into my hip, hollowing me out. Pain radiates up my lower back, jabbing, forcing me back into consciousness. I groan and examine the scientist's handiwork. There's a bloody bandage over a puncture wound on my hip and a new cut on my forearm, with stitches to match.

"Shit, it hurts." The cold cement floor of my cell isn't helping. I shiver and push to my hands and knees, crawling to the toilet, using it to get to my feet.

How could I forget they fucking drug the water? My legs tremble and goosebumps prickle my skin as I struggle to dress in the standard issue loose gray pants and shirt. Every step sends a dull ache flaring up my hip. Crossing the six steps to the partially open door, I push it open with a creak.

Waves of dread wash over me. Many of the cell doors are open. Two men stand near cell 28, talking in hushed voices. Another man shuffles the perimeter of the room, fingers twitching in the air, muttering under his breath, talking to someone only he can see. A smaller man sits on the floor of cell 40 across from mine, knees pressed to his chest, rocking back and forth, a plastic cup gripped in his hands. An older, taller man stands above him, fully naked, grunting and groaning in pleasure, jerking himself off until his contribution fills the bottom of the container. When he's done he leans forward, ruffles the smaller man's curly hair, and whispers something in his ear. The smaller man stands, hands him the cup, and goes rigid when the taller man kisses his neck and smacks him on the ass, propelling him into the common area. As the younger man shuffles away, head bowed and shoulders slumped, subject 40 winks at me and raises the cup, his lip curling into a satisfied smile.

My hands ball into fists at my sides. Shit like this didn't happen when I was a kid, the older men would never allow it. What's changed?

A chair scrapes in the center of the room and Ian rises from the table where he's playing cards.

"Griff, you okay?" He asks, hurrying over, putting an arm under my shoulder.

"I'll survive," I croak, leaning on him as I limp over to his empty chair. "Who's the fucker in 40?"

"That's Dean. He's mostly harmless. Mostly."

Ian stops as I jerk to a halt, my blood running cold.

"He has his favorites, like Sam, but I'm not one of them," Ian offers quickly, dragging me forward again. "Come on, I'll introduce you to the guys. Everyone, this is my brother Griff."

Metal legs scrape on the concrete when I plop into the chair. The group of elderly men examine me with bleak, stoic stares.

"Fletcher's older boy," the frail older man says, tapping his cards on the scratched metal table top. "Never thought we'd see ya again. Weren't you supposed to get to the Free Territories, save the world or some shit?" He gives a dry, hoarse grunt. "Fletcher always was delusional."

"If we work together we can overwhelm the guards and get outta here," I counter.

The frail older man chuckles and wheezes, slapping his spindly leg. "Enforcers are armed to the teeth, stronger than we'll ever be. In all my years, only two ever got outta this hell hole—you and your pa. And look how that turned out."

"This time is different. Enforcers are getting sick, their numbers are stretched thin."

"Shh...please, keep your voice down or they'll hear you," Ian whispers, glancing over his shoulder at the security cameras and leaning closer. "Look, Joe's right, you've been gone a long time, you don't understand how things work around here now. Things are bad, worse than when we were kids. Even if you're right and there's something going on, stirring up shit is pointless and dangerous. If you're caught talking like this they'll put you in the white for behavior modification."

"Behavior what?"

Joe places his hand of cards down on the table. "After you two disappeared there was a string of escape attempts. The Authority didn't waste any time. Behavior modification is what they call it. Their way of using fear to restore order. Anyone who went through the Breaking and wouldn't satisfy their Contribution Cycle...well, they hauled um off. Never seen um after that. Talk is they poke a hole in their head, not enough to kill um, mind you, but enough so you don't cause trouble no more. Twenty-two seen the white room once. Bodies lining the walls, wasting away in their beds, stuck staring at the ceiling. As long as they keep um breathing I reckon they can still contribute."

"Final verdict," says another man, naming Joe's hand laid on the table. He tosses down his cards in defeat. "Shit Joe, how you so good at this game? Counting cards again?"

Nobody responds and the group falls silent, lost in thought. Ian swipes the cards off the table, shuffling the deck for a new round, helpful to a fault. He's refusing to meet my gaze, fixating on the only thing he can control in this situation.

"I can't stay here, I won't do this again. I have someone out there worth living for...and this isn't living."

The crayon bobs behind Ian's ear, and his lips press together in a thin line. It's a gesture that's so like our father's angry disappointment it gives me pause. For a split second, Father's sitting there beside me.

*He's no longer standing in my shadow.*

"Say what ya gotta say," I urge him. Better to get it over with than let his simmering wound fester.

"It's not important," he shakes his head, dealing a new round.

"You're still just a scared kid waiting for someone to protect ya," I murmur, shaking my head.

He stops dealing cards, piercing blue eyes meeting mine. "Funny," he says quietly, "how you think you're something special. I shoulda known better than to hope you'd come back for me. You could care less, right? You and Father left me here to rot."

Fuck! How could he think so poorly of us?

"Ian, that's not true–"

"Subjects, return to your cell for your Contribution Cycle," a female voice barks over the intercom. The lights above every cell in our block blink green. Ian drops the deck onto the table and pushes to his feet along with the other older men.

"Better go or you'll regret it," Ian warns in a deadpan voice, walking away.

"Ian! Wait!" I call after him.

Shit. The last thing I expected was to have to track down and win back the trust of my little brother, the kid who dogged my trail from the moment he could totter around on two legs. He was the one person I should be able to count on in this viper's pit, and I'd already sent him spooked and crashing through the woods.

Grunting, I stand and shuffle back to my cell. As soon as I cross the threshold my cell door slides closed behind me, the light above the door going red. Locked. A slot at the back of the room slides open, revealing a plastic cup.

"Subject, thank you for serving the greater good. Please provide your daily contribution."

No. This can't be happening. I grit my teeth and turn my back on the observation window. There's a reason we call the Authority's Contribution Cycle the Breaking. But Rei showed me I am not broken.

"Subject, provide your daily contribution, immediately." The female voice says in an eerily cheery tone.

"Fuck off!" I scream pounding my fist against the door until I draw blood. Helpless or not, I don't belong to them. Their need for control will never trump what Rei and I have together. For her I was never a resource, a possession, a helpless body drugged into submission. With Rei my desire was built around choice and trust, not fear and control.

"Subject, this is your final warning. Failure to provide your daily contribution will result in a medical extraction procedure."

Rei's big brown eyes, long dark hair, and flirty smile come to mind. My galloping heartbeat slows as I picture the way she flips her hair over her shoulder, bites her lower lip, and laughs with a flippant shake of the head. She pulls my scraped knuckles from the door, examining the wounds with a frown. Slender fingers pull my hand between her breasts, directly over her heart. "So demanding..." she whispers in my ear, sending shivers down my neck. Erect nipples slide over my chest and my other hand brushes the damp tangle of curls between her thighs. Skin meets skin.

My desire for her doesn't make me weak. Or powerless.

It makes me stronger.

And it's the reason I'll do whatever it takes to convince these men to get out of this fucking place.

"Subject, thank you for your daily contribution."

# 43

REI

## Every broken wing is a chance to learn how to fly.

Before I reach the checkpoint, I scrounge around the truck for a forgotten hat in the back seat. Tucking my hair into the blue cap is the best I can do to look some semblance of "normal." The dirt staining my face will help me spin the narrative I've come up with during the drive. There's been no other chatter on the radio, but it's possible I'm just out of range of the signal. Come on, I got this. It's now or never.

The single guard out front waves for me to slow at the gate. Where are the others? Protocol dictates three guards on duty at all times. I sit up straighter as she approaches, her hand on the gun slung across her chest. Without a badge or papers, I'm forced to take a page out of Alyssa's playbook. Strategy is paramount to sell this story.

"What the hell happened here?" the guard asks, brows furrowing at the cracked windshield and multitude of bullet holes.

"Soldier!" I snap my hand up to my forehead in salute. "My Enforcer platoon is under Sympathizer attack. I narrowly escaped with urgent information about their secret base and an assassination attempt. I have orders to report to Commander Lynx, immediately."

The woman's eyes go wide in surprise.

I remember the way Commander Lynx and Alyssa demand absolute obedience as I bark, "Open the gate! Hurry! That's an order!"

She scrambles, pulling the lever to let me through. I salute again as I drive, keeping my eyes pinned straight ahead, grim and determined. Relief washes over me. I'm back in the freaking city, but they'll be looking for me soon, if they aren't already. First priority, get rid of this truck. Next, figure out how to sneak into Mara's house.

Young children run and play as I pull into the marketplace. One of the older, braver girls waves at me as I park and hop out. I toss my hat on the seat before I blend into the crowded throng. Civvies of all ages and backgrounds frequent the market at this time of day. The stalls are full of a variety of seasonal foods and wares on display under the standard issue red awnings for Cleansing day. Two older women haggle in loud voices over rations for a chicken. A baby wails in its mother's arms. The aroma of cooking foods and spices makes my stomach growl.

A trio of soldiers moves through the crowd, civvies parting on either side, giving way to their marching stride. Crap! I pick up a trinket from the stand in front of me, pretending to study it intently, turning my back as they pass by. Good, they didn't notice. My heavy sigh blows strands of hair from my face.

"That's yours for three marks." The young vendor motions to the object in my hand.

The tiny figure has Mischief's black mask and grey ears, but the texture isn't right, it's too soft. Guilt gnaws at my heavy heart. I left them there, but I didn't have a choice. Did I? Tears well in the corner of my eyes. Crying won't solve anything.

"Sorry, I'm outta rations." I say, pulling myself together, suddenly self-conscious of the bandage wrapped around my palm where my tether should be.

"You a soldier?"

I look up sharply. Her gaze is gentle, understanding. What was I expecting? Recognition? Accusation? She doesn't know who I am. Not yet anyways.

Despite my hesitation, I nod. "Yeah, I am."

"My grandmother made that one. Her eyesight is going and her fingers are mostly numb nowadays. It's certainly not the same quality as the things I normally sell," she motions to the other quaint, woven animals and objects.

I set the raccoon down and give her a sad smile. "It's lovely," I say.

"I'll tell you what, since it's almost Cleansing day, you take it. I'm not likely to sell it to anyone. Heck, I don't even know what kind of strange creature it is. Her memories aren't the best, so sometimes we just humor her." The woman picks up the trinket and places it into my palm.

"I can't take this," I say, trying to give it back.

"Of course you can!" she closes my fingers around it.

"Thank you," I whisper, my voice going hoarse.

"Does it remind you of someone special? That's usually why people buy these. Is there a special woman in your life you want to give it to?" She nudges my arm and winks.

I'm too emotional to do more than nod and give her a watery smile.

"Well then, I'm glad I could brighten your day a bit." Her attention shifts as another customer approaches. "Thank the Authority you keep us safe, hun." She hurries toward the next customer.

I rub my fingers over the soft raccoon as I blend into the crowd, lost in thought. A little girl stumbles in front of me and I help her up. She's a miniature Cameron with her two front teeth missing. Her two front teeth are missing.

"Thank yo—" she says, and screams the moment she notices her knees are bleeding.

"Hey, that's enough of that," says a middle-aged woman, I assume her mother, as she marches over and snatches the girl's arm. "I told you not to run around like a cull. Do you know what the Authority does with naughty girls like you? They say no one ever comes out of the GRH once they go inside."

She rolls her eyes as the child wails uncontrollably. "Bless the mother, what did I say?" She drags her away, reminding me of my mother.

I shove the raccoon into my pocket and weave my way through the busy crowd. The more people there are, the less I stand out. Everyone's in a mad rush to do last-minute shopping for Cleansing day. Mara's apartment is on the farthest side of the market. As I get closer to her housing block, I use the cover of activity to scope out the area. I see a soldier every once in a while, but nothing leads me to believe they're surveilling her place.

Three middle-aged women break off from the market heading toward Mara's building. I slide into step behind them, not so close that they wonder what I'm doing, but not so far away either.

"Can you believe the cost of rice has gone up again? How do they expect us to feed ourselves?"

"It goes up every winter, dummy."

"Not this high! It's nearly twice as many rations as before! There's been so many shortages lately."

"If you want good deals, talk to the lazy-eyed old cull who sells carrots and potatoes."

"Ugh, she gives me the creeps. I can never tell where that wonky eye is looking. Do you think she's a spy for the Authority?"

"Shhh—watch your mouth! You never know who's listening," a woman with short blond hair swivels her neck left and right in her unease. Luckily, she doesn't look behind her, a little too close for comfort.

I break off from the friends and take the steps up to Mara's apartment building two at a time. Just as I'm about to press the buzzer for her apartment, the door swings open as someone leaves. I grab it before it closes and slip inside. She's on the fifth floor. Climbing the flights of stairs leaves my legs shaky and aching. The growling of my stomach reminds me it's been more than a day since I last ate.

The number 507 adorns her door in rusted brass. I knock three times and wait, keeping a watch down the hall. There's no freaking answer. What if she's not home? Crap!

Pressing my mouth to the wood I ask. "Mara? Are you in there?" Still, there's no answer. As I consider my options, I hear voices down the stairwell. Booted feet are marching up the steps. Panic floods my body. Enforcers? Did they find me?

I pound on the door frantically. "Mara!" I hiss as loud as I dare. "Please, let me in!"

*Nothing.*

The boots are getting louder, drawing closer. They'll be here any minute. I have to move, to find a way out of here. The long hall of the fifth floor has no windows, only apartment doors. The only way out is back the way I came.

"Dammit!" I clench my fists and lower my stance, preparing for a fight.

Mara's front door opens and a strong hand yanks me inside. It shuts right as the booted footsteps reach the fifth floor. I turn and press my face to the peephole. A teenage girl stomps past Mara's unit, unlocks a door across the hall, and slams it behind her.

Bless the mother, it's not them. My forehead bumps against the door frame and I let out a shaky breath.

"Rei?" Mara asks in a voice thick with raw emotion.

I spin and take in the sight of my best friend. Messy hair plasters her head and there are dark circles under her eyes. Her nose is irritated and swollen with a thin line of snot dripping to her lips. Dried food stains her soggy robe.

She doesn't say a single word as I wrap my arms around her and hug her tightly to my chest. Tears soak the front of my shirt as sobs wrack her body. Her fingers dig into my skin as they squeeze, holding on for dear life. My vision blurs with my own tears.

"Rei, the baby—" sobs cut her off. I let her cry until there's nothing left.

"Look at us, we're a mess," I say, pushing her out at arm's length. "Come on, let's sit down on the couch." I head into her kitchen to pour her a glass of water and stop short. Crap. Without a tether there's no way for me to activate the water. I grab a handful of tissues instead.

"Thanks," she says as she takes them and wipes her nose.

"Tell me what happened."

"I followed all the protocols and went to the birthing center right after I called you. Everything was fine at first. Then the doctor and nurses came in, but there were Enforcers, too. I didn't know what was going on. The doctor told me to push. The pain was so bad I thought I was going to split in half. Then the doctor frowned and the baby started crying. They told me they were giving me a sedative to help with the pain, but then the doctor handed the baby over to the Enforcers. I didn't understand what was going on. Why were Enforcers taking my baby? The doctor told me I had a boy and he died. But I heard him crying, Rei, I heard him crying as they left. The nurses held me down when I tried to get up, to go to him, but the sedatives had my head spinning and I blacked out. I didn't even get a chance to hold him in my a-arms." She shudders and adds fresh tears to the soaked sleeves of her robe.

"I had lots of sonograms the last few weeks before I went into labor. They told me over and over again I was having a girl." Her face becomes drawn and her eyes go cold, lifeless. "They lied to me and stole my son."

I grab her hands and squeeze. "If he's alive we'll find him. We can get him back."

She searches my face and I see the first spark of hope flicker in her eyes since our tearful reunion. She shakes her head. "How? The GRH is heavily guarded. No one's ever escaped from containment, Rei. No one."

"I have to tell you something Mara...and I need you to hear me out. Do you trust me?"

"Of course I trust you. You're my best friend."

Once I tell her this, there's no going back. If she knows, she'll be in as much danger as I am. But I can't do this without her, either. "I–" I say and hesitate, then start again. "I met an escaped survivor near your lake house. His name is Griff. He gave me this." I reach into my bra and pull out the necklace.

Mara takes it and examines the intricate details on the griffin. Her gaze meets mine in confusion.

"They took him to Eastkeep and I have to get him back. I'm willing to do anything, Mara." I say into the silence. After a long pause, I choke out the words I've been holding back this whole time. "I love him."

She stands abruptly and paces in front of the couch. At last, she stops and asks, "how?"

"We need to find the Sympathizers. They helped Griff and his father escape years ago. If they did it once, they can do it again. The Authority is hiding things from us and we need to figure out why."

Metal flashes as I unscrew the top of the necklace, revealing the USB port inside. Mara gasps and puts a hand over her mouth. Her hand shakes as she reaches out and takes it from me, pulling it close to examine the hidden gem.

"Can you load it so we can see what's on it?"

She nods. "Follow me."

I rise from the couch and walk with her down the narrow hallway into her bedroom. There's a desk pushed up against the far side of the wall, away from the rumpled, soiled bed sheets. She sits down in a chair and pulls up a screen on her desk. It's the first time I've seen her work in person. I watch with fascination as her fingers fly over the keyboard. At last she takes the USB drive and plugs it into a hole in the side of her computer. The machine makes a soft humming sound as it loads.

A folder appears on the screen with a triangle and a dot inside of it.

"You ready?" Mara asks.

I lean over the back of her chair and the side of her desk to get a better view.

Mara clicks on the folder, and a list of files appears. She clicks into the first file. A video window appears with a young woman in a white lab coat. Her hair hangs loose around her shoulders rather than pulled back into a typical, thick braid or twisted into a bun. Mara hits the play button.

"This is Evelyn Lynx reporting on our latest test results in our research. Heart disease is the leading cause of death in the world and today I've made a startling breakthrough! I've discovered that by manipulating MMP2, which is involved in the breakdown of extracellular matrix proteins, we can make use of 9p22 deletion syndrome on the 9th chromosome to target the cause of heart disease." Evelyn holds up a small vial and smiles. "I'm calling this Coronix-9. This is going to save so many lives."

The video ends. Mara and I exchange glances. "As in Director Evelyn Lynx?" I ask.

Mara nods. "Look, there's more," she clicks onto the next video. Evelyn is in a sparkling evening gown, a glass of champagne in her hand, standing behind a podium.

"Thank you all for coming today. Coronix-9 is officially in mass production. Our initial test trials blew our expectations out of the water. Without your help and the help of our donors and supporters, we wouldn't be here today."

"That's it?" I ask as the video cuts off. "That was a short one. Play the next one."

Evelyn appears back in a laboratory setting, a pair of glasses askew on her nose. "So, we've had some reports of side effects from Coronix-9. Male patients are reporting chest pain and shortness of breath. I'm pulling my hair out on this one. None of our trials displayed any of these symptoms. Although, on a positive note, we've had over 100,000 reports of Coronix-9 curing severe cases of heart disease. What I don't understand is these medical records for the patients experiencing negative symptoms. Their blood work is strange. I requested some tissue samples from severely affected individuals. I'll have to wait and see."

The video goes black. "Looks like this is the last one," Mara says, clicking on the last video. Evelyn's face is close to the monitor and there are dark bags under her eyes.

"I got the tissue samples three days ago. I tried to isolate Coronix-9 from the samples but I can't. There's been some kind of mutation in the HLA-B antigen. Coupled with the MMP2 protein breakdown, Coronix-9 is rapidly mutating. Worst of all, the symptoms are growing more severe; chest pain and fluid retention in the lungs,, followed by crystalline formations in the bloodstream, and severe blood clots. The president collapsed and died during a broadcast last week. World leaders have declared a state of emergency and locked down their borders, and there's talks of quarantining the affected cities. We had over 5,000 deaths yesterday. They're calling it the Heart Blight virus. So far, it appears that only those with a y chromosome are being affected. If I can isolate the exact genetic mutation, I think I can create a cure. But I need infected test subjects and they're dying left and right."

The video transitions to a different scene in another part of the lab. The camera swings and bounces along as the person holding it runs. Screams and cries fill the air and the movement stops, panning upwards. A middle-aged in a white lab coat grabs at his chest, vomits blood, and collapses to the floor.

"It's in the water!" A male voice screams somewhere off camera. "Don't drink the water!" An older man, also in a lab coat, hurries to help the person twitching on the floor. The moment he touches him, he grabs at his chest, vomits blood, and falls on top of him.

The camera spins around to face the person holding it. Evelyn's blood-streaked face appears so close that I can't see more than her eyes, nose, and mouth. She says, "What have I done? It's killing all the men. Only the men. It's spreading by contact now. They're dying all over the world and there's nothing I can do. I can't stop this. It's mutating too fast."

"Oh, no, it's happening here too!" The camera swings toward the sound of the distressed voice. Young Dr. Martina stands before the bodies of the two dead men, her hands clamped over her mouth. The name tag on her white coat says intern in big block letters.

"We have to burn the bodies." Evelyn says.

"Burn the—what?" Dr. Martina asks.

"If we don't, the virus will continue to spread until there's only women left. We have to do everything we can to stop it or humanity will go extinct. We're the only ones who understand what's going on and have the authority to keep everyone safe."

Dr. Martina lowers her hand and her lips quiver. Tears stream down her cheeks.

"Fire is the fastest way to cleanse the virus. If we want any chance of surviving this, we need to contain and isolate anyone infected. We have to burn the dead and contact every fertility specialist we can. Quick, help me move them. The sooner we do this, the better. Let's hope it's not too late for us, too."

The camera is set onto a flat surface. Dr. Martina stares in wide-eyed horror, then nods. Evelyn grabs the hands of one of the dead men, and Dr. Martina takes his feet. They drag him out the door, leaving a trail of blood behind, disappearing from view. The video stays fixed on the remaining dead man for another three minutes before it cuts off.

"I don't believe it," Mara sits back, astonished. Our eyes lock and a wordless understanding passes between us.

Director Evelyn created a medication that mutated into the Heart Blight virus. The virus contaminated the water and also spread by touch, killing the men faster and faster. The Cleansing holiday was a cover for her efforts to contain the spread of the virus by burning the dead bodies. The men in the GRH were her test subjects in an effort to find a cure before the virus started killing women, too.

The Director formed the Authority to control the population, secure the virus, and solve the problem she created.

That meant the Iron Divide was likely the result of the Free Territories trying to contain the spread of the virus. Does Commander Lynx know? Did Alyssa? What role did the Sympathizers have in all of this? Is this why they killed Dr. Martina?

There were still so many unanswered questions. But one thing's for sure.

The Authority created the Heart Blight virus.

Griff was telling the truth and I would do everything in my power to get him out of there.

# 44

**REI**

## As facts surface, betrayal boils and loyalty drowns.

"This is dangerous information, Rei. If everyone found out about this, there'll be rioting in the streets...." Mara pulls the USB drive from the computer and screws the top back on, handing it to me.

"This explains why the Authority wants to keep the men in containment. Griff said they run experiments on them, but I didn't want to believe him. They're using the survivors to create the cure for the Heart Blight. That also explains why they took your son."

"Tyrese." Mara says.

"Huh?"

"His name is Tyrese." Her chair slides backwards as she stands up and shuts off the computer. "Are you serious about getting them out of there?"

"Yes! We can't leave them there." I grab Mara's hands and squeeze. "Do you have any idea how we can get in touch with the Sympathizers?"

Mara fiddles with the belt on her robe as tears well in her eyes. She shakes her head, no. Now we both know what it feels like to lose someone we love. I wrap an arm around her shoulder and pull her close to my side.

"I'm sure we can figure it out. Griff told me they use this symbol to mark safe passage for each other." I flip the griffin upside down to show her the triangle with a circle in the middle.

Mara goes stiff against me and her head jerks up. She grabs the necklace and examines the mark. "I've seen this before," she says.

"Me too. It's carved on trees all over the Brass Mountains."

"No, Rei. I saw it recently at your house."

"Huh?"

"Your mom was going nuts when you didn't pick up the phone. I went over to your apartment to talk some sense into her, tell her you needed space. She said she had some old things in the nursery I could have for the baby. There was a picture of a tree with this mark on it. When I picked it up, she snatched it out of my hand. I thought she was just over-reacting. She'd been acting so strange since we couldn't reach you. Rei, you don't think your mother's a Sympathizer do you?"

The world tilts on its axis. I knew exactly what picture Mara was talking about. My mother had a similar reaction when I touched the same photo. How could I have missed it? It's been right there in front of my face this whole time. No wonder the symbol felt so familiar.

"I–I feel dizzy. I need to sit down."

Mara guides me into her computer chair. The wheels squeak as I settle into it. All those years of being so distant, of prying me for information, and encouraging me to become an Enforcer and get more lottery tickets when I said I wanted a baby. Had she been using me this whole time?

"I think I'm gonna be sick," I bolt from the chair and race for the bathroom. Foul bile burns my throat as I vomit into the toilet. My stomach heaves a second time and I gag, but nothing comes out. For once, I'm glad I haven't eaten since yesterday.

"We need to call your mother," Mara says from the door to the bathroom.

How could she?

I rest my forehead on the cold porcelain as my stomach churns. I don't want to agree with her. Screaming, throwing a fit, and crying until I can't anymore won't help. But I'm too emotionally exhausted to do more than nod in agreement.

"You better do it," I say with a hoarse voice. "They might be listening to your phone."

Mara gives me a sad smile and walks away to make the call. I can hear her voice down the hall as she tells my mother, "Yes. No, I haven't heard anything from Rei, sorry. Can you come over? I'm still such a mess and I really need someone to talk to. Okay, thanks. I'll see you soon."

Mara comes back to the bathroom with a glass of water in her hand. I take it from her with my thanks. It washes away the bitter taste in my mouth.

"Do you have anything to eat? I'm starving."

Mara holds out her hand to take the empty glass from me. "Sure I do," she says. "Come on, I'll make us both a sandwich while we wait."

The knock on the door startles us both. I shove the last bite of sandwich into my mouth and hide in Mara's bedroom while she goes to the door.

Just in case.

"Oh, poor child, you look awful." Mother says with her usual put on airs. "I'm glad you called. We need to get you cleaned up, and then I'll tell you my news."

The front door clicks shut before I exit the bedroom door and march down the hall.

"Rei finally called back. She says she's fine, but you and I both know she'll say anything to make sure we don't worry about her—Rei?"

She hurries over to me, wrapping her arms around me. "What are you doing here? Are you okay? You've lost so much weight, I hardly recognized you. Where have you been?"

"I'm fine," I choke out, torn between prying her off of me and hugging her close.

She takes my face in her hands and searches my eyes. "Cleary, you're not okay. Tell me, what's going on?"

"I have to ask you something, and I need you to tell me the truth. No excuses or deflections, just honesty." I pull from her grip, putting distance between us. There's no freaking easy way to ask her this. "Are you a Sympathizer?"

My mother freezes on the spot and wild terror invades her face. Her head whips back and forth, looking between Mara and me. It's all the confirmation I need. I pull out a kitchen chair and slide into it, putting my forehead on my crossed arms.

"Why didn't you tell me?" I mutter, afraid to see her reaction to my question.

A chair skids across the floor and I can only assume she's taking a seat. Her hand touches my arm. "Rei, look at me," she says.

I shake my head in my arms, refusing to comply. I'm done following orders.

My mother lets out a heavy sigh and says, "Mara, you might as well sit down, too, this may take a while. I can explain," she says, squeezing my arm.

My head shoots up and I glare at her. "How! Why? Have you been using me all this time? Do I mean nothing to you?"

"Rei! Of course that's not true. I love you! You're my daughter!"

"Then you better explain, so I can understand. Why would you do something like this to me?" My hands curl into fists and my face flushes red and hot. I want to reach across the table and strangle her. All these years she's been so distant, poking into my life, not being the mother I needed. For what?

"Her name was Lyra, Dr. Lyra Solenne. The first time I met her, she was trying to get some new equipment for her lab. She was the most beautiful woman I've ever met. She had hair the color of the sunset, a brilliant reddish-gold, and freckles across her face. What we had started as a friendship, but quickly developed into something more...."

"How come I never knew?" I ask, my fingernails cutting into the palms of my hands.

"We enjoyed keeping it our little secret. It made things more exciting," Mother says with a shrug. "I respected her wishes because I loved her, I wanted to make her happy. You see, she loved the forest, so I found this old road we sometimes used for supply runs through the Brass Mountains. We hiked off the beaten path until our feet ached. That's where we marked the tree with that silly symbol."

She traces an invisible triangle on the kitchen table top and says, "It was around an old knot in the wood where an old tree limb used to be. We thought it was funny, like it was watching us somehow. For my nameday the next year, she surprised me with that photo."

"What does this have to do with the Sympathizers?" Mara asks.

"One day, she asked me if I could help her with a special supply run. She wanted to get rid of some of the older lab equipment and replace it with the new stuff I'd brought in for her. Of course, I signed off on the paperwork without a second thought. I couldn't refuse her anything. Three days later, I heard reports of a containment breach. Two survivors had mysteriously escaped."

She pauses, glancing at us, then lays her hands flat on the table, palms up, and stares down at them. "That's how I found out the woman I loved was a Sympathizer. I could've turned her in, but I didn't. I was afraid they'd kill her and me, too. But I had a child at home who needed me."

There are tears in her eyes as she meets my fiery gaze. "I couldn't leave you an orphan, Rei. I loved her, but I love you, too. And I chose you."

The kitchen chair topples as I jump to my feet. "How dare you say that! Is that why you've been stringing me along and using me all these years?"

"What are you talking about? Use you? I've never used you! If anything, Lyra used me! I was so foolish, I would do anything for her!"

"Have you been feeding them information all this time? Is that why you wanted me to become an Enforcer?"

"N–no! Of course not!"

"I don't believe you," I say between clenched teeth. "You must be working for them. You are, aren't you?"

Her mouth opens, closes, then opens again. No words come out.

"I knew it." I spit with barely contained fury.

"The Authority killed Lyra two years ago," she says, her voice choking back tears. "Somehow, they found out about her involvement in the containment breach. They tortured her to death and then hung her body from the Suppression Line, Rei! I drove past her every day for weeks, do you know what that feels like? Seeing someone you love falling apart before your very eyes? She could've turned me in, but she didn't. I had to do something. She died protecting us!"

"Us! Tell me, how was she protecting us?" I ask in a deadpan voice.

"You have to stop this, Rei. This whole endeavor is so, so dangerous. It's why I tried to keep you out of it. That's why I wanted you to become an Enforcer. If you're loyal to the Authority and they found out I was a Sympathizer, no one would question if you had anything to do with it. It was to keep you safe!"

"Yeah, well, you sure did a horrible job, didn't you?"

"No one is perfect, Rei. Not even you," she says and for the first time her eyes flare with an anger to match my own. "But I'm here, aren't I? I always show up for you when you need me."

"We can't trust her," I hiss at Mara. "We'll have to find another way."

"There's no other way. This is our only option, Rei." Mara says with a calm confidence. She turns to my mother and laces their fingers together. "We need your help to get them out of containment. You did it once, you can do it again."

My mother's face scrunches in confusion. "Them? Who?"

"My son is alive. The Authority took him and a man you and Lyra helped escape from the GRH years ago."

My mother gives me her most famous, detached look. Her eyes bore holes in my freaking chest, but I can't turn away from them. Crap. I meet her gaze and return it tenfold.

"This man, does he mean something to you?" she says at last.

"I love him," I say with a defiant lift of my chin. "I'm getting him out of there whether you and the Sympathizers help us or not."

Mara huffs in exasperation. "Hate each other all you want. I can't do this without the both of you. We'll also need the Sympathizer's help if we want any chance of getting into the GRH. Can you take us to them?"

"You'll get yourselves killed doing this," she shakes her head in disbelief. "It's a terrible idea. The Sympathizers have been trying to break up the Authority since Lyra died without success. We take huge losses for little gain every time."

"Yeah, well, you didn't have this." I place Griff's necklace on the kitchen table.

"What's this?" Mother asks, picking up the griffin. "It's beautiful."

"Proof that the Authority created the Heart Blight virus," I say with eyes full of hope and something more. "A way to destroy the Authority from the inside out. Will you help us or not?"

Mother carefully places it back on the table. "We can't leave together. I'll take you where you need to go. Wait 15 minutes after I leave, each of you. Meet me at the far table in Loyal Grounds."

She stands from her chair. Without another word, she turns and leaves.

"We can't trust her," I say with a growl, picking up the griffin and stuffing it back into my bra.

"If you want to get them back, we have to. Unless you have any other bright ideas?" Silence. "I thought so. You go next. I have to get dressed."

# 45

## REI

**Nothing stays contained forever, so when the truth is revealed, the cost of knowing has a price.**

The coffee shop is crowded this time of the afternoon since entry school has just let out. Cliques of girls gather in groups, their textbooks spread out on the tabletops, as they work on their homework and trade gossip about the day. My mother stands by a tall table in the back, a glass coffee cup steaming in front of her. I head to the back and take up a position where I can still see the front door.

She nudges the cup over to me and I take it, enjoying the warmth of the ceramic from the brief chill outside.

"I'm sorry," she says.

I keep my eyes pinned to the dark liquid inside the cup. It's warm and comforting, reminding me of the way I felt in Griff's hut. Nothing will ever freaking be the same now.

"You can't help who you love," I say.

"You've changed, Rei."

I don't respond. What can I say? The silence stretches between us. Somehow, it feels more companionable than uncomfortable. I frown. Forgiveness shouldn't be easy, right?

I curl my fingers tighter, letting the heat chase away the thought. Mara enters, her hair combed, wearing clean clothes, and heads straight back to us. I offer her the coffee cup, but she shakes her head.

"Thanks, I'm okay," she says.

"Follow me," says my mother, moving away from the table.

I leave the coffee cup and we follow her down a narrow hallway at the back of the store. Mother stops at a door and makes sure no one is behind us, then opens it and slips inside. We enter a small store room packed with shelves full of ceramic mugs, bags of coffee grinds, and filters. Plates and dishes line the other side of the wall.

"Close the door," she says to Mara.

Mara pulls it shut behind us.

"This way," she squeezes past a tall shelving unit. Behind it, there's a narrow space with a keypad on the wall. She punches in a code and a small access door slides open. Ducking her head, she crouches and enters.

Mara and I exchange glances, then follow.

We stand at the top of a long, descending staircase. The space is dark, but faint light at the bottom makes it bright enough to see.

It takes longer than I thought to descend the stairs. In the dim light, its length is deceiving. The light grows brighter as we reach the bottom and find a long hallway with small sconce lights inset every few feet. The cement floor is damp and slimy. A strong, moldy odor permeates the air.

"Are we in the sewers?" I ask.

"No, but close. It's not much further, come on." Mother leads the way down the narrow space.

Panic rises in my throat. It reminds me of the tunnel and cement exploding around us, the sound of gunshots, cloying smoke stinging my nose. Mara notices my distress. She tucks her arm through mine and drags me along.

At the end of the hall, there's another door with a keypad. After my mother enters a code, she turns the big wheel on the front and pulls it open. Together, we enter the underground vault.

Several women look up from the boxes they're sorting and stacking. One yells in warning and goes for a gun on her belt.

My mother throws her hands up in the air and says, "Easy Claire. It's me, Naomi. This is my daughter Rei and her friend Mara."

Claire's gun stays trained on me. "What the hell! You brought an Enforcer and a Surveillance Officer here?" she hisses.

No way. She's the annoyed waitress from Loyal Grounds who brought us water when Mara was pregnant. "We're unarmed," I say, raising my hands in the air. "You can check."

Claire's eyes narrow, and her hand tightens its grip on the gun. "Give me one good reason why I shouldn't kill you where you stand?"

"Claire, stand down!" says a strong, authoritative voice. A tiny, older woman struts around a tall stack of boxes.

I blink in surprise. "Mrs. Wellsly!" The old cull who was always digging through the trash outside our apartment was the last person I expected to see leading the Sympathizers.

"Close your mouth, girl, you're catching flies," she says and chuckles as she approaches. Her gnarled hand lowers Claire's gun arm.

"But—what are you—how?" The teeth in her mouth transform her entire facial structure.

"You think I rifle through the trash by your house because I like to? Passing intelligence to your mother is an art form, girl. No one bothers a smelly, senile, old lady," she says and pats Claire on the shoulder. "Now, what's this I hear about needing our help, Naomi? Follow me, let's talk."

My mother falls into step behind her. Mara and I hesitate, exchanging glances at the sinister look Claire is giving us.

"Claire, that's enough." Mrs. Wellsly barks without turning around.

"I'm watching you," Claire sneers, lowering her gun without returning it to its holster. Instincts tell me I need to keep my eyes on this one. As we inch past, following my mother and Mrs. Wellsly, she pins us with a dark glare.

Behind the boxes, we find my mother and Mrs. Wellsly standing over a large table covered by a map, talking in lowered voices. When Mara and I appear, they break apart, and Mrs. Wellsly clears her throat.

"Your mother tells me you want help to get her son and some other man out of the GRH containment." She traces her finger over the geography and stops on a black dot marked Eastkeep.

The map is nothing like the simple drawings in the Authority's textbooks in entry school, or even the more complex terrain I studied during basic training. This one has a bold, dark line showing the separation between the Authority and the Free Territories by the Iron Divide. In addition, there's a multitude of smaller shapes: squares, diamonds and X's, but they're missing labels.

"That's right. His name is Griff. He escaped containment with his father years ago."

"Fletcher's boy!" she says, and her head jerks up. She runs her hand down to the Iron Divide and past it, to the small section marked Free

Territories. "Most of what we know about the Free Territories came from Fletcher. He was born there before they built the Iron Divide to try and stop the spread of the virus. Here, outside of Boverwick, before the Authority annexed these lands." She traces her finger in a circle around an area where the Iron Divide separates the Authority from the Free Territories.

"That means the information Lyra gave them never made it across. Dammit!" She pounds a fist on the table so hard it shakes. "Lyra thought the Authority created the Heart Blight virus, but we had no proof."

Her words give me pause. What? Lyra gave Griff and his father the necklace with the videos, which means she had everything they freaking needed. Why didn't she tell the Sympathizers what she'd found?

"I don't understand your cause. If you had proof, what would you do with it?" I ask.

"Expose the devious, manipulative Director for stealing, experimenting, and using our boys like livestock. Lies, the lot of it!" She sweeps a hand out, motioning to the stacks of boxes around the open space. "We have enough munitions and supplies to raise a small army. What we don't have is the support to stop this madness. The citizens are so thoroughly oppressed and controlled they honestly believe the Authority is searching for a cure. "

She turns to Mara, "Your name was pulled in a backup drawing, wasn't it?"

"How did you know th-"

"This lottery business is nothing but a propaganda tool to force pregnancies on fertile women. Tethers, water purification, and strict rations keep us dependent and under their thumb. All in the name of preventing humanity's extinction and science." She taps a finger to her forehead. "But our eyes are open to the truth. They claim this deadly virus is rapidly mutating, and it's only a matter of time until we're also infected. After years of needless precautions, not a single woman has been infected by the Heart Blight. The virus–our boys–they aren't contagious."

The conversation I overheard from the Enforcers on the radio gives me pause. Bless the mother! The pieces click like a loaded weapon.

I didn't get sick during my time with Griff because he's not contagious, but a barrack in the MMZ is under quarantine. Those Enforcers left someone in their unit who'd been infected to die in the Brass Mountains. Dr. Martina was terrified, overworked and exhausted the day of the bombing. She'd argued with Commander Lynx about something spreading and risked her life to protect her black case during the attack...because she knew what was at stake. It explained everything; our sudden call to formation, standing in front of her viral research lab, and watching her take off her red hazmat suit.

Dr. Martina must have examined the first infected woman in the history of the Heart Blight that morning.

So Commander Lynx sent our platoon, a group of brand new Enforcer trainees led by Alyssa, to escort the doctor to the GRH. Because there was no one else she trusted and no time to waste. Despite every freaking crazy method the Authority used to prevent the virus from mutating and spreading, the Director's worst fears had come true.

"The virus is contagious. Women in the MMZ are already infected. What if the Director is the only one who can find a cure?"

Mrs. Wellsly's watery eyes study me with fierce intensity, a muscle twitching in her cheek. "Whose side are you on, girl? I thought your mother brought you here because you wanted to join our cause, or have they brainwashed you past the point of no return?" She looks at my mother and raises an eyebrow. Mother lowers her eyes, refusing to meet her accusatory expression.

Dammit! She doesn't believe me.

"You're either an ally or an enemy," she snaps. "If you're our enemy, Rei, you won't leave here alive. I guarantee it." The threat hovers in the charged air.

"I'm not your enemy," I insist, refusing to break her piercing stare. However, memories of the attack on my protection detail won't let me hold my tongue. "But I was in the convoy you bombed."

Mrs. Wellsly snorts and throws her head back. Her wrinkly neck waddles as she laughs. "I've always liked you, kiddo. Always said you got a smart one, didn't I, Naomi?"

My mother gives her a weak smile

There has to be a way to get through to her. To all of them. "Why did you kill Dr. Martina?"

Mrs. Wellsly's face contorts at the mention of the name and she snarls, "she murdered my son! She got what she deserved."

Mara whimpers beside me and lunges for Mrs Wellsly's hand, squeezing tightly. "Please," she pleads, "you have to help me get my son out of there. They wouldn't even let me hold him. Please!"

Mrs. Wellsly shakes her off. "Look around you, stupid girl," she hisses. "All of us have lost sons. You think we wouldn't get our boys out if we could? What makes yours so special, huh?" The bite to her voice is loud enough the women in the room turn in our direction.

"All of them?" I ask, assessing the numbers. There had to be 15 or 20 women here, possibly more. The mothers of the boys and men I'd been training to keep in containment. Thanks to the bombing, I'd never made it inside a GRH facility.

"Most of them," Mrs. Wellsly corrects. "Your mother is one of the few who hasn't. I told her not to encourage you to become an Enforcer, but your mother can be quite stubborn with things involving you."

"Is that your ultimate goal, then? To free your children and get revenge on the Authority?"

Mrs. Wellsly leans forward and smiles as she says, "The Director will pay for stealing our boys, and their murderous, twisted experiments. If you want to call that revenge, so be it."

"If I can give you proof the Authority created the Heart Blight virus, will you help me rescue my son?" Mara begs.

"Get us that and we'll bring the Authority crashing down on its head," Mrs. Wellsly agrees.

"Give it to her, Rei." Mara demands. "You have to. It's the only way we can get them out of there. They have the weapons, the supplies, and the resources we don't. We need them and what they've built here."

My gut clenches and my underarms sweat. Still, I hesitate. Lyra didn't give them the proof when she had the chance, she told Griff to go to the Free Territories instead, because the Sympathizers didn't believe in a cure. Turning this information over would expose the Director for the disaster she'd made, a mutation that catapulted humanity to the verge of extinction. A freaking mistake she'd been trying to fix all these years in her own twisted ways.

These videos may as well be her death sentence, but I wouldn't see Griff again without their help. There has to be a way.

"Rei! Give it to her!" Mara demands, her voice near hysterical.

Dammit, I'm outta time! I pull the necklace from beneath my shirt and place it gently on the table. Mrs. Wellsly picks up the griffin and studies it, confused.

"There's a USB drive inside," I explain. "The videos prove Director Evelyn Lynx accidentally created the Heart Blight virus."

Mrs. Wellsly snaps her fingers. "Linda, over here."

A young woman with large glasses and frizzy hair stops packing boxes and crosses the room. Mrs. Wellsly hands her the necklace. "Linda is our tech expert. She works at the Collective Voice Broadcast Station. I want to see the videos on this as soon as possible. If it contains what they say it does, we'll need to prepare a broadcast," she says, handing it off.

"It'll take a few days to prepare. Unfortunately, we have limited intel on the interior of the GRH. We were hoping Cameron would come through on that front, but sadly she died in the bombing."

"C–Cameron was a Sympathizer?" I ask, stunned. Her silly interest in the GRH seems like forever ago. Did she talk out of turn and piss off Commander Lynx on purpose? Was her son alive, locked away somewhere in containment?

Mrs. Wellsly nods. "We had high hopes for Cameron. She got further than any of the others."

"Others? Did you know she was part of the protection detail for Dr. Martina?"

"No," Mrs. Wellsly says with a frown. "She was an unfortunate casualty. Claire won't forgive me for her death, but I hope one day she'll understand this was all for the greater good."

My reality has been built upon so many freaking lies. But one thing is crystal clear.

If I want any chance of getting Griff out of the GRH and to the Free Territories, I need all the help I can get.

# 46

## REI

**Luck isn't always a part of the draw.**

Stepping inside, I'm assaulted by the sour stench of musty paper, tangy iron, and something darker. Clumps of gray, fuzzy hair and pale, brittle bones, the remains of some rodent, rot in the corner. Metal tins and wooden boxes take up much of the available space, stacked floor to ceiling.

"What's all this stuff?" I ask, wiping a thick layer of dust off the lid of the closest metal box. Gross.

"Most of these hold copies of the MMZ's transport records, courtesy of Naomi. I haven't digitized these ones yet." Linda pries a container open, revealing a stack of papers. "Do you remember the day they took your son?"

Mara nods, picking up a large stack, flipping through. "Last week."

"All transports are logged, if you can find the ones for that day we can narrow down which GRH they took your son to."

"Linda, Mrs. Wellsly needs you," Claire appears in the doorway, hand on the holster of her gun.

"Oh, okay." Linda pushes her glasses up her nose. "Anyways, it shouldn't take you long to find it. The most recent records are in this stack here."

"Thanks," Mara says as Linda walks out and Claire slams the door in her face, leaving the two of us alone in the musty space.

"We have a problem," I hiss.

"What?" Mara asks, leafing through papers.

"I need you to figure out a way to make a copy of the USB drive."

"Huh? Why?"

"They don't care about a cure and that's probably why Lyra didn't tell them about the videos. We have to get a copy to the Free Territories."

"The Free Territories won't care about some old videos of the Director—oh, here! I found it!" Mara rips the piece of paper from the stack and marches over. "Look, here's the birthing center I went to. The transport that day went to Eastkeep. Isn't that where they're keeping Griff?"

"Yeah, that's right."

Mara smiles, gripping the paper to her chest, heading for the door.

"Wait! Mara," I grab her wrist, pulling her close, lowering my voice. "Lyra got her hands on these videos when Griff and his father escaped. But she was a Sympathizer for years before she died. She could have just given it to them but she sent it to the Free Territories instead."

"Honestly, what difference does it make as long as we get them back?"

"Didn't you hear me earlier? The virus is making women sick. What if history repeats itself? How long was it before most of the men were wiped out by the virus? If women are getting sick it could happen to us, too."

"You were out in the woods with Griff for days and you didn't get sick. The Authority has been lying to us our whole lives and now you want me to believe them?"

"Mara, for the love of the freaking mother and all the years we've spent together, you have to believe me."

She sighs and nods, squeezing my hand back and giving me one of her best mischievous smiles. "For once I'm not the one insisting we break the rules. Okay. So what do we do?"

"I have an idea."

Beyond the door there's a hiss and click of static followed by a familiar announcer's voice. Our heads whip around and we follow the sound out of the cramped storage room. A crowd of Sympathizers huddles in front of a fuzzy black and white television screen.

"Loyal citizens of the Authority, this is the CBV coming to you live. Today is code yellow, with a 29% chance of rain. The market will see an increase in patrols and close at 0200 hours this week. Oh, Director, what are you doing here? Here, take mine."

The announcer rises from her chair, pulling it out so Director Lynx can sit. Her tailored uniform is clean and neatly pressed but one button is askew and wispy strands of gray hair have slipped from her typical bun. There's traces of dark circles under her eyes. It's the only time in my life I've seen her unkempt and disheveled.

"Children of the Authority, I come to you today with a message of hope. Effective immediately, all rations are being reduced by 40 percent. Due to increasing Sympathizer activity on our supply lines, this is a necessary step to ensure the health and safety of our citizens. Do not be swayed by their lies and baseless rumors. We will not stop until this threat is completely neutralized.

"Vigilance. Order. Discipline. Together we build a bright future."

Director Lynx stands, salutes the camera, and walks off.

The announcer hurries to return to her seat. "Thank you, Director Lynx. What an unexpected surprise. And now, the big day is here, it's the moment you've been waiting for. Special congratulations to Rei Koss for winning today's lottery! We can't wait to meet your little bundle of joy next year, Rei. That's it for our afternoon updates, now please join me in closing with the pledge of allegiance."

Wait, did they just call my name? No freaking way. Claire turns from the front of the pack, her brows furrowed, lips curling. "I knew you were a double crossing spy!" she screams, lunging forward, hands reaching for my shirt.

"N-no, I-" Fingers curl into my collar, forcing me backwards, slamming me into the rough concrete wall. Stars pepper the edges of my vision as I grab her wrist and use my elbow to break her hold. "Wait!"

Her fist launches for my face but she's much, much slower than the soldiers I've trained with over the past few years. Knuckles hit concrete instead of my jaw, eliciting a gut wrenching howl from her throat. Bracing my hands on her shoulders I shove with my body weight, pushing her off me.

"You traitor!" Claire bellows, face red, spit flying from her open mouth. "You're going to expose our base to the Authority the first chance you get!"

"I won't. I can't go back! Don't you understand, they'll hang me from the Suppression Line the first chance they get."

"They just called your name in the lottery!" There's a wild, dangerous look in her eyes. She wants me dead.

"And? What do you expect me to do about that? I'm here with you! I'm on your side!"

Claire reaches for her holster and I react, shouldering into her, throwing her off balance. Together we careen into the onlooking crowd of Sympathizers. Hands tear at my hair, my shirt, my arms, trying to pull us apart. I use every trick in my book to evade their grasp and disarm the threat in front of me.

"Enough! Girls, stand down!" There's no mistaking who the bark of the authoritative voice comes from.

Hands drag me, forcing me to my feet and away from Claire. Her gun lies on the ground and blood smears her nose from our tussle. The bandage over my tether is unravelling, trailing the ground as I'm pulled backwards.

"What is the meaning of this?" Mrs. Wellsly demands, my Mother hovering behind her shoulder, a worry furrowing her brows.

"They called her name in the lottery!" Claire spits, jerking free of Linda and the other girl holding her, wiping her nose.

"And you think I had something to do with that? The Authority wants me dead," I growl.

"You're a double crossing liar!"

"Claire!" Mrs. Wellsly snaps, "that's enough. Rei brought us everything we needed to destroy the Authority for good."

"She's an Enforcer, she's the reason Cameron's son is in one of those hell holes!"

"I'm not anymore. I've cut all ties to the Authority. That's why I'm here. The man I love is in the GRH and I want him out as much as the rest of you want to see your boys again."

"Let her go," Mrs. Wellsly commands.

The women holding my arms release me. She steps back, her boot catching my dangling bandage, yanking it off of my hand. There's a collective gasp as eyes go to the cut over the top of my palm.

"What is this?" Mrs. Wellsly grabs me, examining the weeping wound. "You've untethered? How?"

"It was acting funny in the woods, so I cut it out..." my voice falters.

They wouldn't understand. How could I explain I'd done it so I could touch Griff again?

"No one has ever untethered before without being suppressed." Mrs. Wellsly mutters, running a hand over her chin. She paces a few steps back and forth, lost in thought. "It happened in the woods, you say?"

I nod.

"Perhaps it has something to do with a weak signal? If that's the case, we could all remove them. There's no signal down here."

A woman beside me makes a high-pitched noise in her throat. Suddenly, she pulls a knife and places it against the bump on her hand.

"Wait!" There were no strange beeping noises, no blue lights.

Damnit, I need to stop her! I reach for the knife.

# 47

**REI**

**The hardest part isn't the ending, it's the ones we leave behind.**

The moment she slices into her skin her eyes roll back into her head, she spasms violently, mouth falling open, foaming white, and collapses. Screams ring out, echoing her death throes, falling silent when she lies still. Crap. As if things couldn't get any worse.

"Well, that didn't work. Stupid girl. You two, take care of the body. Claire and Rei, come with me." Mrs. Wellsly turns and strides away, shaking her head and mumbling something under her breath.

Claire glares bullets. Good thing she's unarmed.

"Now!" Mrs. Wellsly barks.

Turning, I follow. She winds us through stacks of boxes and crates, stopping at an old, military grade truck. How did they get something like this? Had they acquired it from one of their attacks? Or did my mother have something to do with it? Claire pauses beside me a few seconds later, her hand clamped over the gun reset in its holster.

"The Authority has spent years trying to hang us, to break us apart. I'll be damned if I let you two ruin the best shot we've ever had at real progress. This nonsense ends now. The two of you will unload this truck, no," she holds up a hand, "I don't want to hear one word, Claire. Get to work."

Yeah, right, together? Like that will ever freaking happen. Blotchy red spots break out across Claire's face, neck, and shoulders. Without a word she climbs into the truck, and picks up a box. She turns and extends it over the edge of the truck bed, clenching her teeth, fingers white along the bottom.

"Well?" she hisses. "I don't have all day. Get your ass over here."

The edges of the cardboard burn my forearms as she lets it slip, dropping it before I can get a grip. Metal rattles inside as it hits the floor and smashes my toes. So this is how it's gonna be, huh? Hazing and Alyssa's drills in the MMZ made this a walk in the park.

"Where do I put this?" I ask, picking it up as if nothing happened.

"With the others, where else?" Claire takes another box and drops it, aiming for my head.

"You missed. Better luck next time." I stack it with the rest.

"It should have been you," she spits, another box clattering as it narrowly misses my shoulder. It splits as it hits the ground. Small bags of horrible, spicy chips spill across the ground. They crunch beneath my boots, burning my nose.

"These supplies were supposed to go to the MMZ, right?" I ask, picking up one of the unopened bags. Cameron's favorite.

"You spent your whole life bowing to their lies. Cameron was a better person than you'll ever be." Claire's voice cracks and she struggles to blink back tears.

"Maybe she was," I say, gathering the chips into the broken box as best as I can. Collecting the fragments of our short-lived time together. "She was always eating these damn things. No one else in the mess hall would touch them."

"That's why I used them to pass her messages." Claire wipes tears from her cheeks. "She was determined to win you over to our cause because your mother was already one of us. That's what got her killed. You!"

"Hate me all you want," I set the crumbling box on top of the first one I stacked. "When our truck flipped she was pinned by the driver's seat. There was nothing I could do to save her. I stayed with her until the end. She wanted me to tell someone she loved them. I'm guessing that was you."

"Liar!" Claire sobs. "Goddess Lysara, I miss her so much."

"I'm sorry. I'll give you a minute."

"Rei? Rei! There you are," Mara nearly collides into me. "You have to see this." She hands me a piece of paper with a grainy black and white picture. Bold, block letters are printed beneath my basic training graduation photo: wanted for treason.

Bless the mother, what is this? No freaking way.

"Where did you get this?" I demand.

"I was talking to Linda when a Sympathizer came in with one of these. She said soldiers are posting them all over the city."

"Crap! This isn't good."

"But it gets worse. Fights broke out in the market. People are in a panic over rations being cut and it closing early. Apparently the line to get in stretched a few blocks. Add that to more patrols than normal and everyone is on edge. Linda said there were three new bodies hanging from the Suppression Line and none of them were Sympathizers." She leans in close and whispers, "There's a rumor going around that soldiers in the MMZ are sick. I should have believed you right away. Things are getting bad out there."

"Were you able to get what we needed?" I question, keeping my voice low.

Mara's face falls, and she shakes her head. "No go."

"Dammit. We'll have to try again later."

"You don't understand. I had to ask around a bit to figure out where Linda was. I could hear voices inside so I stopped to listen, but I couldn't hear what they were saying. So I peeked around the corner and I saw Mrs. Wellsly destroy the USB drive with the butt of her gun. It's gone, there's nothing left."

"What? Why would she do that?"

Mara shrugs. "I'm guessing they made a digital copy but without access to their system there's not much we can do."

"Maybe my mom can help us with that. Do you think you can find her? I'm supposed to help Claire unload these boxes."

"Yeah, I'll go look."

When I return Claire is gone. Go figure, she's left me to do all the work. I climb into the truck and something skitters underfoot. Reaching down I pick it up off the metal floor bed. On Cleansing day motherlines around the city would use lighters like these to set bundles of wood ablaze and celebrate, remembering the pyres we built 60 years ago for the men we'd lost.

With a press of my thumb flame ignites, flickering in reaction to the soft stir of my breath. Griff won't be one of those, I won't allow it.

Static squawks and a voice chimes on overhead. "Please report to the common area. I repeat, report for a briefing."

I shove the lighter in my pocket, the one thing here that reminds me of Griff, and follow the sounds of the rising commotion to the common area. Sympathizers crowd around Mrs. Wellsly, who stands before the table with the map. Working my way through the crowd I fall in line beside Mara and my mother. Mara, sensing my wordless question, shakes her head. Crap! My mom wasn't any help, either.

After a few minutes, when the crowd has grown to fill the open space, Mrs. Wellsly raises a hand and everyone falls silent.

"In light of recent events in the market, I've decided to launch our attack on Cleansing day. It gives us time to finish our preparations and it's the perfect distraction, everyone's attention will be focused elsewhere. In the meantime, we'll work to increase tensions and riots at the market. Naomi, you're in charge of transport as usual. The rest of you will split into groups. Rei and Mara, you'll be with the rescue team going into the GRH led by Claire and Linda.

"We have lots of work to do and not a lot of time to do it. Let's go get our boys back."

# 48

# GRIFF

**You don't survive a place like this by
believing in kindness.**

Nothing could undo the years the Authority gutted and
drained Ian in the GRH. Like him, these men had lost their
fight, ready to lie down to die, forgetting they still had teeth and
claws. Drugged water and a strictly controlled diet kept us lean,
subdued, and fertile. Helpless. Now I have to show them strength
isn't born out of fear or control, but from love, truth, and the
courage to stand up for our dignity.

*Fuck the Authority.*

The chill of the pitted cement wall seeps through my flimsy gray
shirt where I'm leaning. Waiting. The red light above 51 turns green
when he's finished. Musty heat and the salty tang of flushed, sweaty
skin greets me when I enter.

Ian stands on his stained mattress, crayon pressed to the wall,
shading a section of his drawing. When we were children we dreamed
of going outside, of seeing the world around us. The odd shapes and
colors on the mural, of nature he's never seen but only imagined and
re-created from stories, tug at my guilt.

"I need ya help to convince the others to get out of here."

Great, he's ignoring me.

"Ya draw a lot better than ya used to." Prominently featured above his bed is a portrait of my 12-year-old face beside a younger version of Father. "This is really good." I run my fingers over the waxy surface of the blue stubble on his chin. Even if they're the wrong color, he's accurately captured the overbearing, critical gleam in his eyes.

"Don't touch them," he says in a flat, numb voice.

"For a second, when I looked at ya earlier, I thought ya were him...." My hand drops and I turn to find Ian watching me. "That day haunts me, ya know? I didn't want to leave ya behind–"

"Stop!" Ian shakes his head, "I don't want excuses. Why are you here?"

"To explain what happened–"

"I was there, I know what happened."

"But ya don't understand–"

"I'm not a scared little kid anymore! Stop treating me like I'm stupid. They questioned me for weeks. No matter how much I screamed or cried or begged and told them I didn't know anything they wouldn't let me out of my cell."

"Nothing I do or say will ever make up for what happened," I murmur. "I tried, Ian, I did. Father picked me up and dragged me away kicking and screaming."

"Because that scientist only wanted you." Ian shakes his head, going back to his drawing, scraping the end of the crayon against the wall so hard it squeaks and snaps in half, rolling across the floor. "Shit! That was my last one."

Bending down, I pick up the broken crayon. Huh, what is that? There's something white tucked beneath his mattress. A weapon? The piece of paper slips free when I tug.

"What the fuck is this? Why do you have her picture?"

Ian turns, his mouth falling open, and lunges, yanking the paper from my grip. "Keep your hands off my stuff!" His panicked gaze swings toward the observation window before he shoves the sketch beneath the bed.

"Hey! I asked you a question."

"It's a long story."

"Seriously? An Enforcer?" If he thought I'd let him off the hook for this one he had another thing coming. He better have a good reason for giving her that smile.

Commander Lynx's daughter.

Our sister? Shit!

"Do you remember Craig?" Ian asks. "He was bigger than me and Sam, the round-faced boy who liked to crack all those stupid jokes. Anyway, after you left and they let me outta my cell he took me under his wing. Without him I never woulda survived the Breaking. He taught me the ropes, how to trade, and that who you know makes a difference."

"What does that have to do with her?"

"He liked to test the limits so I would run around making trades to keep the peace. I didn't know he was stocking up to try and escape. When they caught him and dragged him off for behavior modification he started screaming that I was the one trying to escape, not him. Two Enforcers grabbed me, started dragging me off, but she stopped them, said I had nothing to do with it. They took Craig away and I haven't seen her since then. I always wondered what happened to them."

The way he averts his eyes when he talks about her makes me uneasy. There had to be more to the story. Stone-faced Alyssa, the first one to run after Rei when Commander Lynx ordered her killed, protected my brother? And yet, Ian drew a picture of her smiling face.

"Why would she help ya?"

He shrugs. "Dunno. She brought me crayons sometimes. Maybe she liked my drawings. I'd be an empty shell in the white room if she didn't help me."

"I met a woman, Rei, out in the woods and she saved my life. So look, I get it. They're not all bad, but ya can't trust her. She was a part of the group that hauled me here."

"Were you ever coming back for me?"

Shit. The question hits like an arrow to the chest, puncturing, sucking the air from my lungs. He deserves the truth, I can't lie to him. Meeting his stormy blue eyes is my price to pay.

"I didn't think I'd ever see ya again. But the guilt eats away at me every day. Father told me not to let go of your hand. Ya dropped your crayon and wanted to pick it up. I thought there was enough time...I was wrong. It's all my fault. I shouldn't have let ya go. I'm sorry I failed ya."

There, I said it. I hold out the piece of broken crayon. Forgiveness in the form of the one thing that broke us apart.

Will he take it? Can we move past this and start again? The longer he stares at my fingertips, the longer he doesn't respond, the more my chance at redemption flounders, struggling. The noose grows tighter, strangling the life out of whatever remains of our relationship, the connection we once had.

"I don't—"

"There you are!" The loud, obnoxious voice behind me interrupts the unreadable expression in Ian's eyes. I turn, finding the tall man in the cell across from mine leaning against the door frame.

"D-Dean," Ian sputters, shoving his broken piece of crayon behind his ear in a fluid, habitual movement. "You need something?"

"Gotta tooth that's been kicking my ass. You know if Joe got anything that might help?"

"No, but–" Ian breaks off, snapping his mouth shut.

"What?" Dean leers, shoving past me, approaching Ian. "You know who does, don't cha?"

Ian shakes his head, backing up until he hits the glass of the observation window. What the fuck? Even though he's a head taller than Dean his shoulders slump and he curls his body, making himself smaller, less of a target.

Dean's hand slams into the glass beside Ian's head, rattling the frame. His greasy fingers leave streaks behind when he grabs Ian's chin in his fist and squeezes.

Hard.

"Don't lie to me, little mouse. Keep it up and you might tempt me to visit." He hisses, stroking a finger over Ian's forcefully pursed lips.

"Hey! Get ya fucking, slimy hands off him!" I grab Dean's wrist, tearing him off my brother.

Dean stumbles, hitting the wall, face contorting in rage. "You're gonna regret that, little boy! Looks like I gotta show you how things work round here."

He shoves off the wall, hunched low, barreling into my stomach. Stars dance on the edges of my vision as the force of his hit slams me into the wall, head connecting to the concrete. Despite his smaller size he has an iron grip with one hand on my waist, his other pummeling the side of my ribs.

"Fight, fight, fight!" voices chant and a crowd gathers, jockeying for a better position in the narrow doorway.

I drive my elbow down into his shoulder blades, trying to get him off of me. Using my more heavily muscled body, I grab his underarm and twist, flipping him to the ground. The second he's clear I'm on top of him, hammering away.

Dean grins up at me, teeth bloody, as he brings his arms up to block my blows to his face. "Whoo!" He screams and breaks into cackling laughter. "We got a live one here!"

"Shut. The. Fuck. Up!" My knuckles pop and crack, protesting the force of my punches. "Don't ya ever fucking touch my brother again or I'll kill ya, do ya hear me?"

"Griff! Stop! Shit, Griff, you gotta stop! I'm okay. Hey! I said I'm okay!" A hand catches my arm, holding it back.

"Don't stop baby, give it to me good," Dean chuckles, blood smearing his cheeks and chin. "When you're done I'll be sure to give my little mouse a spin." His eyes sidle up Ian's height, stopping on his face, and he licks his lips.

"You're dead!" I scream, going for his throat.

"Enough!" An Enforcer's gun presses against my temple. "I said, enough. The rest of you, return to your cells, lockdown is in effect."

I raise my hands above my head, standing down.

"Both of you, get up! Slowly! You're heading to the maximum security ward." The green-eyed vixen hisses.

Getting to my feet, gloved hands grab me and drag me out of the cell. We're being separated, and once again there's nothing I can do. Whipping my head around, I search for my brother. He's got his hands in the air, standing against the observation window, straining to see me over the other Enforcers in and around the cell.

"Ian!" I shout, "I'll be back, I promise."

His dark head bobs, blue eyes pinned to mine. "I'll talk to the guys, see what I can do."

Then I'm shoved toward the exit for the ward.

Leaving him behind.

Again.

# 49

**REI**

## The enemy of my enemy is a useful tool when it's right for the job.

I stand with a group of Sympathizers and Mara, loading weapons and double checking all the gear we'll need. Claire is directly across from me. Her watchful gaze follows my every movement with hawk-eyed attention. I load a clip into a handgun and check the safety, then slide it into the holster on my leg. A meal, shower, and a fresh change of clothes have done miracles for my appearance. I sweep my damp curls into a ponytail behind my head and continue loading and checking weapons.

"Fifteen minutes, last call, ladies." Mrs. Wellsly says, her voice ringing across the space.

Mara picks up a crate of supplies and heads toward the Authority truck we'll be using to get into Eastkeep. My mother arranged for it somehow, so here it was, ready and waiting for us.

"Rei?"

I turn as my mother approaches. She takes hold of my arm and takes me away from the group.

"What is it?" I ask, not bothering to hide my disappointment.

"Please be careful out there. I wish I could do more," she says and pulls me in for a hug. Something presses into my hand and she whispers against my neck. "Don't look, there's too many people watching. Wait until you're alone. Go straight to the Free Territories and find the Ash Syndicate. You can't trust anyone, you hear me? I love you so much." She squeezes me extra hard and walks off without a hint that this may be the last time I ever see her.

I stand there, trying to process what she said to me, as my hand curls around the paper she gave me.

"Rei? You coming?" Mara asks, standing by the back of the truck.

"Yeah, coming." I say and hurry over, climbing into the back. Mara scoots over on the bench, hidden behind all the boxes loaded inside. Several other Sympathizers sit with us. There's 10 of us if I include Claire, who's driving, and Linda in the passenger seat.

The vehicle lurches and pulls out of the underground base. As we get further from the sewers, the more familiar scents and sounds of the city replace the foul smell. Our goal is to reach an abandoned warehouse several blocks from the GRH. There we'll rendezvous with a larger group of Sympathizers before the broadcast goes out.

The truck pulls to a stop inside the warehouse. From between the boxes I can see a crowd of women has gathered, all wearing dark clothing. Upon our arrival, they gather in a group and walk together down the road.

"It's starting," Linda says. We're close enough to the front of the truck that we can hear the squawk of the radio as she turns it on.

"Happy Cleansing day, good day citizens of the Authority. This is your daily update from Collective Voice Broadcast. Remember that fires are only allowed in approved receptacles and locations.

"If you think today is cold, be prepared for tomorrow! The temperatures will dip another 10 degrees, so pull out your winter coat and gloves. You'll want to dress warm to stave off the chill. In light of the long lines and rising disputes and fights at the market, all residents will be assigned a specific market day for the week. Anyone attending the market outside their assigned day will be arrested and have their rations decreased by half. Tomorrow's specials are potatoes and cabbage.

"As a reminder, spreading false rumors of a spreading sickness is punishable by the Suppression Line. Anyone charged with this awful treason will be punished accordingly.

"Now, on to everyone's favorite part of the day. Birth announcements! Congratulations to Sydney Mier and give a big salute to our brand new citizen, Rachel. She was born this afternoon at a healthy eight pounds and two ounces. That means tomorrow we'll announce another lottery winner.

"Finally, please join me in closing with the pledge of allegiance. Authority keep us safe–"

There's a high-pitched squealing beep as the audio cuts out. I clamp my hands over my ears to drown out the painful noise. If the broadcast didn't have my attention before, it did now.

A recognizable voice breaks through the horrid sound. "This is Evelyn Lynx reporting on our latest test results. I want to thank you all for coming. Without the help from you, all of our supporters, we wouldn't be here today. We've made a startling breakthrough! I'm calling it the Heart Blight virus. This is going to change so many lives for the greater good. Our initial test trials blew our expectations out of the water. It's killing all the men. Only the men. It's spreading by contact now. It's mutating so fast. I need surviving test subjects to isolate the mutations. They're dying all over the world. We have to burn the bodies. If we don't, the disease will continue to spread.

We have to do everything we can to stop it or this will be the end of humanity. We're the only ones who can keep everyone safe."

The horrible sound screeches and the same message repeats a second time. Mara and I exchange worried glances. What's going on? The Sympathizers have doctored the evidence so it looks like the Director created the Heart Blight virus on purpose.

On the third iteration, the sound cuts out and the original newscaster returns. "Well, um, that was...interesting. Please excuse the technical difficulties. Enforcers? Oh, Director Lynx, you're back. Here–"

"A curfew is being placed into effect immediately. Return to your homes. Anyone caught outside will be arrested and detained. I repeat, a curfew is now in effect. Return to your homes right now," the Director's voice seethes with deadly calm. I've never heard her this angry before.

*Boom!*

*Boom! Boom!*

"That's our cue," Claire says, and the truck jerks forward. I smell smoke in the distance. Were those more bombings?

As we approach the front of the GRH, an angry mob of Sympathizers blocks our way. It sounds like they're grabbing at the fence and shaking it, screaming and cussing, and throwing glass bottles. Other trucks pull up with reinforcements.

In the chaos, Claire smashes the horn and revs the engine. The rioting Sympathizers scream as we barrel toward them. Our truck breaks through the gate blockade and continues toward the containment building. When it jerks to a stop, we pile out, guns at the ready.

Down the hill, I can see the guardhouse roof is on fire. Enforcers are shouting and pointing their guns at the Sympathizers as they push forward. Gunshots ring out.

"Quickly!" Claire calls, splitting away with a group of Sympathizers.

I grab Mara's arm as she makes to go with them and shake my head. "This way," I say. I don't wait to see if she follows me or not. I run around the side of the building toward a different door. The light above it goes from red to green as it swings open. I use my elbow to bash the green-eyed girl who exits in the face. Her head snaps back as she crumples to the ground, unconscious. I snatch the keycard from her belt.

Mara appears around the corner, gun raised at the commotion. She lowers it when she recognizes me.

"Rei! What's going on?" she hisses.

I shake my head and say, "No time! Follow me." Together we run down the hall to the next locked door. I swipe the keycard against the reader and the door unlocks. I push it open and we continue on, racing for the next door.

Voices shout down the way, and I skid to a stop. Mara collides with me. It's all I can do to keep from falling over. Damn! I spin, trying to remember details on the map my mother gave me. "This way!" I say in a whisper, back tracking. I stop at the door on my left and swipe the keycard on the wall. It clicks green and I shove it open as the sounds of Enforcers round the corner behind us.

We duck inside with moments to spare. An Enforcer sitting behind a row of monitors spins in her chair, her hand going for her gun. I dive right as Mara dives left. The bullet ricochets around the steel reinforced room and hits the Enforcer in the neck. Blood spurts like a fountain as she gasps and slaps a hand over the wound. Moments later, she slumps to the ground, her eyes glassy.

My ears are still ringing from the gunshot. I feel a trickle of blood down my neck from my burst eardrum. The room spins for several minutes before I stop seeing three of Mara.

"Are you okay?" Mara asks, but her voice sounds far away and garbled. I can read her expression well enough to answer.

"Yeah, I'm fine." I wave her toward the bank of security monitors. "Can you find them?"

If Mara answers me, I don't hear it. I touch a hand to my bloody ear and stand. At least the room is no longer spinning. Mara turns and says something, but I can't hear her.

"What?"

Mara motions me over and points at something on the screen. I step around the body of the dead Enforcer as I take up the space beside her. She taps on the monitor screen again and I squint at the fuzzy black-and-white picture. It looks like a nursery, with several cribs and playpens on the floor. She lifts her finger and pokes again. When she lifts her hand, I see it, the little boy in the crib. His tiny arms and legs wave in the air and his face scrunches in a soundless scream.

"Tyrese?" I ask.

Mara nods and her fingers trail over the image on the monitor. "I think I can unlock the doors from here. Do you see Griff?" Her voice sounds washed out and low, but at least I can hear her again.

I scan the security monitors. "No, I don't see him."

"It looks like they keep most of the men here," she says, bringing the little video I was looking at up onto the largest screen. "That's probably your best bet to find him. I have to go to the children's ward, but we only have one keycard." Mara pushes out of her chair and it hits the dead Enforcer on the ground.

"Not anymore," I say, leaning down and taking the keycard from the unfortunate woman. "Here." I press it into her hand. "Whoever gets out of here first, bring the truck to the furthest door. The one at the back of the building."

I move to leave when Mara grabs my arm. "Rei, what's going on? Why aren't we sticking to the plan?"

"This is the plan," I say. "Just you and me. Understand?"

Mara nods. "O–okay."

"Go get your boy. Tell him his auntie can't wait to meet him. I'll explain later." I squeeze her shoulder and she smiles back at me.

"I'll loop as many security feeds as I can. Be careful."

"You, too."

I leave first, peering both ways out the door before I slip down the hall and start running. I take several turns I memorized from the map my mother gave me. The guardhouse should come up soon. I duck as the glass observation window comes into view, staying low to the ground so no one inside can see me. The men's ward is through the door down the hall, directly within view of the guardhouse. I'll need a distraction if I want any chance of getting inside unnoticed.

I pass the guard area and find the place I'm looking for three doors down. There's a beep as the keycard unlocks the storage room and I slip inside. I grab several buckets and fill them with anything I can find that looks flammable. I tear up rolls of toilet paper on top like kindling. When they're full, I pull the lighter out of my pocket and flick, but nothing happens.

"No, no, don't do this to me, please." I try again. Nothing happens.

"Dammit!" If only I had some flint...I look around at the metal shelves. There has to be something I can use to start a fire. In the back of the room I find a hand axe behind protective glass. I use the butt of my gun to break the glass. Pulling the axe out, I heft it in my hand and return to the buckets.

"I sure hope this works," I say as I strike the steel end of the axe against the metal shelf. There's a loud thunk from the impact. I pause, waiting to see if the noise will arouse suspicion. When a minute passes without incident, I try it again, changing the angle of my strike to imitate the way I hit the flint. Sparks fly and the shredded paper in the bucket smokes.

"Yes!" I drop the axe and blow gently on the ember. The flame gives a small whoosh and grows larger. I light fires in the other two buckets and drag them around the room, spreading them out. Black smoke fills the space. Pressing a hand over my nose and mouth, I slip back into the hallway and duck back under the glass window, waiting.

An alarm blares as thick, choking fog fills the corridor. I hear movement behind me in the guardhouse and then the sound of boots moving off toward the storage room. Keeping low, I move in a crouch to the entrance for the men's ward, happy for the cover the smoke provides me.

The door beeps as I hit the keycard to the lock and slide inside. Several men watch me as I enter. Their loose-fitting clothes hang on their lean frames. Their faces look haunted, gaunt, and tired. Along the walls are rows of locked cells. I stand and race toward the first one, using my keycard to unlock it. The door slides open and it's empty.

"Griff?" I say, calling his name as I run to the next one. "Griff, where are you?" The next door slides open and an older man lies on a mattress, unresponsive. I move on, unlocking them as fast as I can. "Griff! Answer me!"

There's a banging noise in a cell on the opposite wall. Familiar looking shaggy hair frames the tiny window. "Griff!" I make a beeline for him.

The door beeps and slides open. "Gri–" The word dies on my lips. The man is too young and gangly. All arms and legs. His face is wrong too, the eyes are blue, the jaw more narrow, and the nose turns up a bit at the end.

"You're not Griff." I say.

"No, I'm Ian, his brother."

I step back as he steps toward me. Although younger than Griff, he's every bit as tall.

"Do you know where he is? We don't have much time," I say and turn, looking around the room for anywhere else I might have missed.

"They took him to the other ward. Where they keep the more problematic guys. It's on the other side of the building."

I spin to leave when he grabs my wrist. "You'll never make it. We need to go," he says.

"I won't leave him!" I hiss, yanking my hand from his grasp. "Are you going to help me or not?"

An alarm blares. The sprinkler system kicks on overhead, drenching us in water. The door to the ward opens and several Enforcers pile into the room. Backup has arrived and I'm out of options. I have to get out of here, but how?

"Come on, this way!" Ian drags me backwards. Several other men turn tail and run with us at the sight of the Enforcers, their batons and guns drawn. "That door!" Ian says, pointing at one in front of us.

I slam the keycard against it, and he pulls it open. We pile through and race down the hallway, Enforcers fast on our heels.

# 50

# GRIFF

**Tear it down, watch it crumble, make their weakness your strength.**

G unshots punctuate the relative silence of the high-security ward. I bolt up from the mattress and immediately regret it. My head spins and my stomach roils. Whatever drugs they put in the water are still working their way out of my system. I crawl across the floor and use the toilet to pull myself to my feet. There are shouts outside and more gunshots, a scream, more shouts. Vertigo threatens as I force myself to take the steps to my cell door.

I raise my fist to pound on my door and demand what's going on. Before I can, an alarm blares and the sprinklers go off overhead. The light on my door goes from red to green, sliding open. Several other men are doing the same as me, stepping out of their cells and looking around in confusion.

*Boom!*

The ground shakes, a side of the wall explodes. The blast knocks me backwards into my cell. I slam against the glass observation wall and feel it crack under the impact. Pain radiates across my back. A shower of thick dust clouds the air. I cough and each one sends agony through the right side of my ribs.

"Ah," I press a hand against my excruciating side and struggle forward. More gunshots. I have to get out of here. Grabbing the doorframe, I pull myself through the threshold.

There's an enormous hole where the ward door used to be. Three Enforcers scramble into the ward, ducking behind chunks of concrete, an upturned table and an open cell. Plaster explodes near my head from a stray gunshot. One Enforcer falls back, holding her side, blood pouring from the wound. The second is being strangled by the man whose cell she entered. Her feet lift off the floor as he drags her into the line of fire. Her body jerks as she's shot. The man drops her and throws his hands into the air. A bullet rips into his shoulder and he screams, ducking back into his cell.

"Don't shoot the men, you idiots!" says a voice beyond the exploded wall.

"There's only one more," I say, "to the left! Cell five, get back!"

The Enforcer hiding behind the cement flinches at my words. Stark terror contorts her face. She can't be much older than Rei. A shower of gunfire rains down on the left side of the room. It forces her to cower into a ball behind what little cover she has.

"Stop! Cease fire!" The Enforcer screams. When the gunshots stop, she slides her gun out into the center of the room. "I surrender!"

"Put your hands up where we can see them! Stand up slowly!" says the voice beyond the blasted opening.

Her hands raise above her head. Carefully, she gets to her feet.

*Pop!*

Red blossoms from the center of her forehead. A slow rivulet of blood slides down her nose, mouth, and chin before she crumples. Dead. Whomever this was, they showed no mercy.

Black outfitted women clamber through the opening, guns raised. I don't recognize any of them. Who are they? The woman in front lowers her gun and turns. There's a triangle with a circle on the sleeve of her shirt.

"Clear," she says.

"You're Sympathizers," I say, stepping forward.

She nods. "Come on, we're getting you out of here. All of you! Linda, you take point. Let's go!" She steps back through the debris of the exploded wall.

Behind me, the men hesitate, poking their heads out of their cells. They make no effort to follow.

"We have to go," I say, moving into the open space where the bodies of the Enforcers lay. Their blood tints the inch of water on the floor pink.

"It's not safe," says an older man, his arms wrapped in bandages. Beneath his thin shirt you can see the outline of every rib.

"And staying here is?" I say with challenging menace. "I survived out there for years. I can show ya how. We need to go while we still can."

The older man shakes his head and disappears back into his cell.

"What the fuck is wrong with ya? Don't ya understand? If we stay here, they win. Is that what ya want? To curl up and die? Will ya let them chip away until there's nothing left?"

"He's right," says Dean. The crazy bastard is leaning against the door frame of his cell, one hand pressed to a gunshot wound in his shoulder. "I'd rather take my chances out there, fighting, then die in a cell." He shoves himself away from the doorframe and joins me in the center of the room. "I'm not a coward!" He says and his shout stirs several men into movement.

Three more men join us in the center, then two more, then five. Almost everyone. Almost. It's the best I can do. If there's one thing living in the mountains taught me, it's that I can't always fix what's broken.

"Follow me," I say and lead the way.

We creep over the debris on the ground and into the hall. I hear gunfire and fighting in one direction. Do I follow the Sympathizers and put us in the thick of it or go the other way?

"Which way?" Dean asks.

I turn away from the sounds of fighting. "This way," I say, running down the hall. Our bare feet make slapping sounds against the cold floor.

I slow at the split in the hallway. The men who aren't as fit as me close up ranks behind, coughing and wheezing. I look both ways, listening hard. There are scuff marks and boot prints on the left and nothing on the right.

"The Sympathizers came in this way. Where there's a way in, there's a way out. Come on," I say and wave them forward.

We follow their trail back the way they came. The first body of an Enforcer appears around the corner of the hall. More follow as we go and I wince as I step on spent bullet casings and through sticky puddles of blood.

Pushing open a door, we enter a long, narrow room. Beds line both sides of the walls, each occupied by a gaunt, skeletal man, their eyes closed and their arms hooked to machines that blink and whirr. All that's left of them is a shell of the person, a tired husk kept alive after behavior modification so they could continue to collect their fucking quotas. No more than a means to an end.

This is what the Authority did to us, what the future held in store for me, for Ian. "Let's go," I shudder and cross the room.

"Do you smell smoke?" Asks Dean behind me, his voice hoarse from exertion.

Shit. Their trail ends at a closed door. Black smoke billows around the seams. It's too late to turn back now. The only way is through.

"Take your shirts off, cover ya nose and mouth. Keep your heads down. We have to go through. Stay low, and go fast, understand?"

I pull my shirt over my head and shove it in my face, demonstrating. Dean pulls up his shirt and balls it up as best he can, but with his wound, there's no way he can take it off. Scars and incision lines criss-cross his chest and those of the others. Similar to the scabbed claw marks across mine.

Slamming my shoulder into the door makes it give way. The heat is miserable. We've found a laboratory. Flames lick across the ground, consuming desks and papers. Equipment explodes and glass beakers shatter. Huge metal vats groan and buckle. Flames melt the words cryobank storage off their sides. Running forward, I angle toward the open door across the way. Heat blisters my feet, but I ignore the burning and focus on the goal.

I'm getting out of here. To find Rei.

We pile through the open doorway and out into the cement hall. The smoke is thicker here, but there's some relief from the flames. I scan the floor, trying to pick up the trail again. The smoke makes it hard to see, and my chest is tight and aching.

I turn back and see the number of men following me is fewer than when I started. Either they couldn't keep up, or they turned back, or they didn't make it through the fire. Sweat covers those remaining. Patches of black soot streak across their thin arms and lean chests. They look exhausted, pushed past their physical limits. We're running out of time.

"Over there! I see them!"

My head whips around at the voices and sound of boots. Enforcers. A lot of them. I turn the opposite direction and run.

My blistered feet leave bloody smears on the ground. The ragged coughing and gasping of the men behind me drives me onwards.

"That way," says a voice ahead of us, where the hallway splits again.

Dread makes my muscles tense. Someone's running in the hallway ahead. It's too late. They've surrounded us.

Rei collides with me.

"Griff?"

"Rei!" I wrap my arms around her and our lips meet in desperation. Within her arms, my aches and pains fade. There's only her.

*Mine.*

"We have to go!" says Ian, racing to Dean who's lagging behind, putting his arm under his shoulder. "Now!"

I grab Rei's hand and run.

# 51

## How can you tell the truth from a lie when they both sound the same?

My relief at finding Griff is short-lived. His hand grips mine, squeezing tight, as we run. I retrace my earlier steps, turning left, right, and then left again. Without Ian, I wouldn't have made it this far. Now we're so, so close.

The guard house window is empty as we run past it, heading into the last stretch. Only two doors to go. I slam the keycard against the first one and it beeps and swings open. Behind us, the men who came with Griff are struggling. Toward the back, Ian is falling further behind, sagging under the weight of the man he helps.

"Griff," I press the keycard into his hand. "Keep going. You'll find a truck around back. Mara should be there with her son. I have to help the others."

Griff falters and stops. "I'm not leaving without ya."

I look back down the hall. "If I don't, they won't make it. Hurry, go!"

Before he has a chance to stop me, I race back toward Ian.

"Keep going!" I yell at the men I pass, struggling to keep up. "You're almost there!"

When I reach Ian, I wrap my arms under the man's other shoulder and hoist him up. The man groans and almost passes out. Blood oozes from his wound and stains the side of his shirt bright red.

Ian throws me a thankful glance as I take on as much of the man's weight as I can, lightening his load.

"Rei! Stop! You don't know what you're doing!" Alyssa says, shouting down the hall.

She's closing in fast.

*Too fast.*

We're not going to make it.

"Ian, I've got him. You need to run. Help the others." I say, dragging the injured man forward.

"There's no way you can—"

"Ian! I said go!"

I didn't realize how much Ian was supporting the injured man's weight until he lets go and races ahead. He's so heavy I stumble sideways and smash into the wall, struggling to keep him on his feet.

"Come on, help me out here," I growl, gripping the man's side with everything I have.

"Leave me," says the injured man, his voice thick. Blood coats his teeth and his lips are turning blue.

"No!" I reach up and slap him across the face. "Move! Now!"

He pushes to his feet and I use the bit of momentum to propel us down the hallway as fast as I can.

I can see the exit ahead. Light from headlights stream in and breaks through the haze of smoke. A truck screeches to a halt and Mara reaches across and opens the passenger side.

"Get in!" She says to Griff and the men stumbling out after him.

There's only 10 feet to go.

"We're going to make it," I say to the injured man as his blood seeps into the front of my shirt.

"Rei! Stop or I'll shoot!"

I hear the cocking of the gun with surprising clarity. My footsteps falter as I turn. Alyssa has her weapon pointed at me. More Enforcers are closing in.

The injured man and I are the only two things standing between Griff and his freedom.

"You have to let me go, Alyssa." I take a single step backwards.

"Don't move! I mean it, I'll shoot!" She screams and her face goes red.

"They're lying to you. Everyone. You can't trust them, Alyssa. That's why you have to let me go." I say, pleading with the Captain I once reported to.

"I can't do that. You know I can't." She loosens and tightens her grip on the gun, widening her stance. "I can't let you go."

I take another step backwards. Alyssa fires the gun into the ceiling. Plaster showers down on top of us. The Enforcers behind Alyssa are catching up.

"Rei! Come on, Rei!" Griff says, calling for me from the vehicle.

"Thank you," says the injured man. "Run!" He lunges forward, tackling Alyssa. The two of them collide and they fall to the floor, him on top of her. She struggles to get him off.

I turn and race for the open door, toward the truck, Griff, and freedom.

"Griff is immune to the virus, he's the key to the cure!" Alyssa screams from underneath the injured man. But I don't stop or turn back.

I grab Griff's hand. He yanks me onto the seat beside him. Mara peels wheels as we take off away from the building.

I won't believe their lies any more.

# 52

 **REI**

**Rise and fall, ebb and flow, the tides carry us out to sea.**

The rioting Sympathizers at the gate are gone as we careen toward the burning guardhouse. Cleansing day pyres burn, and mangled bodies litter the road as we smash through the gate and head out into the city.

Chaos engulfs the streets. Shop windows shatter as looters throw bricks and steal supplies. Red awnings lie in shreds and Authority flags burn in the hands of the civvies marching in protest. Soldiers are trying and failing to maintain some semblance of order as the violence of the rioting crowd grows. One woman in Enforcer blues is strung up with rope, hands clawing at her neck, her legs flailing as she's strung up from a lamp post.

An Authority truck is being rocked back and forth by the crowd and flips over onto its side. People scream and jump back. Thick, oily smoke billows from under the hood before it bursts into explosive flames.

Mara swerves as a glass bottle shatters against the front window. A gang of civvies runs toward us, faces contorted, broom sticks and crowbars, bats and other hitting instruments in their hands. There's a clang and clack as they batter the sides of the vehicle as we plow by them.

"Aaah!" I scream as a rock cracks the glass in front of my face.

"We have to get out of the city," Griff says, a bundle in his arms, pulling me close against his side.

"I'm trying!" Mara says, yanking the wheel hard to the right to avoid hitting a woman dragging a little girl away from the fray.

A tiny voice wails.

"Shhh! I'm sorry. Momma's sorry." Mara says, glancing from the road to the bundle in Griff's arms.

"Do you want me to take him?" I ask Griff as he rocks the baby, trying to calm him down.

"No, I've got him.”

“Rei, will you tell me what the hell is going on?" Mara demands through gritted teeth.

"We're going to the Free Territories." I say, sitting back and pressing myself to Griff's side. I need reassurance he's really here and not just a dream.

"What about the Sympathizers? We didn't follow their plan."

I shake my head. "Their goal isn't just to crush the Authority, it's taking over in their place. That's why my mother gave me a map of containment before we left. Lyra, the scientist who helped you escape, Griff, she didn't give the USB drive to them on purpose. On the back of the map my mother wrote: Sympathizers don't want a cure."

"That explains it then." Griff says. "When we were trying to get out of containment, we ended up going through a lab. Someone set it on fire." He teases his fingers in my hair.

On the dash of the truck, the radio fizzes with static. I tense, waiting for someone to come on the line. The white noise continues for a minute, then two, then cuts off.

"We're not out of the woods yet," Mara says, stepping on the petal as we clear the outskirts of the city. "There's a checkpoint up ahead." She pulls her gun and places it on the seat next to her leg.

"Griff, get down." I say, sliding past him so I'm sitting next to Mara. Two Enforcers in an Authority truck are easy enough to explain. A man on the other hand.... Turning, I poke my head into the back of the truck. The men we brought with us sit huddled together around Ian. They look so pathetic. Their bodies are thin, without an ounce of excess muscle, on top of their weary, dejected faces.

"Shh! Not a sound." I warn them.

Ian gives me a thumbs up before I face forward again.

Mara slows as we near the guardhouse. The light is on, but no one approaches us. There are no other Authority trucks in sight.

"Uh, I think it's empty." Mara says. She leans out and calls, "Hello?"

There's no answer.

"Maybe they pulled all the troops in to help with the rioting?" Griff says, offering a plausible explanation.

"I'll go raise the gate," I say, sliding over Griff again and opening the passenger side door.

Griff grabs my wrist before I jump down. "Be careful," he says.

But Mara's correct. There's no one inside. I fiddle with the buttons on the console until the gate lifts. Griff holds out his hand to help pull me back inside.

"You're right, there's no one there." I say.

"Let's hope the next one is the same," Mara says, then leans down and brushes the baby's forehead in Griff's arms. I get a glimpse of

Tyrese's coarse, black, curly hair and brown skin. Large brown eyes blink up at us. He coos softly. Mara's face lights up in a smile. My heart swells with happiness for the two of them.

Every checkpoint we pass is the same: empty. It leaves me with a disquieting feeling in the pit of my stomach. We drive through the night, stopping only long enough to refuel from gas cans in the back. During the stop Ian passes out food to everyone from the boxes the Sympathizers loaded. I switch places with Mara so she can get some rest and hold the baby.

Griff lays his head on my shoulder. In the back, the men speak in hushed, anxious tones. Mara's soft snores and the truck's engine are a comfort in the growing silence.

"Oh, I forgot." I say. My hand digs into the pocket of my dark clothing and curls around the soft trinket. "This is for you."

Griff's eyes sparkle with unshed tears as he takes the raccoon from my hand. "Thanks," he says. He leans back in his seat, examining it and running his fingers over the soft fur. His eyes close and a tear slides down his cheek, but he doesn't bother brushing it away.

I reach across and touch his face. He catches my wrist and kisses my knuckles, his breath warm against my skin. I lace our fingers together and let him bring my hand to his lap. The tight feeling in my chest is easing bit by bit as the quiet peace draws out between us. I imagine we're back at the hut, just the two of us, laying skin to skin on the bed, without a care in the world.

We've struggled so much to get here. This all feels too easy. I wonder if this is how Lyra felt as she helped Griff and his father escape. His grip goes lax and I glance over to find him fast asleep. There are dark purple and yellow bruises on the side of his ribs, fresh stitches over a cut on his arm, and a blood-stained bandage over his hip. All of them new and raw.

"What did they freaking do to you?" I whisper and frown.

Fixing my eyes forward on the road, I clench my fingers on the steering wheel. Soon this will all be over. We'll be beyond the Iron Divide and safe within the Free Territories.

I pass the sign on the road for Boverwick. This is where Griff's father grew up as a child. The area Mrs. Wellsly circled as being annexed by the Authority. It all feels so surreal.

The road turns from pavement into gravel and takes us through the woods. The truck bounces along over the dips and ruts. Griff groans beside me and stirs awake. We hit a deep rut and the truck lurches. Tyrese wails, waking Mara.

"Shh! It's okay," she says, running a hand along his back.

"Where are we?" Griff asks, wincing as he stretches and yawns.

"End of the road," I say, hitting the brake. The gravel road has a metal barrier across it, blocking vehicles from going any further. A narrow dirt path snakes beyond the fence into the woods. "Guess we go on foot from here."

"This feels familiar. Kinda like how we first met, huh?" Griff says with a grin as he slides out of the truck after Mara.

Mara makes a funny face at the hot flush creeping over my skin. "I don't want to know..." she says and shifts Tyrese against her chest, going to help the other men get down from the back with Ian.

"I loaded these bags with all the food and water left over from the boxes," Ian says as Griff and I approach. Together they help the last of the men hop down. There's only six of them besides Griff and Ian. I wish we saved more.

"Give them to me," I say. "They'll just slow everyone else down."

"I can take one, too," Mara says, slipping a strap over her shoulder.

Ian scoffs and puts a backpack on. "I'm not a kid, I can help, too."
He throws the last one at me and I catch it and let out an oomph. It's
heavier than it looks.

"He's stubborn, just like you," I say to Griff, looking from one
to the other. Their resemblance is uncanny despite having different
colored eyes. Ian smiles, enjoying the comparison to his big brother.

"Father would have loved this," Griff says, suddenly changing the
tone of the conversation.

Ian's smile falters and something unreadable flashes over his
features. He drops his head and digs his bare foot into the ground.
He's about to say something else when the crunching of gravel under
tires whips our heads around.

"Run!" I scream as the truck appears in the distance. "Run!"

Griff grabs my hand and pulls me down the path. "How did they
find us?" He says, dragging me along. Ian runs ahead of us and Mara
follows. The other men are struggling to keep up, already falling
further and further behind.

"We have to get to the Iron Divide! Hurry!" I say, encouraging
the men struggling behind us. "We're almost there. It's not much
further!"

"They can't keep up," Griff says, panting. Even though the path is
dirt, it's littered with rocks, sticks, and leaves. And the men are all
barefoot.

"If they catch us, they'll kill us," Mara says, running past us as Griff
slows in his concern for the others.

I slam my hands against Griff's shoulders and propel him forward.
"Don't slow down. There's nothing you can do. Run!"

Behind us, I hear shouts and then a scream. Ahead of us, Ian has
come to a stop.

"What are you doing? Run!" I say as we catch up to him.

Griff grabs my waist and stops me, pulling me off my feet. Ian's hands raise into the air above his head as Griff jerks the both of us to a halt. Mara's footsteps falter beside us.

Commander Lynx stands before us, her gun aimed at Ian's chest, blocking the path forward.

"Mara, I believe your name is? Thank you Mara, this wouldn't be possible without your help," Commander Lynx says. "You see, Rei here took out her tether. But you," she leers at her, "you still have yours. Imagine my surprise when I head out to gather more resources for the lab and find you're headed straight for me."

Crap! Footsteps approach behind us. Bless the mother, they're boxing us in. Alyssa and the golden-haired Enforcer have caught up, boxing us in.

"Honestly Rei, I never knew you had this in you." Commander Lynx continues. "I mean, I knew you were leadership material, but this...?" She clicks her tongue and shakes her head. "In some ways you're still so naive. Traitor isn't a strong enough word to describe what you've done–the harm you've caused humanity." Her gun swings from Ian to me.

Griff shoves himself in front of me.

"Move out of the way, son!" Commander Lynx says, baring her teeth.

"No. I won't let ya hurt another person I love."

"Aww, so much like your father, aren't you, son? Do you know what we do to traitors, boy? We hang them by their necks and leave their bodies to rot in the streets so everyone can learn from their mistakes."

Tyrees wails. "No, no..." Mara says in a panic, clutching him tighter to her chest, taking one step backwards. Then another.

"Stop! Don't move!" Commander Lynx warns, turning the gun on Mara.

Mara's eyes go wide with pure terror. She spins and runs. Griff lunges at Commander Lynx.

*Bang!*

The bullet hits Mara in the back and she collapses, face first, into the dirt. Tyrese's screams fall silent.

"Mara!" The anguished cry rips from my throat. She's not dead. We were supposed to go together.

All of us.

Griff and Commander Lynx fight for control of the gun. Alyssa and the other Enforcers stand frozen in shock, dumbfounded.

*Bang!*

Griff stumbles backwards, the gun in his hand, blood all over his bare chest.

"Griff!" My heart stops in my chest. No, no, no! This can't be happening!

Commander Lynx's hand clenches at her right shoulder. Blood slides between her fingers and she stumbles back, falling to her ass on the ground. She meets Griff's gaze.

He raises the gun at his mother's sneering face.

# 53

# GRIFF

## In the mirror I face myself, unsure who is the more savage.

I stare down the barrel of the gun at the face of the woman who murdered my father. For so many years, this is what I wanted. I've imagined it in my head over and over again. Being here now is surreal. This woman, this monster–my mother–needs to die.

Alyssa and the other Enforcer go for their guns.

"Stand down! He's no good to us dead," says Commander Lynx. Pure rage in her eyes mirrors the dark depths of my thoughts. "The Authority will hunt you to the ends of this earth. So go ahead, shoot me, son."

"Why? Why did ya kill him?" I ask, placing my finger on the trigger. Adrenaline floods my body, making my muscles tense to the point of being painful.

Commander Lynx's lip curls. "Your father was a danger to humanity. Your escape jeopardised everything I've worked for. I made the ultimate sacrifice, so one day no one else has to lose a son to the Heart Blight."

My throat goes dry and my arm shakes. "Ya did this! The Authority created the Heart Blight. Ya keep us caged, drugged, and experiment on us like animals! Do our lives mean nothing?" I'm gripping the barrel of the gun so hard my fingers cramp.

Commander Lynx's brow beads with sweat, the color draining from her face. "Do you think you're the only one who's ever suffered? Look around you!" She says, breathing hard. "Your madness is believing we can fix humanity without strict control. I'm fighting desperately to hold the pieces together. I've dedicated my life to protecting our future. And you? You're the punishment for my every failure."

She looks at Rei and sways, struggling to stay upright. "I had such high hopes for you, Rei." Her words are slurring. "Alyssa always sung your praises. Remember your training and the world we're fighting for. Don't do this. You. Will. Cost. Us. *Everything!*"

I take a step forward, ready to end it all. Rei's hand closes over mine on the gun. The warmth of her body against my back relaxes my taut muscles.

"If you do this, you're no better than she is," Rei cautions. Tears stream down her face. "You'll regret it for the rest of your life. I believed their lies for so long, but with your help, we exposed them for who they really are. The Authority will never be the same. The Sympathizers destroyed the lab and the Genetic Preservation Units. Things will never be the same. It's over."

"You stupid girl, what have you done?" Commander Lynx says, wheezing. Her white face contorts, and she topples over. Her eyes rolling up into her head as she passes out.

"Mom!" Alyssa says, rushing to her side, ignoring my gun. She presses her hand against the wound to staunch the bleeding. "Mom, answer me. Wake up! Joy, go get the medic!"

The remaining Enforcer, the vixen, glances from me to Alyssa and back to me again.

"Rei, please! Help me!" Alyssa says, her eyes pleading and frantic as she looks past me at Rei.

Rei lowers my gun hand until it rests by my leg. She nods to Joy.

"Go," Rei says.

The vixen takes a step away from us, another, then hurries past, running down the path. As she does, there's a muffled wail beneath Mara's body. Pitiful mewling cries punctuate the stillness of the surrounding woods.

"Tyrese?" Rei scrambles for her friend. "Ian, help me! I can't roll her over by myself."

The cold returns as soon as she's gone. I keep one eye on Alyssa, who's still attempting to stop Commander Lynx's bleeding.

"Shhh! It's okay, I've got you, little one, you're okay. I'll keep you safe." Rei bundles Tyrese into her arms, holding him close.

Ian stands and the two of them join me, Rei rocking Tyrese and wiping dirt and blood from his tiny cheek.

"If you take pressure off the wound she'll bleed out," I say to Alyssa. "Don't follow us if you want her to live."

Alyssa looks up at me through a haze of tears with puffy, red eyes. It's the first time I've been able to really study her face. We share the same sharp nose and high cheekbones of our mother, but that's where the similarities stop. In the distance, I hear the yell of Enforcers and the sound of boots crunching through leaves and undergrowth.

"If I ever see you again, I'll kill you myself, cure be damned!" Alyssa spits, snot dripping down her nose as she applies more pressure to the wound. On the ground, Commander Lynx moans. "Mom? Can you hear me? Hold on, help is coming!"

"Griff, we have to go." Rei takes my free hand in hers.

I nod and say, "Let's go to the Free Territories."

# 54

 REI

## And here we find ourselves, between the wild lines.

Tyrese's small body pressing against me feels heavier as we go, like the weight of my choices. Mara, the one person I could count on, is dead. My mother is caught in the middle of a city in chaos, greasing the wheels of the Sympathizer operations. I'm leaving.

This is really happening.

For so long, the Authority has been such a major part of my life. I joined the Enforcers, desperate for a child and a family of my own. I'd lost so much to get here, more than I imagined. My home, my purpose, my mother and now...my best friend. Hot tears sting my eyes as we run. Exhaustion helps to dull my senses as my pulse races. Griff's dark head is like a beacon in front of me, holding together the cracks threatening to tear my heart apart. I need freedom from the Authority's oppression, control, and lies.

*I chose him.*

Griff holds up a hand, bringing us to a sudden halt. There's a noise to our left. He lifts the gun, aiming toward the sound. How did the Enforcers catch up to us so quickly? Griff grabs my arm and pulls me behind him. Ian moves up to stand by his side. Together, they make a barrier with their bodies.

"Shit, ya scared me," Griff says, lowering the gun with a sigh of relief.

"Joe! Sam! Brendan! You made it," Ian exclaims.

I peek between the gap in the two broad shoulders and see the lean figures of three men emerge. The smaller, curly-haired guy in front, supporting an older man, is the only one whose chest isn't heaving. "We followed the marks on the trees, like you told us," says the frail old man, pointing to the triangle with a circle carved into the trunk not 10 feet from us. I didn't even notice we'd been following them. Trust Griff to know his way around woods, no matter where we are.

"And the rest?" Griff asks, checking if there were more behind them.

The older man shakes his head. "They couldn't keep up, the Enforcers rounded them up."

"Should we go back?" Ian asks, turning to Griff.

"There's no time," I say, interrupting this brief reunion as Tyrese begins fussing in my arms. "We have to keep going. The Iron Divide shouldn't be far now."

"Give us a minute to catch our breath," the old man says, resting his hands on his knees and leaning over. The others follow suit.

"I'll stay with them. You go on ahead," Ian says, moving toward the man holding the cramp in his side. "Here Joe, let me help you. I've got him, Sam." He slips his arm around the older man, helping to hold him up.

"Are ya sur–"

"Go," Ian says, interrupting Griff. "I've got them."

I lace my fingers in Griff's hand, holding tight. "It's okay. They'll be right behind us. Let's go." I say.

Griff pulls me close and kisses me. "Always so demanding..." he says against my mouth as a smile slowly spreads across his lips.

Ian coughs and clears his throat. I flush, pushing him away as Tyrese kicks his legs between us.

Still holding my hand, Griff gives his brother an intense, approving look. "Don't take too long," he says.

As we scurry down the path it narrows, overgrown with bushes and brambles. Thorns scratch at our arms and legs, tracing wild lines across Griff's bare chest. The sleeves of my shirt catch and tear. A long sticker branch gets stuck in my hair and Griff has to stop to help me untangle it.

"We've gotta be close," Griff says, wincing as a thorn catches his thumb as he pulls my hair free. A bead of blood wells and drips to the ground. The trees press in close around us.

"I haven't seen any of the Sympathizer symbols." I say, following him as he sucks his thumb and sets off again.

"There was one a few hundred yards back, but it was hard to make out with all these vines and underbrush in the way. I think it veered off to the right, but there's no getting through those thorns. This deer track is the best option. We can swing back around that way when it opens up again." He grimaces and turns as another thorny branch catches his pants.

"What's that?" I say as I notice a change in the light. Something down the path reminds me of the rough texture on the buildings in the city.

Griff turns and cocks his head where I'm looking. His brows furrow. "I dunno. Come on, let's find out."

We follow the path another hundred feet to the dead end. I step up beside him and place my hand against the cold, hard concrete. I tip my head back and look up and up and up. The cement barricade in front of us is so tall it reaches higher than the tops of the scraggly trees. I turn my head right and then left. The barrier stretches as far as I can see, the brambles dense and twisted, some even climbing up the coarse texture of the wall.

Griff shakes his head, "No, this can't be right. Shit! How the hell are we supposed to get past this?" He balls his hand into a fist and punches the daunting barrier. His knuckles leave a bloody mark behind.

"Stop! That won't help anything. Maybe we should double back to where you saw the last mark on the tree?"

Griff shakes his head. "It'll take us too long to get through there, even if we could manage it. Look at us, Rei. We're shredded to pieces here." Griff throws back his head and screams, his hands pulling at his hair. He slumps down against the wall, his palms covering his face.

His bitter laughter breaks the silence. "I see why they call it the Iron Divide."

"Get up! We're not giving up, not when we're so close." I say, moving toward him.

Griff lifts his face from his hands and the defeated look he gives me makes my heart skip a beat. I fold him into my arms, pressing a kiss to the top of his forehead.

"I'm so tired, Rei." He says and his breath warms the hollow of my stomach. Tyrese squirms, making soft cooing noises.

"You and I, we don't give up. We're fighters, remember? Besides, I will kick your ass as many times as you need me to. Don't forget, I have a mean left hook." I lift his sweaty chin and press a kiss to his lips. They're rough from dehydration and taste salty. "Now get your ass up. People are depending on us, and we can't let them down. Together, we can do anything."

Griff chuckles against my mouth. Lacing his fingers into my hair, he kisses me deeper this time. My belly clenches and my knees threaten to buckle. I want to feel him against my skin, on top of me, inside me. But now isn't the time.

"I can't imagine my life without ya," he wraps his arms around my butt. His hand squeezes playfully.

"Hey! Come on, get up. We have to figure this out." I pull away from him and step back. A rock throws me off balance and my bad ankle twinges and buckles. I fall backwards onto my ass, gasping in surprise.

Griff laughs, a rich, throaty noise, and climbs to his feet. "I enjoy seeing ya in that position," he says, his green eyes sparkling. He holds a hand out to me.

I roll my eyes at him and let him pull me up. My foot hits something else hard on the ground. "What the hell is this stupid rock?" I say, trying to kick it out of the way. My boot gets stuck underneath it and I almost fall a second time. Griff catches my arms and keeps me upright, his eyes going wide.

"I think there's something under here," he says, stomping down with his bare foot. *Thud.* There's a metallic undertone. He gets down on his hands and knees and scrapes the leaves away from the ground. What I thought was a dull, gray rock turns into a weathered metal handle.

I fall to my knees and help him, pulling away damp clumps of dirt, sticks, and grass. Our hands meet as we trace around the seam of the door, clearing it off. Stamped in the metal is a triangle with a circle in the middle. Griff and I exchange smiles.

"How do we open it?" I ask, examining the handle. It's a solid loop of metal, but I don't see a way to turn or twist it.

Griff wraps his hands around the handle, braces his feet on either side of the door's edge, and pulls. Metal creaks and groans as the hinges resist his strength.

"Maybe we need to turn the handle somehow?" I ask. Tyrese fusses in my arms and I shift him and run my hands through his coarse, dark curls.

"No, I don't think so. I need better leverage. It's just rusty." He stands, grabs the handle, and pulls again, leaning backwards, using his body as a fulcrum. There's a loud crack as the hinges give to the pressure. Griff strains to lift the door and when he gets it high enough, it tips on its own. Letting go, it falls to the ground with a bang.

I stare down into the dark hole. Rusted metal rungs lining one side disappear into the pitch black. I have no clue how deep it goes.

"I'll go first," Griff says, sitting down and scooting to the edge. He dangles his feet into the void and I clamp a hand onto his shoulder, holding him still. My heart is racing and panic looms. Griff grabs my fingers and squeezes. "I'm right here."

I nod and let him slip from my grasp. He disappears down into the darkness as my palms grow sweaty and shake.

"It's not that far down," he says, calling up to me. "Be careful. The rungs are slippery."

I scoot to the edge and dangle my feet into the void. My chest feels tight and my breathing is growing shallow. Tyrese wiggles against me and cries. "Shh, it's okay buddy. We're gonna be okay. I promise I'll keep you safe." I bounce him in my quivering arms until he quiets.

I take a deep, shuddering breath and let it out as slowly as I can. I grab the first rung and turn, lowering down my legs, searching for the next one. The metal feels slick and gritty against my palms. As I descend, the light recedes overhead.

"Only a few more to go," Griff encourages, reaching up and touching my ankle. He guides me down the next few rungs, and his touch spreads a calming sense of reassurance through my body. "That's it, last one."

My boot splashes into a few inches of water. I blink, trying to let my eyes adjust to the darkness. Light filters down from above us. In the gloom, I can make out the long tunnel wide enough for three or four people to walk abreast. Slimy wet muck covers the walls. It smells like moldy bread. Gnarled roots hang from cracks in the ceiling, like reaching, skeletal hands.

For a moment, I imagine the walls collapsing in on me. A flash and boom throwing me backwards. A truck exploding. The blistering heat of flames and the pop of frantic gun fire. My mouth goes dry. I shudder and freeze in terror.

"Ya ready?" Griff asks, pulling me into his side. His hand wraps around my waist until our hips touch.

"Let's go," I say, pulling myself out of my own personal darkness. As his heat seeps into me, I burn away the fear, set fire to the terror, and I drag myself from the ashes. Today I will be born anew.

I take confident steps into the pitch black, bringing Griff with me. The going is slow but steady. We reach the far end of the tunnel as the sound of Ian's voice echoes behind us. They made it, too.

"I think there's a ladder here," Griff says, and I hear him climbing.

Metal rungs groan under his weight as he ascends. There's a loud bang as he attempts to lift the door. Dirt, rust, and afternoon light showers my head. I shield Tyrese's face from the debris. He wails at the loud noise as it slams open. I blink hard as my eyes struggle to adjust.

Griff's dirt-stained face appears at the opening above me, grinning. "Rei, ya won't believe this. Come on." He holds a hand out to me.

I grab the jagged ladder rungs and climb, taking his arm when I can reach it. One powerful tug and he lifts me out of the tunnel and into the light. I shield my watering eyes. Blinking the tears away, I follow the line of Griff's gaze.

An endless cement wall looms behind us.

Griff wraps me in his arms and kisses me until I'm breathless and clinging to him.

We've crossed the Iron Divide into the Free Territories.

# 55

**REI**

## Freedom is a hunter beckoning with long, skeletal fingers.

Ian's discrete cough breaks our lips apart. I blush and disentangle myself from Griff's embrace, pulling my shirt down to cover my exposed back. My skin already misses the feeling of his callused hands where they slipped into my pants.

"I have a feeling this is gonna be happening a lot," Ian says, climbing out of the trapdoor.

Griff chuckles and rests his forehead on my shoulder. Bits of dirt and rust fall from his hair and tickle my neck.

"A little help here?" Ian says, reaching his hand down for Joe who is climbing up after him.

Griff groans and forces himself to let me go. He heads over to Ian and grabs the man under the elbow, pulling him up. Together, the brothers repeat the process until they hoist the last man out of the tunnel.

"Should we close this?" Ian asks, staring down at the hole in the ground.

"Yes," I say. "Even better if we can wedge it shut so they can't open it again."

"Good call," Griff agrees. The brothers work as one, finding a stick to wedge into the far door and then stacking heavy rocks on this side.

"What if the Enforcers follow us?" Ian asks when they're done.

"We're not sticking around to find out." I say, soothing Tyrese in my arms. "Let's go."

"Okay." Ian shrugs and goes to help Joe, the older man, back to his feet.

"Lead the way," Griff says, steadying the smaller, brown-haired man who waivers on shaking legs. Sam, I think his name was.

We're standing in a rolling, grassy meadow of red wildflowers in full bloom. I've never seen anything like them before. They whisper and sway in the chilly breeze. Little white butterflies flit between them, dancing with erratic, carefree abandon. Their scent teases my nose with a soft, sweet, comforting fragrance. Birds chip and call overhead, singing with an easy, joyful abandon. The peace of the meadow permeates my body, releasing the last coils of tension in my shoulders and lower back.

We're finally free.

Together, the six of us set off across the meadow. The flowers and grasses are so tall they tickle my hands as I walk, forging a fresh path ahead. I think back to what I remember of the map in the Sympathizer's hideout. It's at least a day—maybe two—to reach Persham, the capital of the Free Territories. The more distance we put between ourselves and The Authority, the better.

Beyond the hilly meadow, the grade slopes downward into a grove of tall trees and a sparse forest. We approach the first trees and gawk. Their bark is an unusual reddish brown color. With the fading morning light, they seem to bathe the woods and leaves around them in their warm, inviting glow. Up close, they're massive. I could put

20 of Griff's huts side by side and it still wouldn't span the trunk. Standing next to one makes me feel so small and insignificant.

"Have you ever seen anything like this before?" I ask Griff as he comes up next to me. I trail a finger over the bumpy, sun-warmed bark and it thrums with energy, so full of life.

"No, but I've heard of them. Father called them redwoods."

"They even smell different," I say, inhaling the crisp, tangy scent. "Everything about this place feels new. It's so beautiful."

Silence falls between us as we walk, taking in the enormity of our surroundings. Our footsteps slow even as the ground becomes more level and easier to cross. Tyrese feels like 100 pounds. My whole body aches with weariness, but stopping isn't an option. Not yet, not until I know we're safe.

Griff wraps his arm under mine and supports my elbow, letting me lean against him. I entwine my fingers with his in silent thanks. He grins and the smile lights up his face.

I turn back to the men behind me, watching me, trusting me.

"Let's go." I say, dragging him forward, leading my new family into an uncharted future.

Suddenly the birds go quiet and Griff stops, squeezing my palm, pulling me against his side. He holds up a hand in warning, and everyone falls silent. "Do you hear that?" he whispers.

I strain my ears, listening hard, picking up the crunch of boots on leaves and low, muffled voices.

A gun cocks.

My mother's detached voice plays on repeat in my head.

*Don't trust anyone.*

GRETA KRAFSIG

# AMONG
# THE WILD
# LINES

## Among The Wild Lines

Rei and Griff's journey continues Among The Wild Lines.

I hope you loved Between The Wild Lines as much as I enjoyed staying up past 2am every night, pumped full of caffeine, bleary-eyed and writing. Thank you so much for supporting my work and making it to the end. It would really help me fight the algorithm if you could **leave a review** or recommend this book to friends or family.

Need more content? **Subscribe to my website newsletter at https://gretakrafsig.com** and you'll get updates, book releases, and additional bonus content.

Now, seriously, this is it—the end, it's over.

Sending you lots of love and hope from the dark and twisted world we live in,

*Greta Krafsig*

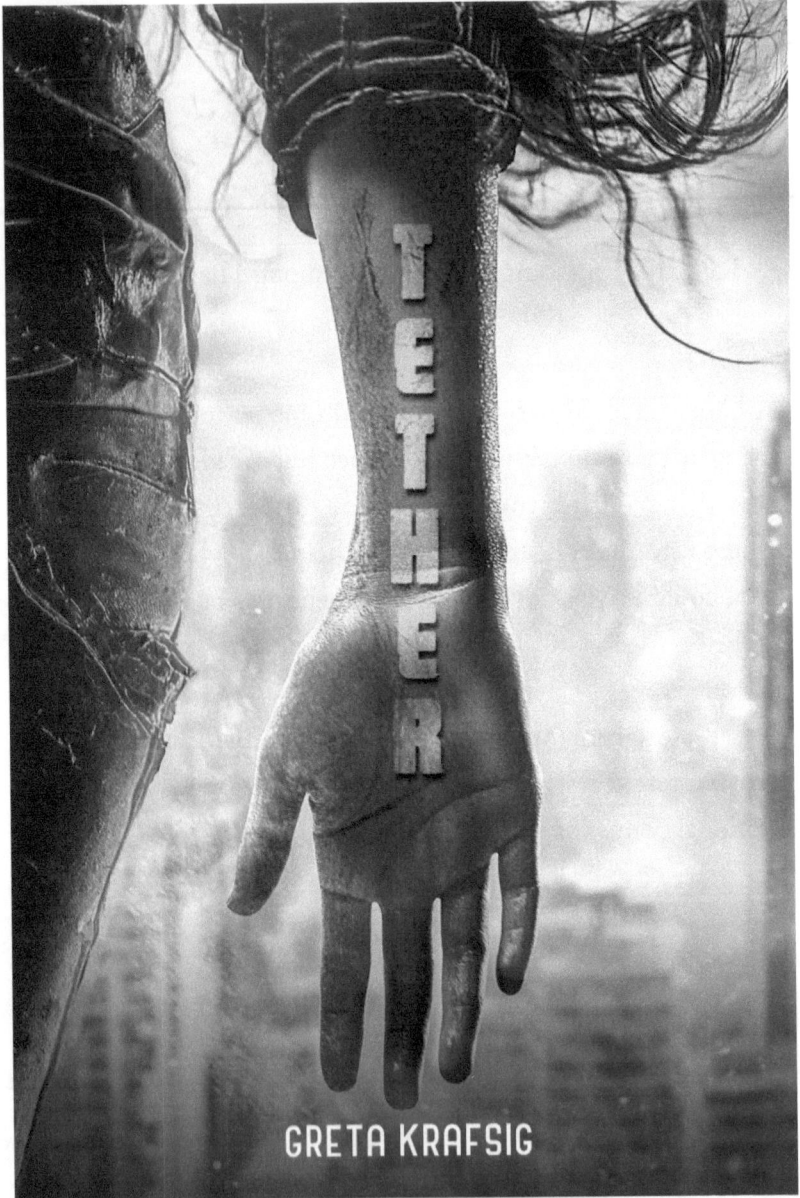

# Tether

**You've unlocked Tether, a secret surprise only available to special readers like yourself.**

Tether has the answer to the question you're dying to know: what's up with the locked room in Mara's lake house? **Grab your free bonus content by going to https://gretakrafsig.com/downloads/btwl-bonus/.**

Oh, sorry, that wasn't your burning question? Ahh darn, well, Rei and Griff's journey continues in Among The Wild Lines. Pick up a copy to find out what happens in the Free Territories.

# Glossary

**Authority** — a country in Phyrros led by an authoritarian government

**Bless The Mother** — a swearing phrase

**Blight Storm** — a disturbance, sometimes violent

**Blight Fallout** — the aftermath of a disturbance or problem

**Civvies** — people who are not part of the Authority's military, earn 1 lottery ticket a year

**Collective Voice Broadcast (CVB)** — provides daily news and radio broadcasts in the Authority

**Core Tenants** — loyalty, duty, mission, taught to all children of the Authority

**Cull** — a woman who never had children or is no longer fertile, end of the motherline

**Discipline Stick** — a spiked metal rod used by overseers to reinforce the core tenants

**Eastkeep** — one of four GRH facilities

**Enforcer** — highly trained soldiers who guard the GRH and go on special missions, earn 3 lottery tickets a year

**Entry School** — the first type of school a young child goes to

**Fatherline** — men in a generation where the father's first name becomes their son's last name

**Fertility Tracker** — an implant given to fertile women in the

Authority

**Free Territories** — a country beyond the Iron Divide

**Genetic Research Hubs (GRH)** — where the Authority contains infected men

**Goddess Lysara** — one of the old gods, their worship is frowned upon in the Authority

**Heart Blight** — a deadly mutating virus

**Iron Divide** — a physical barrier dividing the Authority from the Free Territories

**Linebreaker** — a woman who has no living children and ends the motherline

**Lottery** — how the Authority selected women with fertility trackers for artificial insemination

**Military Management Zone (MMZ)** — a soldier training facility and the head of military operations

**Mother Bless It** — a swearing phrase

**Motherline** — women in a generation where the mother's last name becomes their daughter's last name

**Northkeep** — one of four GRH facilities

**Officers** — members of the military who are not soldiers or citizens with high standing, earn. 2 lottery tickets a year

**Overseer** — the person in charge of a class of children in school, typically a woman with no children

**Phyrros** — a continent separated into two countries

**Platoon** — a group of eight or more soldiers, each led by a captain

**Suppression Line** — where traitors are given justice

**Squad** — also smaller subset of a platoon

**Sympathizers** — a rebel faction

**Tanking** — ruining your chance or a low shot of success

**Terin** — capital of the Authority

**Tether** — a small implant injected under the skin of the hand to monitor a woman's fertility

# Acknowledgements

I want to say thank you to all the people, some of whom I'm sure I'll miss, who helped make this story possible. Without your help and support, the world of the Authority would still sit tangled in my head.

Thanks to my mom, Jill, who has and always will be my biggest and number one fan. To my daughter, Gianna, thank you for pointing out my over-generalizations, plot holes, and putting up with endless repetitions of the story on text-to-speech playback. And to my sissy, Serena, for being my cheerleader of creativity. I love you all.

Shannon Ottmers, I don't think I could have found anyone better to read my first draft faster than you did.

For tearing this story apart so I could put it back together again, there's no one better than Chersti Nieveen. I appreciate your wonderful feedback, attention to detail, and pushing me to make this story hotter, grittier, and the best it could be.

And finally, to the team of authors/writers/mentors/critics who helped drive me to be better in the areas I struggled, thank you so much. Daniel Kaplan, if there's one thing I learned its conflict and character development (with a few acronyms and laughs thrown into the mix). Catherine D. Graham, your constant constructive feedback, hook ums, encouragement, checklists, and knowledge shares were invaluable. Bekah Brinkmeier, your marketing and publishing strategies have already paid off. For midnight sprints, fun image prompts and lots of patience during my editing process, there is no one better than Kat Campbell. And of course, the spice wouldn't be as spicy without or meaningful without Cara Crescent's help to rein in my overused cliches and push the hot so, so much hotter!

With much love, thank you all.

## About The Author

Greta Krafsig lives on her family farm with her daughter and a host of friendly dogs, cats, horses and cows. She started writing when she was six years old and has been doing it ever since. She enjoys writing romance because the world can always use more love. In her spare time, she enjoys horseback riding, computer programming, drawing and all things creative.

Sign up for her newsletter and get all the latest updates, freebies, discounts and release info at https://gretakrafsig.com.

www.ingramcontent.com/pod-product-compliance
Lightning Source LLC
Chambersburg PA
CBHW031417240626
47154CB00001B/80